Dear Will

KARL ACKERMAN

Scribner
New York   London   Toronto   Sydney   Singapore

SCRIBNER
1230 Avenue of the Americas
New York, NY 10020

SCRIBNER and design are trademarks of Macmillan Library Reference USA,
Inc., used under license by Simon & Schuster, the publisher of this work.

Designed by Brooke Zimmer
Set in Caslon
Manufactured in the United States of America

1   3   5   7   9   10   8   6   4   2

Library of Congress Cataloging-in-Publication Data is available.

ISBN 0-684-83953-9

To Jenny, Zoë, and Nell
my three loves
and
To my mother and father

Dear Will

The poor fellow. He has just begun to suffer from it, this miserable trick the romantic plays upon himself: of setting just beyond his reach the very thing he prizes.

WALKER PERCY, *The Moviegoer*

IT HAD BEEN billed as a weekend of rest: two full days of monastic silence, hours and hours of sleep, whole mornings or afternoons spent strolling alone in the dunes at Cape Henlopen. The stack of manuscripts in the trunk of Will's car would remain under lock and key. His laptop, too. He would slow down amid the hurry-up of migrating birds. The ospreys had just returned to the area to nest. No doubt warblers were moving through. Will hoped to add a bird or two to his life list. That was all he considered as he sped eastward through the gritty neighborhoods of northeast Washington, and later, past the outlet malls that clung like barnacles to the shores of the Chesapeake.

He stopped for gas on Kent Island at a convenience store with a huge inflatable crab dancing on the roof. Inside, he bought a cheese sandwich and a six-pack of beer. Will was planning to hold off on the beer until the end of the journey, but succumbed to thirst during the slow crawl through his fourth or fifth Delaware town, speed limit twenty-five miles per hour. It had been years since he had driven out to Lewes, and the last time he had arrived at midday. Now, close to midnight, he drove back and forth on darkened streets, utterly lost until he found himself in the parking lot of the local hospital. By the time he located Michael and Alejandro's large Victorian house two blocks away, a full bladder had him squirming.

In pitch black beneath a droopy evergreen, Will fumbled with the key ring, trying desperately to identify the one that opened the side door of the house. "It's the key with serrations that feel like three-day whiskers," Michael had told him. In the white light of the Amtrak club car this had seemed like a useful tip. But here in the darkened driveway, dancing with discomfort, Will realized that he stood as much chance of locating a key that felt like three-day whiskers as he would have had besting Michael in a Verdi trivia contest. So he abandoned the task and hustled toward the backyard, shamelessly preparing to relieve himself behind a bush. Then he spied steps, and recalled that Michael had mentioned a kitchen door off the deck with a torn screen and a loose pane of glass. Suddenly it occurred to Will that everyone who came out here, straight and gay alike, must have trouble identifying the three-day-whisker key.

So there he found himself a few moments later, noiselessly removing that loose pane of glass, carefully setting it on the ground, reaching through the door to unlock the sliding bolt. He felt for a light switch which was not, alas, where a building inspector would have wanted it. Then he had a foot inside the door, still patting the wall, now wondering if there might be a beaded chain hanging somewhere in the middle of the darkened room. A nearly inaudible murmur—"Shit"—had just escaped his lips, when all at once, as if in *punishment* for this puny curse, Will found himself clubbed to his knees. He screamed out in pain. Then another blow glanced off the side of his head, and he actually saw stars.

Woozily, he tried to escape to the porch, but found himself pinned by the heavy door. He shouted, "Stop! Stop! I'm a friend!" as his assailant continued to pound his arms and back.

A woman's voice called out, "The cops, Hank! Call the cops!"

"Alejo," Will cried. "Michael! I know them!"

The pummeling stopped instantly but the door didn't budge. Will remained trapped like a mouse. "Who are *you?*" the woman demanded.

"Will Gerard. I ran into Michael on the train. He sent me out here."

"Without a *key?*"

Will's head throbbed as he tried to sit up; but he found that he couldn't move. "Michael gave me a key. Gave me an entire ring of keys. I couldn't find the right one. Call him. Ask him. I'll stay outside, I promise." Silence. "Q and Seventeenth," he went on. "202-553-something."

The woman leaned heavily against the door, then let it open just wide enough for Will to scoot backward to freedom. Instantly the bolt snapped shut. Will thought about standing up, but rejected the idea. His head, throbbing in time with the mournful call of a distant foghorn, suddenly felt three sizes too large. His back, shoulders, and arms pulsed with aches. Sprawled on the wooden deck with eyes fixed on the black sky seemed the right position until this mess was straightened out.

"Hello, Michael, it's Annie." There was no hint of panic in her voice. No fear. "Look, I'm out in Lewes and I've got a *huge* problem. Just now a guy tried to break in through the kitchen door. He claims he ran into you on the train, and that you *sent* him out here." Long pause. "Oh," Will heard her say. "Oh," she said again. Another pause. Then: "Jesus." Then: "Well, I don't know. I must've hit him about twenty-five times with that big flashlight." Then: "Sure . . . sure. Thanks."

The cordless phone appeared at the empty panel of the door. "Michael wants to talk with you," the woman said.

Will struggled to his knees.

Michael's voice was shrill: "Good Lord, man, are you okay?"

"No."

"You've got a hospital right down the—"

"I know, Michael. I know. It's not that bad."

"And there's arnica for bruises. In the medicine cabinet. Oh my word. What a screwup!" A ripple of self-conscious laughter followed. "Alejo must've talked to Annie and I talked to you and we never talked to each other!"

"Yeah, right."

"Truly!"

"Let me talk to him."

"He just stepped out." Silence. "He really did." Another pause. "This *was* a mistake, Will. Honestly, I had *no* idea." Michael chuckled nervously again. "And that *flashlight*! Ouch!" Long pause. "Are you sure you're okay?"

"I'll live."

"Thank heavens!" The laughter deepened to a rumble. "Who would've ever guessed that you'd be the sort to break into a strange house!"

"An *empty* house, Michael. All those damn keys—"

"C'mon, Will, take a deep breath." His voice dropped: "There could be an upside to this."

Will gazed at the sky.

Michael, in a whisper: "I know you won't believe this, but last week Alejo and I were actually talking about you and Annie."

"Oh, I believe it."

"We would *never* do something like that."

"He wouldn't."

A snicker now.

"Good night, Michael."

"Who knows, someday you may thank—"

Click.

The overhead light in the kitchen had flickered on. Will's assailant stood beside the stove with her arms crossed. She was tall, with short brown hair and a narrow face. Her neck was elegantly long. She had delicate features which seemed at odds with the image on her oversized T-shirt: Edvard Munch's *Scream*. Will faced her through the door. With the pane of glass missing, he felt like a kid at the ballpark waiting for an order of fries and a Coke.

"Look, I'm sorry," he said. "I had no idea you were here."

"Are you hurt?"

"A little banged up." Will shrugged, and the pain in his right shoulder radiated across his back. "My self-respect, especially."

Her face relaxed. The tiniest hint of a smile appeared. One front tooth slightly overlapped the other. Her eyes matched Munch's blue swirl of water. She still held the huge black flashlight in her right hand, and used it to gesture toward Will. He glanced down to discover a gaping zipper.

He pirouetted. "The long drive," he explained. "After I gave up on the key . . ."

"Sure, sure." The door came open. She was suppressing a grin now. "Look, I'm really sorry about this. I turned off the lights about ten minutes ago. When I heard noises, I thought mice had gotten into the food that I left on the counter. I was already in here when I saw your arm coming through the door. It scared the daylights—"

"Hank," said Will.

Annie bit her lip.

"Where is Hank?"

"Well," she said slowly, "when strangers come around, Hank generally, um, retreats to the litter box." Long pause. "When he's with me, that is." She smiled gamely. Then her gaze narrowed and she lifted her chin to examine the lump on Will's forehead. "I think that needs ice." She shook her head. "I can't believe I actually clubbed another human being."

Will asked about the downstairs apartment. Annie reported that it was in the process of being repainted: plaster dust, drop cloths, empty paint buckets, soda cans overflowing with cigarette butts.

"I can sleep in my car," he said.

"Don't be silly. There's plenty of room. I have the Turkish harem; you can take Martha Stewart-does-Montana." Another smile, a wry smile this time. "By the way, my name is Annie Leonard."

"Will Gerard."

She looked at him. "Am I supposed to know who you are? What I mean is, on the phone Michael made it sound as though you were some kind of celebrity."

"There was a piece in the paper a few days ago," he replied. "Michael seems to think . . ." Will paused. *Think what?* He didn't know, couldn't guess. "My fifteen minutes," he said weakly.

There had been an article in the *Washington Post* three days earlier, a splashy Style-page profile of Will Gerard, literary agent. Every writer and would-be writer in town, it seemed to Will, had read the story, and then dusted off a manuscript to send to him. The boxes and padded envelopes that used to arrive on his doorstep in ones and twos suddenly started coming by the dozens. Over the course of that miserable week the telephone never stopped ringing. Will's fax machine burned up. His assistant, Teddy, who was also his nephew, vowed to quit; and this vow was repeated hourly, like a mantra. Will felt trapped, like an old bass in a small pond, its favorite spot in the shadows identified, now subjected to the relentless torment of line weights and fishing lures. Friday morning, with just one appointment in his book, he fled to New York. Late that afternoon he found himself on the platform at Penn Station, heading home.

"Will Gerard? Is that *the* Will Gerard? The famous literary agent?"

Heads turned. Will found Michael Phillips, an old friend, pushing toward him through the crowd with a broad grin on his face. Will put a finger to his lips, which Michael took like the flick of a riding crop.

"So what in heaven's name does it feel like to be the toast of the town? Are the young ladies lined up at your front door?" Michael took Will's elbow and steered him toward the club car. "Admit it: you love it."

Will grimaced.

"For God's sake, young fellow. I know folks who pay flacks tens of thousands of dollars in the mere *hope* of getting publicity like this."

"Who do I pay for a good night's sleep?"

Michael laughed. "Sleep is for babies and for people who are unhappy and depressed." Then, in a whisper: "Not for a young man with a soulful look in his eyes." He began to fish around in the attaché case that a moment earlier had yielded two airplane bottles of Johnny Walker Black. Soon Michael produced a ring of keys, which he pressed into Will's hands. "Everyone sleeps better at the beach," he said.

Will had clothes in the trunk of his car, gas in the tank, Teddy at home to feed the cat and ignore the ringing telephone.

"You sure you don't want to check this out with Alejo?"

"Go!" said Michael.

"And so I went," Will told Annie. "I picked up my car and drove straight out here."

They were standing in the hallway outside a darkened room, Will with a small bag of ice pressed to the side of his head.

Annie said, "Alejo talked to me and Michael talked to you, and they simply forgot to mention it to each other!"

"It does sound a little fishy, doesn't it?"

"Yes, it does."

She was addressing Michael's well-known reputation as a match-maker, and Will was recalling the wide smile on Michael's face as he pressed the house keys into his hands.

He said, "You really think he'd do something like that?"

"Probably not." Then: "Actually, he might."

Annie reached for a switch. When the overhead light came on, the first thing Will saw was a huge bed with a tan spread. A bedspread made of leather, he realized. It had a ragged, faded American flag tattooed at the center, and an elaborate fringe of coiled silver wire. In all it looked as if it must weigh two hundred pounds. There were saddlebags hanging from the rough-hewn bedpost. The small bureau set against the far wall was covered with cowhide. Beside it, on a display stand in the corner, was a western saddle. There was a bullwhip tacked to the wainscoting, two framed "wanted" posters, a set of antique revolvers in a velvet case. No doubt the bookshelf between the windows held the entire Louis L'Amour oeuvre, Zane Grey first editions, signed copies of *All the Pretty Horses* and *Lonesome Dove*.

Will stepped inside. "Why are gay men so relentlessly thorough?" he asked.

Annie, in the doorway, shrugged. "Probably just another thing to blame on their mothers," she replied. "Feel free to sleep on the couch in the living room if the smell of buckskin gets to be too much for you."

The living room was farther down the hall. There at least the decor reflected the local scene: dried beach grass in straw baskets in each corner, photos of a fog-shrouded coast hanging on the wall, sisal carpet trimmed in teal green, a beige sofa as broad as a dune, a bookcase filled with shells, various nautical devices, and books about the sea.

Will said, "So how long have you known Michael and Alejo?"

"Years and years," Annie replied. "In fact I'm renting from them right now."

"On Q Street?"

She nodded.

"Wonderful apartment," he finally managed.

"You know it?"

"I, um, used to live there."

"Oh," she said.

"Years ago," he added. "Years and years ago."

"It's a great place."

"Beautiful woodwork."

"And so convenient."

"You can walk everywhere."

"I guess that was the main reason I took it. That, and the two of them."

It was like a dance, a modern minuet.

"Back then," said Will, "I was traveling all the time. Two weeks on the road, and I'd get back home and find a pot of Michael's chicken soup on the stove. Homemade bread on the counter. Salad in the fridge."

"I believe the word is *nurturing*," offered Annie.

"With Michael you'd need a full paragraph."

"A whole book."

Will smiled. The smile froze. All at once he lost confidence in small talk. Some innocent remark about Annie's apartment—how much he'd enjoyed the sunsets on the back porch, say—would end with him describing the time he'd locked himself out and had to squeeze through the high window above the refrigerator. "Um, could you point me toward the bathroom?" he said.

"Down the hall. On the left." Again she studied the side of his head. Then she reached out and gently touched the bruise on his cheek. "There's aspirin in the brandy snifter on the shelf beside the window."

"Let me guess," said Will. "Roaring Twenties?"

Annie smiled, shook her head. "Fin de siècle," she replied.

THE HOUSE FELT empty when Will awoke. His brain sloshed about painfully as he pulled on a pair of jeans and a flannel shirt, and staggered into the bathroom. The sink was an old one with two spigots. Will filled it to the brim with hot water. He scooped handful after handful onto his face—washing, rinsing, massaging, scrubbing again—before daring to lift his eyes to the mirror. There was a striking purple lump on the side of his forehead, and a matching bruise on the opposite cheek. In his toilet kit he found a plastic container of Tylenol, and swallowed three. Then he hunted around in the back of a closet for a warm jacket and a pair of binoculars, and drove out to the highway. The young waitress at Dunkin' Donuts stole glances at his battered face as she filled his order: two large cups of coffee and a heart-attack cruller.

Afterward, Will drove out to the beach.

It was still early, a frigid March morning with ice glinting from the tips of the marsh grass. A flat winter sun stood like a brilliant coin on the horizon. Will stopped at the fishing pier, deserted but for a few gulls. The bait shack remained boarded up, the vending machines at its front door wrapped in tattered plastic. There were no ducks in the shallows of the Delaware Bay: just cormorants and a few grebes. Farther into the park, Will saw killdeer at the tennis courts, and in an adjacent field, a flock of small birds with black, harness-like markings.

The parking lot at the tip of Cape Henlopen had one car, a green Taurus with D.C. tags. Annie, Will presumed. He drove to another section of the park, to a lot beside the ruins of a World War II–era gun battery set on a dune high above the blue Atlantic. He sat in the car in the warming sun and finished the second cup of coffee. Then he descended to the beach through heather and wind-stunted pines, and walked among the bickering gulls and skittery sandpipers. Will wandered the beach for several hours. He sat on his heels pitching stones into the incoming tide. On the drive back to town, he spotted a Volvo station wagon parked at the side of the highway. An old woman stood beside it peering through binoculars at an osprey platform attached to the top of a utility pole in the adjacent marsh. Will pulled his car to the shoulder.

There was a female osprey perched on the nest. A male circled high above. The old woman's binoculars stayed fixed on the nest as Will approached. She was white-haired, tall and thin—heronlike, thought Will, with her gray down vest worn atop a light blue windbreaker.

"Illegal to park here," she called out. "Cop comes by, he'll ticket you."

"What about you?"

"My car was overheating."

Will looked out at the nest. "Mine, too," he said.

The woman turned to him, a smile tugging at the corners of her thin lips. Then she noticed his bruises, and frowned slightly.

They returned their attention to the birds.

Will lifted his glasses. "When did they get back?"

"Day before yesterday."

"In the park, there was a flock on the field—"

"Turnstones," the old woman said.

"What else is around?"

"Brants in the cornfields. Skimmers, buffleheads, goldeneyes, gallinules, yellowlegs at Prime Hook. Had eagles there, too. Nesting. But they're gone." She looked at him again, more intently now. "So what happened to the other guy?"

Will worked hard to appear nonchalant. He gazed up at the male osprey, still circling. "It wasn't a guy," he admitted.

"Some gal."

"Well," he said finally, "I guess my car's probably cooled off by now."

The old woman's thin smile reappeared. "Not mine," she replied.

Will headed north on Route 1. He was planning to spend the rest of the morning at Prime Hook National Wildlife Refuge. But a few miles down the road, he changed his mind and decided to drive back to Washington. It was a snap decision. He would let Annie have the house to herself. He would go home, take a walk on the towpath, get to bed early, tomorrow nurse his wounds and set up a triage table to sort the stack of manuscripts which had no doubt grown ten feet taller in his absence. He called Michael and Alejandro's house from a gas station on the highway to say good-bye to Annie.

"Are you okay?" she asked.

"Fine," he said.

A truck at the traffic light bucked into gear.

"Really?"

"Really."

"You don't sound fine."

"No palsy, no amnesia: I remember my name, my birthday, the names of my brother and sister. I can still count to a hundred in Spanish."

"You sound tired, Will."

"Exhausting dreams," he admitted. "First, some weird gaucho stuff, then a nightmare in which I had turned into Mr. Potato Head."

She laughed. "I've put away the flashlight. I promise."

"Careful now. If Michael calls and finds out that I went home, he's liable to send somebody else."

"You're not serious!"

"Probably not."

"Oh, Michael," she said.

"We should call him up and demand an explanation."

"He's a lawyer. He'd deny everything."

"And enjoy every minute of it," said Will.

"Yes, he would."

The snap decision to head home suddenly felt like a big mistake.

Annie said, "Look, I have a confession to make. I stopped into the town library this morning and read a newspaper profile about this successful young literary agent who is in search of the perfect marinara." The highway stoplight went to yellow. An eighteen-wheeler braked hard, clattering to a stop. "The search is over," she went on. "I'm about ready to put it on the stove."

Will said, "For some reason I thought leaving would be the gentlemanly thing for me to do."

"Only if this was a Henry James novel, which I sincerely hope it is not."

Any response he might make, whether witty retort or chuckle or dry remark, felt positively *Jamesian*.

"There's your favorite Sierra Nevada Pale Ale in the fridge, and fresh bread about to come out of the oven." When he didn't respond, she added, "If you don't come back right this minute, Will Gerard, I'm going to have to call the *Post* and ask that reporter to make a correction."

His ears were on fire.

Annie said, "You don't understand. I'm *impressed* by men who bake bread."

"It's the Style page," he said. "The writer is ostensibly coming to your house to ask you a few questions about what you do for a living. Then she all but pokes around in your underwear drawer."

"You were baking bread when she *arrived*. You should have been hunched over a manuscript by the next Patricia Cornwell."

"Patsy, we say in the trade."

"Or been parked on the telephone."

"It was Saturday morning."

"For goodness sakes, Will. You're a high roller. High rollers don't pay attention to the concept of weekend. Most of the lawyers at my firm would have rented a furnished mansion in Potomac for an interview like that. You had a *Washington Post* reporter out to your house on a Saturday morning while you baked bread."

"And tossed off a few shrewd observations about the hot new literary genre."

"While you were *kneading*."

"It was time to knead."

"You don't get it, do you?"

"Something about men who cook?"

"A western omelette for brunch would've been perfect. Baguettes and focaccia are definitely over the top."

He laughed. "So what was the message I was sending?"

"You'll have to come back," said Annie. "I can't do this on the phone."

At the house, Will found a pot of chicken soup on the stove and a note on the counter—"Eat, eat!"—so he ate two bowls. Then he lay down on the couch in the living room, a three-year-old copy of *National Geographic* propped up in his hands one moment, then flopped open on his stomach like a saddle the next. Will's fifteen-minute nap stretched on to two hours. He awoke feeling completely disoriented. In the kitchen he brewed himself a cup of coffee and watched Annie, who was sitting out on the deck in sunglasses and a hooded sweatshirt. She was reading a fat, orange-spined Penguin paperback. Annie looked so absorbed in the book that Will couldn't bring himself to interrupt.

He took a walk instead.

The sun passed in and out of the clouds as he headed toward the marsh north of town. There he spotted another pair of nesting osprey, and a marsh hawk hovering above the wide expanse of spart grass. He saw killdeer at the roadside, and an egret poised like a statue in a tidal creek, waiting to snap up its supper.

Dusk brought Will back to the house. He sat on a stool beside the kitchen window, sipping a beer. Annie worked at the stove. She wore black leggings and thick red socks, a black apron over a red flannel shirt that Will guessed she had borrowed from Michael and Alejandro's closet. Her arms were long, hands graceful. She was trim, and though not obviously muscular, she seemed strong—strong enough to drop a grown man to his knees with a single blow. Will took a sip of beer. The sort of gal who would make short work of a piñata, he thought.

The pasta water had achieved its rolling boil, and the marinara was gently bubbling. The smell of garlic embraced the room.

Annie glanced at him from the corner of her eye. A moment later she spoke to the sauce pan: "'Gerard is tall, with deep-set eyes and a tangle of dark hair. In a crew-neck sweater and blue jeans, he has the casual look of a Saturday morning carpenter. He owns an old pickup truck that rarely leaves this quaint neighborhood of Sears bungalows, starter homes, rundown farmhouses, and modern Victorians. He keeps his thermostat set at sixty-two. This is a man who chops wood for exercise, who built the potting shed that sits behind his house beneath a towering maple. But don't be fooled by the country charm. Will Gerard is perfectly at ease in the big city, be it Washington or New York.'"

Oh dear Lord, thought Will.

She turned. "You know, you come off much better in person."

"Thank goodness."

"Still, you came through. A little defensive about your father, though that seemed understandable." She paused. "By the end, I thought you sounded sweet. In a Southern way." She shrugged. "I think."

The reporter had noted that Will lived alone. (She neglected to inspect the "potting shed" out back: nephew Teddy's abode.) She went on a bit too long about the stray cat named Newt that had taken up residence in a wooden crate beneath Will's front porch. That Will had Newt altered and regularly fed the old tom seemed to qualify him as some sort of modern-day St. Francis of Assisi. Will had ducked the reporter's questions about his late father, whose long and storied career at the CIA was old gossip in Washington circles. All of this was dutifully reported, of course: Jamie Gerard's years in Berlin after World War II, his involvement in the 1954 coup in Guatemala and the disaster at the Bay of Pigs, the years he spent in Bangkok during the Vietnam War.

The table had been set in a dining room that was done up in various shades of yellow: seat covers, curtains, napkins, label on the wine bottle. Will regarded the steaming plate of butter-colored pasta that Annie had set before him.

"So what about you?" he asked.

"I'm a lawyer."

"Besides that."

"Don't tell me you want to see the legal thriller I just finished!"

He winced.

She grinned. "Not me," she said. "Just every guy I work with."

It was dark outside. There were yellow candles burning at the center of a yellow pine table, apricot place mats, heavy cutlery with amber handles.

"What else?" he asked.

"I grew up outside Chicago. A brick house with a hipped roof, neat lawn, white picket fence, miniature poodle." Annie shrugged. "Pretty boring, all in all. No ancestors arriving on the *Ark* or the *Dove*, no spies in the family, no childhood in the exotic East, no Pacific crossings on ocean liners."

At that moment Will made a very explicit promise to himself that he would never again submit to a personality profile. "The marinara is delicious," he said.

"The search is over?"

"Definitely top ten." He took another bite, and savored it. "Make that top five."

"One thing that surprised me about that article was what was left out. Any hint of Mr. Will Gerard's *private* life, for example."

"People just want the dollars and cents," he replied with a shrug.

"Nuts," she said. "At least half the reason you read a piece like that is to *snoop*."

He poured wine into both their glasses. "It seemed tacky to mention the string of divorces, the bankruptcy, the fraud conviction, all those years in tax exile."

"Liar," she whispered.

He smiled. "I'll bet you grew up in one of those midwestern suburbs with an Indian name that hasn't seen a person of color in the past two hundred years."

"Next town over." Annie shrugged. "We got stuck with the French explorer."

"So why did Michael take so long to introduce us?"

She picked a kernel of wax from the base of the candlestick, then looked up at Will. "The obvious answer, I suppose, is because I'm married."

Will stopped chewing. For one brief instant he thought she was kidding. There was no ring on Annie's finger, no aura of settledness or guilt about her, nothing remotely indicative of marriage at all.

"Married, soon to be unmarried," she added. Her expression seemed more vulnerable all of a sudden. "My life is a little complicated right now."

"This must be a rough time," he replied. "I'm sorry."

Annie put down her fork. "It's sad. But it isn't a tragedy. Just one of those things that happen. Life goes on."

Rob was her husband's name. He was a lawyer, too, sixteen years older than Annie, with teenage children from a first marriage. Only the bare facts were mentioned. Annie spoke softly, without affect.

The conversation rambled.

Will described the string of jobs he'd had in the book business before launching this new career as an agent three months earlier. Annie talked about law school, which she hated, and the practice of law, which she loved. She was one of three women partners at a big Washington firm. She talked easily about her job as a litigator: the strategizing, the competition, winning. She liked to win. She said this with an easy smile. She didn't mention her first marriage, just out of law school, a marriage so brief and sad she rarely mentioned it at all. Nor did she offer much more about the second one, at thirty-one, to Rob, until Will gently steered the conversation back to it.

Annie sat back in her chair. "We were friends before we got together. Rob was easy to be with. I loved that about him. I thought it would be enough." She shrugged. "Turned out it wasn't. Not for either of us."

Annie told Will that as she thought back on the relationship she was struck by the fact that the two of them hardly ever sat still. Most nights she and Rob dined out. They traveled to Europe two or three times a year; they entertained; they took in the opera, films, theater. Early on this life had seemed glamorous and exciting to Annie, but now she considered the emotional distance that had always existed between them. She and Rob were good companions. She had shared the world with this man for ten years, and somehow that was the most they could achieve. It was this realization, she admitted, and not the breakup, that left her saddest.

"So how long have you been separated?" he asked.

"Five months."

"Second thoughts?"

"None," she replied.

More wine was poured.

Annie took a sip. "I think it's your turn to tell me something about you," she said.

Will thought.

"Anything," she added.

"Birds," he offered.

She looked puzzled. She didn't process what Will was saying at first. At that moment she was thinking about the birds you eat: Peking duck, stuffed quail, twenty-five-pound turkeys.

"My dad was a birdwatcher," Will went on. "It's something we used to do together. I got hooked."

"Why?" She seemed genuinely curious.

He shrugged. "I like to keep track of what's going on in the world. Watching birds taught me to pay attention. To stay in the moment."

"The zen of nature?"

"The zen of wet tennis shoes."

Their plates were empty. The bottle of wine was empty.

Will reached for Annie's hand across the table. "Let's go look for owls," he said.

There were matching trench coats in the front closet. Annie rolled the sleeves on hers, and the two of them trudged out into the cold foggy night. Lewes felt deserted. At the center of town, they passed antique shops, a Tru-Value hardware store, a bank; they walked out onto the town dock, and stood for a moment at the edge of the canal, gazing out at a line of white-hulled boats rocking in their slips. The wind had picked up. It was brisk enough to catch the rope on a flag-pole in front of the post office and ring it like a bell. At a wood-and-brass faux English pub with two regulars perched at the bar, Annie and Will took a table by the front window. Outside, the wind had begun to howl, vibrating the plate glass. A pizza box cartwheeled down the street.

Over Sambuca they talked genealogy: Annie's ancestors on her father's side had been among the first Jews west of the eighty-seventh meridian, as she put it. "Tinkers, tailors, a few soldiers in the old country I was told, but that's it. No spies. None we knew about, anyway."

"But that's the point," said Will. "You wouldn't."

"Is it true that your family actually has a coat of arms that wasn't designed by a mail-order house?"

"My family brought Catholicism to America," he said quietly.

"This is something to be proud of?"

"*English* Catholicism," he murmured.

She grinned. "You know what floors me? That hundreds of years later, it still matters."

"Of course it matters," he replied.

"I thought the whole point of America was to check that sort of baggage at the gate. Lefcowitzes get to become Leonards. Everybody gets a clean slate."

"Only if you want one."

Will was smiling. He had a hand on the table, fingers spread. Annie reached over and placed her hand beside his, fingers interlocking. She traced a vein across the top of his hand, then shook her head in disbelief. "My God," she whispered, "it *is* blue."

He laughed.

At the side door to the house, Will was able to identify the correct key this time, but now he had trouble with the lock. So Annie took his hand to demonstrate the proper technique: "You slide it all the way in," she coached. "Then pull it back a smidgen, and wiggle it till you feel it catch." "Ooh, baby," he whispered. "Ooh, baby, baby, baby." She laughed to wake the neighbors. At the top of the narrow stairway, Will wrapped his arms around her. Annie turned, still smiling, and they sank together to the floor. She caressed the side of his face. "Where in heaven's name did you come from, Will Gerard?" He kissed her cheek, her nose, her lips. "Lady," he said, "I was just about to ask you the very same question."

There was really no choice of rooms. Which is not to suggest that Will felt that he and Annie *needed* the Turkish harem atmosphere of her room. But there, at least, they would be able to keep straight faces, which would have been impossible for them in Will's little bunkhouse by the sea. "Not to mention," he told Annie, "that I forgot to pack my chaps."

The lamp shades were rose-colored with blue beadwork and tassels that looked like something a stripper might wear. The bed was a plush battleship: a mahogany four-poster with drooping canopy and silk sheets. Annie adjusted the lights to establish a mood that Suleiman the Magnificent might have favored. Then she disappeared for a moment into the bathroom. Will, meanwhile, rifled the drawers of both bedside tables, the bureau; he searched the saddlebags hanging on the bedpost in his room, and the medicine cabinet and brandy snifter in the bathroom. *Nothing.* He was confounded. It just didn't seem possible in this grim era that two socially responsible gay men (men who stocked extra toothbrushes for weekend guests, various colognes, breath mints, disposable razors, six brands of pain reliever) would not somewhere have laid in a small supply of condoms.

Will made a report of this to Annie as they lay stretched out on the bed, the good news about their HIV status already exchanged. He added that he was willing to make a run to Happy Harry's All-Night Discount Drugs on the coastal highway.

"That's up to you," she replied. "What I mean is, it isn't necessary."

A midnight run to Happy Harry's was the last thing in the world that Will wanted to undertake at this particular moment. So he heard in Annie's comment what he wanted to hear. He defaulted to the good old days of birth control, when a remark like this (or so the assumption went) meant the woman was protected.

"Up to me in what sense?"

Will had intended this as a follow-up question, though it arrived late, nearly ten minutes late, as the two of them lay sprawled across the bed, half-undressed, locked in an embrace. Annie was kissing Will as if she would never stop. His eyes were closed. She rolled on top of him, and slowly began to rock. Then he looked at her, his eyes wide open. He was startled by how familiar she looked: like someone he had known for years. Which was when Will recalled that he and Annie had met just twenty-four hours earlier.

And so he whispered, "Up to me in what sense?"

"All of them, I suppose."

Now she was lying beside him with a leg draped over his. Will kissed her neck, her chin. A moment later Annie touched him. She did something with her thumb that nearly lifted him off the bed. She kissed his chest, his shoulder, his fingertips. He was afloat on the wide Sargasso Sea, naked in a noontime sun, as Annie gently traced the lump on the side of his head, kissed it, kissed his forehead, an eyebrow, that roguishly bruised cheek, his chin, his lips.

"Will," she whispered.

"Hmmm."

"Will, look at me." His eyelids fluttered open. As his vision came into focus, he noticed a tiny mole above her lip. He kissed it. "You need to know something," she said. "I'm not using birth control." Will closed his eyes, rested his cheek against Annie's small breast. It was soft, soft. "My diaphragm," she added a moment later. "I don't use it anymore." Another pause. "I threw it away."

The news that a thirty-nine-year-old woman who was ending a childless marriage had destroyed her birth control device should have connected the dots for Will, but right then he wasn't in a dot-connecting frame of mind. Instead of processing what she said, he pictured her standing on the catwalk over Great Falls, sailing her diaphragm like a Frisbee into the roiling waters of the Potomac.

"What you're saying," he finally managed, "is that we're taking a chance."

"Yes."

"Oh." He tried to think. "Big chance or little chance?"

She looked at him. "Maybe not so little."

Again: "Oh."

They held each other and listened to the foghorn. They kissed again, lovingly. Will inhaled the sweet smell of Annie's skin.

"And, um, you're willing to take that chance," he finally said.

Her blue eyes said *yes*. She nodded.

"What you're saying," Will went on, "is that you want to get pregnant."

This nod was more tentative. "Don't get the wrong idea. I didn't plan this or anything. Tonight just happened." She looked at him. "And for what it's worth, I want you to know that whatever happens, I would live with the consequences. I'd never ask you for anything." The foghorn bleated again, and this time Will heard in its tone the condemnatory voice of an Old Testament prophet. "What I'm trying to say," Annie went on, "is that this is completely up to you."

In Will's mind, having unprotected sex with a woman he had just met ranked right up there with sky-diving and open-heart surgery: activities to avoid. So there should have been nothing to think about. A simple *no*, respectful and unequivocal, was the only possible response. It was what he expected to hear himself say. But for some reason he couldn't speak. He was too stunned to speak. Or maybe he just needed time to collect himself, to think about what Annie had just said, and what he would say.

"Will?"

It was madness. How could she even ask such a thing! And how could he lie there like a slug as though actually considering the request, which of course he wasn't. Instead, he was trying to think of some artful way to decline without hurting Annie's feelings. Because Annie's feelings mattered to him. He liked her. Liked her a lot. So much, in fact, that in the midst of this long awkward moment a new thought, like a bubble from the depths of the sea, bobbed up into Will's consciousness: she wants *me*. Annie Leonard has just met me and she wants to have *my* child! And most amazing of all, Will's first response to this thought was to feel flattered. Deeply flattered. More flattered, he suddenly realized, than he had ever felt in his whole life.

"Would you please say something, Will?"

"If I wanted to make a run to Happy Harry's—"

"That would be fine with me."

"You'd still be here when I got back?"

"Of course." She kissed his ear. "I'd go with you." Then she whispered, "I want this. That's where it all started."

"You want to get pregnant, too."

"I told you the truth. I wouldn't have felt right if I hadn't. Chances are it won't matter. But it might. So I had to be honest with you. And to let you know that I could live with that. Alone, if that's how it turns out."

A smile came to Will's face, a smile he didn't understand at all. Nor could he fathom why Annie's words stirred him so, even as a voice within still argued for a speedy trip to the highway. But this was a voice that could be ignored, as it turned out. Blame it on the wine and the Sambuca, or the lust. Blame it on the queasy sense Will had right then that he was falling for Annie, and that he was old enough to take a chance. Blame it on the fact that Happy Harry's All-Night Discount Drugs was miles and miles away.

"Kiss me," Annie whispered. "We don't have to decide anything tonight."

He kissed her. And he thought, of course we do. And not just tonight, but *now.*

Will felt jangly. He figured he had fifteen seconds to sort things out, twenty at most. What Annie was asking was crazy and impulsive. Unequivocally *wrong.* It would be a huge mistake. Will knew that. But then he looked into her blue, blue eyes and said to himself, for God's sakes, man, this is life as it has been lived on this planet for *millions* of years. Be a mensch.

He ran the tips of his fingers across Annie's belly, the belly she wanted to swell up with a child. For years now some ancient region of his brain had pressed him for a moment like this. And Will had always resisted. Now, beside him, was a woman of the highest caliber, the sort of woman he could *marry,* and she was naked, and she wanted him, and she wanted his child, and yet, and yet—

And yet, an outright *no* was simply not in the cards tonight.

It's a gift, he told himself. The greatest gift I can give.

To Annie, he whispered, "Do you promise to respect me in the morning?"

She laughed softly, kissed the tip of his nose.

Will had seen those blue movies where the men and women cavort about like sexual athletes. For all the energetic lust of those films, none had ever seemed particularly erotic, not like this anyway, lying atop a long-legged woman, moving upon her as if grooving to the nastiest Barry White tune. Annie's eyes were closed. Her expression grew a tiny bit severe, and Will had to banish the sudden thought that he was making love to a woman who might one day become a federal judge. Then all was quiet, and they floated together. The bedroom window was cracked open, and Will could smell the tang of salt and marsh. This very bed he lay upon seemed to be rising and falling with the rhythm of the sea. Once, as a boy, Will had been on an ocean liner as it sailed through a typhoon; the huge ship rode the swells and troughs of the Pacific like a dinghy. It was an electrifying experience, a feeling of helpless ecstasy for Will as he gripped the rail at the stern, gazing up into the sky at a mountain of dark water.

Then Will and Annie were moving again, urgently, the act of love suddenly frantic, intense, *larger* somehow. The first hint of panic left Will puzzled—he was still that awestruck boy at the ship's rail, suddenly drenched by a crashing wave. Then he sensed panic again. And fear. The skin on his arms tingled, and all at once it felt to him as if he were a thousand miles away.

"Hold me," whispered Annie, kissing him hard on the lips.

The previous night—a mere twenty-four hours ago!—this very lady had assaulted him. She had dropped him to his knees in the kitchen doorway with a single blow. Now it seemed she could read his mind, every single thought. Another wave of panic crashed over him. "It's okay," said Annie. But it wasn't okay. It was awful. Erections weren't things that suddenly vanished, never in Will's experience anyway. But this one had. Not even a ghost of it remained.

IT WAS STILL dark outside when his eyes came open the next morning. Annie slept beside him. Will listened to the hum of traffic for a moment, and then remembered that he was many miles from the highway. He listened closer, and realized that what he was hearing was the muffled honks of a thousand snow geese migrating overhead. It was stunning to Will to think that he and this beautiful stranger beside him suddenly had a history together. They had life issues to mull over, hugely embarrassing events to avoid mentioning, a future to contemplate. Already they were partners of a sort: *accomplices*. Annie had described the loot just sitting in that bank vault, and Will had hopped behind the wheel of the getaway car with hardly a second thought. But now he was full of second thoughts. At that moment his mind was consumed by second thoughts.

Will's next impulse was to flee. He lay there listening to the high-flying geese and considered gathering up his clothes and stealing off in the dark to Dunkin' Donuts. Annie would understand. For all he knew she might have drifted off to sleep the previous night intending to wake before him so that she could steal off herself. She might even be the sort who left good-bye notes taped to the bathroom mirror: *Such a mistake on my part, Will. A terrible, terrible mistake. How could I expect you to process so much so quickly? How could I even ask! The sad, sad truth is that we have nowhere to go from here, except back to our respective lives. Farewell, dear man . . .*

But Annie slept. She slept and slept. Will sat on the edge of the bed and watched her in the half-light of dawn; and later, sipping coffee, he watched her as the morning sunlight suddenly flooded the room. Annie slept on her side with a corner of pillow clutched in her hand. She stirred when the sun hit her face, and smiled briefly, still asleep. It was a mischievous smile, a smile that left Will smiling, too. That was the moment he realized he wouldn't flee: not today, nor tomorrow, nor the day after that.

"So what *happened?*"

"I called her this morning."

"I thought you called her yesterday."

"I did."

"Annie never called you back?"

"Nope."

It was May, nearly seven weeks later.

"Is she mad at you?"

This wasn't pure nosiness. Teddy actually seemed troubled, even worried. Concerned enough to have set a half-eaten baloney sandwich on his knee as he waited for his uncle to answer.

Will shrugged.

"You love her, don't you?"

Another shrug. Will didn't know. Or wouldn't say. Apparently didn't want to address this particular question at this particular moment.

"That means *yes*."

Will looked at his nephew. "Since when does a shrug mean yes?"

"A shrug means you don't want to talk about it. Not wanting to talk about it means yes."

They were sitting side-by-side in wicker rockers on Will's front porch. Will was dressed in blue jeans and a white shirt. He had a laptop propped on his knees. Teddy wore his customary black: T-shirt and jeans, Doc Martens, the scruffy baseball cap with the word *Linux* embroidered in silver.

"Look," said Will, "this isn't about whether I love Annie or she loves me. It's about our situation."

"She wants to have a kid and you don't."

"She knows she does and I'm not sure that I do. Not yet anyway. For God's sakes, we've only known each other forty-seven days."

Teddy's eyes widened.

Will scowled. "It was forty-three on Sunday. Annie mentioned that. Today's Thursday. Forty-three plus four equals forty-seven. Okay?"

"She *mentioned* it?" Teddy gazed out at the vine-shrouded trees choking the untended lot across the street. A blue car rounded the corner. The driver was a young woman—pretty, Teddy noted, as he watched the Toyota roll past and continue down the street. He turned to Will. "You want some advice?"

"No thanks."

"I think you should call her again."

Three goldfinches sailed through the yard, sailed straight past the bird feeder that Will had filled with thistle seed that very morning. Even the birds were shunning him today.

Teddy went on. "Could be this is exactly what you need."

"Why on earth do I need a child right now?"

Softly: "Not a child, Uncle. All the stuff that comes with a child. You know, a *life*."

"I love my life." Will gazed around. "This is a great life."

Teddy picked up his sandwich and took a bite. He chewed and chewed, chewed so slowly Will felt as if his last remark was being chewed to pieces. At last Teddy swallowed. "Maybe you should tell me what *really* happened on Sunday," he said.

Not much. Not enough, as far as Will was concerned, to explain four days of silence. Which isn't to say he thought they'd had a wonderful time together on Sunday. The mood was apprehensive, and so Will had suggested a long walk. He figured he and Annie could use a change of scene, exercise and fresh air on a cool spring afternoon. He was hoping that a leisurely stroll together among the blossoming dogwoods and azaleas might somehow unlock their trunk of troubles, even point them in a new direction. What he got instead was silence.

The silence had come in stages, like a bicycle race: the wordless trek down Seventeenth Street, the mute hike past the White House, the quiet stroll through the new FDR Memorial. A mistake, Will realized instantly. At every turn, etched deeply into the granite walls, he and Annie found themselves standing before yet another pithy quote from FDR about war, poverty, racism—in short, some Large and Important issue against which their own dilemma seemed trivial indeed.

Nine days.

It wasn't as if Will had a red *X* marked on his calendar; nor did he need to put one there. He had done the math. The previous month, Annie's ovulation had commenced on the eighteenth. Eighteen plus Annie's twenty-six-day cycle meant the next day of reckoning would arrive on May 14. Sunday was the fifth. Fourteen minus five equals nine.

Nine days.

Let me assert my firm belief that the only thing we have to fear is fear itself.

Will saw pregnant women everywhere. They were lumbering along the wide pebbly paths of the Mall with water bottles strapped to their hips. They sat together on benches in front of the Smithsonian Castle, nibbling saltine crackers while their gleeful toddlers and slightly seasick husbands spun around and around on the nearby carousel. One glance at these suffering moms and dads left Will wondering if parenthood was simply too difficult a job. And this thought led to another: perhaps it was time to admit that he might be one of those men who simply isn't cut out for fatherhood.

Ahead, approaching, he spotted a husky dad in madras shorts. What little hair the man had left was pasted to his round head. His face was bathed in sweat. This overworked father had a folded-up stroller in one hand, a picnic basket in the other, a Hula Hoop draped over the left shoulder, and two dolls wedged under an arm. His fanny pack (a *fanny pack*!) bulged with disposable diapers and a half-eaten bag of Goldfish. And worst of all, as far as Will was concerned: the poor bastard was shuffling at full speed in the wake of two small children, and they were *outrunning* him. This was a portrait of misery, pure and simple—a caricature of misery. And yet, Will knew, were he to stop this fellow and press him on the issue of fatherhood, the man would smile broadly. Then he would rhapsodize. Fathers could be counted on to do this. These men would strap packs to their fannies; they would transport dripping bottles in dress shirt pockets; they would lug all manner of plastic gear over hill and dale; they would scream at their children in public, and rail inwardly at the layer of graham crackers that had petrified in the crack of the backseat of the Ford Windstar—and still these dads would rhapsodize. *Best thing that ever happened to me,* they would tell you. You could count on it.

It was significant to Will that no man ever said having a child was the best thing he had *decided* to do. It was the best thing that *happened.* A fine distinction, but an important one. Fatherhood isn't something most men actively choose. It seemed necessary to Will that fate be involved. The element of surprise, too. Like any stunning development in life (winning the lottery, flunking an exam, getting a grim report from the doctor), the news arrives like a thunderbolt, and one's first thought is to hold oneself together. You don't ask yourself how you feel because at that moment it no longer matters how you feel. You carry on.

In the old wing of the National Gallery, in a room covered floor to ceiling with paintings of the Virgin and Child, Annie finally took Will's arm, but in a grandmotherly sort of way that left him feeling even more deeply depressed. He gazed at the Madonna and Child before them, in a painting entitled *The Rest on the Flight into Egypt.*

She said, "So you're off to that conference next weekend?"

"Friday in New York. Then on to Boston Saturday morning."

"When do you get back?"

"Late Sunday."

In the painting, the Virgin Mary and baby Jesus rested in the foreground. Far in the background Will noted the tiny figure of St. Joseph with his walking stick upraised, whacking ineffectually at the high branches of a date tree. He turned to Annie. "Can we talk about what's going on?"

"Sure." She moved on to another painting.

"You're angry."

"Oh, please. It's just not that simple."

Was this comment addressed to him or to Lorenzo Lotto's *Maiden's Dream*? This painting featured a forest scene with a recumbent young woman being showered with flower petals from a hovering Cupid while a female satyr behind a tree gazes longingly at a male satyr who is swilling a jug of wine. All at once this room seemed to Will the absolute worst place in the world to be attempting this conversation. If only, somehow, he could have transported them down the marbled hallway to that suite of rooms filled with the sullen work of the Dutch masters: the unsmiling merchants and burghers, the dead game, all those lonesome windmills.

Annie was mad. At him. Probably furious. And she had a right to that fury. Will would have granted her that. Understood it, even. So why couldn't she empathize with his own difficult position? Both of them had their thorny issues, which, right then, beneath the beatific gaze of so many divine babies, seemed all the more irreconcilable.

At Massachusetts Avenue Will and Annie stood together in gloomy silence waiting for the light to change.

Will said, "I suppose it was crazy to think we could come to a decision about this in the first place."

For one brief second it seemed that Annie might respond, but then her expression went cloudy, and Will found himself staring at the two blue sapphires posted to the lobe of her left ear. The light turned green. In the middle of the intersection she said, "Of course it was crazy."

"I'm not good at crazy."

"I think you've mentioned that. Three or four times now."

She picked up the pace. Will stayed with her.

He said, "One minute I'm sure this is a terrible idea, and the next I'm trying to convince myself that it's not, and the minute after that I'm worrying about what would happen if there came a time when you wanted me to go away, and I wasn't willing to go away." He took her arm. "Have you thought about that?"

She nodded almost imperceptibly. "Yes, I have," she said softly.

"And?"

"I don't know, Will. I guess sometimes in life you have to take a chance."

"Talk to me," he said.

Annie stopped. "Okay, here it is: you're right. This is crazy. It was crazy to start with, and it's even crazier right now. The problem is, we can't do anything about that. *If* we want to have kids, I mean." She paused. "The only way this isn't crazy is if one of us walks away. If that's what you want, say that. *Do* that."

"That's not what I want." He took both of her hands. "I want you. I want to live with you. And I don't want to screw up our life together by having a child right now."

"So you're saying *no*."

"I'm saying *I don't know*. I'm saying we just met. That we need time. That there's this paradox that we can't get around. This is the sort of decision you can't make until you really know someone, but you can't really get to know someone with a decision like this hanging over your head every month."

She stopped. "You know me, Will. You know who I am. What else do you need to know?"

Softly, he said, "Look, if I was one of those guys who's known all his life that he wants to be a father, maybe I would see things differently. But I'm not one of those guys." He paused. "The other day it occurred to me that for all I know I might never have another chance at fatherhood, and I thought, *why not?* And then the idea of creating a child with a woman I've known for two months seemed like the most irresponsible thing in the world."

"Not two months," Annie replied. "Just forty-three days."

By the time they arrived at her apartment, Will figured that it was actually forty-two days. Forty-two days, sixteen hours, and ten minutes. Suddenly the conversation seemed absurd to him. The answer had to be *no*. Even if that meant he would risk losing her. But he wasn't brave enough to say that to Annie, not then.

"I want what you have," he told her. "Your certainty. Your fearlessness."

"I'm scared to death, Will." She looked at him. "This isn't something I decided to do. It's something I suddenly couldn't turn away from." There were tears in her eyes. "It's bigger than wanting to have a child. It's about living my life. Which is something I haven't done for a long time." She started up the steps, stopped, turned, sat down, stared straight ahead. Will sat down beside her. They sat together in silence for a full minute before Annie went on: "I had a boyfriend in law school. His name was David. I adored him. He was one of those young guys who had his whole life planned out, all the way to the Supreme Court. And I was part of that plan. Me, three kids, great careers for the two of us in and out of government, a big old house full of music and books, all of it. We got married the day after we graduated. David had never seen the ocean, so we drove a U-Haul with all our stuff to Washington, moved into a little apartment near the zoo. Then we rented a car and drove down to the Outer Banks for our honeymoon. Two weeks. Afterward we came back here to begin our jobs—to begin our lives. And a week later, David was out at lunch with one of the lawyers in his office, waiting to cross K Street, when a pickup truck jumped the curb and hit him. He died instantly." She looked at Will. "I was a kid. And suddenly I was all by myself, with no plans, no future, nothing. I didn't know anybody. I didn't know what else to do, so I threw myself into work—sixty, seventy hours a week, the more the better. A few years later I met Rob, and we became friends, and somehow I got folded into his life. I wanted that actually. It felt safe. And then one day I realized that I couldn't do that anymore." She paused. "Once I woke up I started feeling better about myself. As if I was in charge of my life. And then I met you, and it seemed that you and I might find a way to make some kind of a life together. Part of me really wanted that and another part of me was scared to death by the very thought of it. For a while, I thought it might happen. And now I'm not sure. And I'm really sorry about that. But I'll get over it. I'm not a dreamer, Will. Not anymore."

Monday morning Will telephoned Annie and left a message on her voice mail. He didn't expect to hear back from her until late in the evening, since Mondays at her office were generally crazy. But Monday night came and went; and then Tuesday, too. By Wednesday Will had a knot in his stomach. Late in the afternoon he called Annie at home, intending to leave a message on her machine. But the sound of her voice on the tape unsettled him, and he hung up before the beep. Thursday morning—still no word—he telephoned Annie's office again and left a message with her assistant.

By noon, the continuing silence had ballooned to such large and ominous proportions that even young Teddy must have sensed it, or so Will assumed when his nephew joined him on the front porch, baloney on Sunbeam in hand. Apparently Teddy had decided to forgo his regular lunchtime Internet round of Hearts to sit with his despondent uncle. But quiet commiseration was not Teddy's strong suit.

"Does this mean she's *dumping* you?"

Will considered the question. He looked at Teddy. Then he nodded. "It's beginning to feel that way," he replied.

"Wow." There was a long, long pause. Then: "How come she didn't tell you?"

"She did." Will gazed across the street. "Apparently I wasn't paying attention." He shrugged. "Sometimes bad news can take a little while to sink in."

Teddy chewed, shaking his head.

Will's eyes fixed on a quarrelsome band of starlings on the front lawn. He thought, so what exactly is wrong with my life?

Teddy swallowed. "Let's say I was God," he said. "And let's say somehow I let you know that you and Annie were going to spend the next forty years together. Would that change how you feel about having a kid?"

"Right this minute?"

Teddy nodded.

Will thought. "I don't think so," he finally said.

Teddy brightened. "So then this isn't about Annie *at all*."

Of course it was. It had to be. At some level. At least a little bit. *Didn't it?*

Will wasn't one of those men who knew with certainty that he would never have kids: didn't like children, or didn't want the responsibility, or didn't have room for them in his life. But as to agreeing to conceive a child with a woman whom he had known forty-seven days? No. Not even this woman, whose voice right then he was dying to hear, whose quick wit and sweet, mischievous smile, both absent of late, he adored. Annie Leonard fascinated Will. He loved her wry sense of humor, her blue eyes and short brown hair, her forthrightness, the degree to which she knew her own mind about everything, it seemed, including having a child. His child.

This inconceivable child.

Okay, so maybe the solitary life he'd led these many years made him a poor candidate for marriage and fatherhood. Not that this had ever troubled him particularly. The fact was, Will did love his life. He had friends and family nearby, work that suited him, a funky little house in the shady suburbs, a lawn to mow, wild birds to observe and feed—a nephew to observe and feed, too, for the moment anyway. So what if this wasn't a life that young Ted could admire? Teddy was just a kid, a kid filled with strong opinions about any number of subjects about which he knew almost nothing.

So why was Teddy's observation so troubling?

Because it stung.

The quarrelsome starlings flew away.

WILL WAS NOT a morning person, but with the arrival of Teddy the night owl the previous January, he trained himself to get up with the sun. These days he was out of bed at six. He would splash cold water on his face, brew himself a strong cup of coffee, and plunge directly into work. The early morning hours were the precious ones. The phone was quiet, the answering machine unblinking; the computer slept, as did Teddy, in the shed out back. Like some sort of long-legged grazing animal, Will would wander from manuscript to manuscript, pausing here to nibble fifteen pages of a coming-of-age novel, there to consume fifty pages of a war story. One morning might find him reading the outline and introduction for a biography of a little-known American nominated for sainthood; the next, stretched out on the couch, he would skim three chapters of a self-help book on how to survive a tax audit.

At around ten each morning Teddy would stumble through the back door into Will's kitchen, and soon the house would echo with knocks and scrapes, shuddering pipes and muttered expletives; and then moments later, as if in response to Teddy's arrival, the phone would ring, the fax would beep; finally came the whistle of a kettle and the whir of a computer: the Gerard Literary Agency, headquartered in a shady Maryland suburb just west of the nation's capital, was open for business.

On sunny days Will abandoned his office in the spare bedroom for the front porch. There, settled in a rocker, glass of water and birding binoculars at his feet, laptop on his knees, he would set to work on his correspondence, tapping out a dozen letters of every stripe: pitch, rejection, solicitation. Inside the house the ringing telephone marked the passing hours like a ship's bells. And young Teddy, as boatswain, would pop outside at regular intervals to deliver another in an endless string of comments and questions:

"Does anybody still care about the Korean War?"

"Just got a novel called *The Gay President!*"

"Listen up, Uncle: a woman wants your hand in marriage, and oh-by-the-way could you find a publisher for her roman à clef?" Pause. "What's a roman à clef?"

At noon, if the weather held, Will would lace up his running shoes and jog down the street to the Potomac River for a half-hour run alongside the C&O Canal. Or else he might pass the time in the backyard hammering lumber together to make raised beds for a garden, or a new compost bin. Afterward came a bite of lunch, and then Will would spend the rest of the day on the telephone.

Thursdays tended to be frenetic, as most Fridays Will caught an early train to New York to make the editorial rounds. But this Thursday was the exception to the rule. Teddy's photocopying had been wrapped up by eleven, Will's Friday lunch date already confirmed. And so, at two o'clock on a summer-like afternoon, a well-exercised, freshly showered Will Gerard again settled himself on the front porch of his brick bungalow. *Annie still hadn't called.* Will watched a pair of nuthatches grooming a mottled old sycamore and gave some thought to Teddy's suggestion that he call her again. But he rejected this idea: either he would be leaving another message with Stephanie, or else Annie would pick up her line and—

And what?

He didn't know. He couldn't imagine what either of them might say, but after four days of silence he could be sure the conversation would go badly. Will had a stockinged foot resting on the newly painted white rail, a mechanical pencil in his left hand, a stack of padded envelopes and manuscripts on the floor in front him. He decided to tackle the mail instead.

This was mind-numbing work. To stay focused Will liked to imagine himself on the same sort of hunt as, say, a floppy-hatted pale-ontologist wandering the windswept hills of northeast China, eyes ever alert for the whitish lump of fossilized bone that would turn out to be the remains of some fantastically old bird-dinosaur. In Will's case this meant keeping his wits about him as he sifted through the desiccated gray oatmeal of a split-open Jiffy bag, awake to the possi-bility, slim though it might be—*nonexistent*, Teddy loudly insisted— that this was the manuscript whose first sentence would quicken the pulse, even announce the arrival of a new voice on the literary scene.

What Will heard instead was the shriek of a pileated woodpecker. He quickly found the red-headed bird attached to the trunk of a tulip poplar across the way. Inside, the telephone sounded—four rings before Teddy picked it up. At the conclusion of the call, Will listened for the scrape of Teddy's chair, and the sound of his approach. There was nothing but a private whistle, and then Teddy's ack-ack-ack laugh, softly this time. The next call brought no heavy tread of Doc Martens, nor the next, and when Teddy finally did arrive at the screen door, it wasn't to announce that Annie Leonard was holding for Will on line one, but to register his baffled contempt for the folks some writers thought worthy of a biography.

"Who the hell is Spiro T. Agnew?" he asked.

Will looked up. "Who's the letter from?"

"A guy named R. C. Parrolan."

"Robert Chancellor Parrolan?"

Teddy studied the piece of paper in his hand. "It says here that he wrote a book about a guy named A-D-L-A-I—"

"*The Summons*. It won a Pulitzer."

"I guess that means you want to take a look at this."

Will nodded. "Train mail," he said.

"Aye, aye, Captain." The screen door slammed. Then, at the open living-room window, came a whisper: "You know something, Uncle? If you ever want to make some *real* money, all we'd need to do is figure out how to get you on *Jeopardy*."

Teddy was nineteen.

That spring was to have been the second semester of his freshman year at Princeton, only Teddy had saddled himself with a fall semester course load that turned out to be the academic equivalent of tackling Everest on one's first hike in the mountains (Chinese, upper level courses in linguistics and philosophy, etcetera, etcetera). To make matters worse, Teddy had spent most nights in the computer lab designing Web sites for anybody on campus who might need one. Early in December he came down with the flu. He slept through one exam, failed another, and arrived home for the holidays with the news that he had been "advised" to take a leave of absence from school. Will had a report from Teddy's mother—his younger sister, Marianne—when he ran into her at the food co-op up the street. This was a few weeks after Will had launched his career as a literary agent. Dark-haired Marianne deftly steered the conversation from Teddy's academic travails to the headaches that *must* be facing a man who was trying to run a new business *all by himself.*

She shook her head sadly as she began to scoop organic flour into a plastic bag. "No one to answer the phone. Nobody to sort the mail. Or set up the computer systems, the accounting systems, the bank accounts—what else?"

"I thought I'd look for an assistant with some publishing experience," Will explained. Someone I can *fire,* he was thinking.

"Ted's quick on his feet. You know he's a fast learner."

This was true. But Will was considering several adjectives that did not apply to young Ted: neat, polite, conscientious, to name a few.

Marianne gently set the bag of flour in her shopping cart beside the bags of raisins and dates, a slab of rennetless cheese, a huge box of multicolored pasta, a tub of honey, jars upon jars of vitamins and homeopathic remedies.

"We're both Aries," Will went on. "Hiring Teddy would be a disaster."

"So you'll butt heads a little bit. Jonathan and Dad were both Leos, but they worked it out eventually, didn't they? Besides, it'll be good for you. For both of you."

How could Will explain to his sister that he was too far out on a limb already? Real literary agents are supposed to live and work in

New York City. An agent based in Washington, D.C., is, by definition, second-string. A Washington agent who operates out of his house in the suburbs with a nephew for an assistant must be considered beyond the pale.

Marianne took his arm as they moved toward the check-out line. "Just this morning I was reading an article which said that among some Native American peoples it's the mother's *brother* whose job it is to guide her sons on the path to manhood."

"I'm sure it's the oldest brother," replied Will. "This definitely sounds like a job for Jonathan."

"But Jonathan doesn't have the patience for Teddy." Marianne gave him a winning smile. "Not to mention that he isn't hiring."

"Where would Teddy live?"

"With us. In his old bedroom." Marianne and her husband, Tom, lived in Glen Echo, less than a mile from Will's house in Cabin John. She was a sculptor. "When you don't need him he can help me in the studio," she added. Another bright smile. "Think about how convenient that would be!"

A few days after Teddy came to work for Will, venetian blinds appeared in the windows of the shed out back. ("To let me work late without disturbing you," Teddy explained.) A gleaming dead bolt soon adorned the shed's door. ("Your machine isn't big enough for what we need to do, Uncle. I brought mine.") He had also brought a duffel bag of black clothes and a trunk filled with homebrew equipment. Next, Teddy's toothbrush showed up in the bathroom alongside Will's. Then early one frosty morning in late January, as Will sat working at the kitchen table, Teddy appeared at the back door in parka, pajamas, and mukluks. With his eyes closed, he looked like a raccoon on its nocturnal rounds. "Toilet," he whispered as he shuffled past the refrigerator. "Still nighttime," he muttered on the way out.

Teddy's literary sensibility was unreliable, but the last thing Will needed right then was an assistant with the soul of a poet. Teddy's genius for systems (computer, filing, mail sorting, office design, coffee brewing, you name it) more than compensated for his surly presence. He was a wizard on the telephone, able to adopt the voice of whatever authority figure need be summoned to shield Will from the persistent and the rude. This is not to suggest that Teddy was anything like a model employee. His hours were irregular. He was crotchety in the same way that Will's late father had been crotchety. An autodidact, too. Teddy took instruction with all the grace of a cranky two-year-old.

"So what's missing from this manuscript?" Will might muse aloud. "A grasp of the English language," Teddy would mutter without taking his eyes from the computer screen. Or: "A story that anybody in the world would want to read."

Sorting the mail was Teddy's job.

On sunny days Will sent him up the street to the post office, and Teddy would return red-faced and angry, dragging one or two dirty postal sacks. Other days the pristine or battered boxes arrived singly, or in small flotillas that collected on the front porch. Four months into the job and Will still couldn't predict the volume of his mail. A listing in a trade publication for writers or a talk at the National Press Club (not to mention that gossipy piece about Will in the *Washington Post*) inevitably spawned something akin to what the warm sands of the Sahara stir up in the cold waters of the Atlantic. Like hurricanes, these letters and manuscripts seemed to coalesce in the mouth of the Potomac and crash ashore at Will's door. "Dear Mr. Gerard, My father recently passed away and I was sorting through his papers when I came upon the most fantastic story. . . ."

Frank, the regular UPS driver, was tall and suave, with dark glistening hair and a trophy mustache. He had a dancer's body and moved with elegant restraint in his back-protecting harness as he wheeled a hand-truck up the walk. Sally, of FedEx, displayed the raw strength of a kayaker. She was frenetic and reckless in the white water of her appointed rounds, Will's house just another of the many upcurrent flags to be furiously approached and circled. From her departing truck she would lift an arm like an exhausted competitor passing beneath the colored flags at the finish line. Wade Peggett, Will's postman, was the Robert Duvall of mail carriers. He would park his diminutive truck at the entrance to Will's gravel driveway, emerging these days in shorts and calf-length socks or, if there was a hint of rain in the air, in a broad-brimmed helmet covered with tightly fitting plastic and a sheer poncho. Wade whistled as he made his way across the lawn. There was a broad hint of west Texas in his dry chuckle.

Wade would cradle each day's stack of manuscripts as if they were breakable things. Will was touched by his care. Sometimes Wade set the mail on the top step and read aloud the handwritten name and address as he passed each padded package to Will. Wade had been with the Special Forces in Vietnam in the late 1960s; he had spent two tours of duty in the Ia Drang Valley. This exchange always felt to Will like a military ceremony: "Anderson. Carefree, Arizona." Will could almost hear the lone bugle playing taps. It saddened him that so much of his mail came from towns in the Sunbelt with relentlessly upbeat names: Celebration, Paradise Valley, Sunrise Harbor.

> Dear Mrs. Aringham, Like your book group, I too was
> moved by your reminiscences of Chiang Mai. And yes, it is
> incredible to think that in all the years you lived there neither
> you nor your husband ever came into contact with opium or
> anyone involved in the opium trade. The title you have
> chosen—*The Hidden Chiang Mai*—does address this
> paradox. Your description of the U.S. Consul's house came
> alive for me, as I have been there. But I found myself
> troubled by the anecdotal nature of this book—what you
> describe in your letter as its "episodic" structure. I'm sorry to
> have to report that this is not a manuscript that I can sell. . . .

Teddy regarded the mail as a dog regards its fleas, a source of fascination and irritation even on the lightest days. After just a week on the job, he stormed into Will's office waving an envelope, saying, "You are asking me to look for a needle in a haystack. One needle per two hundred haystacks, Uncle. If I'm *lucky*."

Will smiled. "So get lucky."

Sorting through the slush pile requires the touch of a prospector, he explained. Look for stories. Pay attention to the voice. Each sentence, each word should be surprising *and* inevitable. We don't want books written to recently departed spouses, or to the guys at the watercooler, or to lost parents or unborn children. Nor do we want books animated exclusively by the plaintive cry *I lived* or *I loved* or *I lost*. (Teddy emerged from this chat with three new rejection categories, and soon had manufactured three rubber stamps.)

Who's to say that a literary gem isn't hiding under that sheaf of autoerotic poems, or beneath the cassette labeled *The World in all its Chaotic Complexity Fully Explained?* ("I feel I am freshest when speaking into a microphone while biking twenty miles to and from my job at the Bureau of Standards," huffed its narrator.) A treasure might be lurking underneath that folio of sheet music ("I assume, Mr. Gerard, that you represent composers, too"), or the blue binder with a garishly colored image of the Virgin Mary glued to the cover, or the plain white envelope with the tiny handwritten note ("Enough sand has passed through the hourglass, Mr. Gerard. I am at last willing to reveal the true story of American involvement in quashing the Hukbalahap rebellion"); or, perhaps strangest of all, beneath the marriage proposal that served as a cover letter for a hefty saga of family strife set in the hills and hollows of southwestern Virginia. ("P.S.," wrote Miss Luanne Swink, "I have just finished a long, long novel about the past six generations of strong women in my family. Whether you are or are not able to accept my proposal of marriage, Mr. Gerard, I am sure I can count on you to forward this manuscript to a publisher who specializes in romans à clef.").

That Will actually read a few pages of this novel on this particular Thursday afternoon was an indication of his frame of mind. He was killing time waiting for the phone to ring. Enclosed with Ms. Swink's mauve-colored, lilac-scented correspondence was a copy of her family tree. Will scrutinized that, as well. It resembled a mushroom cloud. The names of her relatives were memorable: Hilda Mae Groom, Noel Fortune, Winston Tayloe, Grafton Spotswood. Will's eye was drawn to the edge of the diagram, to the lineal cul-de-sacs of spinster aunts and bachelor uncles. Each name seemed to dangle inertly, like a dead tree limb ready to snap off in the next breeze.

It was close to four when a hiccup announced Teddy's presence at the screen door. He reported that Annie's assistant had just telephoned to say that the boss's afternoon had gone haywire: Annie had told Stephanie to tell Teddy to tell Will that she would try to reach him later in the evening.

Will considered his options. Perhaps this was the moment to telephone Annie and invite her out to dinner. Or else he could call her up and get mad. Howl a bit. *Four whole days!* He could rush downtown to her office, bust in on a meeting, and spirit her away. *To the beach!*

He did none of those things, of course.

Instead, in the soft light of the late afternoon, gazing up at the darting swallows and martins, Will came to the glum conclusion that there was nothing he could do. The relationship was doomed. It was too late for bold declarations of love, too late for anger, too late even for the miracle of a road trip. If only he and Annie had met two years earlier. Or five years later. If only she already had a child, or he had somehow managed to have his own epiphany about parenthood. If only!

Will was awash in self-pity now. This was the moment to undrape himself from the rocker and start packing for his trip to New York. Or, at the very least, to admit to himself that he had begun to brood.

Brooders miss everything.

The screen door creaked open and slammed shut. Young Teddy collapsed into the other rocker. "Catch this," he announced. "True story. Young woman who was adopted is searching for her birth parents. Sort of a quest. Sounds intriguing."

"What's the hook?"

"Part detective story, part memoir, part how-to, I guess." He scratched the stubble on his chin. "The main thing I like is her attitude."

"What else has she written?"

"Doesn't say."

Which meant: nothing. Which meant that this proposal had to be considered the longest of long shots. Will listened to the sad call of a mourning dove. He recalled a book he must have read a thousand times to a much younger Teddy, the story of a baby bird that hatches alone in its nest and then goes off on a journey, stopping along the way to ask a kitten, then a hen, then a dog, a cow, a boat, a plane, and finally, a steam shovel, the question at the front of its mind: "Are you my mother?"

Teddy went on: "More than a hundred thousand kids adopted in the U.S. each year. Sounds like a pretty big market. It wouldn't be hard to reach."

Still.

Will had opened up shop four months earlier with the belief that as a literary agent based in Washington, D.C., he ought to concentrate on the few subjects that were native to the town: journalism, history, politics, travel, memoirs and biographies related to those topics; fiction, too. He was looking for novels about presidents, great wars, grand American themes—not to mention tales of greed, lust, treachery, and scandal of the sort that regularly appeared on the front page of the *Washington Post*.

"Couldn't hurt to look at what she's got."

Will shook his head. "Thanks but no thanks," he said.

"When this turns out like that book on adult incontinence that sold three hundred thousand copies, I am going to remind you that you didn't even look at the damn letter."

Will smiled. "To the bridge."

And so Teddy departed. But on the way back to his desk, he didn't drop the envelope with the stylish handwriting into the red plastic crate labeled *Thanks but No Thanks*. Instead, he left it with the mail that Will was planning to read the next morning on the train to New York.

Friday morning the alarm didn't sound. Or else it had sounded, and Will had slept through the awful buzzing noise. Or maybe he'd forgotten to set it. Or it had broken. Or he'd sleepwalked and turned off the damned thing in the middle of the night. Or else—

He flew around the room stuffing clothes into one bag, then dashed into his office and jammed a stack of paper into another. The laptop was zipped into its case. In three minutes Will was spinning up gravel as he backed out of the driveway; fifteen more found his car racing into Georgetown. Only then did he gaze through the windshield and note the darkness: *middle of the night* darkness. Only then did he glance down at the dashboard and discover that he had misread the clock on the bureau.

It was quarter to five now, not quarter to six.

At Union Station, feeling deeply grumpy, Will bought coffee and a bagel, orange juice, three newspapers. He couldn't help but note a theme that morning in the *Washington Post*, one that was nicely squared with his own frame of mind: a story about the president's fading memory concerning a series of Oval Office meetings, news of a bone chip that would end the racing career of the previous week's winner of the Kentucky Derby, a report of a forty-year-old tennis champion who was taking his ancient wooden racket to the Senior Tour. The Arts page featured a review of a book entitled *Getting Over Getting Older.*

Forty had seemed young enough to Will, no big hurdle. It was a momentous birthday only in the sense that it had felt like an achievement: he'd reached a summit of some sort. But then he crossed over into a new watershed. Forty-one arrived like a slap to the back of the head. First came a pair of drugstore reading glasses, long needed and long refused. Suddenly Will could read things that he had once just guessed at (the warnings on pharmaceutical labels, for example). But he couldn't help thinking that this clarity of vision had come at a price. His dignity, for one thing. Somebody would shove a newsclip in his hands and instead of just glancing at it and roaring along with the crowd, he would now go into the grandpa routine, hunting up the glasses, fumbling them out of their case, by which time the joke had been lost. (*If* he found the glasses, that is: now he had a third vital object, in addition to his wallet and car keys, to misplace.)

Nobody had warned Will that these glasses would reveal far more of the world than he might actually want to see. An unshaven Teddy parked at the kitchen table, for example: a Chuck Close portrait come to life. Or any part of his own anatomy. These days the skin on his hands seemed a suitable covering for luggage. In the shaving mirror he noted a permanent crease on his forehead that looked like an old fencing scar. And all those stray whiskers on his cheeks! There were stray hairs on his ears, too, one of which he had discovered growing horizontally, almost an inch in length! It was as if he'd woken up one day to discover that he had become grizzled. For some reason these rogue follicles bothered Will more than the idea of a thinning hairline. Not that he *had* a thinning hairline—no evidence of that, none whatsoever. But the mere fact he was making an occasional tour of his own scalp with a hand mirror, well, to him, that said it all.

Will felt old. And the reason he felt old, he now realized, was that he *was* old. Old enough to stumble from bed under the assumption that he had forgotten to set an alarm, and then not have the presence of mind (or the glasses at hand) to check the clock and discover that it was an hour earlier than he had thought.

Heading off to the train Will sensed Father Time trailing behind him, gaining with every step. He picked up the pace, but a stab of pain in his lower back slowed him to a walk. In the concourse he experi- enced short-term memory loss regarding the track number of his train. The loss of one hour of sleep had turned him into a doddering old man! He half-expected the Amtrak porter standing beside the courtesy wheelchair to note the confused expression on his face, take his elbow, and sit him down. Instead, the porter's eyelids lowered drowsily, and the younger man took a seat in the chair himself. Will soldiered on through the carpeted hallways, his knees cracking like gum.

Nothing had prepared him for suddenly finding himself in such a state. Nobody had warned him of the sudden downhill slide. Perhaps that was because this didn't happen to other men. His own father hadn't seemed old at forty-one, not by a long shot. He was dapper. No creaky joints, no back pain—no physical complaints at all. This was a man who had spent his twenties parachuting into trouble spots around the globe, who had trained Cuban freedom fighters in the jungles of Guatemala, and God only knows what else.

Will pictured his father at forty-one: suit and tie, his regular cos- tume even on the hottest days in Bangkok, hair slicked back with a lit- tle Brylcreem, a Kent in his left hand. The year was 1968. At forty-one, James J. Gerard's government service stood at a year short of two decades. He was the CIA station chief in Thailand. Jamie Gerard was a man to be reckoned with. *Established* was the first adjective that came to mind. At forty-one, Will's father had been married for fifteen years; two of his three children were already teenagers. He had a life filled with awards, accomplishments, letters and photos signed by presidents; a life vigorously *lived,* and still a young man!

Will's own life, by contrast, seemed to him a jerry-built affair full of fits and starts. Take this new career, for example, which couldn't be considered off the ground until he had enough of a regular income to rent a proper office. Twenty years of adulthood and all Will had to show for it was a well-mortgaged house in the suburbs. No wife, no kids—no dependents at all unless one were to count Newt the cat under the front porch, and Teddy the nephew in the shed out back.

On a descending escalator, it hit Will that this seven-week-long discussion with Annie over the issue of procreation might have been a complete waste of time: he had never submitted to a sperm test. For all he knew, at his advanced age, fatherhood might be out of the question. That microscopic army of his was certain to behave less like a well-drilled Tour de France racing team than a placid herd of grazing cows.

The Amtrak Colonial sat quietly on the track, doors flung open. The platform smelled of hot wires and disinfectant. This definitely wasn't anything resembling a Hollywood departure scene of steam and train whistles and billowing regrets, but Will felt a sharp twinge of sadness nonetheless. At a pay phone, he punched in Annie's number without a second thought.

Four rings brought in the answering machine, then Annie's message, at the end of which Will's mouth felt as dry as powdered milk. The instant he spoke, the real Annie—a very sleepy Annie—picked up.

"I figured it had to be you," she said. "Nobody else calls me at the crack of dawn."

At least I call, he wanted to say. But he didn't.

Annie went on, "I meant to call you back last night. But I got home late." She paused. "It seemed like a lousy thing to do to a guy with an early train."

"I was hoping we might have a conversation before I headed out of town." He sounded formal, unhappy, hideously stiff. Even he could hear this in his voice.

"Will, don't be angry at me."

He gazed around at the boarding passengers trailed by their leashed luggage. Not angry, he thought. Disappointed. Upset. Depressed by the very circumstances surrounding this call. Okay, maybe a little pissed off, too.

He said, "Things went sour on Sunday. I call you on Monday and you don't return my call. We don't talk all week. Now I'm off to New York and the Cape. I had this crazy idea that maybe we should talk before I left. To find out where things stand. Just in case we're still hanging by a thread."

"You don't get it, do you?"

What he got, mostly, was that it was best never to try to answer a question like this. "I guess not," he said.

"All the focus has been on you. Which made sense at first. I want to get pregnant, and you're not sure you want to be part of that. So you think it over. You think it over and over and over. First you decide to go along with it. Then you change your mind. Then you think *that* might not be the right decision. Time passes and things between us change. Suddenly the issue of my wanting to have a child becomes a conversation about *us*. Then it isn't—that is, we agree that it doesn't have to be. Then you decide that we should wait six months. We don't talk about it, you don't ask for my opinion, you just blurt that out one day. And I'm supposed to go along with it—all of it—no questions asked, no complaints, no bad feelings. You know how that makes me feel, Will? Like a bystander."

He didn't know what to say.

"Sunday I couldn't take it anymore. I wanted to check out for awhile."

"I got the sense that this was bigger than *a while*."

Annie said, "The truth is that I've been busy—"

"You've been busy all along. But somehow you always find fifteen minutes—"

"I wanted to be busy. Staying busy seemed like the right approach this week."

"Four days," he said. "I called you. You could have called me back."

"And you want to know why I didn't? Because I was afraid of *this*."

He sighed. "It doesn't have to be like this."

"But it is. And I knew it would be. You did, too. Which is why I figured we'd be better off waiting till you got back on Sunday. Face next week next week." She paused. "Maybe that was a mistake."

The conductor on the platform was checking his watch, just like in the movies.

Will said, "Look, I could wrap things up after lunch with Barry. Grab an early train. We could do something tonight."

"But your conference on the Cape—"

"I'll cancel."

Silence.

Will said, "If you've got something else—"

"It's not that." Annie sighed. "Last night I went to a meeting. Single moms. Sort of a support group. Pretty depressing all the way around." She paused. "I came away with the idea that it would be good for me to take a few days by myself. To think about things. Try to sort them out."

"What kind of things?"

"Every kind of thing."

"We wait till Sunday," he said gravely, "and we're toast."

Annie didn't reply.

"A quiet dinner," said Will. "Afterward we'll go to a silly movie. Just be together. No talk about next week."

A moment passed. Then Annie said, "Do you ever wonder where we'd be without this cloud?"

"All the time," he replied.

"So where would we be?"

"Without this cloud, we'd be living together."

"You really think so?"

"Absolutely."

"I don't know. One minute I think that, and the next I'm sure it's just wishful thinking." And then, an instant later: "Come back, Will. We'll grab a late bite."

"You mean that?"

"I'm still asleep. Of course I mean that."

ON THE TRAIN, Will commandeered a table in the dining car and spread out his work: he had three book proposals to consider, a contract to review, the latest issue of *Publishers Weekly* to skim, a rubber-banded stack of mail to read and toss, two manuscripts to pass judgment on. Before him lay one of those. It was a work of fiction that had been written by a reporter who had sent it to Will at the suggestion of Will's older brother, Jonathan, who was also a journalist. *Pass Christian* was the title. The cover letter described the novel as the story of a group of Vietnamese boat people who settled on the Mississippi Gulf Coast, started shrimping, and suddenly found themselves in conflict with a group of American shrimpers who happened to be Vietnam vets. As a favor to his brother, Will was planning to read the entire manuscript, which explained why he had lugged all of it along with him. This he regretted the instant he flipped it open and read the first sentence that caught his eye: "Giap moved like a tiger on the deck of the old boat, nostrils to the wind, recalling the awful days he'd spent drifting helplessly in the South China Sea."

Will plucked the rubber band from the mail. No doubt there would be a solicitation from a stockbroker pretending to be an old school chum, a request or two that Teddy couldn't (or wouldn't) handle, query letters that he wanted Will to read, be they charming or peculiar or even interesting. For most of Will's adult life the afternoon mail call had been a predictable collection of bills and junk. But nowadays he found surprises every day. There were notes from old friends or the parents of old friends, invitations to parties, lecture requests. The profile of Will in the *Washington Post*, complete with photographs of the literary agent at work, had resulted in a surge of interesting mail: a call for his presence at a fête at the Swedish Embassy, at a piano recital at the Kennedy Center, at a literary salon on Cape Cod. There had been news via Will's mother that his fourth-grade teacher had read the piece. (His mother had also reported that the once-intimidating Sister Mary Bartholomew, who had left the convent long ago, had earned a Ph.D. in sociology and was writing a book.)

Everybody was writing a book.

Will had grown up in a family that cherished books. He was a voracious, eclectic reader: Walker Percy on quiet Sunday afternoons, Colette in the wake of romantic catastrophe, Dashiell Hammett on trains, George Sand's *Intimate Journals* or Sy Hersh's Camelot at bedtime. He had spent his entire working life in the realm of books. His first job, at seventeen, was as a reshelver at the local library. Later, he worked in a variety of bookstores, everything from the fussy literary shop with a carriage trade to a remainder warehouse that sold novels by the pound. After college, at loose ends on the issue of career, Will took another bookstore job and five months later found himself managing the failing shop. This had led to a stint as a salesman for a large trade publisher, which in turn led to a partnership in a small press that specialized in travel guides. Each of these jobs began with a honeymoon period while Will learned the ropes. But once the ropes were learned, complacency would set in, and then boredom, and in the midst of that Will would find himself surreptitiously reading novels at work.

It was during just such a stolen moment nearly a year earlier that he had been seized by a thought: reading ought to be a much bigger part of his day. This flash of insight behaved like a virus, burrowing into his brain and slowly infecting the place. As luck would have it, around this same time, the first chapters of a novel arrived out of the blue. It was a Civil War story. Across the top of the first page, in a cramped scrawl, the highly eccentric Norton Tazewell had written, "This any good?" It was good. So good, in fact, that Will saw this book as a bridge to a new career. Within months he had sold his share of the publishing business to his partner and opened up shop as a literary agent.

What pleased Will most about this new job was its simplicity: he trafficked in *words*. Writer to agent to editor. There were no printers to pay, no warehouses to supervise—indeed, no sales reps, no wholesalers, no booksellers, and, most blessedly of all, no direct contact with a fickle book buying public that could drive a small publisher or bookseller into bankruptcy in the course of a single season. All that a person needed to succeed as an agent was a good set of eyes, a modest array of telecommunications equipment, some publishing contacts, and a stack of promising manuscripts. The job was elegantly straightforward: everything depended upon literary taste and intuition. Either you respond to a piece of writing or you don't. *Yes* or *no*.

Will felt temperamentally suited to this new role. He was prepared to act decisively, to bluff when necessary, to play the high-minded man of letters or the bottom-line scold. He was not, however, prepared for the mail. All these heartfelt letters and manuscripts! A dozen more the next day! There were strange letters, too. Notes from cranks and obsessives, whistle-blowers real and imaginary. Most of this mail Will tossed out immediately, but some of it he couldn't help puzzling over. What would a query letter from Sylvia Plath have looked like? Or Mark Twain? Or young Fidel Castro?

> Dear Mr. Gerard, There is no return address on this note for
> one very good reason: agents of the federal government open
> my mail. You see, I know the truth of what happened in
> Dallas. And I am ready to talk. My mother's closest friend
> was a client of Tom Clancy back when he was in insurance
> (Clancy, that is), and I was planning to offer this story to

him. But then I saw that article about you and figured I
would try you first. All I require in the way of compensation
is $135,675 in cash, which I can assure you is a bargain.
Shortly I will call you from a pay phone using the code name
Mockingbird. . . .

Dear Mr. Gerard, You don't know me but I suspect you
might have heard of my husband, Earl Waring, who is now
deceased. He was the U.S. Consul in Chittagong, which I am
certain I don't have to tell you is in Bangladesh (East
Pakistan as we first knew the country). My husband and I
lived there for ten years, through the struggle for
independence, through typhoons and floods, the cholera, the
terrible assassination of Sheik Rahman, you name it. It was
quite an exciting life I can tell you that. But then you would
know all about the overseas life, from the time with your
family in Bangkok. We loved Bangkok.

Do you believe that God works in mysterious ways, Mr.
Gerard? I do, and I will tell you why. I still subscribe to the
Washington Post, of course, and the very day I read about you
and your new literary enterprise was the day I began this
short (just 74 double-spaced pages!) memoir, entitled *Our
Years in Chittagong*. As if that weren't coincidence enough,
here is another: I believe I met your mother when we were
evacuated to Bangkok from Dhaka (Dacca then) in 1968.
That time the reason was smallpox. We were all so grateful
for the sandwiches and coffee. . . .

The next envelope was handwritten, the letters so stylishly printed
that Will assumed the writer must be a graphic artist. The ink was
dark blue, almost black. Will noted the College Park, Maryland,
return address and the postmark from St. Mary's City, far to the southeast. The name in the upper left-hand corner meant nothing to him.

Dear Mr. Gerard, I just read the article about you that
appeared two months ago in the *Washington Post*. In it you
described a book as a journey. I was intrigued by this idea

because I am presently involved in a journey myself. You see, I am adopted, and I have begun searching for my birth parents.

What you said in the article made me think about writing a book about adoption. (More than 100,000 children are adopted in the United States each year.) This book could describe some of the new directories and techniques one could use in the search for birth parents, focusing especially on the World Wide Web. But most of the story, as I imagine it right now, would be about my personal experience. A memoir of sorts. I liked what you had to say about memoirs—that they aren't *the* truth but *a* truth, less about what happened and more about how we experience what happens, and how this experience makes us who we are. Adopted kids are always struggling with the issue of who we are.

I set out on this journey in the hopes of meeting my birth parents, but as I enter adulthood (I turn twenty-one on December 23) I have come to realize that what I've really set out to do is come to a better sense of who I am. I have no romantic illusions that a reunion with my birth parents will lead to any sort of deep or long-lasting relationship, I simply wish to meet these people, and learn something about where I come from. Growing up, all I knew about my past came from the information that my parents picked up at the time of my adoption. For example, that my birth mother spent the last trimester of her pregnancy with me at a Catholic home for unwed mothers in Silver Spring called St. Jerome's, and that her father had died in the Vietnam War.

To know so little about my past is no longer okay with me. I want to know why I was given up for adoption (the circumstances, I mean), and to see myself in the context of extended families about which I know nothing. (I don't even know for certain that my birth father knows that I am alive.)

Does any of this make sense to you, Mr. Gerard? I hope so. And I would very much appreciate any thoughts or advice you might have for me.

Sincerely, Charlotte Cameron.

Will stared at the sheet of paper for ten or fifteen seconds. His mind had gone blank. Glancing up at last, he caught the eye of an Armani-suited lawyer across the car, another regular on the Friday morning run. The lawyer's nod was so tentative Will knew that his own face must be drained of its color. He took a deep breath and turned slightly toward the window, sat there numbly as the train rolled through another in the string of sad towns northeast of Baltimore, past sagging porches and swinging gutters, old cars and woodpiles, the vaguely depressing backyards of so many lives.

Near Philadelphia, Will glanced at Charlotte Cameron's letter again. He imagined she was a junior at the University of Maryland. Her phrasing suggested someone more practical than theoretical, but scientific, somehow. A psychology major, he guessed. He wondered about her family, wondered if her adoptive parents lived in St. Mary's City and if so, whether she had grown up in southern Maryland. But most of all he wondered why she had written this letter to him. And why it had had such an impact on him.

To distract himself, he considered checking in with Teddy. But it was still early for Teddy, which meant Teddy would be grumpy. Nevertheless, he would have appreciated Will calling home from a train. Just a week earlier, Teddy had browbeaten Will into buying a cell phone, which now lay folded up like a dead beetle at the bottom of his bag. Teddy had ripped that phone from its tiny cardboard case like a child unwrapping his favorite Christmas toy. Its weightlessness delighted him; he cradled the device as if it were a small, fragile pet. Will, on the other hand, hated the look and feel of the phone, hated the whole cell phone culture, in fact: the one-handed driving, the arguments which had once been private affairs that were now conducted beside strangers on park benches, the parade of humanity talking into their palms as they sauntered down the street. Having come of age in the era of poles and wires, Will found it deeply disturbing to be untethered from the grid.

Outside Trenton he looked at Charlotte Cameron's letter for a third time. By some bit of visual alchemy, three lines—her birth date, the sentence about the Catholic home for unwed mothers and her birth mother's father dying in Vietnam, and the comment, "I don't even know for certain that my birth father knows that I am alive"—

stood out as though colored with a highlight marker. "Does any of this make sense to you, Mr. Gerard?" Will took another breath. Of course it did. In that instant it felt as though he had been waiting for this letter all these years. And just as quickly he dismissed that thought. He reminded himself that the mere fact that he *could* be the father of this young woman in no way proved that he was.

Besides, Lucy Vitava's father hadn't died in Vietnam; he'd gone missing in Laos.

AT PENN STATION, the crowd from the train attacked the escalator like salmon on a fish ladder. The passengers were all from points south, so in addition to tightening their ties and smoothing the wrinkles from their laps, they had to adjust their facial expressions to blend in with the hard-bitten natives of this big northern metropolis. The terminal had the wet newspapery smell of despair. Will felt the usual amount of Manhattan anxiety—inadequacy, incipient danger, the same fluttery feeling he'd had as a boy whenever he climbed too high in a tree. There was another staccato burst from a loudspeaker, so perfectly unintelligible the announcer might as well have been speaking Urdu.

On most of his visits to New York, Will's meetings ran back to back, but today his agenda was light. The main event was lunch in the park with Barry Valentine, Will's oldest friend in the publishing business. Will had a manuscript for Barry. It was precisely the sort of dark, lyrical, well-plotted story with obvious film potential that Barry couldn't resist. At a bank of pay phones Will set his bags between his feet and punched in Barry's number.

A young man answered on the first ring: "Mr. Valentine's office."

"Is Barry there?"

"Who is calling, please?"

"Will Gerard."

"May I tell him who you are *with*, Mr. Gerard?"

The pseudo-Continental accent ruined Will's telephone manners. Quietly, he said, "I'm alone." Silence. "Okay, okay," he added. "Tell Barry her name is Mona. She's tall, blonde—"

"One moment, please."

Barry came on an instant later: "Guillermo!"

"Another new assistant?"

Barry's voice dropped to a whisper: "Young Stevens from *Remains of the Day*. Name of Trevor." Pause. "I didn't think Americans were allowed to name their kids Trevor."

"We still on for lunch?"

"I've got three chores to wrap up. We're talking thirty-four minutes tops."

"Noon, then?"

"Just after," said Barry.

"Big hand closer to the two or the seven?"

"Four." Barry paused. "Five," he said.

"You're late and you don't get to see this manuscript."

He laughed. "Is that a promise?"

In Central Park the sun was out. It was hot for May. Will settled himself in a patch of shade near Fifth Avenue. Feeling self-conscious, he removed the cell phone from his bag and punched in his home number. Eventually Teddy picked up.

"Okay," said Will, "here's the scene: on the park bench across from me is an old guy smoking a cigar with his eyes closed, a couple making out—genders unknown at present—and a fellow your age with a lightning bolt of blue across his scalp who is lacing up a pair of Rollerblades."

Teddy said, "Are you ready to admit that you were a jerk for fighting with me about buying that phone?"

"Depends how much this is costing."

"Don't ask." And then: "So what happened to you this morning? The place a wreck, alarm buzzing—"

"Don't ask. What's up?"

"Two calls of no consequence and a very agitated editor holding on the other line."

"That would be Rita?"

"Who else?"

"Patch us together."

"Aye, aye, Captain."

Rita Corelli sounded tentative, as though standing in the doorway of a darkened house. "Will? Will, are you there?"

"Right here," he said.

"Right where?"

"Central Park."

"Down the *street*? But I called you in *Washington*."

"We live in a miraculous age," Will replied. "The global village and all."

What more could he say to a woman who, not two years earlier, had been debating the merits of *word processing*? Rita had telephoned Will for advice on software. In the course of the conversation she had announced that she felt certain she would continue to compose the *really important* letters to her authors on her trusty IBM Selectric.

Rita said, "Ted gave me the news about the network miniseries! Is this true?"

"Production company is on board. My guy in L.A. reports that ABC is close to a preliminary green light."

"Wonderful, wonderful news, Will." Then a long, long pause. "So now all we need is Norton's manuscript."

"Ha, ha," replied Will.

"No joke," Rita said sternly.

"I talked to him a week ago. He was on his way out the door to drop it in the mail."

"Did you remind Norton about stamps?"

"Have you called him?"

"*Nine* times, Will. I have left messages at a bank, at a newspaper office, at an airport, and at the front desk of a motel which I assumed Norton owned, but only now discover he uses as a mail drop." Rita paused. "Can you please tell me why he doesn't have a telephone?"

"He's a character," said Will.

"A character or a *nut*?"

"A *bit* of a nut."

Norton Tazewell was a retired newspaperman. These days he spent most of his waking hours, literally and metaphorically, wandering the battlefields of the Civil War. The Wilderness, near his home in Orange, Virginia, was a particular obsession. Thus, in Norton's mind, the month of May was permanently fixed in the year 1864. The fourth of May would no doubt find Norton at the muddy banks of the Rapidan, reliving the arrival of Grant's invaders; the fifth and sixth he'd be tromping through the piney woods, imagining the blood and smoke of battle. Yesterday, the ninth, he'd have walked through the second day at Spotsylvania. So it went each and every year. The highway might be widened across that stretch of Virginia countryside; the strip malls in Fredericksburg might creep another mile westward; new curio shops might open their doors and old clapboard farmhouses might fall to ruin, yet come May all of these reminders of the present would vanish from Norton's mind, and the ghostly armies of Grant and Lee would return, like swallows to Capistrano.

Will and Norton had met some six years earlier, the day Will, in his role as publisher of Tiber Creek Press, approached Norton about writing a series of battlefield guides. The Tazewell guides to Gettysburg, the Wilderness, Fredericksburg, Antietam, and Bull Run quickly established themselves as Tiber Creek's perennial bestsellers. Unknown to Will, in addition to the battlefield guides Norton had been quietly composing a novel, too. The riveting adventures of Confederate spy Moses Cadwallader Pugh (a.k.a. Lincoln Smith) had the sweep of a Civil War epic.

Will's first thought was to pass along the project to a top-notch agent who could sell the book. But soon a grander plan presented itself: he would sell *Pharaoh's Ghost* himself. At the time Will had been mulling over something Barry Valentine had said to him when he complained about his current job: "Face it, my friend, you'll never be happy unless you're *out there.* Publishing and bookselling are waiting games. You do your work—put together a list or create a store—and then sit back and hope somebody notices. Sales reps and agents, though, make things happen. They bang on doors. Every title has its own bottom line. Let's not forget that you never had much trouble selling the books you liked."

The previous January Will had sent a packet containing his pitch letter, a detailed outline of Norton's book, and the first hundred pages of the manuscript to eight editors, Rita Corelli among them. She read the pages overnight, and the next day sent word that CastleBooks would make a preemptive bid: $300,000 for the hard- and soft-cover rights to this novel and a sequel. Will was stunned. It was as if he had stepped up to the plate hoping to make contact with a pitch, and he had smacked a whistling fastball out of the park. He told Rita he would talk to Norton and get right back to her. Only he couldn't reach

Norton. So he chatted up Wade the postman, hammered a few nails, sauntered up the street to the food co-op and bought a thick wedge of pecorino for his lunch salad. At home, his heart was still pounding and Norton was still missing. So he called Rita back and said, "Looks to me like you've got a deal."

"Norton's on board?"

"Momentarily."

Will finally tracked down Norton at a horse farm near Brandy Station. The news stunned him, too, so much so that upon his return to Orange, he stopped next door at the Wilderness Motel and asked Ruthie Ann Staton to hold on to his mail for a few days. Then he disappeared. Will's worst moment closing this deal involved tracking his client to a catfish house in Richmond, and cajoling him into signing off on terms that had been more or less agreed to. He recalled a red Naugahyde booth, a pale-green Formica table dotted with cigarette burns, the white-haired and white-bearded Norton Tazewell sitting across from him, elbows on the table, eyes fixed on a plate of fish bones, jaw sliding side to side as he chewed. Upon swallowing Norton resolutely shook his head.

"Don't know for certain that I can finish this one," he finally said. "Can't promise 'em another."

"Sure you can," Will replied. "Just think of it like that column you wrote every week for forty years."

"That was a thousand words."

"Plus a thousand, plus a thousand, plus a thousand. A few months of that and the numbers start to add up."

Norton remained unconvinced. He took a sip of Wild Turkey.

Will said, "Look, friend, they'll take this book a whole lot further if they're on the line for a sequel. That's just the way this business works."

Norton harrumphed. His dentures slipped forward, signaling the beginning of another round of head shaking. Will sat back, hands poised prayerfully on the edge of the table. A waitress approached, and Will ordered two more shots of Wild Turkey. They arrived in small jam jars. Will nursed his drink while Norton continued to pick through the fish bones with fingernails as thick and chalky as clamshells. The one thing you could say for Norton Tazewell was that the man was consistent. Sitting there, Will considered all the reasons why this deal would spook him. For one thing, the money wasn't an inducement. Money didn't move Norton. Money couldn't be expected to move a man who favored Confederate currency over federal notes. Not that Norton ever *spent* those bills. (Though he could, he liked to point out, since these days Confederate money traded at face value.) Norton lived rent-free in a trailer at a small airstrip outside Orange. He had no debts that Will knew of, no credit cards, no utility bills, no taxes that he would admit to—nobody but his own abstemious self to feed. In short, Norton had none of the pecuniary ties that bind the rest of humanity together, and force us all to behave like free-market-driven adults.

Will called for another round of Wild Turkey.

"Just doesn't set right with me," Norton said. "All that money on a promise."

This man hadn't worked a day in his life for anyone but himself. No doubt Norton hated the thought of taking money from a stranger—a stranger from *New York,* no less!—and thus agreeing to be bound to her terms and deadlines. The central issue, Will finally realized, was freedom. So he tried a different approach: "How about if you sign this contract and I escrow the money. That way, whatever happens, you can pay them back."

Much, much later that night, bent over the hood of Will's car, Norton finally signed.

"So where is our favorite author?" Will asked Rita.

A pigeon had landed on the arm of an old woman who was sitting at the base of a statue nearby. The bird was taking popcorn from the woman's hand. Her jacket was flecked with guano. Rita sighed theatrically. Will shifted the phone to the other ear.

"Out of town," she said.

Of course he was. Today would find him still at Spotsylvania. Will figured that Norton wouldn't be available to the twentieth century until Monday at the earliest. Not before Grant's soldiers had been repulsed at the Bloody Angle.

"A little more research," said Will, in his most reassuring tone of voice.

"Funny, that's exactly what Norton's friends are saying, too. You want to know something? This is beginning to sound like a conspiracy."

"A thousand details, Rita. And Norton is the sort of writer who has to get every single one of them right."

"I recall you telling me once that Norton Tazewell has eaten and breathed this war for so many years he doesn't *need* to do research."

"It's May," said Will. "The battle month. Norton's walking the woods to see what's in bloom."

"The manuscript is overdue."

"It's a week late."

"First it's a week, then it's a month. Then you call me for an extension. And then suddenly the whole thing vanishes in a puff of smoke." She paused for effect. "Listen to me, we aren't living in the good old days anymore."

"Which means what?"

"I need the manuscript *right now*."

Rita Corelli was innately grumpy, but lately her mood had been downright rotten, ever since the news, two months earlier, that Castle-Books had been sold to a giant software company. A number of editors had already been laid off. The rest, like Rita (the so-called *lucky ones* who had managed to hold on to their jobs), now found themselves answering to a crew of accountants who had descended upon the place to assess all of the forthcoming projects and jettison any that looked unpromising. *Pharaoh's Ghost* had survived the first round of "housecleaning." In fact, it had been pronounced "a winner" by Castle-Books' new publisher. That was the good news. The bad news was that the *new* publisher was now the *old* publisher: the previous week he had been fired.

"What's up?" asked Will.

"I met with Kathie yesterday," Rita said quietly.

Kathie Link was the *new* new publisher. All that Will knew about her was what had been reported in the *Times* a few days earlier: before taking this job she'd been a television producer whose singular achievement was the creation of an outtakes comedy program called *Hollywood Follies*.

He waited.

"She has concerns about this book." Long pause, then a rustle of paper. "Here's the thing. She wants to know if Moses has to be *from* the South? Also, does he have to have the nickname *Weedy?* Kathie thinks Moses Cadwallader Pugh sounds, well, um, a little downmarket. She suggested he might just go by his last name—Harrison, say, or Ingram."

The pigeon left the old woman's arm and another took its place. Will's face felt hot. He had trouble keeping a grip on this slippery wafer of a telephone.

He said, "Wouldn't it be awkward if Moses didn't come from the South, given that he's a *Confederate?*"

"Kathie told me that she wants us to think about the word *Confederate.* About the demographics. And the associations. You know— slavery, ignorance, racial hatred, that *flag,* and all the rest of it." Another long pause. "Kathie suggested a tweak."

"A *tweak?*"

"What if Moses—or Ingram—came from southern Pennsylvania? Say he was visiting *cousins* in Virginia when the war broke out."

"Why is he spying for the Confederacy if he's from Pennsylvania?"

Long pause. "He came with his mother. She's being held hostage."

Now Will sighed. Sighed and sighed. Sighed until the rage trapped in his chest had begun to break apart. Soon, no doubt, a pigeon would land on his arm, and shit all over his sleeve. And he would sigh at that, too, smile even, suffused with a weird sort of contentment at the realization that swallowing all this rage had not killed him, not yet anyway.

Finally he said, "You didn't mention this *tweak* to Norton, by any chance, did you?"

"I thought I'd try it out on you first," said Rita.

"Promise me you won't mention any tweaks to Norton until we get our hands on the manuscript."

"You make it sound as though that might be a difficult thing to do."

"Piece of cake," replied Will, a bit too quickly.

Rita said, "I want this book. I want it right now. I need it right now. That may not suit Norton, but I can't help that. He has to deliver."

"The final touches of a perfectionist," said Will.

"Why doesn't he return my phone calls?"

Will thought: Why does Norton Tazewell eat johnnycakes for breakfast? Why does he wear drop-bottom britches? Why does he ride the reenactment circuit as Robert E. Lee?

"At the moment he must be out of the loop," he replied.

"He doesn't call in for messages?"

"Rita," said Will. "Let's walk through this one more time: Norton Tazewell *lives* in the nineteenth century, late spring of 1864, to be precise. Back in 1864 people didn't call in for messages. They didn't have telephones. To get a message to someone, you had to get on a horse."

"Did you see his author's questionnaire?"

Will hadn't.

"Thirty-two pages. Single-spaced."

"He's a writer," said Will. "Writers like to write."

"It rambles."

"Norton sometimes rambles."

"Thank God he sent it directly to me. The publicity department would have gone nuts. Does Norton drink?" Momentary pause. "Of course Norton drinks."

"At home," said Will.

"I'm out on a limb. *Way* out on a limb."

"Sit quietly. I'll get in touch with Ruthie."

"From now on I only talk to you. Not Ruthie, not Grover, not Lester, not Dewey—not even crazy old Norton himself."

"I'll track him down."

"The book," she said.

"Loud and clear."

"When?"

"I'll call you Monday."

"Monday morning," she said.

WILL WAS DAYDREAMING as he wandered through an empty playground in the park. He was trying to picture Charlotte Cameron. Charlotte struck him as a blond-haired name, but he imagined the young woman who had written to him to be dark-haired. He saw strong features and a steady gaze. Responsible. She would be living in one of those low-slung postwar brick apartment complexes in College Park. Seven months shy of twenty-one, near the end of her undergraduate years, a bright, independent, upstanding young woman. Charlotte Cameron would have a boyfriend, a cat, a roommate or two, an elderly lady living upstairs whose mail she regularly carried up, whom she shopped for, and made time to chat with once or twice a week. She would have a part-time job in a research lab of some sort. A good kid with a shy smile.

And yet—

Occasionally, she would find herself gripped by a peculiar sadness. Some mornings this sadness felt suffocating, like depression. She might stay in bed those days, skip her classes. Charlotte knew what was bothering her, had understood it for years. Life was good, but something was missing. Important facts about who she was, where she had come from. Faces. Names. Places. Stories. Now that she was an adult, she knew she had to confront this issue. She needed answers to all these questions. (Not a psychology major, Will decided. Perhaps anthropology, one of the quantitative branches.) He recalled a segment from a television news magazine about a young man who was attempting to locate his birth parents. The camera records the telephone call this fellow makes to the woman he believes is his birth mother. He introduces himself and then immediately says, "Does the date June 12, 1976, mean anything to you?" There is a pause on the other end, then the unseen woman begins to cry. After a moment she says, "Yes. Yes, it does."

That Charlotte Cameron hadn't posed the question directly—*Are you my birth father, Mr. Gerard?*—suggested to Will that she wasn't certain that he was. Or else she knew he was her father, and also knew that he wasn't aware of her existence. ("I don't even know for certain if my birth father knows that I am alive.") Or else she was a cautious kid, afraid of spooking him, and so was proceeding slowly. *Or else, or else* . . . Had she already found Lucy? Might Lucy have revealed his name? What would she have told Charlotte about him? Will gazed out at the trees. *Nothing,* he thought. He felt dead to Lucy Vitava. There wasn't a chance in the world that Lucy had directed this young woman to him.

It was possible, too, that Charlotte Cameron knew nothing of Lucy. Perhaps she had located Will through extraordinary coincidence. The *Post* article, say. Wasn't this how everybody found him nowadays? Will imagined that someone—a professor—had referred Charlotte to that day's book review in the *Post,* a collection of natural history essays set on the Atlantic shore. (Her field is marine biology, he thought.) She was the sort of kid who would act on a professor's suggestion. So there she was, late one night in the library, rooting through a stack of newspapers, finally locating the right one, which she took to a wooden table. She flipped to the Style section. There was the photograph of Will. It might have stopped her, and she didn't know why it stopped her. Perhaps then she read the piece. She could have noted Will's age. That he had spent four years in Bangkok in the late 1960s might have raised the hair on her neck if she'd known that her birth mother's family had lived in Bangkok those same years. Perhaps she had specific clues about her birth father which she hadn't mentioned in her letter. That *his* father had been a well-known government official, for example, or that his family was from southern Maryland. An old established Catholic family. It was a long shot, to be sure, but how many clues would it take to pique the curiosity of a person in Charlotte's situation?

It was possible.

The longer Will considered that he might have a grown-up daughter living a short spin around the Beltway, the more likely it seemed. He found himself suddenly transformed by this idea, at one moment giddy, then stunned, then weepy. Imagine, out there, a twenty-year-old woman who was his daughter! *Dear Ms. Cameron, Do you have any reason to think you might be my daughter? ... Dear Ms. Cameron, Is it possible that I am your father? ... Dear Ms. Cameron, I couldn't help but read between the lines of your letter, and ... Dear Ms. Cameron, I am intrigued by your book idea and thought we might meet to discuss ...*

The rusty merry-go-round turned stiffly in one direction, but not the other. Will leaned against it, pushed hard, and continued to push until he felt something break loose; then the merry-go-round turned smoothly. He thought: This is all in my head. What was the chance that Lucy had been pregnant all those years ago? That she had carried a child to term, a baby girl, and had given her up for adoption? That he had never had news of this, never even suspected it?

No, Charlotte Cameron was just one more person with a story to tell. He had blathered on in the *Post* about the current popularity of the memoir. It made sense for her to write to him. Describing to Will the journey that she was about to undertake would confirm its significance in her own mind. So, too, mentioning the book she wanted to write. Charlotte had ambition, drive, and that beautiful youthful preoccupation with self. Twenty-one was a benchmark year: no doubt she had mentioned the date of her birthday as an act of exuberance. Vietnam, Vietnam, Vietnam: how many hundreds of adoptees had lost a grandfather in that war?

BARRY VALENTINE was late, of course. It was close to 1 P.M. when Will spotted him across Fifth Avenue, mobbed now with the lunchtime crowd. Barry paused at the curb, held aloft a bulky white bag, and then grinned. When the light changed, he shambled forward like a grumpy old bear.

"You've put on a few pounds," he announced.

"My whole life I've been needing to put on a few pounds," replied Will.

He had been a skinny teenager, lanky in his twenties, rangy in his thirties. These days he was still better described as *tall* as opposed to *big*. But his metabolism had slowed, no question about it. Will had arrived at that age when a second slice of cheesecake or a small plate of chocolate chip cookies migrates directly to the waistline.

Barry was shaking his head. "*After* you get married, my friend. Single women want the thoroughbred look. God knows it's probably an evolutionary thing: the hunter who can stay on his feet all day. Just because we've done away with the spear doesn't mean we trash the concept."

"I'll get right back on the bike."

"A road bike," instructed Barry, as they headed into the park. "Push-ups are okay, too, but in moderation. No lifting or you'll end up with a neck like a bouncer." He put an arm around Will. "After you settle down you relax into the pasha mode. Climb onto the treadmill three times a week to keep the heart pumping. But that's it. At that point, you're proud of your Sansabelt slacks."

"Look at my face," said Will.

Barry stopped. He glanced around. The request clearly made him unhappy.

"My eyes," said Will.

Barry squinted. "I don't see anything."

"You don't see a soulful look?"

Barry grimaced. "What the hell is soulful?"

"That beneath the surface is a guy with an active emotional life." Will shrugged. "An old friend mentioned it. I looked in the mirror. I didn't see it."

"You're talking to a married man, Will. I'm lost."

Barry was Will's mentor. Over the years he had taught Will much of what he knew about the publishing business. (About life, too, Barry would have been quick to add.) These lessons went back to the mid-eighties, to the day the two met in the front room at Tenleytown

Books. Barry was a sales rep for Simon & Schuster, Will was managing the shop. This was a sales call, but Barry refused to play the role of salesman. He and Will weren't going to be adversaries, he all but explained: they would be partners. It was a partnership based on trust. Barry's job was to steer a savvy bookman like Will to the worthy titles in the spring catalog; and Will's job, in turn, was to stock those books and sell them. The relationship blossomed, as much due to a shared passion for good books as for the cuisines of Asia, indulged upon at dozens of lunches and dinners courtesy of Barry's expense account.

A year after they met Barry took a job in New York with Random House, and a few months after that he hired Will to work for him as a sales rep in the lower mid-Atlantic region.

They celebrated the new relationship at an Indonesian restaurant in Georgetown. A large, cold Balimbang had loosened Barry's tongue and raised his voice, much to the annoyance of the couple dining at the adjacent table. "People don't think they *need* books," Barry cried out at one point. "But my God, look around! Who can't tell at a glance the folks who don't read them?" He leaned forward. "Books are the backbone of civilization, Will." There was a momentary pause while Barry consumed the last piece of satay. "Well, perhaps not *every* book." He shrugged. "It's a guerrilla war out there, kid, so hit the ground running. And remember the catch-22 of this business: you can't get distribution without the promise of sales, and you'll never get sales without distribution."

Over dessert, Barry disclosed to Will a few other secrets of the trade.

"You want to size up the bookseller right off," he said. "Depressing, but necessary. First thing you'll discover is that there is hardly an entrepreneur in the lot. For the most part you're dealing with clerks and librarians. If you ever have the good fortune of selling to an entrepreneur, throw down the gauntlet. That's rule number one. Convince the fellow to order some ungodly expensive title—a seventy-dollar two-volume biography of an obscure Czech composer, say. Make him take two, and tell him how to sell it. When those books go out the door, that bookseller will feel like he's died and gone to heaven. Rule number two: never, ever try this with the clerks and librarians. Any sales tips, or talk of increasing store traffic, units-per-customer, point-of-purchase sales, and the rest of it makes these folks feel as though their briefs are suddenly too tight. These are the men and women who will tell you that they just aren't in it *for the money*. For what, I would love to know? They can't say. A hint about those shops: no computer. You're lucky to find a cash register sometimes. The lighting is awful and there's no music, or else it's the same damn flute solo every time you walk into the place. The poetry books are next to the front door. Not to cut down on shoplifting, I might add, but as an aesthetic statement."

He laid a hand on Will's arm. "With the clerks and librarians, the pitch has to be subtle: peer pressure, literary reputation, community needs, the semiotics of publishing—"

"The *semiotics of publishing*?"

Barry shrugged. The words had just tripped off his tongue one day. This was in the early eighties, during a sales trip that saw Barry pushing a book about how to make a million bucks in the real estate market. Barry blithely suggested to one buyer that this title was further evidence of a profound shift in the national mood: solar power, marijuana, baseball, spiritual malaise were on the way out; gas guzzlers, basketball, cocaine, personal computers, junk bonds, and greed were on the way in.

The bookseller, a bearded child of the sixties, snorted in disbelief.

"Check out our catalog. Check out everybody's fall catalog." Barry shrugged. "It's the semiotics of publishing."

The bookseller pursed his lips. He agreed to take four copies of the book. In the end, he upped the order to eight, at Barry's suggestion, to get a better discount.

Will loved the life of the commercial traveler, the days and weeks spent cruising from one bookstore to another. He genuinely admired a few booksellers, too—their idealistic belief in the power of books, and their stubbornness. But over time the enjoyment diminished, until finally it occurred to Will that it was time to think about doing something else. He never tired of the road, not even the pointless visits to moribund shops on permanent credit hold ("showing the flag," Barry called it), or the hour spent arguing the merits of various vegetarian cookbooks over a cup of cashew chili to die for at a lesbian bookshop tucked into a renovated arts factory in a working-class neighborhood in Baltimore. Something perverse in his soul even enjoyed the three-cheeseburger lunches with Edith Boyd, trade buyer at Books & Bibles (*Bucks 'n' Bubbles,* in the vernacular), a small chain based in Norfolk, Virginia, all the while getting hammered by Edith about how the publishing business was being ruined by a bunch of Ivy League know-nothings who could not absorb the fact that the marketplace did not need *one more* Southern gothic novel, but desperately needed a dozen new books by or about Richard Petty, Rusty Wallace, Ricky Rudd, and the rest of the NASCAR brotherhood.

No, the real reason Will finally left this job was that Barry Valentine had gently shown him the door.

Will never had trouble selling the books he liked, but for some reason he couldn't move the ones he hated. And generally speaking, the books he hated were the blockbusters he had to sell. The first season it was a Great Plains saga about a young woman and her unfulfilled dreams, which featured endless car rides, a cast of worthless men, and several explicit scenes of female masturbation. Barry had pitched this first novel at a sales conference as "Judith Krantz meets Ellen Gilchrist." Will loathed the book. Every sentence rambled; even the sex scenes drooped beneath the weight of adjectives. The six-figure advance that had been paid to acquire this book resulted in sales quotas that Will knew would be impossibly high.

His numbers came in consistently low.

At one point Barry suggested that he wasn't properly framing the sale. He told Will to pitch this book as "the most exciting debut novel in a generation." Will knew he wouldn't be able to say those words and keep a straight face. His orders remained dismal. Barry threatened him with probation. Will asked to see the other reps' sales numbers. Barry changed the subject. They fought via voice mail. At the next sales conference, Will asked Barry to lunch to clear the air. They ate Japanese. Over miso and two giant Sapporos, Will gently steered the conversation toward the previous season's titles. He inquired about the book which he had sold so miserably. Proof that it had died on the vine came an instant later when Barry Valentine, a walking edition of *Books in Print,* suddenly could not recall the title.

Will swallowed a piece of tuna. "So tell me, Chief, what were the final numbers on our *debut novel for all time?*"

Barry smiled blandly. "Everybody agrees that you're a sweet fellow,

William. But something tells me you don't have enough fire in the belly to climb the ladder on this end of the business."

"Not to mention that I don't want to live in New York."

"We say Manhattan." Barry reached over and placed a meaty hand on Will's shoulder. "You can't be coached. You need to know that about yourself. Think of that as a strength." Long pause. "While you're weighing all of your options."

Away from the noise of midtown traffic, Will thought wistfully about the good old days: tallying orders in some noisy roadhouse, phoning up Barry with good news at all hours of the day and night. A few times the two had even traveled together: Butch and Sundance. With Barry riding shotgun, Will's orders shot through the roof. Every sales call had seemed to Will like a grand scam, one clever heist after another.

Barry had settled himself on a bench. He regarded his bagel with nova and tomato as if it were a work of art, turning it in a full circle before settling on where to take the first bite. A gentle wind rustled the new leaves overhead as Barry chewed. The sky was pale blue, the air more humid now. Barry swallowed. He placed his sandwich on the deli paper and took a sip of iced tea.

Finally he said, "We saw that puff piece in the *Washington Post*. The 'Literary Intelligence' headline was very cute. That reporter certainly rode the nag about you being a son of a spy and a young Catholic aristocrat." He leaned forward. "It seemed thin for a gossip page. Di and I were disappointed that there wasn't even the hint of a domestic angle aside from that Dickensian business about having a nephew for an assistant."

Will shrugged. "I guess she missed the soulful look in my eyes."

"We assumed you had something going with her," said Barry.

Will laughed. He gave Barry the background on the *Post* article: the sale of *Pharaoh's Ghost* to CastleBooks made the local literary gossip circuit, and got the attention of Will's journalist brother. Jonathan and Will met for lunch to talk about Jonathan's current book project, a memoir of his boyhood in Thailand during the Vietnam War. Will read the book proposal and the first twenty pages. They talked by phone the next day.

"It's beautifully written, evocative, even haunting in a way. But somehow the focus feels tight. I wonder if there's some way to get outside yourself here. Even add another voice."

"Another voice?" Jonathan sounded defensive.

"To fill in the story. And to get at some of the things you couldn't have known as a kid. Why we lived there, and what was going on outside the compound, so to speak."

There was a long pause. Then Jonathan said, "You mean Dad's voice?"

"It did occur to me." Will paused. "He wrote everything down. The barn's full of his papers."

"Let me ask you something. Writer to agent. Do you actually think I could pull that off?"

"Yes, I do."

"I can't imagine Mom going for this."

"Maybe not right off, but she'll come around once she understands that a book like this would humanize Dad."

"I don't know, Will. It's not at all what I had in mind."

"It's a bigger story, Jon. Professionally, it would put you in a new place."

The ongoing silence indicated that Jonathan liked that idea.

"Talk to Mom," said Will. "And think about it." And then: "You could pick a year. Tell your story, our story, the American story—what was going on. All the things we knew and didn't know. Follow some of the lives of your friends, the music. It was a strange life, Jon. Somehow you need to get your arms around all of it."

"*Bangkok 1969.*"

"I like that."

"Maybe you're right." Jonathan paused. "I'll make some notes. See where it goes. And listen, one other thing: I need a new agent." Another pause. "Any chance that might be you?"

Early in March, Will sent two chapters and a revised proposal for *Bangkok 1969* to eleven publishing houses. An auction quickly ensued. In the end, Jonathan received an advance that was three times the advance of his previous book, an exposé of the dirty world of campaign fund-raising. He was ecstatic. He spread the news to friends, one of whom happened to be a reporter at the Style page of the *Post*, with a book idea of her own: *The Wives of Jack Kent Cooke.* She called Will and suggested a profile.

To Barry, Will said, "She had the piece written before the interview. All she needed were a few quotes and telling details." He paused. "It did lift the quality of my submissions, so I guess I shouldn't complain."

"Business," Barry intoned morosely.

Barry was the publisher at a company called Garrison & Reed. In seven years he had transformed a family-owned, six-million-dollar crafts-and-cookbooks operation into a fifty-million-dollar, publicly traded, general trade-book publisher. When he took the job he reported to twenty-six-year-old Nelson Reed. Now G&R was a division of book publisher Avery Tice, which was owned by British-based communications giant Hayward Heath, which was a subsidiary of the Dutch conglomerate Odoorn-Eerbeck, which in turn—Will recalled—was controlled by a fellow in Singapore named R. C. Feng.

Barry's brow furrowed. He dropped his half-eaten sandwich into the bag. "Lately it seems like it's the same damn manuscript going around and around. Please show me something I haven't seen before."

Will tapped his bag. "You'll like this. A first novel. Exotic. Written by a woman named Iris Swan."

Barry looked thoughtful. "Iris Swan. I like the sound of that. Go on."

"A journey," Will said. "A young woman escapes from an abusive husband and takes off with her daughter to Central America. This story has beaches, jaguars in the jungle, Mayan ruins, good guys in red bandannas and bad guys in camouflage. Emotional upheaval, physical danger, and at the heart of it, a mystery: the narrator is looking for clues about what really happened to a great-grandfather who was supposed to have died of yellow fever at the beginning of the century while he was trying to make his fortune growing bananas on the Mosquito Coast—"

"There's a title," said Barry.

"Been used, I believe."

He shrugged. "Got a better one?"

"Still working on that," replied Will.

Naming books was Barry's favorite pastime. He would anoint a manuscript with a title like a priest applying a blackened thumb to a parishioner's forehead on Ash Wednesday. Will knew this about Barry of course, and he was baiting him. When Barry hit on the perfect title, it meant he had to buy the book.

Barry leaned forward. "Too bad *banana* is such an unacceptable word. Maybe something with *fever*?"

"Too hot. This is elegant. Cool in a way. Literary."

"Harriet Doerr meets *In Patagonia*?"

"Harriet Doerr meets *Thelma and Louise in Patagonia*," said Will.

An outstretched hand beckoned. Will passed over the manuscript. Barry flipped to page one and settled against the bench. His cheeks sagged, his breathing grew audible. Will closed his eyes for a moment and tried to rid himself of the image of an old man dozing beside him on a park bench. He heard an airplane overhead, then a line of Rollerbladers whishing past. The paper rustled. Eyes still shut, Will counted two, three, four pages.

"Not awful," said Barry finally. "Too bad it isn't a memoir." He read the first page again, feigning mild interest. "So who's seen this?"

Will waited.

Barry looked up. "Exclusive. Otherwise I don't waste my time."

"I mentioned it to Rita Corelli."

"Next weekend Rita can read it for herself. No doubt she can even buy it."

"Chances are she'll want to see it today."

"Well then, my friend, you will just have to be firm."

"Look," said Will. "This is your copy. The other one goes to my messenger service with instructions to deliver it to Rita next Tuesday."

"Friday," said Barry flatly.

"Wednesday noon."

Barry addressed the heavens: "Why do I put up with this shit?"

"There's one small complication," Will added.

Barry's smile froze.

"Hardly worth mentioning."

The smile vanished.

"In her former life Iris Swan freelanced for some travel magazines. Ten years ago she sold the idea of doing a travel book on the Caribbean. A guidebook. It never happened."

"How much?"

"Fifteen," said Will. "Thirteen-five to Iris after the agent's cut." He paused. "It was Avery Tice's thirteen-five."

"Oh, that's wonderful."

"Ten years ago."

"This belongs to them."

"They signed up a travel guide, Barry. This is a novel. We're talking about different books."

"The manuscript never looks like the proposal. My God, one clown who was into us for thirty-five grand for an inside look at the future of space exploration tried to submit a *narrative poem*."

Will leaned forward. "Iris runs a lodge in the jungles of Guatemala," he said. "Five or six cabins with thatched roofs, a generator for electricity, right next to a Mayan ruin. Great birdwatching, she said. She sent me a photograph." Pause. "I think it's safe to say that Iris doesn't have thirteen-five stashed under a mattress. I'm willing to bet she doesn't have a mattress. She did say that she intends to repay that debt as soon as she can."

Barry shook his head. "So let me get this straight: I'm supposed to buy this book, pay Iris with G&R's money—money that belongs to Avery Tice—some of which Iris may or may not use to pay back Avery Tice." He frowned. "Could somebody tell me what I don't like about the sound of this deal?"

"Barry, that advance was written off years ago. The editor has had two jobs in the meantime. Nobody at Avery Tice even remembers the name Iris Swan. So let's go back to square one. I have a novel that I am going to sell. I brought it to you first because I think you're a wonderful publisher and I happen to know that you will love the story. You don't want to see it, fine. Say the word and I'll send this one to Rita and the other one to Sally Stevenson."

"This goes straight to Gwen," Barry replied. "But first we take a blood oath that you haven't breathed a word to me about the sordid history of Ms. Swan's contractual obligations."

"Who's Gwen?"

"My new editor-in-chief."

Will produced his cell phone. "How about if you call Gwen right now and tell her that I'll drop off the manuscript in an hour."

Barry whistled through his teeth. "*Muy* gangsta," he said.

Afterward, Will dispersed a crowd of pigeons as they started toward Fifth Avenue.

Barry dropped his trash into a wire bin. "What else?" he said.

"I have a dozen memoirs of the Foreign Service, in case you'd like to see one of those."

"This is the Age of the Memoir," Barry intoned.

"*Our Years in Chittagong.*"

Barry grinned. "What else is going on in your *life?*"

"I'm headed to the Cape tomorrow. A literary conference. The Falmouth Institute."

Barry stopped. "Falmouth Institute." His nostrils flared as the wheels began to turn. "Rich lady," he said.

"Dee Dee Abad." Will continued on. "Dee Dee stages 501C literary get-togethers a couple of times each year. This one's called *Art from Past Lives.*"

Barry laughed out loud.

"For the inconvenience of delivering a twenty-minute talk," said Will, "I go home with a thousand bucks plus expenses, plus fabulous food and wine, and who knows, maybe even a new client."

"What else?" said Barry.

Will thought about the letter from Charlotte Cameron. He thought about his troubles with Annie, whom Barry had never met, had never heard mention of. All of it seemed too complicated to explain during the short walk to Barry's office. So Will shrugged.

Barry draped an arm around his shoulders. "Let me explain something. When I arrive home tonight, my dear wife will say to me, 'So how *is* Will?' " Barry paused. "When Diane says how *is* Will, it means that I'm required to say something *meaningful.* I need a little juice, pal. Something that involves sex or matrimony. Preferably both."

"How much time do you have?"

Barry studied Will. "Now that you mention it, maybe I *do* see a soulful look in your eyes."

"It's complicated."

"Of course it's complicated," Barry whispered. "Adult relationships are always complicated."

Will shook his head. "In this case complicated means that the relationship is teetering on the brink of the abyss."

Barry's smile was blissful. "I dimly recall that those were the best."

"Fact is, I think it's over," said Will.

They watched in silence as a horse-drawn carriage rolled past, Barry waiting for Will to continue, Will hoping that Barry would let the conversation die. Barry didn't look at Will. He didn't need to look at him to know that Will's relationship with this unnamed woman, troubled though it might be, was not, strictly speaking, over. *Over* would have been indicated by a dismissive comment about the lady in question. ("She's read all the Mars and Venus books.") Or else, more likely, no mention of her at all.

Barry said, "Here's the deal: I head back to the office and clear off my desk. You stop by and schmooze Gwen. We cut out early and run around at the gym for a half hour, then meet Diane for an early bite."

"There's one problem," Will replied.

Barry tapped the pocket that held Will's cell phone. "Fix it," he said.

Once there had only been black-and-white TVs and rotary telephones; now there were answering machines, faxes, call waiting, e-mail, pagers, cell phones and all the rest. The communications revolution was supposed to make life better, but as Will saw it, things had just gotten progressively worse. For one thing, a person couldn't get lost anymore. You couldn't hide out. Gone was the era when you could send a brief telegram to cancel a dinner engagement that had been made under the influence of a broken heart, fatigue, and too much caffeine. Every small and large mistake in life nowadays had to be discussed.

And so Will found himself strolling the sidewalks of the park, hand pressed to his ear like all the other movers and shakers. He reached Annie's voice mail, then the switchboard operator, then Stephanie, who sweetly and professionally exiled him to hold. He took a seat on an empty bench. Two minutes passed. Holding on a park bench was a brand-new experience for Will. He gazed around, feeling uneasy. The blue sky overhead, the soft breeze in his face, the Frisbee and mutt sailing together across an open field, the clip-clop of horses and *whish* of bladers, the sleek black man with the Walkman dancing alone at a fountain: each of these observations seemed to heighten Will's anxiety. He felt like a shady character. *Muy* gangsta about summed it up. Another minute ticked by. Will thought about how much easier it would have been to make this call from a graffiti-covered phone booth on the street, every fourth word lost to a tire squeal or a horn: *What? WHAT? You'll have to speak up . . . Listen, I'm really sorry but I can't—*

It occurred to him that one reason for the on-again off-again nature of his romance with Annie had to do with the simple fact that so much of the communications between them had been conducted by telephone. Phone conversations are inherently unreliable, confused, one-sided, impulsive in all the wrong sorts of ways. And so easily derailed. One's mood could be transparent on the telephone; or worse, could be *assumed* to be transparent. Yesterday Will had telephoned Annie: he wanted assurance that she might still be willing to help him bail their leaky rowboat of a romance. (More precisely, he wanted to know that Annie hadn't ditched her bucket.) Stephanie had delivered his message, perhaps had even mentioned the note of panic in Will's voice, and Annie's response was . . . *nothing*. When most of the day had passed, and Stephanie finally returned the call on Annie's behalf, Will believed that Annie had delivered a message. It was over. He went to sleep an angry young man, and woke up feeling old and in despair. Despair had goaded him to make the impulsive call from the train station. He couldn't decide if that had been a good or bad move on his part. Then, it seemed fine; right now, not so fine.

He was staring morosely at a crowd of pigeons gathered at his feet, the pigeons staring back, ten seconds away from hanging up, when Annie picked up.

"Will! Are you still there?"

"Right here."

"I'm really sorry. This day has been utter hell—"

Toward the end of the wait Will feared he might open with some petulant remark. *I guess if I were paying for your time . . .* But the sound of Annie's voice derailed him. It wasn't quite breathless, but something like that, a voice directed at him: she didn't talk to other lawyers in this breezy tone.

"—utter and complete hell." She was snarling happily. "Six lawyers arguing with each other about a divorce settlement in which every-one—including the six of us—is going to end up with more money than any of us deserves. Just your average Friday afternoon." She paused. "After we talked this morning, I went for a run. It didn't help at all. I woke up in a bad mood and I'm still in a bad mood. I keep thinking about what you said about us hanging by a thread."

"Does that mean we're still hanging by a thread?"

"I didn't think so," she said softly, "but I guess I was wrong."

"You know what bugs me? That our time together is running about ten to one on the telephone."

"Five to one," said Annie. "It's only ten to one when things get unhappy."

He had the whole excuse scripted in his head: that Barry Valentine had put the finger on him for dinner—Barry, who Annie understood was something of a professional lifeline to the Gerard Literary Agency. That would segue into mention of Barry and Diane Valen-tine's social life: how it required a two-year calendar, how nothing spontaneous occurred in their lives. They had the kids, and the beach house and country house that had to be visited on something approx-imating a custody schedule. Barry had asked Will to dinner and he had accepted. He had to. He simply couldn't refuse.

But Annie never gave him an opening.

"Will, there's something I need to tell you. Something I should have said this morning. It's about that support group I sat in with last night. It wasn't just for single moms." Pause. "It was for single moms who had conceived through artificial insemination. You see, last Mon-day I made an appointment for myself."

Will gazed up at a dense white cloud. With bowsprit and wispy sails it resembled a pirate ship. He stared at it, just stared at it.

"It seemed like a way out," she continued. "For me. And for us."

I get the woman of my dreams, thought Will, and she gets the Nobel Laureate-to-be.

An old lady in a white tennis dress sat down beside him. She took a sandwich from a straw purse. The crust had been trimmed from the bread.

Annie went on: "I canceled this morning. The whole thing suddenly seemed so pathetic. Doing that, I mean. How would you explain something like that to a child? And who's it for, really? And *why*, what with all the kids in the world who need homes?"

Why hadn't she talked like this before? Or had she? Will was confused. He suddenly felt humbled. And shamed by the purpose of this call. All at once he wanted to see Annie. But to say what? She seemed so far away from him right now.

Will said, "I keep thinking, what if you hadn't said anything that first night? What if you were six weeks pregnant right now?"

She didn't say a word.

"We'd handle it," he added. "It's something real. We'd do okay with something real. I'm not saying that we'd never have a bad moment, or that in the end we would live happily ever after, but we would be talking to each other. Every day, I bet."

"Will, I *had* to tell you."

"I know you did." And then softly, "That doesn't mean I can't wish you hadn't."

"Why is this such a big deal?"

"Having a child with a woman you've known for forty-eight days?"

"No, Will. Just having a child."

Once she had told him that the key to her success as a litigator was that she didn't look the part. The faces of opposing lawyers relaxed when they met her. There was no steely gaze from Annie Leonard, no sneer, no bark, nothing grave or remotely dangerous at all about this attorney on first glance. Just a forthright expression and an easy smile. But the thing to fear, these lawyers would learn, was something they couldn't see: Annie could read her adversaries as well as she could read herself.

She had been an athlete, and one didn't spot that right off either. Ice hockey at Cornell, full scholarship, freshman starter on the varsity team. When she first mentioned this to Will, she'd said it casually, and he thought she was kidding. But then they went out to a rink, and even as she was lacing up her skates, he saw that it was true. She moved effortlessly around the ice, elbows rocking as though carrying a stick. She was extraordinarily graceful, and deceptively fast.

He wanted to say something to Annie about the letter from Charlotte Cameron. If she had a few minutes to spare, he would have liked to read it to her. She would have good instincts for what it meant, and for how he should proceed. But he couldn't bring it up. Not now. Not today. The letter wasn't related to their situation at all, and yet, oddly, it was. Or rather, his reaction to it was. There was still so much personal baggage that he had to sort out. Past and present.

"I want to see you," he said. "I want to talk. Honestly. About us. About something else, too, which may bear on the question you just asked."

"Not tonight," she said. "I'm just not up to it tonight. I'm sorry."

"Sunday, then. We'll have dinner."

"Call me when you get home."

Will sensed despair. Something terrible was happening. Something terrible that neither of them seemed to want, but were powerless to stop. "Look, maybe we can start over."

"I wish I thought we could."

"We can," he said. "I know we can. This is up to us, isn't it?" *Wasn't it?* And then: "We could drive out to Lewes. Roll back the clock. You know, revisit the scene of the crime."

Despite everything, she laughed.

Diane Valentine was a serious greeter—wet kisses full on the mouth—and Will felt ashamed that his first thought in the grip of her welcoming embrace as they stood beneath Magyar Siam's green-and-gold awning concerned the health status of Barry Junior and baby Lila. "It's been months!" Diane cried. She kissed Will again, this time on the cheek. In one arm she was carrying a huge bouquet of flowers. Her thick blonde hair flowed like water over a black suede jacket.

Inside the restaurant, a young waiter tried to guide the three of them toward a table at the back of the room beneath a tapestry of crossed swords and a Wehrmacht eagle. The instant Barry saw where they were headed, he steered Will and Diane to the only empty table at the front window. Diane waylaid a passing waiter for the three beers on his tray. Then she smooched the side of Barry's face, and dropped into the chair beside him, an arm draped around his neck.

"What a treat!" she told Will. "This place is fabulous."

"Thai food with extra paprika," Barry added, with a shrug.

Diane leaned forward. "So what have I missed?"

Barry was already studying the menu. "Will's in love," he said matter-of-factly. "But he doesn't want to talk about it."

"Do we have a name?"

He shrugged. "We're not to trouble ourselves. It's almost history."

Diane's eyes widened in disbelief. She looked at Will. "Name, please."

"Annie Leonard."

Diane's green eyes beckoned for more.

"Annie is a high-powered lawyer in Washington," he added.

"Age?" She seemed ready to wince.

"Thirty-nine."

A bright smile from Diane.

"Barry's right," Will said. "At the moment things are looking pretty bleak."

"This is a bad match?"

"Let's just say that Annie and I are grappling with an intractable dilemma."

Diane took a sip of beer. "Honey, at your age, dilemmas are never *intractable.* Especially not that one."

"Which one?" asked Barry.

She smiled tightly. "Darling, don't be thick."

Barry's eyes remained fixed on the menu. "If it's more serious than Will's refusing to share his feelings, then I say he should think about throwing in the towel."

"Throw in the towel?" Diane scowled. "For pete's sake, the man's in love. Look at his face."

Barry glanced up. "Looks to me like the flush of three sets of racquetball," he said.

"Baloney, darling. It's love."

Barry gazed sadly at Will. "A glow on his face *and* a soulful look in his eyes."

"It was a gay friend who mentioned the soulful look," Will explained to Diane.

She leaned forward. "Was this before or after you met Annie Leonard?"

"A few hours before."

Her smile was triumphant. "And you boys think these things happen by *chance*? Let's start with the basics. How long has this been going on?"

"Since the day after we met."

"Which was when?"

Will took a sip of beer. "March twenty-second."

Barry's head snapped to attention. "Sweet Jesus, Mary, and Joseph, Di. He knows the *date*." He shook his head sadly. "How about if I order the squid with paprika and green chilis; Will gets the *pad thai györ;* and sweetheart, you get chicken curry *miskolc;* then we share." He turned to Will. "Is this Annie person the sort of woman you marry?"

Diane rolled her eyes. "Of course she is. Otherwise their dilemma wouldn't feel intractable." To Will, she said, "So how did you two meet?"

"We bumped into each other at the beach."

"Sounds romantic."

"Not exactly," replied Will. "Not at first." He described the breaking-and-entering scene at the kitchen door of Michael and Alejandro's house, and Annie's assault on him with the big flashlight.

The waiter arrived. Diane collected the menus. "Three, twenty-nine, forty-four. Extra rice. Three Singhas and a pitcher of water," she announced. And then to Will: "I hope you're planning to stay at our place tonight. I want the whole story."

Will described how the flirting with Annie began over the telephone, how the courtship commenced in earnest over marinara and a full-bodied merlot. He described their unsuccessful late night search for owls, the sparks over Sambuca, the fiddling with the keys at the back door and then with each other at the top of the steps, the retreat to Annie's harem chamber, the revelation that she had forsaken birth control, the reckless, glorious sex that followed, and the panic that had derailed him at the critical moment.

"A little too much vino," said Barry. "Can happen to anybody our age." He smiled earnestly. "So I hear."

Diane leaned forward. "Your brain woke up. You started thinking. You lost concentration. Trust me, I've been there."

No, thought Will. Dear sweet woman friend, you have not been there. This wasn't about losing concentration, or getting distracted, or not being fully engaged. What had happened to him with Annie that night was more in line with what the white shirts at NASA would describe as a "catastrophic failure." The catastrophic failure of a certain male body part commonly described as one's *manhood.* One's manhood is designed to behave as predictably as a moth at a flame. Will's hadn't. That such a thing could happen once—well, best not to finish that particular thought.

When the food arrived, Barry served portions to each of them, tasting as he went. "Let's eat," he said. And then to Will: "So we can infer that the rabbit didn't die?"

"Sweetheart!"

"Baseline question." He sounded defensive. "It needs to be asked."

"It's a lousy expression, since the rabbit *always* died." Diane leaned forward and whispered, "And anyway, Will said that he lost his—"

"No dead rabbits," mumbled Will, through a mouthful of chicken.

Diane set down her fork. "So then what happened?"

He swallowed. "We talked. We started dating. It was on again, off again. And right now things are looking way off."

"Dating could be the right approach," said Barry.

"Darling," said Diane, "Will and Annie had *poetry*. A couple that has poetry doesn't suddenly shift to dating." And to Will: "I don't get it. You like her. There's a chemistry. You're both bright, sensitive, thoughtful, caring people. How often in your life have you met a woman like this? Not to mention that if the thought of having children has even crossed your—"

"Oh, it has."

"And?"

"I don't know, Di. Basically I've talked myself into a corner."

Diane sat forward. "So stop talking." And, in a whisper: "The reason nature has endowed us with these impulses, dear sweet William, is in the hope that someday we might act upon them."

"For some reason I keep thinking that before we get to *that* we need to settle the issue of *us*."

Her look of exasperation was dismissive. "Foolish man, that's for kids."

"Tick, tock, tick, tock," said Barry.

"Let me ask you something," said Diane. "Do you want to have children?"

Will considered the range of possible responses: *I love other people's kids. I've never thought of myself as someone who* wouldn't *have kids.*

Maybe I'm too old to be a father. Or else the bombshell: *Good chance that I might already be a father!*

He smiled weakly. "Right now it seems like a bad idea."

Hungry crowd at the door notwithstanding, this was the moment to tell them about the letter from Charlotte Cameron. But Will couldn't bring himself to do that. The timing was all wrong. To bring up that letter right now would derail this conversation. It would ruin the end of their meal together. Diane's expression would sag; all at once she would look ten years older. Then would come the barrage of questions that Will couldn't answer, the same questions he had been asking himself all afternoon: Why had he never known about Charlotte? How did it happen that he had lost touch with Lucy Vitava at the precise moment she became pregnant with his child?

Barry said, "For me in this situation, the bottom line is: Do I trust her?"

"Of course he trusts her," said Diane. "Annie Leonard is a trustworthy person."

"I mean *really* trust her." Barry went on: "Think about it. What's worst-case if Will decides to go along with this?" He looked at both of them. "How about this: the magic disappears, and two weeks later Annie Leonard finds herself pregnant. Let's imagine that the relationship has ended on a frankly awful note. Child support isn't an issue for her. So what happens? When does Will get the news? In two days or two months or twenty years?"

Diane closed her eyes. "In the event," she said wearily, "Will can always hire a private investigator."

A smile appeared on Barry's face, grudging at first, then spreading out in all directions as he celebrated the good fortune of having married such a winningly practical woman.

Diane rapped on the table with a knuckle. "The point *I* have been trying to make is that all this talking is going to take some time. And time is the one thing that Will and Annie don't have. That first night at the beach he was ready to let nature take its course. Doesn't that tell us something?"

Will said, "It seemed crazy, and then not so crazy. I wasn't thinking about the child. Just about Annie. About the fact that for the first time in my life I had met someone whom I would have been willing to move in with the very next day."

"But you didn't," said Diane.

"No." He paused. "We did spend a lot of time together."

"With or without birth control?" Barry asked.

"Without."

"And?" asked Diane.

Will smiled tightly. "Never at the critical moment," he replied.

In April Annie telephoned Will one afternoon to invite him to join her for a weekend in the mountains of western Virginia. Ostensibly, this was a judicial conference. Had such an event been booked at, say, the Marriott in Crystal City, few lawyers in Washington would have attended. But since this gathering was to be held at a resort that featured golf, trout fishing, skeet shooting, hot springs, aromatherapeutic massages, high tea, activities for kids, and so forth; since the smattering of seminars about tort reform and judicial activism would be non-taxing (and would make the entire weekend tax deductible), the Homestead would be jammed with attorneys.

Will consulted his calendar while Annie disappeared to field another telephone call. He was free on Thursday and Saturday, and with a call to New York could be made free on Friday as well. Then his eye fixed on the date: April 18. He counted backward from the eighteenth to the night they met in Lewes: twenty-seven days.

Annie was back: "Are you in town, Will? Are you free?"

Mere coincidence, he reminded himself. Annie's room at the Homestead would have been booked for months. And anyway, this weekend would be fun. They'd hike, bike, fly fish, skeet shoot, soak in the healing waters, eat waffles and venison, get to know each other a little better. Perhaps they might even sit outside under the stars sipping mint juleps, and have the heart-to-heart conversation about parenthood that Will had been studiously avoiding these last weeks.

He took a deep breath: "Sure."

Just imagining that microscopic egg preparing for its incredible journey—maybe it was already on its way!—left Will momentarily thrilled, and then paralyzed by doubt. There were moments during the week that followed when he was prepared to stroll forward into this brave new world; and other moments—many, many more of them, it should be said—when Will thought forward to this Homestead week-end and saw himself hiding out in a remote cave in the Allegheny Mountains for three consecutive nights.

He drove. A half hour into the journey, with the Blue Ridge Mountains standing off in the distance like a great wall, Will felt the first wave of queasiness. Soon he was lightheaded, and then extraordinarily dizzy as they passed through Thornton Gap. He was seconds away from pulling to the side of the road and turning the wheel over to Annie. But the nausea passed, and a dull headache took its place. He picked up an apple, but put it down after one bite.

Annie touched his arm. "You okay?"

"Tired, I guess."

On the climb toward Hot Springs, Will had to work hard to keep the car alongside the yellow line. Annie looked at him with alarm and laid a hand on his clammy forehead.

"Honey, you look awful," she said. "Pull over."

She drove the rest of the way. At the main entrance of the hotel, Will stood unsteadily at the car door, unaware of the dozens of late-model sport-utility vehicles arriving and departing, each one disgorging another freshly shaven attorney in khakis and Ray-Bans. Annie took his arm. "Let's get you to the room," she said. "You're burning up."

At three in the afternoon, Will lay down to rest while Annie went to register for the conference. Next thing he knew it was the crack of dawn. Annie was asleep in the other bed. Will's head was pounding, his mouth was full of cotton. He closed his eyes. When he opened them, the room was awash in sunlight. Annie was gone. There was a room-service cart at the foot of his bed with cereal and juice; and on the table beside him, a huge pitcher of water and an unopened packet of Sudafed. The TV remote lay next to his hand.

Annie came and went over the course of the day, as did Will, the only difference being that he remained flat on his back. She took his temperature several times, and announced the same reading in the same grave voice: 102 degrees.

Will's primary recollection of that weekend was the steady drone of basketball—the NBA playoffs were under way—though he couldn't recall which teams had been playing. At one point he thought he heard Annie laughing outside the door, and felt a weak stab of jealousy: either she was chatting with a tightly worsted comrade about some humorous loophole in the new tax code, or else she'd given up on Will, and was out trolling the red-carpeted hallways for an unattached, healthy, reasonably attractive, potent young man.

Or else he was hallucinating.

The fever broke early on Sunday morning, but Will remained so weak that Annie had to help him into the shower. This angel of mercy laid out his traveling clothes and packed his bag. She fetched a bagel for him from the breakfast buffet: plain, well-toasted, cream cheese on the side. And to her everlasting credit, not once during the long drive home did she utter the word *psychosomatic*.

"I flunked," said Will.

"A lousy virus," Annie replied. "If I had an ounce of religion maybe I'd take this as a divine sign." She shrugged. "I guess that means I don't."

It was the wrong moment for Will to admit that in his delirium he had come to the conclusion that this might actually *be* a divine sign. Flat on his back in the hotel room, Will decided that he and Annie had to put aside this crazy plan. Put it off for, say, six months, he explained a few days later. Enough time for the two of them to get to know each other. Annie looked down at his hands, which were holding hers. She listened without saying a word. But she went along with him. And so suddenly Will quit thinking about pregnancy, parenthood, biological clocks, and all the rest of it. All at once he felt as if they could act like any other couple who had just fallen in love: they took in the museums, went out to the movies, ate dinner at a dozen restaurants near Annie's apartment. When the clouds briefly parted during what had been nearly two straight weeks of rain, and the sun emerged, they drove out to the National Arboretum and watched the azaleas and dogwoods come into bloom. And all the while they made love with what was, for Will, the blissful feeling that love was the only thing they were intending to make. It was sublime.

"The calm during the storms," Will explained to Barry and Diane. Then he described the previous Sunday's excursion to the FDR Memorial and the National Gallery, the four days of silence that ensued, and the two telephone conversations with Annie earlier that day, both of which had ended on a note of despair.

Ninety minutes had passed.

Barry sat like a happy potentate before an empty plate. Will's plate still held a mound of rice, which Barry had begun to casually strip-mine with a fork, oblivious to the waiter who was now circling the table, removing every stray piece of flatware, every untended glass. Diane ignored the waiter as well. She sat back in her chair, arms crossed, lips pursed, her expression knotted in concentration.

Barry, the consummate problem-solver, suddenly brightened. "It hit me while Will was talking: the problem isn't *them*. It's sex."

Diane closed her eyes. "Honey, that's brilliant."

"Listen up. Pee Wee's word for the day is *indirection*. This current approach is way too . . . I don't know, Catholic or something. Bottom line is that it has to feel queer to someone who came of age in the sixties. *That's* what undid Will. And that's what's dredging up all these doubts." He turned to Will: "Up till now sex has always been pretty straightforward—consenting adults, foreplay, contraception, a few minutes of frolic, then a short nap." He addressed Diane: "That's what he knows. Then one fine day, the rules of engagement suddenly change. Suddenly sex isn't good old-fashioned fornication anymore; it's procreation. What happened here is that our boy lost his nerve." He leaned forward and whispered: "You know what I think's missing? Mr. Monkey's rainhat."

Diane said, "Somehow I get the feeling that might interfere with the plan to conceive a child."

Barry's head was bobbing excitedly. "Exactly."

She frowned. "I am completely lost."

Barry said, "Way back when, us guys might pinch a rubber from somebody's father and carry it around in our wallets for months, years even. Not that we thought we might need it. But for confidence. To know that whatever happened, we'd be ready. What's crucial here isn't Mr. Monkey actually *wearing* the rainhat, but the fact of one being available." He turned to Diane: "The illusion of control. To put a little iron in the spine. Why do you think they package condoms to look like badges?" And to Will: "There's a *farmacia* next door. This will be my treat."

He was gone.

Diane grinned. "I can't help it. I know it doesn't make any sense, but I just love that guy." They sat together in silence for a few moments before she leaned forward. "Intuition," she whispered to Will. "If the answer is *yes*—"

"We are talking about bringing a human being into this world."

"Of course we are. It's a big decision. All I'm suggesting is that you need to *make* that decision." She put a hand on his arm. "Sweet man, you are forty-one years old. You have never been married. This is not something that was of concern to Annie when you two met. Now it is. If you care about this woman, she needs to know that. She needs to know where you stand. Right now. Six months will be too late." She pinched his arm. "Admit it: you would love to have a child."

The truth right then was that Will was dying to find out if he already *had* one.

"What about you?" he asked. "How long were you and Barry married before you decided to have children?"

"Four years."

"And what happened? One day you just made the decision?"

"One day my period was late. My period was never late. I was sure I was pregnant. The thought terrified me—for about fifteen minutes. Then suddenly it wasn't terrifying anymore." She looked at Will. "I wasn't pregnant. So we started trying. Nothing happened at first. Four or five months went by. I was taking my temperature every morning before I got out of bed, driving both of us crazy. And so was the fact that we weren't getting pregnant. I don't think either of us had a clue as to how much having kids meant to us until it looked as though we might not be able to." She paused. "Barry had a sperm count. I had an endometrial biopsy. And we got lucky. It just happened."

"Nothing just happens with Annie and me," said Will. "Everything has to be talked about, mulled over, analyzed from every vantage point. That's one of our big problems."

"That's everyone's problem." She leaned forward. "You can't figure out the right thing to do here. Nobody can. All you can do is look at the different paths in front of you and pick one. That's how life works."

Barry was back. He dropped into his chair and placed the mauve-and-silver condom packet before Will as if presenting him with a fortune cookie. "Trust me," he said. "What we're looking at here is a simple quarry jump."

"A quarry jump?"

"You know, just like when you were seventeen, cruising with the guys on a hot Saturday afternoon. You head out to the place where everybody swims. Someone dares you to go off the Tarzan cliff. You don't even think about it. There is nothing in the world to match the feeling of hitting the cold water. Right now you need to tap into *that* part of your brain."

"A quarry jump is over in two or three seconds," said Will.

"*If* you land in the deep water."

"Love as spinal-cord injury," said Diane. "Darling, that's beautiful." Then to Will: "You have to understand something. This lug and I have been married for fifteen years. Fifteen years and we're *still* not sure. You're never sure. The little secret nobody mentions is that this whole marriage enterprise is a huge leap of faith. In some ways the person you live with gets stranger to you by the day." She took Will's hand. "You have to trust your heart."

"For some reason mine just hasn't been very communicative," Will replied.

"You go on like this," she said quietly, "and one of two things happens: either you'll talk yourself out the door, or you and Annie will run out of time."

An hour later found Will and Barry alone in the dark on the small patio off the living room of Barry and Diane's co-op. Diane was upstairs putting the kids to bed. Barry had an unlit cigar clenched in his teeth. Will was peering at him through a thicket of bamboo. At last he said, "Look, there's something else I didn't mention."

Barry's eyes widened. The end of his cigar lifted like the tail of a stalking bird dog as Will began to describe the letter he'd received from Charlotte Cameron. Soon Barry beckoned with a hand: he wanted to examine the letter. Will retrieved it from his bag. Barry held it up to the moonlight and skimmed it in four seconds.

"The birth date," said Will.

Barry nodded. "It corresponds?"

"It might."

Barry looked puzzled. "Are you in touch with the mother?"

"We haven't spoken in twenty years."

Barry frowned.

Will said, "I walked away at the critical moment."

Barry gazed at the note again. He studied it. "This *is* peculiar. But then you're in a peculiar business, so that in itself doesn't signify anything. What I don't get is why she doesn't come out and say—"

"Could be she knows that I never knew about her."

"Or else she saw your handsome face in the newspaper and is in fact one deeply disturbed young lady."

"She could be my child, Barry. I've done the math."

He sat forward. "I'll let you in on a little secret, friend: we've all done the math. Every single guy who has lost touch with a woman at the critical moment has done the math. God knows that's a lot of us. By now it's probably a Jungian thing: at forty-something you suddenly start feeling that there's someone out there looking for you. Not to mention that some fellows *are* getting the call." He held up Charlotte's letter. "I'm not saying you're wrong, just that this doesn't constitute any sort of proof."

"It's a feeling," said Will. "I can't shake it."

Does any of this make sense, Mr. Gerard? Of course it made sense. How could it not make sense? Charlotte's birthday made sense. What were the odds of that being a coincidence? Small, thought Will. Tiny. Infinitesimal.

"So call up the old girlfriend and ask."

"Assuming I can find her." Will paused. "And then what if I'm wrong? I can't imagine Lucy being wildly excited to hear from me."

The unlit cigar moved in a wide oval while Barry mulled over Will's situation. Finally his head began to nod. "I've got it: tell her you're in A.A. On step six, or whichever one it is when you go around and apologize to everyone for being an asshole. Call her up. Be vague. You just want to make amends."

Will shook his head. "I need something else before I talk to her. I was thinking I might try to get a look at Charlotte Cameron. If she looks like me—"

"Of course she'll look like you. Or her roommate will look like you. Or the young woman in the next apartment. Or none of them will." Barry scowled. "Let's not forget that despite the family history of espionage you are not exactly the sleuthing type. You'll screw it up, Will. You'll be hunkered down in your car in front of her apartment, and somebody will call the cops."

"So what do I do?"

"Step back. Take a deep breath. Go slow."

This was not useful advice. Will had been going slow, so slowly his life of late had begun to seem like one long demonstration of the lotus position. That phase was over now. Will sensed his life revving up. Just consider what was on his plate this next week: one last chance to throw caution to the wind and embrace fatherhood (Annie and the good Lord willing), a long-lost girlfriend to locate, an unknown daughter to meet, the manuscript of a forthcoming bestseller to pry from the hands of its reclusive author. And what was Will doing to prepare for these tumultuous days ahead? He was flying to Boston and driving to Cape Cod to spend a weekend with strangers discussing *art from past lives*, whatever that meant. He wondered aloud if he should bail out on the literary conference.

Barry shook his head. "You have to go. If you think for one instant that I'd let you head home to D.C. tomorrow morning, you can forget it. In this frame of mind you would make a complete mess of things."

He was right of course.

Will would go to the Cape, rest up, even try to enjoy himself. He would view this weekend as it should be viewed: as a sideshow. What, after all, could be more diverting than two days of conversation between writers and artists and quasi-literary types like himself about Art and Truth and Beauty and God-knows-what-else over fish and fowl and four varieties of wine? Alexis Pine, an old school friend, had organized the conference. She had promised Will a good time.

Barry said, "Just don't forget to bluster. Overdo it a bit. Maybe drink a little more than you should." He grinned. "This could turn out to be the perfect weekend. With any luck you'll be involved in a scuffle in the parlor. Come away a new man."

"A deeply embarrassed new man," said Will.

"Don't kid yourself," Barry replied. "The right sort of self-disgrace can be tremendously uplifting."

Diane stood in the gated doorway. "The heirs await." As Barry shambled off, she added, "Behold the guilt-free man." He lifted a weary arm in response.

"I come home and wait on them like a servant," she told Will, "and all I feel is lousy. Like I'm never doing enough. Then Barry saunters in to give the nightly papal blessing and he emerges looking as if he's just been nominated for father of the year."

"All depends on where you come from, I guess," said Will.

"I guess that's true." She stood at the rail. Across the courtyard, framed in a wall of windows, there was a party in full swing. "Look, I feel lousy about what I said to you back at the restaurant. I shouldn't be pushing you. You have to do what you think is best." She turned. "I'm just rooting for the two of you, that's all."

"I keep wondering how Annie would react to my asking if I could bring along this packet of condoms to leave next to the bed as a sort of good luck charm."

Diane grinned.

Will said, "When I spoke to her today, she sounded pretty sure that she was ready to bag the whole thing."

"The woman who was desperate to have a child suddenly isn't desperate anymore?"

"She's thinking about adoption."

"She's thinking about everything, Will. And who could blame her?" She looked at him. "So where, um, exactly, do things stand?"

The tightness around her mouth indicated to Will that Diane wasn't inquiring about Annie's current frame of mind; rather, she wanted a full accounting of the peaks and valleys of Annie's basal temperature chart.

"Just four days," he said grimly.

"Four days can seem like a lifetime."

"If it isn't already too late."

Diane paused to kiss Will on the forehead before she headed inside. "Could be that this is the moment when *somebody* has to go out on a limb."

Two THOUSAND FEET above the rocky woods of Massachusetts, Will found himself trying to recall why he had begged off when Alexis offered to meet his plane at Logan. The fact was, he loved being met at unfamiliar airports. Nothing could match that blissful moment of surrender, when a guardian angel took your arm as you stumbled out of the metal cocoon, as disoriented as a possum in the noonday sun. With a guide, Will wouldn't have to try to make sense of the concourse maps. The loudspeaker announcements would become like white noise, the icons and arrows pointing the way to the baggage claim area and car rental counters, mere wall decoration.

But he was alone that Saturday morning at Logan, forced to make sense of all those things. At the razor-wired Hertz lot, Will had to endure an hour's wait as he inched forward through a velvet maze. Then followed a polite battle with the young man behind the counter who was insisting that he had to imprint Will's Visa card, even as Will pointed out that the box on the confirmation form had been marked *prepaid*. The standoff continued until finally the manager had to be summoned from her glass box within a glass box, and shortly Will found himself released into the spring sunshine, not simply a free man in a red Dodge Intrepid, but a free man with a free upgrade from the

Intrepid to a cobalt blue Crown Victoria with gray velour seats and a car phone.

The instant he emerged from the tunnel beneath Boston Harbor, he telephoned home. Teddy answered with what sounded like a mouthful of Lucky Charms. "Young suburban *professional,*" Will scolded.

"Not on Saturday morning," Teddy replied, still crunching. "Besides, I'm working. Working so hard I nearly collapsed from hunger."

"Then let the machine pick up the call."

"I knew it was you. I wanted to tell you about this fabulous manuscript that came in yesterday."

"You found something?" In Will's mind's eye young Teddy had suddenly morphed into Maxwell Perkins, the spiky black hair gone steely gray, the oval Frogskins now scholarly wire rims.

"This guy is the next William T. Vollmann," Teddy announced.

"The next who?"

Dead silence.

"Are you asking who is *William T. Vollmann?*" Teddy's tone of voice was incredulous. It was as if Will had drawn a blank on, say, Bob Dylan or J. D. Salinger. "*The Rifles,*" he said. "*Fathers and Crows, Whores for Gloria.*" When none of these book titles elicited a response, he whistled through his teeth. "I can't believe how much you need me, Uncle."

"And I thank God I have you. Any messages?"

"Four calls from writers who wanted to kiss the hem of your robe, and that's about it."

"Knock off early, young fella. Do something fun tonight."

"Something fun?" Teddy's tone was slightly defensive. "I don't think so. Not with all this code to write."

"It's Saturday night," said Will. "Put that stuff on hold. Go out and run around a little bit. That's an order."

"Run around where?"

Will couldn't say. Teddy should head down to a bar in the District, someplace where he could buy a beer. But as to where the kids from American University or Georgetown or George Washington hung out, Will hadn't a clue. It was the image of Teddy holed up alone in the shed writing code on a Saturday night that had prompted this suggestion. He figured that sundown on a spring weekend ought to bring out the pack instincts in a nineteen-year-old American male. Teddy should be making plans to gather with friends for a night of raucous laughter, and a little howling at the moon.

"What's this all about, Uncle Will?"

"I guess I must be worried about you."

"Why?"

"Well, for one thing, you spend too much time on the computer. I read somewhere that you need to go easy on that. Especially at night."

"How come?"

"Electromagnetic radiation." Will shifted the phone to the other ear. "From the screen. And it's a lot worse at night, I hear. Bad for you. For your glands," he added.

Teddy snorted.

"There's depression, too. Much higher incidence for regular computer users. Especially solitary ones." Will paused. "Maybe you should ask somebody over. Have somebody write code with you. Even a woman friend."

"I don't know any women who write code."

"There must be hundreds of women your age who would love to see how code gets written."

"Hey, I could put up a notice on the bulletin board at the co-op!"

"Not the worst idea."

Teddy snickered. "Listen, if things don't work out for you and Annie, we could put up a notice for you, too."

"Thanks, pal."

"Two hands on the wheel, old fella."

There was a sign for Plymouth Rock, and later, Sagamore Bridge. The tarry smell of the city had given way to the sea scent of salt and pine. The shoulders on both sides of the black highway were sandy now, rising upward in humps, like old dunes. Will sensed the great ocean off to the left, just beyond the low rise. It occurred to him that he had begged off Alex's offer to meet him at the airport because he wanted to make this drive alone. No chatter about school days in

Bangkok, no march through the intervening years, no gossip about the conference. Just cruise control, Bob Marley, and a thousand clouds racing across the open sunroof, like clouds in a cartoon.

He passed a bait shop and a gas station, a stretch of newly planted grass, and then, set in the middle of a gravel lot, a bright orange Chinese restaurant with a gold pagoda-style roof. No matter where in the world you find yourself, thought Will, there is always a Chinese restaurant.

Near Falmouth the highway narrowed and became a tree-lined street. Every half mile there were signs for the ferry to Martha's Vineyard. Beyond an overflow parking lot—3.4 miles beyond, according to Alex's directions—Will turned east on a state road. Soon he arrived at a gravel driveway that snaked through scrubby woods to an imposing brick gate post. Beyond it was a lawn the size of Rhode Island. Gatsby's mansion, with gabled roof and turrets and a four-tone paint scheme, sat off in the distance like a jeweled mountain surrounded by the deep blue sea. The driveway made a cautiously reverential approach to the magnificent house, looping to the right and hugging the rocky coast. There were dozens of sailboats just offshore bouncing awkwardly in the chop.

Catching sight of a dark head moving among the rocks, Will pulled off the driveway and stopped his car. He stepped across a border of stones, and descended between large boulders to a sandy beach that was still wet from the retreating tide. The dark-haired woman was coming toward him now, sunglasses perched at the tip of her nose. The heart-shaped face and dimpled smile he recognized instantly.

"You made it," called Alex.

"I'm pretty good at following directions."

She hugged him, then leaned back slightly to have a look at him. "Gosh, this is weird. I don't even know where to start."

Will said, "We shake our heads and marvel at how long it's been. Something like thirty years."

"Twenty-eight." Alex's grin was still the grin of a teenage girl. Or that was how it looked to Will. She looked the same to him. It just didn't make sense that twenty-eight years had passed since they had last seen each other. "Have you been up to the house?" she asked.

He shook his head. "Just drove up. I pulled over when I spotted you."

"Oh, dear. Something tells me you didn't read the information packet. Why am I not surprised?"

"There are rules?"

Her smile became a scowl. "Of course there are rules."

Right then a voice called "Surf! Surf!" and Will looked up to find a white-coated man gesturing from the rocks above. "Sir! Sir!" he was calling.

"Your car keys," said Alex. "Let's see what's left of that Little League arm."

Will heaved the keys, and the white coated man stepped forward gingerly to retrieve them from the rocks.

Will said, "Does this mean I'll be sent to bed without supper?"

"Don't make fun, Will. It's Dee Dee's house. And her event. She likes things just so."

"And that's all in the information packet, I take it."

"In a manner of speaking."

"So why does she spend her money on this?"

"She likes to bring people together—local folks, friends from Boston, writers, artists, filmmakers, people like yourself. I guess you'd call this a salon. That, and she wants an audience for her paintings." Alex grinned. "But you didn't hear that from me."

"You should have warned me."

"I did."

"I should have listened."

They had started together down the beach.

"I'm sure I didn't bring the right clothes," Will added a moment later. "Definitely not the right attitude."

Alex took his arm. "Still the rebel," she said.

Will laughed. "When was I a rebel?"

"Weren't we all? Or didn't we think we were? Or was it just that we were teenagers?"

"Teenagers far from home," said Will. "So who do you hear from from the good old days?"

Alex shook her head. "Practically no one besides Susannah

Hamilton. She's a professor at American University. The divinity school, if you can believe that. Talk about a high achiever."

The name was familiar, but Will couldn't summon a face to go with it. One of the oddest aspects of his childhood overseas was the constantly shifting web of friendships. So many American families left Bangkok each summer—some for three months of home leave, some for good—that all these departures had blurred in Will's mind. He could recall dozens of hot afternoons at Don Muang Airport seeing off his friends, but few of the faces of the kids whom he had gone out there to say good-bye to. Friends would simply disappear, and new ones would arrive to take their place. This was how life went in Bangkok. Come each September Will would set off for school eager to discover who was still around, and to begin to sort out all the new faces.

He had lost touch with almost all his old friends from Bangkok, though occasionally in Washington he would spot a familiar face in a movie line or at a grocery store. These encounters produced visceral reactions in Will—joy or annoyance or some other emotion that was linked to some forgotten memory of childhood. An old schoolmate turned up next to Will in a discount wine warehouse, and Will sensed rivalry that he couldn't explain. Another had sauntered into Tenleytown Books, and Will sensed that he and this fellow whose name he couldn't recall shared a secret: later he remembered that they had collaborated on homework assignments in Mr. Reeves's eighth-grade science class. Will might grab a beer with these old acquaintances; and he would keep in touch with them for a year or two, when they would vanish again. Word would filter back somehow that this one had gone off to work with Southeast Asian refugees, and that one had commenced a trip around the world; another had joined the Peace Corps, and someone else had moved to Los Angeles and disappeared into the Church of Scientology.

"Have you been back?"

Will shook his head. It had never occurred to him to go back. For one thing, Bangkok just didn't seem like a place you could go back *to*. In Will's mind it seemed less a location than a time in his life, and a collection of kids now grown to adulthood and scattered to the four winds.

"How about you?"

"With a small child?" Alex grimaced. "Completely out of the question." She put her head against Will's shoulder. "I miss those days a lot," she said.

Will recalled Alex at thirteen: the same dark hair, the same eyebrows that met above the bridge of her nose, the same soft features. Back then she had seemed more womanly than the other girls. She was the sort of kid who was always taking younger children under her wing. A caretaker, nosy but good-hearted, and always terribly efficient: the seventh-grade class secretary. It hadn't surprised Will at all to learn that these days Alex was an event planner, a PR consultant, a newsletter publisher, a freelance writer specializing in Women & Business. She was divorced, and remained on good terms with her ex-husband. She had a five-year-old son, two cats, a condo in the Back Bay.

Alex said, "Susannah went to Chiang Mai with a church group a few years ago. She loved it. Not at all like Bangkok, she said. When Joseph is older, that's where I'd like to take him."

Will had been to Chiang Mai twice. The first trip, with his family, was billed as a weekend vacation, though as Will thought back on the outing he wondered if his father had had business to attend to: meetings with Thai officials and American expatriates, CIA informants of one stripe or another. The drive north from Bangkok had taken two days on unpaved roads through dense tropical forests. Will remembered nothing of the trip but an occasional logger trailed by an elephant swaying beneath a load of teak, and the fine red dust that covered everything: the leaves of the trees at the roadside, their turquoise station wagon, themselves. He recalled that he was washing that dust from his hair for days. They spent the night on the road in a government cabin at the base of a hydroelectric dam. In Chiang Mai Will and his family stayed two nights at the home of the U.S. Consul. The house looked like a relic of the Raj, with wide verandas, wicker furniture, and gleaming teak floors, set back on a dark green hill overlooking the small town. Will's second visit came one year later. He had flown to Chiang Mai with a delegation of students. They huddled together in the freezing belly of a DC-9 that was loaded with Christmas presents and medicines that Will and his classmates would distribute to the impoverished children of the indigenous hill tribes of northern Thailand. *Operation Santa Claus,* it was called.

Alex and Will had attended the International School of Bangkok—ISB, in the vernacular. It was a huge school, some three thousand students from kindergarten to twelfth grade, three-quarters of them American, the offspring of diplomats and soldiers, businessmen, journalists, Fulbright scholars and civil engineers, many of whom had settled their families in Thailand while they attended to the war in Vietnam. Will and his classmates had enough of a sense of protocol to know whose father was the U.S. ambassador, or the commanding general at MACTHAI, but that was all. Aside from the embassy families, Will often didn't know whether a classmate's father worked in an air-conditioned office in Bangkok, or built roads in the Mekong Delta, or flew helicopters through the foggy mountains of Laos.

In Bangkok few kids knew about the precise nature of Will's father's work. Jamie Gerard was officially listed as a political attaché at the American Embassy. Will understood that this job was a cover. The other political attachés didn't live in houses with swimming pools. They didn't receive U. S. congressmen and senators at their homes. There were other signs of high diplomatic status as well: the parade of young men with crewcuts who came most evenings to speak with Will's father, the black limousine he rode to work in, the late-night telephone conversations with the U. S. ambassador. But nobody talked about Jamie Gerard's real job, Will included. At home and at school, the fact that his father was the CIA Station Chief in Thailand was never mentioned. Discretion was the fundamental tenet of Will's childhood.

Alex and Will had reached the stretch of beach directly behind the house, and now walked in sand so fine-grained and sparkling white that Will suspected it must have arrived the previous day in the bed of a dump truck. Ahead, a gigantic Nazca-like bird and turtle had been etched with a rake in the sand, each figure outlined with smooth black stones. On the headland above the beach sat a cedar-shingled gazebo. There were a dozen people inside it scuttling about like a flock of shorebirds as they bobbed and pecked at the platters of food laid out before them. Beyond the gazebo, the shore face of Dee Dee's mansion looked unrelated to the turn-of-the-century house that Will had viewed from the driveway, with its fussy scrollwork and peach and salmon shingles. This side was glass. So much glass it seemed to Will that he was looking at a cross-section of a house.

Inside, in an atrium with a magnificent flight of marble stairs that was brightly lit from an octagonal skylight three stories above, Dee Dee's conferees had been immortalized in photographs, bio sheets, newspaper clippings, exhibit posters, book jackets. It seemed to Will to be quite an illustrious group. There was the sculptor Mal Franco, National Book Award–nominated writer Mary Alice Neel, filmmaker Czeslaw Kiedzierzyn-Kozle, poet Carlos Tul, who, Will surmised, was at that moment testing the acoustics in a nearby room. Two conferees went by single names: Nereus (a performance artist) and Moriki (a painter). There were two photos of Rudolph Sweatt (pronounced "sweet," his bio sheet informed), a "world-famous biologist turned paranormal researcher studying morphic resonance and the etiology of reincarnation." No matter what sort of intellectual and artistic nonsense lay ahead, Will resolved to maintain a sense of humor. (Which meant that he would definitely have to boycott Dee Dee's art show— "Past Lives" announced a gaudy red banner hanging at the entrance to her private gallery.) With enough wine, he had every reason to believe that he could convince himself that this was just a brief detour into the theater of the absurd. Another glass or two and he might even enjoy himself.

Alex had gone off to check her messages. So Will wandered. He studied the six-foot-tall leather cross at the base of the marble staircase; he strolled through the burgundy-carpeted club room with its wall of morocco-bound books and plush green reading chairs and billiards table; he stood in the open doorway of the rustic hall opposite. "Hark now! Hark now! Hark now!" Carlos had begun chanting. And right then Will thought wistfully of home: a sunny Saturday afternoon stretched out in a hammock in the yard, perusing an awful novel or two, sipping a cold beer, watching a pair of goldfinches tidy up their nest. The radio at the kitchen window would be tuned to an Orioles game. The truth was that he would have preferred to spend a full day driving into the heart of Virginia to retrieve Norton Tazewell's overdue manuscript than spend it here. Dee Dee Abad's wall of photographs had a zoo-like aspect, a collection of rare birds that would soon be expected to sing for their suppers. Whores for Dee Dee, Will thought, gazing around the room at all the faces, every single person— himself, too, he was chagrined to note—posing like a sullen peacock.

Alex came up behind him. "Not exactly what you would call happy campers," she whispered.

He shook his head sadly. "I guess one can't presume to traffic in Art and Truth without making a diligent effort to remain in a bad mood."

The second-floor landing featured a piece of sculpture that resembled a staircase made from broken baseball bats. At the end of the hallway, Alex opened the door to a room that looked out to sea. Will's overnight bag sat on a luggage rack at the foot of a chrome bedpost. Alex went to the sliding glass door and stepped out on the narrow balcony. Beside her, Will felt like a passenger on a great ocean liner, ready to set sail for some exotic port.

"So what about you?" she asked. "No wife? No kids?"

He shook his head. "I'm slow on these things. Still working on it."

She rolled her eyes. "Am I too nosy?"

"Sure. But that's okay." He looked at the sea. "Let's just say that lately I've been negotiating a patch of thin ice."

"When it starts out thin, it just gets thinner. Take it from someone who's fallen through a couple of times." She grinned.

"You survived."

"Of course I did. And you will, too. Life just goes on, doesn't it?"

He watched the rocking boats. "So who else from Bangkok?" Names that Will couldn't have recalled if he'd set his mind to it just popped into his head: "Charlie Allan, Gerrie Anne Walker, Bitsy Chang, Davy McKeon, Frank Tucker, Meg Morris—any news of them?"

Alex was shaking her head.

"What about Lucy Vitava?"

"I figured you might have some news from Lucy."

"Not for a long time. More than twenty years."

Alex was gazing down at the gazebo, still noisy and crowded. "Susannah ran into her years and years ago. In a hospital." She turned to Will. "Lucy was almost finished with medical school."

The news stunned Will. Lucy the doctor was beyond the scope of his imagination. Now that he thought about it, the Lucy he would imagine from time to time had hardly aged at all. She was fixed in his mind in her early twenties. Lucy the orphan. The survivor. It hadn't occurred to Will that she had gone to college, much less to medical school. Lucy had her father's milky Slavic coloring, his blond hair and rangy build. Years and years ago she had said something to Will about wanting to take flying lessons (her father had been a helicopter pilot), and Will had long assumed that she had followed through on that. The drumbeat of a traffic chopper racing out to the Beltway would remind him of Lucy, not every time but often.

"So how was Lucy?" he finally managed.

"As I recall she asked Susannah about you."

Will waited for Alex to continue.

"Susannah said she seemed pretty frazzled."

"Medical school," offered Will.

"I suppose so."

Alex lifted her sunglasses to the top of her head. Her eyes were green. At their corners were faint wrinkles that lent her face an endearing note of sadness. Alex was somebody you could talk to. Her smile beckoned. She said, "I wasn't at school the day she left. I must have been home with a cold or something. I don't recall the last time I saw her, but I do have this vivid memory of you a day or two later. Funny how some things stay in your head. You looked so sad, Will, so sad I felt as though *I* might end up in tears."

This was March of 1968, the spring of eighth grade. Lucy and Will had been in history class. She was summoned to the principal's office. A secretary had come to get her. That in itself was odd. After a moment, Will asked to be excused to the bathroom. He stood in the open hallway, looking out through the metal grate at the parking lot below. Suddenly he caught sight of Lucy's blond ponytail. She was walking between two men, heading toward a black sedan. The men were Americans. They weren't in uniform but Will knew from their stiff gait that they had to be soldiers. He couldn't imagine why these men had come for Lucy, but he had enough of a nose for government protocol to know that being summoned from school by two military escorts meant something terrible had happened.

The next day Lucy was absent from school. Rumors raced around

ISB: her mother had been in an accident—no, her father, someone reported. Someone else had seen a moving van parked in front of Lucy's apartment building. Will telephoned her, but the line just rang and rang. Later that evening he gathered the courage to ask his father for news about Lucy and her family.

Jamie Gerard listened quietly, his expression tight. Then his face softened. "I'm afraid Lucy's dad had an accident up north," he said.

Up north was Chiang Mai. It was Laos and China, too, though at the time those countries lay beyond the borders of Will's mental geography of Southeast Asia. He was confused. "In his helicopter?"

A sad nod from his own father, but nothing more.

"Lucy and her mother went there?"

Softly: "It seems to have been a tragic accident, Will."

Ernie Vitava was dead. Lucy's dad was dead. His helicopter had fallen out of the sky. In his mind's eye, Will saw it falling. He saw the helicopter hit the ground and burst into flames.

"The chopper disappeared in Laos," his father went on. "Search teams are out looking. Looking everywhere. But it'll take some time. A long time, maybe. It's a big country."

"He's missing?"

A nod. "Doesn't look good, son. Not at all." He put a hand on Will's shoulder. "Lucy's mom made the tough decision to go home to wait for news. They left this morning on the early Pan Am flight."

One day Lucy had been summoned from class by the news that her father's helicopter had gone missing in Laos, and the next day she too had disappeared. Will felt devastated. He and his friends were children of nomads. They were pilgrims of the transit lounge. This tribe of kids had few rights and rituals, but one had always seemed inviolable: departing friends must be seen off. Just as the dead pharaohs of Egypt made their journey to the underworld with a retinue of servants, an American boy or girl departing from Bangkok required a crowd of well-wishers, pretzels and Orange Fanta, cameras and yearbooks, tears and promises.

Lucy had been denied all of that. She had vanished.

That evening Will swam alone in the family pool, swam and cried, swam until his arms ached and his eyes were bloodshot from the tears and chlorine. And then he toweled off and went inside the house. His parents were out. In the top drawer of his mother's vanity he found thirty baht, which he slipped into his pocket. The next morning at dawn he walked out to Sukumvit Road and hailed a cab, and had the driver take him to Don Muang. There he stood alone on the airport's observation deck for almost an hour, stood silently, eyes dry now, unblinking, unwilling to leave until that morning's Pan Am jet had finally rumbled past him, and lifted slowly into a dense white sky.

THE BATHROOM down the hall was a baroque affair with flocked green wallpaper, polished brass, a claw-footed tub, a commode with a ceiling tank, and a sink the size of a small goldfish bowl. Will slapped water on his freshly shaved cheeks, and gazed into a tiny oval mirror. Figuring that Alex's parting instructions to "get settled in" should include a bit of preparation for the evening ahead, he had at last begun to consider what in the world he was going to say to this gathering. In the program, his twenty-minute talk was entitled "Writing a Life."

Dee Dee wanted Will to talk about memoirs. From a literary agent's perspective, Alex had said. So what should he say? Where to begin? Perhaps he should suggest that the current popularity of the memoir was a reflection of these times: our collective voyeurism or appetite for public confession, or simply a preference for what is perceived to be true. He could digress here, and talk about memoir and fiction; he could remind the audience that the two forms have been linked for centuries: just as once it was de rigueur to cast one's novel in the form of a memoir (*The Life and Strange Surprising Adventures of Robinson Crusoe, of York, Mariner*, for example), so too nowadays the serious postmodern novelist often includes himself (a character *named* for himself, that is) in his own works of fiction. Even unlettered old Norton Tazewell had been bitten by this bug: he wanted to call his Civil War spy Norton Cadwallader Tazewell, though Will was finally able to convince him that Moses Pugh was a stronger name, much more evocative with its biblical associations, which became all the more resonant after Will persuaded Norton to change the title of the book from *The Sojourner* to *Pharaoh's Ghost*.

Will studied himself in the mirror. Perhaps he should open the talk with Barry's line, delivered with all the gravelly seriousness of a football announcer: "THIS IS THE AGE OF THE MEMOIR." He smiled. There was something perverse in his soul that preferred to stumble into talks like this one, to throw himself in front of an audience with a sublime sense of detachment from the whole proceeding—to become two selves, as it were, the poor clown trapped at the podium and the spectator curious as to what the poor clown would say. Inevitably, Will the speechmaker would fumble around for a moment or two. He would sense the rising anxiety of the crowd in front of him, take a sip of water, allow the audience to sense his own nervousness, which soon ballooned into panic. Then, miraculously, he would seize on an idea, stumble forward to another one, and, with any luck at all, to another.

Soon he would skirt the abyss. He would note a tentative nod somewhere in the room, a puzzled smile, the touching expression from someone in the crowd who suddenly realized that this speaker was not, in fact, going to fall flat on his face. This was by no means the smoothest sort of public oratory, but it was far better than the alternative: Will Gerard, waxy-faced at the podium, thick tongued, clutching a well-thumbed stack of note cards, droning on in the halting style of a State Department spokesperson.

He might tell this gathering that the line between fiction and nonfiction naturally blurs in a society where hardly anyone thinks twice about sharing a deep, dark secret with millions. The urge to invent becomes impossible to resist. Some novels are fundamentally true, he might say, and some memoirs wholly imaginary. The truth of a piece of writing doesn't depend on form or fact-checking, but on the quality of storytelling. A coming-of-age novel about a girl searching for her birth parents, for example, might be as true as a memoir by the same young woman. The memoir might appear to make the claim that the events described in the book actually occurred. But really, a memoir is nothing more than a story that a writer believes to be true. Belief makes it real. Ask me, thought Will. Ask Lucy Vitava. Ask Charlotte Cameron.

The printed schedule on the bedside table had the conferees gathering on the back patio at five-thirty for cocktails and hors d'oeuvres. Will dressed and assembled among a depressingly homogenous group, nearly everybody clothed in black or gray with angry splashes of color—purple mascara and purple scarf, say, or blood red tie and matching argyle socks. Nobody talked above a murmur. The bartender was still polishing glasses. The Vineyard ferry passed close to shore, and the passengers on deck gazed down in envy at the gathering. This, of course, proved to be the precise moment the champagne was uncorked and Dee Dee Abad made her entrance. She appeared as Will had pictured her: a dark-haired woman, once beautiful, but whose face was now hidden behind Kabuki makeup. She wore nested strings of pearls and a billowy gray gown. Her lipstick was the same peach color as the paint on her window sashes. Watching Dee Dee work the crowd, greeting each guest by name, Will finally understood that he and his cohorts had been assembled not as performers but as an audience. Dee Dee was the main event.

The guests parted before her like the Red Sea, the writers fleeing to the bar in the gazebo, while the artists and sculptors (those whose incomes depended on the sale of a relatively small number of expensive units, Will surmised) remained at her side like tick birds on a water buffalo. Dee Dee brushed them off, and instead went after the people who were trying to avoid her. Folks like Will.

"I can't tell you how much I am looking forward to your talk tonight, Mr. Gerard."

He smiled, straining hard at affability. Dee Dee smelled of exotic oils; she wore three tiny gold rings in one nostril.

"Of course I've been thinking about writing *my* memoirs. (*And why shouldn't I*—her sneering expression added—*since any boring day in my life would be much more fascinating than a good day in yours!*) We stayed in Beirut through the worst days. I saw everything: courage, cowardice, barbarism, gentleness. *I am a camera.*" She lowered her banded eyelids and smiled sadly, pausing to see if Will had caught the Christopher Isherwood reference. "You will want to read it the moment I am finished."

"I look forward to that," Will replied, instantly hating himself.

"I know you do. You've seen my paintings?"

She knew he hadn't. Will saw that right away. She had a list, and she had checked it twice. She was daring him to lie.

"I couldn't help but think that with the morning light—"

"I will give you a tour myself!"

Her gaze drifted away from his face, fluttered off. She scanned the entire room before finally bringing her scowl to rest on Carlos Tul, who had taken up a position on the wrong side of the bar.

The actor among them, a strapping blond fellow with the chiseled features of a soap-opera star, performed a monologue in the gazebo: the last will and testament of an aging Lebanese patriarch, which had been written (surprise, surprise) by Dee Dee herself. Afterward, the conferees and invited guests filed into the library to watch a short film. It was set on a beach: crashing waves, screeching gulls, atonal music, then a couple arguing about how much time they had before the arrival of the afternoon bus. It went on and on, interrupted finally by a voice-over that considered the existence of God and the meaninglessness of any form of work other than manual labor, carpentry and agriculture especially. At the end of the film the couple is still waiting for the bus, though not speaking to each other anymore. Finally the man heads off on foot out of the frame. "Where are you going?" the woman cries. "Africa," the unseen man replies. "Bastard," the woman calls, flinging a handful of sand, which the camera follows all the way to the ground, the focus becoming so tight it is hard to tell whether one is looking at one square meter of beach, or an overhead shot of a sandstorm in the Sahara. There was the sound of drums, then a voice-over in French, bleating in its anger.

Fade out.

Dee Dee rose to her feet to lead the applause as the film's writer, director, cameraman, editor, and composer, Czeslaw Kiedzierzyn-Kozle, wearing a black jumpsuit tied with a turquoise belt, climbed to the podium. He agreed to take a few questions. There were no questions. He admitted that the film had been inspired by Beckett and Camus. An homage, he called it. He was hoping to secure funding to turn the short into a feature, he added, fixing his intense gaze on Dee Dee.

She promptly sat down.

DINNER WAS vichyssoise, marinated beets, and a rabbit stew with seared little bunny-like lumps of meat served on a bed of saffron rice. Will had arrived early and switched his place card with that of Guy

Spicer, a psychologist specializing in sand-tray therapy, who was seated beside Alex. Dee Dee strode into the room at the moment the last of her guests had taken his seat, and instantly flashed Will a sour grin to let him know that she had picked up on his act of disobedience.

The soup was delicately flavored, the beets a bit mushy, but edible, which was not true of the seared bunnies. One glance at them sent Will's stomach into a cartwheel. He considered the napkin trick, but good fortune had placed the ravenous carnivore Carlos Tul on the other side of Alex. Whenever Dee Dee turned her head, Alex was kind enough to shuffle one of her bunnies onto Carlos's plate as Will shuffled one of his bunnies onto hers.

According to the schedule Will was to speak after dinner, following Carlos's reading from his new memoir, *Forcing Myself.* Carlos's highly refined Latin machismo act failed to endear him to the crowd. The passage he read was filled with violence, vitriol, and coarse, sexist language. Carlos described his ex-wife as an "angry little man," which brought howls of protest from a number of women in the audience. Which led to Carlos's angry retort, "I azure you, ze shoe feets!" This brought further shouts and recriminations. Through it all Will remained on the sideline. He had decided to be amused by Carlos's routine, in part because it felt like an act, and in part because Carlos had been such a sport about eating his bunnies.

Suddenly it was ten-thirty, ninety minutes past the hour that Will was to have addressed the group. Carlos announced gravely that he would conclude with a recitation of his epic poem, *The Blood of Cortés.* He would recite from memory.

In Spanish.

He called for the lights to be dimmed.

"*La Sangre de Cortés,*" he growled.

Will went on at eleven-twenty, utterly exhausted. Later, all he would remember of the event was the roomful of weary eyes, eyes connected to brains that had already wandered off to bed, to the bar, to the night beach. Will's internal call-and-response speechmaking style suffered dramatically before this group: two minutes into the talk, he could hear himself beginning to drone.

Only Dee Dee, seated front and center, eyeteeth flashing, seemed remotely, if aggressively, interested. There was nowhere for Will to go with this talk, no safe harbor from which to hold forth. He was doomed, and he knew it almost instantly. But he stumbled on, gamely hoping for some sort of deliverance. After a fifteen-minute paste-up job (paraphrasing letters he had written, plagiarizing Barry, reprising what he had said to the *Washington Post* reporter) he suddenly had some momentum. He felt a surge of optimism. He related conversations he'd had with editors on the subject of memoirs. Then he rushed headlong into a sentence at the end of which he realized he had no place to go: "It's so much more difficult for a writer nowadays, with so many memoirs being published, and each one claiming to be the next *Angela's Ashes* or *The Color of Water* or whatever." *So difficult in what way? To write a memoir? To sell it? To get on Oprah?* Will took a sip of water and rued not having a text even as, setting down his glass, he considered that a text would not save him here. He was tapped out. He took a breath, and another sip of water. Then he pushed his face into a smile. "Questions?" he asked.

Nobody moved. The air in the room seemed to freeze solid at that moment. Dee Dee cleared her throat. Her lips puckered. She was obviously disappointed: she had not gotten her money's worth.

"Above all," she said, "the *literary* memoir must be intensely creative, don't you think, Mr. Gerard? As a *literary* agent? What I mean is, a life put in service to art."

Will nodded. His jaw suddenly felt too heavy to open and shut.

Dee Dee grew visibly angry. "Borges," she spat. She invoked the name like a large pistol being withdrawn from its holster, "If I recall, Borges once wrote . . ."

She droned on and on.

Will had to resist the urge to close his eyes; he struggled to stay on his feet, to keep an expression on his face that might be perceived as being vaguely interested. Jorge Luis Borges was a brilliant writer, clever and inventive, but too often nowadays it seemed to Will that Borges's name popped up at the awkward moments of social events—at dinner parties, say, during a rocky transition from dessert to cheese. Thus, the very mention of Borges acted as an opiate on Will's brain. *Borgesian* had a worse effect: it produced in Will the symptoms of narcolepsy.

"Maybe we should look at the issue of truth," Will managed. "The truth of a memoir needn't be literal. There isn't a formula. Books are sustained by language. The writing either works or it doesn't. Look at Bruce Chatwin: *In Patagonia* works, in my opinion; *Songlines* doesn't."

"Rather obviously put, Mr. Gerard. I must admit I expected subtlety."

The expression on Will's face felt queer to him, as though someone had jabbed a knitting needle into his back and whispered *smile*. Dee Dee was spoiling for a fight, and Will knew that he would refuse the challenge. It wasn't simply the lateness of the hour, or Alex at the back of the room apologetically blowing him a kiss before she rushed home to Boston to relieve the baby-sitter: it was the precariousness of the moment. And the rising swell of anger in his blood. Will despised this sort of literary conversation. More than anything he wanted it over. And so he summoned to his face the most affable smile he could muster, and stood there like a guy waiting for a train. And said nothing.

Dee Dee rose menacingly to her feet. "Thank you, Mr. Gerard. Thank you for illuminating the intersection between art and truth." She gathered her ample dress and stormed from the room.

The abrupt departure stunned the gathering to silence.

"Thank *you*," Will said finally, one eye on the open doorway, still considering that Dee Dee might have gone to fetch a baseball bat from the sculpture on the landing, and would shortly return to teach him a lesson he would never forget about literal and figurative truth. A moment later he drifted away from the podium. The applause was tepid at first; then it built, becoming gracious, exuberant, and finally giddy, as the forty-odd people in the audience clapped themselves back to their senses. The party geared down briefly as the conferees rearranged themselves in other rooms, then it blazed back to life when Carlos, who had been off making a tour of the lower depths, returned with a case of wine, a two-iron, and a bucket of golf balls.

"Focking Borges," he whispered to Will, and then roared with laughter.

Hours later, after billiards and darts, after a round of bocce and a makeshift three-hole golf tournament with Carlos on the front lawn, Will sat alone on the rocky headland beyond the gazebo and marveled at what he would do for a little money. What sort of indignity might he have agreed to had Dee Dee offered *two* thousand dollars?

The stars were out. The night had grown cool enough for a sweater. Will drank a well-aged cabernet sauvignon from the bottle. He thought about what else he had left out of his talk. *Inevitability.* Good stories always seem inevitable. But not predictable. What else? He had foolishly neglected to consider the word *memoir.* He should have *deconstructed* it for Dee Dee. It came from the Latin word for memory, though Will had always felt the genre had more to do with making a story of one's past than recollecting a sequence of events. A narrative needs the sort of tension that is frequently missing from life, he could have explained. Real life is messy, boring, haphazard, the dramatic moments often so separated in time as to seem independent of cause and effect. Stories unfold purposefully, while the unfolding of a life is constantly muddied by chance events: a forty-seven-year-old man's heart gives out one day; a young father's helicopter falls out of the sky; a letter from an unknown child arrives out of the blue.

It seemed peculiar to Will to realize that, over the course of this one day, he had come to think of Lucy and Charlotte and himself as a family, three strangers connected together by nothing but the most powerful threads that connect all families. He gazed at the water. The rising tide had reached the Nazca bird. Dark stones outlined the animal, and each time a wave retreated, the head of the bird seemed to magically emerge from the foam until it finally slipped beneath the sea. He wondered where Lucy was—and wondered who she was, and who she had become. How would she react to news of this long-lost daughter, if indeed Charlotte was her daughter?

And how would she react to him?

WILL WAS NOT, strictly speaking, a doomsday air traveler. He had an intellectual grasp of the risks of flying. He knew that the chance of any particular flight ending in a fiery crash was negligible, that the knot in his stomach before takeoff had more to do with his situation (being locked inside a large metal tube that would shortly be hurtling through the upper reaches of the atmosphere) than any intuition that his hours might be numbered. Still, he was plagued by morbid thoughts that Sunday afternoon, cooped up inside a Boeing 737 that sat for an hour on the runway at Logan.

A good measure of Will's equanimity in airplanes depended upon the orderly progression of the flight. Parked out there like a broken-down bus, the cabin air stinking of jet fuel, he found himself gazing around at his fellow passengers, and imagining the lot of them reduced to a grim newspaper manifest of names, ages, and hometowns. To purge this thought, he buried his nose in the Sky Shopper catalog, with its array of ultrasonic teeth cleaners, pocket-sized travel irons, exercise aids, pillows, rainslickers. Such an odd impulse to shop at thirty thousand feet, but then this plane wasn't even off the ground, and Will felt the urge, too. When his eyes fixed on the perfect birthday gift for Teddy (a personal air-conditioner that hangs draped like a towel around the neck), he felt a surge of hopefulness. The mere act of filling out the order form had a calming effect, as if copying the numbers and expiration date from one's Visa card would guarantee one's survival, at least until the bill was paid.

Could there be a person alive whose life was so full (loved ones so well-loved, affairs so well-ordered) that thoughts of an imminent demise would seem in any way acceptable? For Will, right then, such a thought was not acceptable at all, what with his own life like a desert cactus that blooms every forty years suddenly showing traces of color.

He was staring straight ahead at the Airfone, unaware of the device, when the plane lifted slowly over the brown waters of Boston Harbor. Will's regular habits didn't include making telephone calls from airplane seats. But Teddy had ratcheted Will's life forward a few notches on the telecommunications front, and so he considered making a phone call. It was startling to realize that what would have been a wild extravagance two weeks ago was now just another one of those lifestyle upgrades that inexplicably seem to happen: the tin of Maxwell House is replaced by a sack from Starbucks, the Oral-B goes electric, the new car has power windows, then a CD player, then a heating element in the driver's seat. In one month or two or ten, Will could easily imagine finding himself with a dual-nozzle shower, a lap pool, Egyptian cotton underpants.

He called Annie from twenty-eight thousand feet. After the third ring, he hit the disconnect.

THREE RINGS HAD to be Will: Will who wanted to talk to a real person or nobody at all.

Of course she could have turned off the ringer and turned down the answering machine, or done the old-fashioned thing and unplugged the telephone altogether. She had thought about doing that, about absenting herself for the entire day. She thought about renting a car and driving somewhere. But she didn't. And so now, at four o'clock, she stood in her kitchen, and counted the rings—one, two, three only—puzzled at first, because it seemed too early for Will to be calling.

Still, three rings.

A few minutes later the phone rang again, and this time Annie grabbed it on the first ring. It wasn't Will, but her sister in Chicago.

"So what have you decided?" she said. "What are you going to do?"

"I'll come and hear what they have to say," Annie replied.

"Seriously?"

"Of course."

"Have you told Will?"

"No." She paused. "Who knows, it may be a lousy job, or . . ." Or perhaps by next week there would be no obligation to tell him anything, she thought.

"This must be an awful time, sweetie."

"Yeah, well." She looked out the window.

"Listen, I'll pick you up at the airport."

"Five fifty-five in the afternoon at O'Hare? I couldn't do that to you."

"You aren't. I'm doing it to myself. What airline? What day?"

"United," said Annie. "On Tuesday."

"You take care."

"I'll do my best. Give that little girl of yours a kiss for me."

AT FOUR O'CLOCK Will's plane was crossing the muddy waters of the Delaware Bay, then the glittery Chesapeake. He gazed down on toy bridges and toy boats, on tea-colored creeks and emerald marshes, imagining as he often did flying south to Washington that somewhere below, submerged no doubt, lay a spit of land where the first American Gerard had come ashore in the New World some three hundred and fifty years earlier.

The family story had it that Will's ancestors arrived with the first Maryland colonists, Catholic runaways from Protestant England. But there the trail cooled. The history books indicate that there were Gerards about, but to Will's mother's profound embarrassment the most prominent among them was a Jesuit priest. Will's father displayed a sly sense of pride in roots that were at once holy and tainted. Jamie Gerard was this sort of Catholic: a Sunday churchgoer who never followed the priest's instructions to kneel or stand, and seemed lost in thought as he converted the church bulletin into a private acrostic, yet could recite the morning gospel on the short ride home. He was a student of Vatican history, a scholar of the sociology of intrigue, a devout believer in the medieval Catholic notion that life was an unending struggle between the forces of good and evil, and a man who never lacked for a credible cover story. The suggestion that their line descended from one Thomas Gerard, S. J., neatly explained why the family lacked tangible proof of early passage: there were no seventeenth-century deeds to tobacco plantations or ruined manor houses, no portraits of English noblemen, no foxed ledgers filled with the names of slaves.

Will's great-grandfather was born into the working class. He was the son of a blacksmith who as a young man decided that he would make a better life for himself. He crossed the Potomac at Pope's Creek and went by horseback to Charlottesville to read the law. From there he went to Washington, D.C., became a judge, and rose through the ranks of society to become a shooting buddy of Teddy Roosevelt. His son graduated from Princeton with honors, sailed off to fight in the Great War, and then went to Wall Street, where he grew wealthy, drank heavily, abandoned his wife and young son for long periods of time. (This Thomas Gerard was rumored to have a second family.) In the late twenties, he nearly died from a bad batch of gin.

In the spring of 1929, on a trip to Europe to take the healing waters, a chance conversation in London sent Will's grandfather on a different sort of grand tour: the family spent two months traveling from the Baltic to the Adriatic, stopping along the way to survey the American goods that had begun to pile up in warehouses at every major port. Returning to New York City in late September, Will's grandfather immediately converted his stock portfolio to gold. This was three weeks before the Crash. That winter Thomas Gerard journeyed south to Maryland and bought three thousand acres of land near the village of Port Tobacco. He hired a New York architect to oversee the renovation of the run-down manor house. This was to be a grand gesture, a return to roots. But the triumph was short-lived: Will's grandfather died suddenly two years later, leaving behind a reclusive widow, a shy five-year-old son, and an estate of one and a half million dollars.

It struck Will, gazing down at the water, how all of life's large moments are hinged to small ones: an exile's new home and final resting place determined by a gust of wind that strands a ship on one particular stretch of shore; or by a chance conversation. This was true in his own life, too. The decision to turn left or right at a street corner, to return a phone call, to duck into a newsstand on the way to catch a train: that Friday in March he might have paused for two minutes at Penn Station and never run into Michael Phillips, never gone to Lewes, never met Annie. Just as all those years ago, he might have skipped the newspaper on one particular morning and never spotted the photograph of Lucy's mother. Had he missed that photo of Judy Vitava, in all likelihood he would never have found Lucy, never called her, never gone to see her, never slept with her; and twenty years later, never received this letter from Charlotte Cameron.

Somewhere below was the town of La Plata, and Port Tobacco, and nearby, set above the river, the family homestead. Will thought about his own father, a taciturn man whom Will had felt he understood, and yet who still seemed like a stranger, hermetically sealed in the secret world of his work. Will missed him right then, missed him so fiercely he could feel the tears pressing at his eyes, as if his father had died just days or weeks earlier. This was how grief played itself out in Will: months would pass, even a year, and then suddenly he would find himself gripped by the magnitude of the loss. Right then he longed to hold his father, and even more, to be held by him, held tightly, something he could not recall having done, nor wanting particularly, while his father was alive. He gazed out the window and thought about all these genes and chromosomes that scientists had just begun to locate: for left-handedness, aggression, a weakness for the bottle; for problem-solving, too, perhaps, and concealment.

St. Jerome's, he thought.

Why would Lucy go to a Catholic home for unwed mothers?

He picked up the Airfone.

"You are *where*?" cried Will's mother. She spoke with such delight Will felt like Neil Armstrong phoning home from the surface of the moon. "Darling, how marvelous!"

She was in her rose garden. Will saw her garbed in outdoor clothes and a broad-brimmed hat, Brookstone tool caddy and colored kneeling pads arrayed around her. He could tell from the way her voice changed that she was gazing up at the sky now, as if hoping to spot his plane as it passed overhead.

"Just calling to say Happy Mother's Day."

Mary Gerard laughed. "And to think I used to be happy if you remembered to send a card! Sweetheart, thank you. Nobody's ever called me from an airplane. Your father would have adored the thought of making telephone calls from airplanes."

"He wouldn't like the bill."

"No, he wouldn't." She laughed again. "It's amazing, isn't it, how much things have changed. It used to be we dressed up to fly. Nowadays we just get on an airplane at the drop of a hat. Why Ginny Wheeler called me last week to ask if I wanted to go with her on Tuesday to Ramsey Canyon in Arizona to watch the hummingbird migration, and I said yes. Just like that. Morrie was planning to go, but he was called off to Japan at the last minute. Imagine, it used to take weeks to sail across the Pacific, and now Morrie will go to Japan and be home by the weekend! He's off to Tokyo, and Ginny and I are off to see fifteen or twenty species of hummingbirds."

"I'm jealous," said Will.

"So was Bart. I was on the phone with her yesterday." Mary laughed. "She thinks I've become a nomad."

"No reason not to. It's not like you have to lose touch with anyone. Not with telephones in airplanes. Won't be long before everyone has one in his pocket."

"I've got mine."

"So do I." He looked out at the sea of clouds. "How is Sister Mary Bart?"

"Wonderful," his mother said. "Big, big changes in her life. I'll tell you all about it. Or maybe she will. She'll be coming to visit the second weekend in June. I would love to have you and the young lady that Marianne keeps—"

"Annie," he said.

"Annie who?"

"Annie Leonard."

"Any chance you and Annie Leonard might be free for dinner on the eighth?"

"I'd love to come. I'll ask her."

"By the way, Bart is almost finished with her book. A history of capital punishment in America. A rather astonishing story." Will's mother's voice took on a conspiratorial tone: "I'm not certain, but I think she needs an agent."

"Who's this a favor for, Ma?"

Mary laughed out loud. "Both of you," she replied.

Will mentioned the conference on the Cape, which his mother had had news of a few hours earlier; she had spoken to Teddy.

"It must've been awfully exciting."

"Awfully strange," said Will. "Though I did get a chance to spend a few hours with Alexis Pine." When the name didn't register, he added, "Alex Pine. She was in Bangkok."

"Pine," said Mary. "Her mother was Greek?"

"That's the family. We talked about the old crowd." He paused. "Alex said that Lucy is a doctor."

Silence.

"Lucy Vitava," he added. "I don't know why that was such a surprise to me. But it was."

"People do surprise you."

"I guess they do."

"How is Lucy?"

"Frazzled. This was years and years ago. Another friend ran into her at a hospital."

Mary said, "Your brother was out this morning. Carting away boxes."

"And how is Jon?"

"So excited about that book it has me worried sick."

"He'll be fair."

"I hope you're right."

"I am."

"I don't want to run up your bill," Mary said. "Travel safely, honey."

"You, too, Ma. Say hello to the hummingbirds for me."

She laughed. "I will."

The plane dropped through the clouds. Dropped and dropped. Had she changed the subject from Lucy to Jonathan? Or was that just the way their conversation had gone, like a stone skipping across the surface of a pond.

Now the river was just below them, olive green, shiny as glass.

Will thought about Lucy, about how the two of them had been kids when they first met, about how the people you know in childhood stay with you in some oddly powerful way throughout your life. You lose touch, run into each other, lose touch again; you go off to college, to medical school, get married, have kids, buy and sell houses, divorce, remarry, serve on a school board, declare bankruptcy—whatever—and still some strong thread remains. To know someone in childhood is to know her forever. Lucy the doctor suddenly became imaginable to Will. She would be a hands-on doctor. An orthopedic surgeon, say, or an ophthalmologist. Not a pediatrician, he thought, not a family practitioner. How could he know this? Who's to say that in twenty years Lucy hadn't become someone new? Someone he didn't know at all.

Will had received a letter from Lucy some months after she and her mother left Bangkok. She was spending that summer in Michigan with relatives. He wrote back, but there the communication ended. By the time Will and his family left Bangkok, two years after Lucy, he hadn't a clue as to where she and her mother were living. Then, by chance, he opened the *Washington Post* one day and stumbled upon a story about the troubled lives of the wives and children of U.S. airmen still missing in Southeast Asia. There was a photograph of Lucy's mother. The caption said that Judy Vitava lived in Fairfax, Virginia. Will got her telephone number from directory assistance. He called Lucy. This was 1972. He was seventeen. They met at a McDonald's near her house. The conversation was awkward at first, in this sea of American faces, so far removed from their familiar context. Lucy's blond hair was long now, pinned back with a leather barrette. She looked beautiful to Will, years older than he felt himself to be. She had her father's bright eyes, her mother's high cheeks. She didn't talk about either of them, and Will couldn't bring himself to ask.

They spent most of an afternoon together, though as Will looked back on that day he hadn't a clue about what they might have talked about. Old friends, probably. New schools, this new country that both of them were trying to understand. It was blissful just to be with Lucy, not talking, just cruising in a car, listening to the radio, being

American kids in America, something Will dreamed about in Thailand, but which always felt out of reach, just beyond the horizon. In Bangkok, he and his friends would arrive at parties with tapes of Top 40 radio shows that someone had recorded on home leave, and they would make copies of these shows, listen to them again and again, as if aware that just beneath the surface of these sounds—the music, the DJ's patter, the ads, the requests and dedications—lay clues to their own identity.

Perhaps it was nothing more than the narcissism of youth, but Will viewed Lucy's remoteness on that long-ago day as something they shared, for he too understood the ineffable sadness that followed all of them home to America from their posting overseas. In Bangkok, sneaking onto the racetrack at the Sports Club to watch the horses run, or making out with Lucy on the roof of the Rex Hotel, or walking with her on a dusty road to the beach at Pattaya, Will felt grounded in a life. Back in the States he could never shake the feeling that he would always remain on the periphery.

Two years passed before they met again. This time it was at Will's father's funeral, late in the winter of 1974. For all the Le Carré stories that had been written about Jamie Gerard, one would have expected a lurid end—poisoned by an umbrella stick during a rendezvous with a foreign agent somewhere in the heart of Europe, say. But Will's father's passing wasn't dramatic at all. It began with chest pains that were thought to be indigestion, but which finally drove him to the emergency room where tests indicated that he had had a heart attack. He had a second heart attack the following morning in his hospital bed, this one massive, which had killed him. He was forty-seven.

The funeral mass was held on a cold, rainy February afternoon. Will was shell-shocked, so numb he could hardly make sense of the endless stream of condolences: *such a great man . . . a patriot . . . so sudden . . . terrible, terrible loss.* The only person to reach through his grief to touch him that day was his grade-school teacher, Sister Mary Bartholomew. "Don't let anyone tell you how to feel. Go through all of this at your own pace," she had told him. "Assume that the healing will take a long, long time." Will sleepwalked through the day. His memory of the funeral was of moments that played through his mind like a collection of photographs: the steel gray casket beaded with raindrops;

the sudden eruption of umbrellas at the grave site, like a release of gaily colored balloons; Sister Mary Bart at his mother's side, physically supporting her with both arms; and later, holding him, too, this time by the shoulders. "Don't hide from your grief," she whispered. Later still, as they stood together in the driveway of the family house: "If life teaches us anything, Will, it's that we all must eventually let go of the things we love."

Will spotted Lucy at the grave site, standing beside his sister. He finally spoke to her at the window of her car, just as she was leaving, both of them getting wet in the rain. Later that night Marianne told Will that Lucy had told her that Judy Vitava was drinking herself to death.

Lucy wrote to Will at Washington & Lee. He wrote back. She wrote to him in Alaska that summer, where he had gone to hike and climb mountains and make some money picking crabs. She wrote constantly. Will learned more about her from those letters than anything she had ever told him. He didn't know, for instance, that Lucy had quit high school in the middle of her senior year, or that she had gone to work in a photography shop, and then had taken a second job waitressing at night. "I tell people that I'm doing this because I need the money," she wrote. "But the truth is that getting a high school diploma and going off to college is something people do when they have a plan for the future. I don't have anything like that right now."

That fall the mail from Lucy picked up. Sometimes two or three of her letters would cross one of Will's. She had become a voracious reader, and she wrote long descriptions of the novel, biography, or collection of essays that she had just finished. Once she even sent along the book itself: a first edition of Lewis Thomas's *Lives of a Cell*, which Will still owned. Aside from the news about her mother, which was always delivered obliquely ("Judy's looking worse," or "In the past month Judy seems to be drinking less, whatever that means"), Lucy's notes were full of warmth, more warmth than she had ever expressed to Will in person. At Christmas time that year, when they met for dinner at a Thai place in Arlington, he was stunned to discover that Lucy considered him among her few close friends. He was surprised when she reached across the table and took his hand. Exhilarated, too. Lucy was like none of the Hollins or Sweet Briar girls that Will had met; for one thing, she seemed like an adult. And she had this extraordinary history. She could take care of herself. Life had tested her, and she had survived.

That night they kissed, the first time since they were kids in Bangkok. They sat parked in Will's brand-new truck in front of Lucy's mother's house. It was a split-level suburban home, with a spindly maple tree out front and the same casement windows as on every house up and down the street. That was the night Lucy told Will that she was thinking of taking flying lessons. She didn't talk about Judy at all.

A few months later, the last week in March, Lucy telephoned Will at school to tell him that her mother was dead. The next morning he drove to northern Virginia for the funeral service. Judy had become such a recluse in her last years that Will expected only a handful of mourners at the Unitarian Church, but there were nearly a hundred people in the crowd, most of them the wives of American airmen missing in Southeast Asia. Will gazed around the church at all these stoical women who had been waiting five or six or seven years for news of a lost husband; he looked at the children of these men, too, some of whom were already adults with small boys and girls of their own.

Judy Vitava's funeral service was brief, and not nearly as tragic in tone as Will had expected. For one thing, her death was incontrovertible. There was closure. The watch was over. Lucy would not be spending her afternoons with the curtains drawn, alternately hoping for and dreading the sight of a military chaplain on the doorstep. About the wives of the missing, Lucy had once written to Will, "Half their waking hours are fantasies. The other half are nightmares." Her own mother had never believed that Ernie would be coming home. "Not for an instant," Lucy wrote. "But she could never say that to the others. These women are the only people my mother knows who actually care about us, and I think it is tearing her up to have to pretend that she, too, is keeping the faith."

The few older men at the service turned out to be either journalists or airmen who had served with Ernie, several of whom he had plucked to safety from the jungles of Laos. One reporter, a shaggy fellow with an orange Bic pen and dog-eared notebook, claimed to be writing a book about MIAs. He stood at Lucy's side and furiously scribbled the name of every person who stepped forward to express a condolence. At Will's introduction, his eyes widened: "Will *Gerard*? Jamie Gerard's son? Wow! What was *that* like?"

Only two dozen of the mourners continued on to the cemetery. Lucy didn't cry at the church, nor at the grave site, but in Will's truck afterward, as the sun came out, she was suddenly rocked by tears. She cried hard for fifteen minutes. Will sat there humbled, fighting off tears of his own. "In a way it's a huge relief," she finally said. "To have it over at last. After all these years. But I feel so bad." She looked out at the dripping trees. "For her. And for me, too."

"You'll do fine," said Will. "Just give yourself plenty of time." The words came from his throat. It actually hurt to speak. He put an arm around Lucy, held her tightly. He wiped each eye with a tissue, clumsily, which brought a smile to her face. He kissed her on the forehead, and was rewarded with another smile, which made him want to kiss her again.

They drove to Judy's house. Inside, there were cardboard boxes everywhere. The beige walls were bare. From the look of things Will would have guessed that Lucy and Judy had been living here for weeks, not seven years. Lucy read the expression on his face. Her rueful smile indicated that she, too, had always seen this place as he was seeing it now.

"Let's get out of here," he said.

Her eyes brightened. "Where should we go?"

He hadn't a clue. So they drove into Georgetown and held hands through a five-thirty show at the Biograph, then ate dinner at a restaurant up the street. The film they saw had long since vanished from Will's memory, but for some reason he could recall that they both had pasta that night: Lucy's red, his white. Together they finished a bottle of Chianti. Lucy talked about Judy. "My mother gave up years ago. Even before my father disappeared. She hated Bangkok. She hated every day there. I didn't want to leave the way we left, but when the men who came for me at school told us that there wasn't any hope of finding my father, my mother just started packing. She was so angry. At everybody, my father included. But she couldn't let out the anger. It got packed up in all of our boxes and came home with us." And later, huddled together in Will's truck, waiting for heat: "I've always wanted to believe that my whole world was inside me, that the outside world couldn't touch what was inside. But deep down I knew that was wrong. I think that's why I wrote so many letters to you. Writing those letters gave me a place to go to get outside my life. For years I've worried that I might end up like my mother, but then I realized that she would never have written letters like that. They were proof that I was different."

The first kiss was Will's idea. Lucy froze for an instant, but then he felt her lips relax. She smiled. Her lungs filled with air, and suddenly Will felt himself pressed against the driver's door, making out like a kid again.

She wouldn't go home. She didn't say this, but Will understood. He knew that she would not spend another night in her mother's house. So he drove her to his mother's house instead, and they spent the night together in the tobacco barn that once had served as his father's office and had lately been converted into a guest house. Will's mother was asleep when they arrived. When he telephoned her from the restaurant to let her know he was coming, she had commended his good sense at not attempting to drive back to Lexington in the middle of the night. So instead, in the middle of that night, Lucy and Will lay together beneath the huge window that Will's father had lovingly restored, a full moon fractured into pieces behind the panes of old glass.

Will knew that he should control himself; he sensed how hungry Lucy was for comfort. So he held her, and they fell asleep in each other's arms. Somehow, in the murk of sleep, they kissed again. Lucy pressed against him, and then Will found himself lying on top of her. They kissed in the dark until their mouths hurt. For hours, it seemed. Lucy's face had always shown a hint of reserve, but that night in the moonlight she looked relaxed, beautiful. Sex happened suddenly. Nothing was said, but it was clear to Will that both of them wanted this. Wanted it badly. They were greedy with each other, then quiet as deer, which made Lucy laugh softly. Somehow they had managed to get that far away from themselves.

But the next morning Will awoke in the grip of despair. Lucy must have felt it, too. Driving back to town, they hardly said two words to each other. The truck was filled with gloom.

Lucy called Will at school six weeks later. It was the exam period, and he felt buried beneath a mountain of notebooks, take-home tests, whole books to read, essays to prepare, a forty-page paper that he hadn't begun to write due in five days. Suddenly there didn't seem enough time in the day for regular meals, showers, conversation. Lucy said, "I know you must be busy—"

"It's awful. Three all-nighters in a—"

"Will, I need to see you." There was anguish in her voice.

"Are you okay?

"No," she said quietly. "No, I'm not."

Will was in the living room of an untidy house that he shared with four other young men, the phone cord snaking across an orange shag rug and a scarred pine floor. He sat on an old leather couch. There was a bowl of potato chips on the coffee table before him, and a marsh-mallow resting atop of the pile of chips. Will couldn't have said how long this bowl of chips had been sitting there. Three days? A week?

"It gets a little easier each day," he said. "Not that it ever goes away."

She sighed. "When are you finished? When can we talk?"

He took a breath. "The thing is, the minute I'm done I'm off to Europe."

Silence. To his everlasting shame Will could recall that during that awful moment of silence he had actually considered hanging up the telephone.

"I could see you on your way through Washington," said Lucy. "Or I could drive out there."

One of Will's housemates, deeply ensconced in his own end-of-semester funk, had begun pacing in the doorway. He wanted the telephone.

"It's a charter," Will said. "It leaves from New York. A few hours after my last exam."

Silence.

"When do you get back?" asked Lucy.

"End of August."

She didn't make a sound.

"We'll talk then," he said. "Promise. I'm really sorry, but I've gotta run."

He hung up the phone, left the house, spent that night and the next at work in the library.

WILL'S FATHER had left money for each of his children, actual manila envelopes with their names scribbled on the flaps. The envelopes were filled with francs, deutsche marks, lira, kroner. It was enough money to live like a king in postwar Europe, and like a down-at-the-heels prince by the time Will headed off with his allotment in the mid-1970s. These envelopes also contained a list of tourist sites: the cathedral at Chartres, the Louvre, Michelangelo's Sistine Chapel and statue of Moses in Rome, Fra Angelico's frescoes in Florence, the Van Gogh Museum in Amsterdam, the Munch museum in Oslo, some two dozen destinations in all.

So Will spent that summer fashioning his own grand tour: he sipped real ale in London pubs, ate fish and chips in Dover, smoked hashish in Amsterdam, drank most of a bottle of Rioja on the upper deck of an overnight ferry off the coast of Barcelona while gazing up at a field of stars the likes of which he had never seen before. The glory of the Italian Renaissance lifted his heart, and the grim gray specter of Dachau drove a stake through it. Oslo, in summer, was draped in blue, a winter land gorging on its endless days. Will had brought four or five books along with him, classics all, and he struggled mightily for weeks with *Crime and Punishment* before giving up on it. At a second-hand bookshop in Rome he traded that paperback for Terry Southern's *Blue Movie,* which entertained him through the Alps. *Gulag Archipelago* had been likewise exchanged for *The Sotweed Factor.*

Will didn't write to anyone that summer except Marianne, who had inherited her father's dark views of humanity, and thus had insisted that Will leave a paper trail in the event that he should vanish from the face of Europe. He survived, of course, even thrived in this atmosphere of splendid isolation. It was nothing less than a profound relief to check out of his life for three solid months.

He arrived home two days before the start of classes, well after midnight. Marianne awoke him at ten the next morning. They had coffee on the patio with their mother. It was a sultry August day, the air already ringing with the metallic buzz of cicadas. Marianne had spent that summer working on Capitol Hill. She talked about her job. Will, stunned by the five-hour time difference and the previous day of travel, sipped his coffee and listened. Marianne announced that she had met the man she would marry.

A second mug of coffee brought Will a small step closer to consciousness. "What else has been going on?" he asked. "What did I miss?"

"There's a stack of mail for you in the front hallway," his mother called from the kitchen doorway.

Had she been unnaturally quiet that morning? Had she known something *then?* Or was her silence simply an expression of her disappointment at the news that Will had to head back to Washington & Lee directly?

The patio bricks cooled Will's bare feet; the taste of cold, sweet, U.S. grade A whole milk poured over crunchy American cereal lifted his spirits.

Marianne headed inside. She returned with the newspaper in hand, scanning the front page. "By the way, Lucy called."

Will stopped chewing. "When?"

"Yesterday."

"Did she leave a number?"

A shake of the head. Marianne flipped through the various sections. "I told her you'd be getting in late. She said to tell you that she'd stop by in the afternoon." She looked up at Will. "To tell you the truth, she didn't sound good."

"Poor girl," said Mary Gerard.

After breakfast, Will made a feeble attempt to contact Lucy, but the phone number in his book was out of date and directory assistance in northern Virginia reported no listing. He began to fret. He helped Marianne load suitcases and cardboard boxes into her green VW fastback, whose color reminded him to root through his backpack for the matching silk scarf that he had bought for her at a trendy shop in Milan. They kissed good-bye in the driveway, and Will stood beside his mother as Marianne beeped four times and then sped off to Swarthmore. Then Will transported his mother's well-stuffed carryall to the trunk of her Mustang convertible. She was off to a steering committee meeting at one of her charities: the church, the local hospital, the parochial school. Will leaned into the car to kiss her good-bye as well.

"When will we see you?"

"I'll call as soon as I have a phone number."

She turned her head quickly as tears welled up, and then she was gone, too.

Will spent the rest of the morning washing clothes, scrubbing his backpack and setting it to dry in the hot noon sun; he changed the oil in his truck, flushed the radiator, charged up the battery. Three months idle, and it started instantly. Then he loaded the bed with boxes that were filled with books and clothes. And he continued to fret. After the dryer buzzed, after the stray basketball and lacrosse stick had been stowed in a canvas sack and pitched into the back of the truck, he poured himself a cup of coffee and drank half of it standing at the stove. He had been on the road for so many weeks now, he told himself, that he had simply lost the knack for waiting around. If Lucy were really coming, she would have called. Anyway, she could track him down in Lexington. He poured the rest of the coffee into the sink, scrubbed the heavy mug, dried it, set it back on the shelf.

Then he wrote his mother a farewell note, and drove off to school.

At National Airport, Will decided to collect his car and drive straight to Cabin John; he would call Annie from home. But he made the mistake of letting habit guide his route, which meant that instead of turning right as he exited the parking garage near Union Station—and taking Constitution Avenue to the parkway to White-hurst Freeway and Canal Road—he turned left and drove out Massachusetts Avenue. A quick detour at the Peruvian Embassy brought him to Q Street. There was an empty parking space directly in front of Annie's building. Not once this spring, not once during the two years that Will had lived in this building, had he happened upon an empty parking space directly in front on a Sunday evening. So again he let habit guide him: he parked.

The lights in Annie's apartment were on. She was home.

Will sat there wondering if he had the nerve to march up those steps and press the buzzer on her mailbox. In a moment came the inescapable conclusion that he didn't have that much nerve.

So he telephoned Annie. From his car.

Her front window was open and he could hear the phone ringing. There was a shadow on the wall in the living room, a shadow in the elongated shape of a person's head. When the phone sounded a second time, this shadow moved. It glided across the wall like a ghost, and disappeared through the doorway of the kitchen. The phone rang two more times before Annie picked it up. Will could see her now. She was standing with her back to the kitchen window.

The lights were on so I figured you had to be home—

"Annie, it's Will."

"You're back."

"Just got in." *Just pulled up in front of your apartment.* He felt silly, like a character in a TV sitcom. "How was your weekend?"

"Quiet. How about you?"

"Not so quiet. Loud, in fact. Noisy." He paused. "I missed you."

"Will—"

"Have you eaten?"

She switched the phone to the other ear. "No."

"Let's do something," he said. "I'll come get you."

"You sure you're up for that?"

"Yes."

"Can we talk for a minute? Just so you know where I am? I've been doing a lot of thinking this weekend. A lot of thinking." She paused. "I don't know how to say this, Will, but I think everything between us has to change."

"I agree one hundred percent."

"You do?"

"Yes, I do."

"Oh," she said. Then: "What things?"

"Everything. I want us to start over. Go back to square one."

"Can we do that? Even if we want to, I mean?"

"I think so. And yes, I think we can."

"I don't know, Will. I keep thinking that these things are fixed, that you can't go back, no matter how much you might want to. And that if you try to, all you're really doing is sidestepping the issues that screwed you up in the first place."

"What if you're wrong?"

"I don't think I am."

She sighed. She turned toward the window, gazed out at the leafy branches of the trees. In a moment her gaze dropped to the street. Which was when she noticed the black Acura with the Thule bike rack parked directly in front of her building. Will's face was framed in the driver's window. He grinned sheepishly. Then he waved.

"I realize that this doesn't look very serious," the voice in the telephone said. "But I am serious."

She felt the prickle of tears, tears of frustration and regret, tears of anger, too. Anger at Will, and at herself. She shook her head, wondering what to say in response. And what to do. Time alone hadn't clarified anything for her. But she had made a decision. And she thought she would carry through on it. But right now the notion that she would pull back for a while, or spend some time alone, or whatever words she might use to explain herself to Will—and to herself— seemed all wrong. All weekend she had been alternately missing him and dreading what a conversation this night would bring.

They ate at a French restaurant on M Street, at Annie's suggestion, a place new to Will, or so he thought, until he stepped through the front door and realized he had eaten there once before with his mother. This restaurant was across the street from George Washington Hospital. Will and his mother had met here one evening a long, long time ago, as his father lay resting in the cardiac unit at the hospital, the day before he died.

Annie ordered what Will had ordered all those years ago, trout *en papillote,* which Will had assumed was a potato wrapping of some sort. It turned out to be parchment, and the sight of the brittle paper once again took away his appetite. He sipped a glass of wine, and then set it on the table. "Flying home," he said, "I kept thinking: What if you were two months pregnant right now? What would we talk about tonight?"

"I'm not, Will. So it doesn't matter."

"But what if you were?"

"I can't imagine."

"We wouldn't be talking about us. Not like this."

"You don't think so?"

He shook his head resolutely.

"That's a guess." Then: "Anyway, what's the point?"

"The point is that I've twisted myself up these past weeks trying to decide whether I want to become a father." He looked at her. "It's an impossible question. This weekend I came around to realizing that it wasn't even the right question. The question I should have been asking myself is: How do I feel about you? How do I feel about *us* becoming parents?" He leaned forward. "I adore you. You're the finest women I've ever met. I should be thanking my lucky stars that I met you." He paused. "I've had my head in the sand. About you. About us. About a whole lot of things, if you want to know the truth."

And thus began a slightly windy consideration of how it was possible to know things about oneself that one doesn't actually know—has never been *told*, that is—how it might be possible to process something subconsciously and deny it consciously. To be skittish about fatherhood, Will explained, not because he wasn't cut out for the role, but because of a deep, dark secret that he had been unable to confront for the past twenty years. Annie seemed puzzled at first, but she didn't interrupt. And so Will lumbered on. He sensed himself as an oversized truck, gear in reverse and alarm bell clanging, as he inched backward toward Friday's revelation on the train. Finally he reached into a pocket and produced the letter from Charlotte Cameron.

Annie read it slowly. Unlike Barry, she said nothing at first. She read it, she looked up at Will, then back at the page, just looked at it, then read it again. Her face was slack. She looked up a second time. "You think this woman is your daughter?" she asked.

"Maybe. That is, it's possible." He sat back. "I think so."

Annie looked stunned.

"Her birth date is right," Will said. "And I get the sense she had a reason to write to me."

"You never knew about her?"

He shook his head. "I was never told. But deep down I knew. It was something I never admitted to myself."

"What happened, Will?"

He walked her through the significant events of that long ago spring and summer. Annie listened quietly. "After that," he concluded, "Lucy and I lost touch."

"You never spoke to her again?"

Will shook his head.

"She never wrote, never tried to contact you?"

"Not that I know of."

Then came questions for which Will had no good answers: Why

had he immediately taken off for school that August day? Hadn't he tried to get in touch with Lucy that fall? Had he thought about her at all? Why had it taken this letter twenty years later to bring home the news that she had been pregnant?

"Fear, denial, guilt, cowardice." He shrugged. "I don't know. I honestly don't know."

Annie speared a piece of broccoli. She chewed slowly, put down her fork. Then she looked at him, studied him. She asked herself why he was telling her about this—*why now?*—and soon came to realize that she was glad he was telling her. And yet she still felt unsettled, as if this news involved her as well. But it didn't. Not really. Not unless she allowed it to. And that wasn't possible, not now. She took a sip of wine and read the letter for a third time. Then the lawyer within asserted herself: "You know something, Will, it's possible Lucy never came to your mother's house that day. You could be all wrong about this."

"It's possible," he said.

"You're convinced that she did come."

He nodded.

"Then let's assume she did. The next question is *why?*" Annie listed the possible reasons: "Let's say she did get pregnant. In August she would be coming to tell you that she had miscarried, or that she'd had an abortion. Or to tell you that she was five months pregnant. Suppose she *was* pregnant. What happened?"

"My best guess?"

Annie nodded.

"Lucy came to my mother's house. She arrived after I left. She waited. My mother came home. Lucy told her."

"And your mother helped her get into this Catholic maternity home?"

"It's possible."

"Wouldn't she have told *you?*"

Quietly, he said, "I disappeared. I think she understood that I needed her help. That I didn't want to know."

"And you never asked."

"I was at school."

"Hiding out."

He nodded.

He had arrived home from Europe having scribbled his way across the Continent, fired up with the idea of becoming a writer. He took an attic room in a group house in Lexington, and immersed himself in the bildungsromans of Goethe, Flaubert, Mann, Dickens, Salinger, Styron, etcetera, etcetera. So completely was he wallowing in the garreted life of the *artiste* that he didn't make it home until Thanksgiving, and then only for one day. His mother had applauded this sudden burst of creativity; it was just the sort of energy that his father would have wanted him to bring home from his travels, she said.

Will was one of those writers who couldn't write until he was moved by inspiration, who needed six sharp number 2B pencils lined up on the desk above a brand-new yellow legal pad, a steaming mug of coffee at his right hand, the telephone unplugged, no music within earshot, no Baggie of pot anywhere in the house to lure him out on the back porch. Still, even with perfect conditions, truth be told, he spent most of his free time that autumn reading, not writing. In addition to novels, he was drawn to philosophical works, among them Thomas Merton's *Seven Storey Mountain* and St. Augustine's *Confessions*. So curious, thought Will, how a person seeks out the advice he wants to hear. He was thinking about the bastard child that Merton abandoned in England, and about all the children that young Augustine had carelessly fathered before finding his way to the Church. Who better to serve as a role model that fall than the patron saint of deadbeat dads?

By the middle of the spring semester, having completed two experimental (which is to say, *dreadful*) short stories and fifty pages of an aimless novel, Will had concluded that fiction was not his metier. He auditioned for a play and got the role; and when his portrayal of a self-destructive young radical received favorable mention in the local paper, he gave some thought to pursuing a career in the theater.

Annie was shaking her head. "I don't buy it," she said.

"Don't buy what?"

"Your mother's involvement. I could imagine her keeping a secret like that for a month or two. But not all these years."

"It might have been Lucy's decision."

"Or maybe your mother didn't help her. Or maybe there was

someone else. Or no one. Perhaps Lucy came to the house, saw that you weren't there, and left."

Will shook his head.

Annie took a breath. "How much of the story do you think your mother knows?"

"That Lucy was pregnant. That the baby was mine. That Lucy spent her last trimester at St. Jerome's."

"You haven't asked her?"

"It's a guess," he said. "What if I'm wrong?"

"So now you find Lucy and ask her."

"I suppose." The very thought of confronting Lucy filled Will with dread. It was as if, after all these years, this child was no longer any of his business. The statute of limitations had run out. He tried to explain this to Annie.

"Not that you think the father might be someone else."

He shook his head.

She gazed off across the empty room. After a moment, she said, "I still don't see how your mother could know something like this and never breathe a word about it to you. Not then. Not later. My God, not in twenty years."

"She did that for me. She thought I didn't want to know."

"Your child," whispered Annie. "Her grandchild."

"She would have been focused on the situation—on helping Lucy—and the shame. I'm not sure she would have thought about me at all at first."

"And later?"

"The baby was adopted. There was nothing to say, nothing anyone could do to change that. It would have been easier just to keep that secret. My mother was always good at keeping secrets."

Annie considered this for a moment. "Surely she must have had second thoughts?"

"Second, third, fourth, fifth." Will shrugged. "But in the end, what else could she do but live with the consequences?"

"She could have told you the truth."

"She didn't."

"And so now you want to find out if this young woman is your daughter."

He nodded.

"Then we come back to the fact that there's one person who knows. So find her. Ask her."

"Not yet," he said.

"There's a legal procedure. You could start there."

Will touched Charlotte's letter. "If I'm right, I don't need that. I know who my daughter is. And where she is. And that she wants to meet me. I just need to be sure that I'm right."

"Then get Lucy's address and write her a letter. Lay out what you've said. Be honest."

"And she throws it away. What then?"

Annie considered this.

He went on: "I've come around to the feeling that I have to take a few steps on my own before I can question Lucy or my mother. It's probably a Catholic thing—the road to Calvary, or something."

She picked up the letter. "Why are you telling me all of this? Why right now?"

"Because it's on my mind. Because it's something I've been running away from for a long time, and didn't even know it. Because all weekend I've been wondering if running away might have gotten to be a habit with me. And if I could change that. Which brings me back to what I said about us starting over." He took Annie's hand across the table. "I want us to do that. Right now. This week."

She shook her head slowly.

He waited.

She pressed her lips together, didn't say anything.

"It's like you said," he added. "Sometimes in life you have to take a chance."

"I can't."

He waited.

She went on: "Look, when Rob and I separated, and I started thinking that I would raise a child by myself, I thought it would make sense to be closer to my mother and sister. A few months ago I sent out feelers to some lawyer friends in Chicago. Last week one of the firms called. The managing partner wants to talk to me. I set up a meeting with him on Wednesday morning."

Will sat back in his chair. "You're moving to Chicago?"

"That was the plan." She paused. "Up until about a month ago."

"But you're going out there for a job interview."

"To hear what they have to say."

"So let's say it's fabulous. More money, a corner office with a view of the lake, a team of brilliant young associates, great cases, nobody leaning over your shoulder." Will looked at Annie. "Do you take it?"

"I honestly don't know."

"Put them off. For a couple of weeks, anyway."

"I can't. It's all set up."

"Sure you can. Get a note from your doctor."

She met his gaze. "I don't want to put them off, Will."

He thought about this. He looked around the empty restaurant, looked at Annie. "I can't talk you out of this?"

"No," she said quietly.

When the check was paid, they walked in gloomy silence to Will's car. He had no destination in mind as they set off, and no desire to talk. Nor did Annie, apparently. So they cruised in silence. Will drove out to Hain's Point, then circled around the Tidal Basin; he rolled past the darkened museums and the empty memorials. Finally Annie reached over and touched his arm. "Look, what I was trying to say back there is that right now I need some time to myself. To sort things out. To figure out how I get on with my life."

"Beginning with the issue of where in this great land of ours you might choose to live."

"Knock it off, Will."

"I'm a little surprised," he said. "That's all."

"Well, to be honest, moving to Chicago is not something I really want to do."

"Then don't. And don't go interviewing for a job out there."

"I agreed to it. I have to go."

On M Street, Will turned away from town. He sped through the green light onto Canal Road without a second thought. Annie sat beside him like a stone, her eyes fixed straight ahead.

Finally she said, "If you want to know the truth, I feel like I need to come to terms with the idea of *having* a child." She looked at Will. "I have to get over it, is what I mean."

"How do you get over something like that?"

"I don't know, Will. I don't know." And then, a moment later: "Maybe you can't. But that doesn't mean you don't try."

Will moved right to skirt Chain Bridge. He knew exactly where this conversation was headed. He knew that whatever future he and Annie might have together would depend upon what transpired in the next few minutes. On what *he* said or did, since Annie seemed locked up as tight as a drum right now. He knew this unequivocally. Every romance that Will had been involved in (which is to say, some dozen failed relationships spanning two decades) had pivoted on just such a moment. And Will had to admit to himself that he had always handled these conversations badly: his first instinct was to retreat.

Years earlier, in his mid-twenties, he had been madly in love with a woman he worked with at a bookshop in Georgetown. Robin was her name. Will and Robin started living together. Six months later, she moved to Cambridge to attend a summer publishing workshop. They were planning to reunite in New York in the fall. But when Will visited her during that summer, she announced gravely that she'd had second thoughts about that plan. They were sitting in the bleachers at Fenway Park on a breezy July afternoon. It was the bottom of the ninth, the Sox losing 7-6. Robin suddenly wanted to talk about their relationship. About their future. Perhaps all she wanted was reassurance, some effort on his part to bridge these weeks apart. But Will didn't understand that. What he heard instead was the distant drumbeat of bad news. And his response was to close down, focus in on the game. Finally Robin said, "I just don't think it would be good for either of us, Will. Not right now." The last Red Sox batter struck out on three pitches. What else to do but collect his bags and head off to South Station?

To Annie, he said, "No."

They had come to a halt at a three-way stop on MacArthur Boulevard.

"No, what?"

"Splitting up right now is a terrible idea." He made the left turn, eyes staring straight ahead.

"Were you listening to me, Will?"

"I heard everything. I think you're making a big mistake."

"You're not in charge of my life," she said softly.

"For some reason I thought I was part of it," he replied. "I hoped I was."

They rolled along in silence.

Finally Annie said, "So what you think we should do is just throw caution to the wind. Whether or not we even have a future together?"

"I think we do." When she didn't reply, he added, "Let's put it this way, without a little effort on our part, there isn't a chance that we have a future together." His hands kneaded the top of the steering wheel. "And be honest about one thing: a little time apart is going to lead to a lot of time apart."

Annie spoke in a whisper: "I am not suggesting this because I think it'll make me happy, Will. It's what I think we *ought* to do."

"Well, I think we ought to do what we want to do."

"You've been back and forth on this for the past two months and now you're suddenly comfortable? I don't get it."

Comfortable wasn't the right word to describe Will's current frame of mind. *Terrified* was much better. Terrified and all of a sudden . . . willing. Recklessly willing.

"Let's go somewhere. Tomorrow. Spend the day together."

She was shaking her head. "I can't."

"Sure you can. You're about to quit your job. That means you can do whatever you want."

She looked at him. "Okay, Will. It isn't that I can't. It's that I don't want to."

Will felt the fear and anger well up like a balloon inside his chest. He saw nothing but the sparkly flecks of quartz in the road as he made the turn onto Seventy-ninth Street. There wasn't anything else to say now, nothing that would change the course of this conversation. Will sighed. So determined was he to keep a lid on his emotions right then that it never occurred to him that this roundabout cruise with Annie through the avenues and boulevards of Washington was about to end in his own driveway.

He cut off the engine. Neither of them moved.

"What I've been trying to say is that I care about you," he finally said. "That I know that, even if I'm not very good at expressing it. And the thing is—"

"We started in one place, Will. And now we're someplace else. We

have to make sense of where this new place is. And what it means."
She looked at him. "I care about you, too. Way too much."

He thought, a woman cares about me way too much, and thus has
decided that she needs to spend some time by herself.

He sighed. "I feel like there's finally some sort of bridge between
us. It's a creaky little thing, I admit, but it's there. Finally. We tear it
down right now and I can't imagine that we'll ever get it built again."

"Wouldn't that be up to *us*?"

He was shaking his head. "We'd like to think it was. We'd say that.
We might act as if it were. But it wouldn't be. Relationships aren't gov-
erned by what people think or say, just what *happens*."

"Will," she said gravely, "there's something else you need to know."
He looked at her. Annie held her chin so high he thought his heart
would break. Quietly, she said, "I'm thinking seriously about adoption." He waited. "I spent yesterday afternoon with the friend of a
friend who adopted a little girl in China last year." She paused. "This
firm in Chicago," she went on. "I interned there. I know most of the
senior partners." She faced him. "It's a whole different culture. I think
I could negotiate some flexibility. For a few years, anyway."

"You're planning to take that job."

A moment passed. Then she nodded. "If it's what I think it is," she
said.

"Oh." Then: "You know something? You might have said that
right off. When I called." Will paused. "I mean, what's the point of
this conversation if you've already made up your mind to adopt a kid
and move to Chicago?"

"I haven't made up my mind to do anything."

"Sure you have. You're calling it quits, but you're not being straight
about that. You're making it abstract: your need to *get on with your life*.
As if there's only one way to do that. Without me."

"I didn't start this conversation intending to call it quits. But you
know something? Maybe you're right. Maybe that's all we can do right
now."

He was shaking his head. "No, no, no," he said softly.

"I don't get you, Will. Not at all. I don't know what you want. I
don't think you know what you want. I don't think you've got room for
me in your life, if you want to know the honest to God's truth. But I'm

not completely sure of that because I don't know you. And the reason I don't know you is that you've never let me get close to you." She paused, then softly added, "You may be a wonderful man. You might even be the right guy for me. But I'm never going to know. And you know what? I'll live with that. I'll live with knowing that I did what I had to do. Sometimes in life nobody wins. I think it's time for us to admit that this is just one of those moments."

"Take a week," he said quietly. "Take two."

"I don't need a week. Or a day. Or one more minute. All I need right now is a *cab*. It's over, Will."

He looked around, and was surprised—no, *stunned*—to find himself parked in his own driveway. He started up the engine and backed slowly into the street. And they drove the length of MacArthur Boulevard, all the way to Annie's front door, without saying another word.

SURELY IT wasn't *over*.

Surely there must be something else to say, something important or heartfelt, some small clarifying thought to communicate to her. He could offer to go with her on this trip to Chicago. *No.* Or suggest they see a counselor together. *Perhaps.* Will figured he would think of something. He hoped he would, anyway. For right then, as he moved gingerly across the damp lawn in front of his house on this pitch-black night, the situation seemed hopeless. Will could not imagine any words from him that would cut through Annie's steely resolve. Not tonight, certainly. Tonight was lost. Tonight would be given over to a bowl or two of Special K, and thirty minutes with the sports page, aimlessly perusing the high school box scores. Then he would shower and brush his teeth and go to bed.

It wasn't until he had a foot on the steps of his darkened house that Will noticed his front door standing wide open. He smelled a sweet pungent odor, like marijuana. He froze, scalp tingling, hands suddenly balled into fists. Then, from the corner of his eye, he caught sight of a burly figure sitting in a rocking chair.

"Ho, ho, ho, Merry Christmas."

Teddy.

Will was furious. Furious at Teddy for smoking dope on the front porch where Mr. Richmond next door or anybody out for a stroll might smell it, and call the cops. Furious, too, at being ambushed. Of course the real cause for his anger stemmed from embarrassment; for in that instant Will sensed that his nephew had been parked in that rocker for the past hour. No doubt he had overheard the whole sorry conversation with Annie in the driveway.

Teddy said, "I hope you don't mind that I opened a bottle of red wine."

"It's delicious," another voice added. It was a woman's voice, husky and subdued.

"Oh," said Teddy, "this is Julianna. Julianna, my Uncle Will."

Julianna was seated beside Teddy, hidden from Will's view. She leaned forward, and murmured hello. At once Will felt proud, Teddy's good fortune having trumped his anger and shame. Teddy's smile lit up in the dark.

"Who's smoking?" asked Will.

"Nobody," said Teddy. "It's aromatherapy."

"Somebody sick?"

Julianna's rocking chair creaked. "Strictly speaking it's an herbal incense. It helps to balance the ions. Also, it keeps away bugs."

"Ah, the bugs."

Now Will recognized the husky voice. Julianna worked at the food co-op up the street. Fruits and vegetables, he recalled, and herbal remedies. She wore a red bandanna and a large button promoting hemp. He recalled a slender woman, dark-haired with a faint mustache, a few years older than Teddy.

"Julianna's just finished a novel," Teddy said. "I told her you'd take a look—"

"To be honest," said Julianna, "I'd like to think about putting this out on the Web, Theo."

"That was my other idea," added Teddy, a bit sheepishly.

"The brave new world of publishing," Will said. "Keep me posted on how it goes. Any calls?"

"Just Annie a few hours ago." Everyone on the porch observed a moment of silence. "I guess you already got that message."

"Certainly did," replied Will.

There was more awkward silence.

Teddy said, "We couldn't really hear all of it, by the way."

"Arguments are perfectly natural," added Julianna. "Quite healthy, in fact." She paused. "And if they become unhealthy, there's always St. John's Wort."

"Something to remember."

Had he not been operating on six hours of sleep, Will might have fetched a beer for himself and conducted a quick front-porch seminar for these youngsters—"Spats, Tiffs, and Brouhahas: The View from Forty-one." Right then he certainly had a few thoughts on the subject. At your age, he would have told them, one should argue with gusto. There's so much energy, and so much to learn, especially about one-self. So by all means let the sentiments fly and speak from the heart, even at the risk of making an ass of yourself, or losing the partner of your dreams. Twenty years later, however, the whole notion of self-improvement no longer seemed to Will to have any practical applica-tion. Quarrels at forty had to be tended with all the care of an urban garden: weeded, mulched, watered daily, and each lovely blossom clipped at the first opportunity.

This was not a subject that Romeo and Julianna cared a whit about, so Will opted to sip a beer alone and let his thoughts wander where they would. He stood in the kitchen and considered the solitary course of his life. Twenty-six and alone had felt right and proper to him, thirty-four and alone only a little bit troubling; but forty-one and alone, he had to admit right now, was deeply depressing. It felt perma-nent. After forty, one is—and will forever remain, it seemed to Will—rich or poor, upbeat or glum, hairy or bald, fat or thin, single or married, a jazz lover or an opera buff, a parent or a child. It seemed to Will that somehow, when he wasn't looking, his life had managed to settle over him and thicken, like old yogurt.

On the plane ride home he had decided that if he loved Annie at all—and he did—he ought to take a leap into the unknown and try to conceive a child with her. That was the path before them, and there was simply no good reason not to take it. At that instant, he had even managed to convince himself that this was what he wanted to do. But now, again, came second thoughts. Glancing around this neatly ordered home, Will had to admit that it did not look like the house of a man who was hungry for family. Even Teddy, who *was* family, didn't reside here, but in the shed out back. Not once had Will suggested that Teddy move inside to the guest bedroom. While he genuinely liked the concept of having Teddy around, he had never gotten completely comfortable with his presence. Teddy's midnight flush, his morning shower song, and the late-night clinks and scrapes in the kitchen: none of these noises were actively resented, but they were always noted.

Impulsively, Will picked up the telephone. Directory assistance had a number for C. Cameron in College Park. It didn't occur to Will to punch it in; he just wanted Charlotte a bit closer. Now she was ten buttons away. He wrote her name and number on an index card, and tacked the card to the cork board beside his desk. He stared at the name. It was a stranger's name. The name of a young woman who may or may not be his daughter, but in either case was a stranger. On the one hand it seemed beyond the bounds of coincidence to suppose that this young woman simply shared a birth date with a child he *might* have fathered. But it also strained coincidence to suppose that at the precise moment that he and Annie were wrestling with the idea of planting a seed, who should appear on the scene but this full-grown flower. It was the sort of plot twist one expected from O. Henry, which didn't mean that it couldn't happen in real life. But it was peculiar.

Will didn't intend to eavesdrop, but the front window was open, and he stood fifteen feet away in the lighted doorway of the kitchen. "You know, I'd really love to see your machine," he heard Julianna say, to which Romeo started hemming and hawing about the lateness of the hour and condition of his abode. The hesitancy in his voice was touching; it made Will smile. It was a voice he hadn't heard in years.

Teddy was called Teddy because he had always been called Teddy, but the truth was that the name belonged to a fresh-faced boy who would shriek a warning if his uncle had forgotten to strap him into his car seat. This nephew with the mordant sense of humor, the ack-ack-ack laugh, the bushy eyebrows and five-o'clock shadow, seemed suited to any number of names, but *Teddy* was not among them. A barrel-chested homebrewer with tufts of black hair peeking out from the open collar of his shirt could be called Sal, or Stu, or Lou, or Gus. Julianna called him *Theo*, which Will had thought sounded effete at first; but already the name had begun to grow on him. Theo gave the profusion of chest hair a whole new spin.

"Well," said Julianna. "Will you or won't you?"

"Let's go," answered Teddy.

Will stuck his head out the front door to say good night. Julianna was wearing one of Teddy's black-checked flannel shirts. Her walk was as distinctive as her voice: tentative, as though wearing heels, which she was not. Teddy gave his uncle a manly nod—their first exchange of manly nods—which nicely set up what happened next: as Julianna started down the front steps, Will affectionately grabbed Romeo by the hand and passed along Barry's mauve packet of condoms. Teddy didn't blink. At this particular moment Will could have left a burning coal in young Theo's mitt, and he wouldn't have uttered a sound.

Will was no voyeur, but that night he had to actively resist the urge to spy. He was dying to know what would happen next, though he felt certain, and with a touch of sadness, that he could guess. A peek through the crack in Teddy's curtains an hour later would not have found Romeo and Julianna trysting madly, nor even languidly swaddled in a sheet. Instead, they'd be huddled like space travelers in front of Teddy's enormous color monitor. Will felt sure of this, even as he caught sight of Julianna quietly departing the premises the next morning at the crack of dawn.

Hours later he was in the kitchen making coffee when he heard a shout: *"Uncle Will!"* Then again, *"Uncle WILL! UNCLE WILL!"* Teddy had begun to scream his name in utter panic. Will dashed out the back door in time to see his nephew leap from a ladder. Will stopped short on the flagstone walk just as Teddy hit the ground. He landed with a thump amid a pile of wood. Not a pile of wood, Will realized, but a long two-by-eight that was balanced on a sawhorse. Teddy landed squarely on the end of the wide board. Then, above, Will spotted something sailing toward him through the air. It was grotesquely fat and writhing, translucent. It looked alive, like a sea creature, one of those vicious eel that hides among the rocks and chews the hands off unsuspecting scuba divers.

The hideous serpent landed at Will's feet. It hit the ground and exploded, its awful juices covering him from head to toe. Then Will looked closer. He bent over the tattered remnants of his attacker, and saw that it wasn't a flying serpent at all, but a condom. A condom that had been filled with a gallon of water.

Teddy lifted his arms in surrender. He was roaring with laughter. "It wasn't supposed to go that far. Honest. I tried it with a rock and it only went ten feet. You were just supposed to get a *little* wet."

Had the young man not tripped and turned an ankle as he stepped off his crude catapult, Will would have fired him. Had Teddy's laughter not ceased abruptly as he limped forward, Will would have ordered him off the property. Had the humor of the moment not penetrated Will's soaking wet mop of hair, he wouldn't have noticed the sad, slack expression of romantic disappointment on Teddy's face. It demanded consolation.

"Okay, Romeo, so tell me what happened."

"I don't even want to talk about it," Teddy replied.

IT WAS HIGH spring, summer warm, a sunny Monday of elegant cardinals and stately irises. White dogwood blossoms littered the yard. Will and Teddy sat on the front steps with their steaming mugs of coffee set between them, peace restored, ostensibly commencing their regular Monday morning staff meeting to sort out chores and set an agenda for the week ahead. Today's assembly had opened with Teddy's return of Will's packet of condoms. He had the tight-lipped look of a soldier surrendering a field decoration that he hadn't earned. Without even a glance inside the packet Will knew for certain that only one of the condoms was missing.

"It turned out that Julianna is computer illiterate," Teddy said sourly. "How the hell was I to know that there would no such thing as a *quick* tour of the Web. I couldn't get her to log off."

"Don't blame yourself," said Will. "You can't compete with cutting-edge technology. Nobody can. You ought to know that better than anyone. I guess there's something to be said for doing things the old-fashioned way."

"You won't believe the novel."

"Sci-fi?" Will would have guessed *environmental refugees from Earth living on another planet in the year 2200.* Or else a post-apocalyptic civilization growing hemp in a bubble under the sea. Definitely an eco-parable of some sort.

Teddy said, "It's called *The Word*. The story of Jesus told in our time, only Jesus is a woman. Her name is Justina." He paused, his expression grim. "Justina works in a *food co-op*."

"Blessed are the cheesemakers," said Will, and Teddy laughed. It wasn't his hard-boiled, sarcastic laugh, but softer in tone, full of remorse. The kid had had high hopes, and his high hopes had been dashed on the sharp rocks of life. Will put an arm around his nephew's shoulders. "Happily ever after only happens when a hack is writing the story," he said. "Even the original Romeo found the last hurdle a bit too high."

"Warring families," muttered Teddy. "Big deal."

Will said, "I know it's no consolation, but I salute you. At your age I would have been able to convince myself that this green Jesus concept was a brilliant idea. Probably would have sat up all night and read the whole damn novel."

"That's the nut," snapped Teddy. "I *would* have. But she wouldn't *let* me. I didn't even get to first base with her *book*." He turned to Will. "You have to admit that's pretty pathetic."

"We push and they block," Will replied. "It's an old, old story. I'm sure it goes back to the beginning of time."

"Why'd it have to be me who fell for Ayn Rand in a red bandanna?"

Will said, "When I was your age I went out with a woman who reacted as if I was William Shakespeare when I told her that I worked in a bookstore. I actually asked her out again. Three times in all."

"Jeez, really?"

"I was lonely," said Will. "And flattered. It didn't occur to me that she and I might not be on the same wavelength until she dumped me for a guy who installed swimming pools. It was a job with security, she told me. People always need swimming pools."

"What bugs me the most," said Teddy, "is that I was falling all over myself to convince Julianna to let me read her lousy book, which is something you have to *pay* me to do. What does that say about me? What would I have done to *sleep* with her?"

"Better not to ask."

Teddy sighed.

"Look," said Will. "Don't think you're alone. We all do that. The good news is that you're figuring this out now. I wasn't clued in until my mid-thirties."

"Yeah, well, I'll bet you weren't a virgin when you were my age," Teddy said glumly.

"Almost," Will replied.

"Almost means no." Teddy gazed up at the heavens. "I could die in a car wreck before this day is out. Do you realize how horrible that would be?"

Will nodded. He did. He understood absolutely.

"Maybe I'm gay."

"Could be. Still a virgin there, too, I'd guess."

"True enough."

"Could be all you need to do is get out and around. Maybe think about doing something a little more exciting this summer than hiding away in that shed. Get a job with some folks your own age. We could brainstorm for ideas, if you want."

Now Teddy put an arm around Will's shoulders. "I appreciate the concern, Uncle. I really do. And the advice. So please don't take any offense when I say that I've got to consider the source. Mom calls you the poster boy for serial monogamy, and even there I think she feels she's always given you the benefit of the doubt. The thing is"—he gazed around Will's quiet domain—"this sure isn't where I want to end up."

"You end up where you end up," Will said softly. "It's not like this was some sort of goal."

"But you're a loner," said Teddy. "Living with you, I'm always flashing on the stories Mom tells about Granddad. How he liked to get up before everyone, eat his breakfast alone, walk alone, that kind of stuff."

"So far this just about characterizes both of us, amigo."

"You're both lefties," said Teddy. "Not me."

"Who chose to live and work in a miniature replica of his grandfather's lovingly restored tobacco barn?"

"Jeez, that never even occurred to me."

"Could be you should consider a career at Langley."

"Too late. I've already hacked my way into the place. I'd never get past the lie detector test."

Will shrugged. "From what I understand, all it takes is a little chutzpah and a few shots of single-malt scotch."

"I wish I'd known Granddad," Teddy said.

"He would have loved you and your computers."

"Lord knows he might even have understood the value of having a Web site."

"You want us to have a Web site," said Will, "then let's have a Web site."

Teddy beamed. "Are you serious?"

Will nodded. Whatever he might need a Web site for, God only knew. But simply because you don't need something is no reason not to have it, not for an American.

"You're in charge of it," said Will. "This is information and queries only. No cyber-manuscripts."

"Hypertext," Teddy corrected. "We could agree to look at sample chapters of *edgy* novels."

Designing a Web site might not be as wonderful as discovering the glories of sex, but it served to lift Teddy's spirits considerably. All at once he seemed grounded again, if not quite his old wisecracking self. That morning he seemed five years older to Will.

"Did you and Granddad talk much?" Teddy asked a moment later.

Will shook his head. "Not much at all."

"Why not?"

He shrugged. Who could say? Perhaps the trickle of communication that Will and his father had shared had always been enough. They seemed to understand each other. Pushing for deeper intimacy probably would have scared the daylights out of both of them.

"Then Mom's wrong? It *wasn't* because of a difficult relationship with him that you've had such a hard time settling down?"

Now it was Will's turn to let his gaze wander the porch rails and gutters of this place he called home. The thing was, he felt settled down, as deeply rooted as anyone he knew. Sure, Mr. Richmond could claim more exemptions on his tax return. But did that mean that he was more settled? And anyway, thought Will, why was settling down the goal? Just look at the long march of history! Look at how the world was populated! As creatures we humans are driven by curiosity, and a taste for adventure. If you've got two years to spare, Will would have told his young charge, spend it before a thirty-foot mast, not an eighteen-inch color monitor.

Teddy said, "Last night, with Annie, you were, uh, pretty forceful."

"I made an ass of myself, if you want to know the truth."

"How come?"

The question was genuine. Will understood that this was one of those pivotal moments in the uncle-nephew relationship. Were he to duck this question, Teddy's pupils would shrink to the size of pin-pricks, and he would strike Will's name from his personal list of adults worth listening to. So he told him the whole story: about Charlotte Cameron; about the bout of unprotected sex with Lucy all those years ago, and his cowardly flight to Europe; about his suspicion that Lucy had come to see him the day he returned, and had seen his mother instead; and finally, for reasons he didn't fully understand, that all this news from the past had opened his eyes to his relationship with Annie. Opened his heart.

Teddy's eyes were nearly bugged out by the time Will finished speaking. He was rapt. This was so much better than any dinner table homily from Mom and Dad. This was real. The kid couldn't listen hard enough.

"So what makes you think this Cameron woman is your daughter?" Suddenly a deeper significance dawned on Teddy: "My *cousin* Charlotte."

"A hunch," said Will. "She's exactly the right age. She was born here. Her birth mother was in a Catholic maternity home. Her grandfather and Lucy's father both died in the war."

"Uncle—"

"That's just the surface. I'm sure there's more."

"How many men died in that war?"

"Fifty-eight thousand, more or less."

"The odds," whispered Teddy. "The odds."

"My hunch, dear thick Nephew, is that Charlotte Cameron had a *reason* to write to me. That she knows who I am."

"Or else she's just another troubled individual who thinks she might actually want to write a book. Which means that none of this would've come up if I hadn't disobeyed orders and forced that letter of hers on you in the first place."

"Maybe that was intuition," said Will.

Teddy scowled. "She's my age. I liked her handwriting. I figured I might get a chance to meet her."

"You might."

"What if all of this is in your head? I mean, we don't even know for certain that Lucy had *a* child, much less *your* child. Maybe somebody should check that out."

"Somebody is going to," said Will.

"Who?"

He pointed. "You."

Will figured this would be a great test of the capabilities of Teddy's much-revered World Wide Web. Not that Will had any clue as to how this Web actually worked. Nevertheless, he had a few suggestions for his nephew. Teddy listened silently, growing ever more sulky. Finally, in what seemed a hugely symbolic act, he flung the dregs of his coffee cup into the bushes.

The boss had been ruminating about databases. How there must be a half dozen obvious ones to search: organizations of MIA families, dependents who receive pension benefits from Air America, birth mothers in the Washington area looking for their adopted children (perhaps Lucy had already begun the search), alumni offices at, say, George Mason University or the University of Virginia (in the event that Lucy attended college at a state school), area medical schools.

Teddy stood, suddenly no longer able to contain himself. "What exactly do you mean by *searching* databases?"

Will shrugged. He didn't know. "Whatever it is you do with them. Call up the list on your computer and scroll through it for Lucy's name?"

"What about her credit report? That would have an address."

Will smiled.

"Mastercard, driver's license, motor vehicle registry, Social Security."

The smile grew.

"You don't get it, Uncle, do you?"

"Get what?"

"That what you're asking me to do is perform the computer equivalent of breaking and entering."

"Oh."

In his mind's eye Will flashed on Richard Nixon, commander-in-chief of all these sovereign states, storming around the Oval Office. His instructions to draw up a list of enemies and plant a bug in the Watergate must have seemed about as ominous as an order to his limo driver to double park.

Teddy said, "If you're telling me to hack my way into these databases, well, that's another story. I *might* be able to do it. But as a first option it seems a bit severe."

"So then what is our first option?"

He went to the kitchen for pencil and paper.

"Name?" he asked.

"Lucy V-i-t-a-v-a."

"Any addresses?"

Will rifled his desk for the old address book with Lucy's mother's street and house number in Fairfax, and Lucy's three subsequent apartments. He gave Teddy the last phone number he had for her, the number he had dialed the day Marianne reported that Lucy was coming to see him. Teddy copied down her parents' names, and Judy Vitava's hometown—Manistee, Michigan—which Will recalled. He studied a newsletter that Will had received from an alumni group at the International School of Bangkok; he fetched a magnifying glass to examine the grainy photograph of young Lucy Vitava from Will's seventh grade school yearbook, the *Erawan*. Teddy was glorying in the Sam Spade routine, licking the tip of his pencil as he made notes, filing scraps of paper in a brand-new manila folder, all the while offering nothing in the way of an explanation as to how he might proceed.

He disappeared into the shed, presumably to go on-line. This took all of three minutes. Returning to the house, Teddy wore the expression of a doctor emerging from the sickroom: cautiously optimistic— or was it *troubled*?

"What's the news?"

"A possible lead." Teddy smiled blandly as he headed for Will's old truck, parked at the curb. "Hold down the fort, Uncle."

Will grew annoyed. "Where are you going?"

"Into town. Correct me if I'm wrong, Uncle Ebeneezer, but I believe I'm still allowed a lunch hour."

"So what did you learn?"

Teddy turned on the walk. "There are three L. Vitavas of some renown in these United States. One of them happens to live in our fair city."

WILL TELEPHONED Ruthie Ann Staton to begin the hunt for his fugitive writer.

The line rang and rang. Will pictured Ruthie Ann in her white dress with the tiny blue and yellow dots, glancing piquedly at the ringing telephone as she finished her business accounts. Ruthie looked to be in her late seventies. Her thick white hair would be pushed back with a plastic headband, lime green or magenta. She would be wearing opaline glasses, faux pearls, and, given the warmth of the day, plastic jellies.

Finally Ruthie Ann picked up. "Is that you, Will Gerard?" she screamed, reminding Will to shout back.

"I'm looking for Norton," he yelled.

" 'Course you are. You and everybody."

"Have you seen him?"

"Hold on there, Will Gerard. I got a customer."

Will grimaced. The Wilderness Motel hosted a dozen guests during any given week, and he had the serious misfortune to telephone Ruthie Ann at the precise moment she was beginning the laborious process of registering one of them.

He couldn't hang up. He had made the mistake of hanging up

once before, when he had called for Norton and Ruthie offered to fetch him. This was before Will had visited Orange, before he understood that Norton's trailer, which Ruthie had described as being *just next door*, sat adjacent to the hangar at an airfield nearly a half mile from her motel. When she returned from the fifteen-minute car trip and discovered that Will had hung up on her, she refused to take his calls for months.

Suddenly, from the background noise, he realized that Ruthie was about to register *another* guest.

"Ruthie Ann!" he called. "Ruthie ANN! RUTHIE ANN!"

"Will Gerard, I got twelve people standin' in front of me in a line that's stretchin' right out the door."

"What's going on?"

"A re'nactment," she said.

"A *Civil War* reenactment?"

"Folks around here don't see much of anything that was civil about it. All I can tell you is that we're set to have ten thousand folks in town for sure. And so far most of them seem to be stoppin' in here."

Will's mind's eye saw farm fields and hillsides thick with humanity—zealots, all—folks who had driven their vans and campers through the night in their desire to see this hallowed land come alive again with soldiers from another time. The huckster within saw Norton attired as Moses Pugh, Confederate butternut beneath Union blue, declaiming in the first person about his adventures: how he had talked his way past Union pickets and crossed the Rapidan on a black night to bring news to General Lee that Grant's Army of the Potomac was preparing to march into the Wilderness. Norton would sell *thousands* of books at each reenactment site. This could go on for years. When the paperback edition of *Pharaoh's Ghost* came out, and CastleBooks remaindered the hardcover, Norton and Will could buy up the entire stock and continue to sell it at the full cover price. They could collect names and addresses, and sell it through the mail. Teddy could set up a Web site for them—www.pharaoh.com—and many years from now they would reprint the book themselves and sell it to a new generation of Civil War buffs.

"Ruthie Ann," he hollered, "I need to find Norton, and I need to get my hands on that manuscript of his. Can you help me?"

"With the book," she said. "Real nice fellow who's set to play Jeb Stuart is sittin' on the couch in the parlor reading it right now."

"You've got it?"

" 'Course I do."

"Bless you," said Will. "Would you call Dewey and figure out how to get the manuscript to him? Call a cab if you need to. Ask Dewey to walk it over to Grover's bank and have him put it in a safe deposit box for me. Could you do that right now? And check to see that he gets *all* the pages?"

"No sir, I can't," she said flatly.

"Why not?"

"Well, because of the roomful of folks in blue uniforms who are waiting to get into their rooms, for one thing. And for another, I don't got the *whole* book, only most of it. Norton took off with the tail end of it."

"When?"

"Round about a week ago."

"Did he say when he'd be back?"

Ruthie laughed. "Well, it's got to be tomorrow night, considering that's when he and the fellows play cards."

"I'm on my way. Tell Dewey to look for me tomorrow. I'll stop into his office at the end of the day. And if you see Norton before I do, you throw a leg iron on that man. You tell him that I said he's got to stay put."

She laughed again at the very thought.

Norton was so damn predictable. He was out on the battle trail, no question about it. From the spot on Clark Mountain where Lee and his generals had gathered to assess the strength of Grant's army, to the crossing at Germanna Ford (which Norton had swum twice before, once nearly drowning in high water), straight through the Wilderness to Spotsylvania and beyond. Twentieth-century property rights meant nothing to a campaigning Norton Tazewell. He'd fought through bramble, been chased by dogs, stalked by hunters and shot at dozens of times, all in a quest to know his native land as the men who fought and died there had known it: to stand where Lee had stood, to whittle beside trees that Grant had whittled beside, to gallop afoot where Little Phil Sheridan had galloped ahorse, to fall at Yellow Tavern where

Jeb Stuart had fallen. No doubt now he was taking one last walk through the terrain of his epic novel, the literary equivalent of a homicide detective taking a final stroll through the crime scene. Will checked the date on his watch. Yesterday, at Spotsylvania, Norton had stood at the Bloody Angle. In a couple of weeks, he would spend two nights at Ox Ford on the North Anna, reliving the awful night that Moses Pugh spent with a rifle barrel pressed to his forehead—the spy discovered—unable to get word to Lee to begin the attack on Hancock's II Corps, praying to live to see the light of dawn, and for news that Grant had decided to keep him alive for a few more days anyway, to guide his troops along the western shores of the Pamunkey to a place called Cold Harbor.

On Will's desk lay a library copy of William T. Vollmann's *Rainbow Stories* with a Post-It note from Teddy: "Check this out. There will be a quiz." Beneath it was a manuscript, the novel by the next William T. Vollmann, Will surmised. He opened the book, noting the queer footnotes and typefaces, the Poe epigraph; then he riffled through it, reading pages at random. It had the smell of dirty socks about it; the writer who had spent too much of his adolescence locked in a bedroom. Teddy's find had a similar feel: no title on the title page (a bold statement, perhaps?), a table of contents dominated by mathematical equations (and Teddy's penciled "Wow!"), and a peculiarly breathless writing style, enlivened by frequent hints of sex and violence. Will skimmed. When he looked up he was startled to discover that he had read fifty-five pages. Perhaps Teddy was right. Perhaps this was the real thing. But how could he know for sure? And more to the point, was there an editor in his Rolodex whom he could send this to?

At twelve-twenty the kitchen buzzer sounded. Will telephoned Rita Corelli's office, certain that he would be talking to voice mail. He left an upbeat message saying that Norton was hard at work on final revisions, that he had an editorial conference scheduled for Tuesday evening to walk through the manuscript, that said manuscript would then be transported to New York via Federal Express. "Look for it on your desk Thursday morning," Will chirped. "*Ciao*."

The phone rang the instant he hung up, but he didn't answer it, didn't even listen to the message once he had ascertained that the caller was not a certain lanky, brown-haired, blue-eyed litigator. He was feeling jumpy. He went out back and split a few logs. But the short round of exercise only awakened deeper feelings of agitation, an emotion closely tied to carelessness. Give himself ten minutes swinging an ax in this frame of mind, and Will figured he stood an even chance of serious injury. So he gave up on the ax, changed into a pair of shorts and Nikes, and went out for a run.

He was furious with Annie.

He was even more furious with himself.

The first pounding steps down Seventy-ninth Street were inflicted upon the pavement as if intended to be heard by her. Then Will was gripped by the fear that he and Annie would never speak again, and he ran light as a feather. He was not a serious runner. He didn't truly enjoy any part of the jogging routine other than the final ten steps leading to the shower. But an aerobic workout does have its uses, the chief one being the release of anxiety and bile: by the time Will reached the C&O Canal towpath he knew he would be miserable enough from the exercise that any gloomy thoughts about the future with Annie (or the absence thereof) would seem part and parcel of his general state of being. And so it went. He plodded along the storm-ravaged path for miles, the long shadow of his misery slowly dissipating until it became no more bothersome than a dull toothache. Will was alone. Under the guise of trying to locate an owl he thought he'd heard, he wandered into the woods. But then another bird called, Mick-EE, Mick-EE, which he recalled was Annie's nickname as a kid. Will jogged back to the towpath. He sprinted for half a mile.

Beyond lock 12, beneath the concrete trestle of the Beltway, he stopped. With the canal empty of water, the stone work of the lock and sluiceway resembled the newly excavated walls at an archaeological site. This would have been the holiest place of the ancient Beltway people, site of their portal to the Otherworld. The voices of their Gods still echoed in the sounds of the traffic overhead: FOOL, FOOL, FOOL, FOOL, FOOL. And then, from a speeding eighteen-wheeler: FOOOOOOL.

It was at this moment, at last, that Will could admit to himself that it was entirely possible that Annie had made the right decision. It was one thing for a desperate woman to conceive a child with someone like himself, but something else again to do so with the idea of including the unreliable fellow in her life plans. The news about Charlotte Cameron—more to the point, his reaction to this news—cried out for a moratorium as well. Anyone at all could see that he didn't have room in his life for a significant other. Not right now. He sweated freely, and thanked God that Annie had had the wisdom to give him the shove. Then a mile further on, he missed her. His heart ached for her. He simply couldn't imagine life without Annie Leonard.

Like a storm-tossed gannet, he soon found himself approaching Widewater, miles from home. He slowed to a walk as he climbed past racks of kayaks, and a group of kayakers dressed, it would seem, for a production of Shakespeare in the park. By the time he reached the roadside telephone at Old Angler's Inn, he was chuffing like an old angler himself, supremely grateful to have discovered two quarters in a pocket. He punched in Annie's number first. Her assistant picked up.

"Stephanie, this is Will. I really need to talk to her. Is she there?"

There was an uncomfortable pause. "I—I'm sorry, Mr. Gerard. She's in with a client at the moment."

"Could you buzz her?"

"I could take your number."

"Are you willing to raise your right hand and swear that your boss isn't sitting in her office right now eating a blueberry yogurt?"

"I'm sorry, Mr. Gerard."

Will called home and left a message for Teddy to rescue him. "Bring my wallet," he commanded. For the moment there was nothing to do but wait. So Will took up residence at a table on the flagstone deck at Old Angler's. He admired the petunias and nuthatches, and gazed at the couples seated around him conversing in low tones. Spies and philanderers, he was willing to bet: the women wore sunglasses and head scarves, the men all seemed to be about ten years older. Will ordered what he took to be the chef's tongue-in-cheek special—the plowman's lunch—and a beer.

Afterward he waited for Teddy. Waited and waited.

When the last BMW exited the lot, he went inside to use the house phone and make arrangements to drop off a check to pay his lunch tab. There was still no answer at home. So Will gave up on his nephew and started down MacArthur Boulevard on foot. The air was drier now, and suddenly much cooler; a warm, humid morning had given way to a gusty afternoon. The wind pushed him along. This change of weather, celebrated by squawking crows and jays, did nothing for Will, who with each step found himself growing ever more glum. Here was the man recently celebrated by a newspaper of record as a "rising star in high-stakes publishing" trudging alongside the dusty shoulder of a secondary road on the outskirts of Washington, dumped by his girlfriend, shortly to be dumped by one of those high-stakes publishers, perhaps; wondering what if anything he might do to salvage either of those relationships; wondering, too, what to do about Charlotte Cameron. Perhaps the best course now was to take Barry Valentine's advice and ignore her letter. Sit tight. Catch his breath, so to speak.

The path Will was currently on was the path to a full-blown midlife crisis. He needed perspective. He had to get back on track, and the proper way to do that, he felt certain, was to spend the rest of the day on the telephone. He would shake some trees. He should set the tone for his recovery by calling Barry to say that he was getting pressed on the Swan novel: tell him that he would need a bid by noon tomorrow. Just imagining Barry's indignant howl instantly lifted Will's spirits.

Work had always been his salvation. It anchored him. While he had never made the sort of lifetime commitment to a single job, as his father had made to the CIA, it was interesting to note that, like his father, Will had found his profession early, and had remained committed to it all these years.

In bookshops, he took pleasure in unpacking the cartons of new books, cracking them open to read a page or two before the reviews and ads and customer comments had anointed each of them with something like an identity. First novels, especially: all those earnest authors peering out from the dust jacket. Working as a sales rep in the days before the look-alike superstores, he loved first visits to new towns and new shops. He was young enough then to enjoy the travel, and the eating alone on the veranda of a grandly faded Southern hotel beside a stack of reading copies, or in a grubby diner next door to a crummy motel. He loved the give-and-take of the sales call, the thrill of opening a new account and walking out with an order. As a publisher, he liked the grand scheming, the packaging of ideas, design conferences, selling the commission reps and distributors, and, most of all, marrying the writer to the project.

Will would never forget an excursion to Richmond early in his partnership with Samantha Rogers, so early that Will and Sam were still operating under the brief, misguided notion that they might prosper as lovers *and* co-owners of Tiber Creek Press. Sam had been cross most of the day—her regular mood, Will soon came to realize. It was his birthday, and he had planned the outing: lunch at a restaurant overlooking the James, a walk in an old park, a visit to the Museum of the Confederacy, and a stop at the ballpark to catch a few innings of the Richmond Braves. Sam had seemed bored to death at the Confederate Museum. (This was years before the War of Northern Aggression had proved to be a category unto itself in trade publishing.) But Will already had an inkling of the burgeoning national obsession with this war. He had visited some of the battle sites and observed the Union and Confederate partisans in the field, the hordes of cheerful middle-aged men trailed by weary spouses and children on their long march from cornfield to peach orchard to sunken lane.

A series of Civil War guidebooks.

Will suggested the idea to Sam, who wrinkled her nose. Sam's taste in guides ran more to those that rated B&Bs, garden tours, or weekend getaways. Will imagined a series of books that arrived every few months, like a magazine, with blow-in cards to place orders for the ones you've missed, or lost. One in the bathroom, one on the bedside table, one in the glove box of the Ford Expedition. The key to a successful series, he believed, was the voice: the books should sound as if they had been written by someone who had been there.

At the Museum of the Confederacy there was a tour guide—at least Will's first impression was that this Southern gentleman must be a tour guide. But the blue-haired daughter of the Confederacy at the front desk asserted hotly that Mr. Tazewell *was not* an official museum guide, just a frequent visitor. Will sidled over to Mr. Tazewell and his group. Tazewell himself was rail thin with a gorgeous white beard, hair that almost touched his shoulders, sunken Confederate eyes, and a gift for language. His stories went on and on. "If he can't write, I could just tape record him," Will whispered to Sam. Having finally realized why he was insisting they remain inside this hall for most of a sunny April

afternoon, she replied grumpily, "I can't believe you are even considering this."

Will and Norton exchanged business cards. His listed him as
editor and publisher of the *Orange Gazette,* a job he had held for some
forty years and would shortly relinquish to his nephew, Dewey. At
Will's urging Norton sent him a few clips of his Civil War
ruminations. He was a master of the thousand-word newspaper essay.
Will asked Norton to show him all of his work, and it arrived shortly
in a tomato crate. It turned out that Will had a gift for marrying these
columns, organizing them according to the particular battles, lopping
off endings, suggesting transitions between columns, abbreviating
some pieces and using them as sidebars; for fashioning, in short, Tiber
Creek's bestselling series, *Tazewell's Blue & Gray Guides to the
Battlefields.*

Near the entrance to the parkway Will heard the rattle-and-hum
of an old engine: a ferocious, unmuffled acceleration followed by a
volley of backfires, and then silence. Suddenly there was Teddy in his
rainbow reflective Frogskins, hunkered over the steering wheel of the
old Dodge. It squealed to a stop.

"It wasn't me," Teddy called. "It's this damn truck. I couldn't get it
started."

"It never starts," Will said. "It *can't* start all by itself. The bushings
in the starter are worn out. That's why we roll start it."

"I couldn't roll start it. A Plymouth Voyager had me boxed in."

Will climbed into the passenger seat. "Haven't I already heard the
excuse about the inconsiderate matron of West Bethesda returning her
overdue library books?"

"Not the library this time." Teddy popped the clutch and the truck
rattled onto the road. "And not a matron of West Bethesda." He
glanced at Will. "An au pair to a matron of West Bethesda." A tiny
grin tugged at the corner of his lips.

"Bullshit," said Will.

They bounced along MacArthur Boulevard on the old, old
shocks, every crack in the pavement experienced as a jolt to the spine.

"No bullshit," Teddy replied. Two hands on the wheel, he stared
straight ahead. "Her name is Krista. She taught me how to pronounce
Malmö." A wide grin now.

"I'll bet she did."

"You'll never guess where Krista and I met."

Will looked at him.

"At the emergency room. You see, little Caitlin, Krista's charge, had to spend the morning there getting some stitches in her chin. Nothing too serious. Mom was in with Caitlin, and Krista was sitting all by herself. She looked upset. So I cheered her up."

"What were you doing at the emergency room, Teddy?"

"Getting a positive ID on Caitlin's doctor."

Will had been expecting to learn that *yet again* Teddy been holed up after lunch in the shed, eyes glued to his monitor, surrounded by dirty laundry and an open bag of Chee-tos, writing code for his beloved Web site in such an orgiastic frenzy that, for the 1,244th time, he had forgotten to check the answering machine at regular intervals.

" 'An easy cricothyrotomy approach: the rapid four-step technique.' " Teddy glanced at Will. "*Academic Emergency Medicine,* November issue," he went on. "Maybe you missed that one." Then: "It was one of the titles that popped up when I plugged in the name Lucy Vitava. The author was Dr. Lucy Vitava of Georgetown University Hospital." Now he paused for effect. "When I walked into the emergency room, she was talking to Krista and Caitlin's mom. It's her, Uncle. No doubt about it."

"How did you know she'd be there?"

"I'm a genius," said Teddy. "I called ahead." He handed Will a scrap of paper with an address on Thornapple Street in Chevy Chase and a telephone number. "Just so you don't think I was fooling around with Krista the whole day," he added.

"What's this?"

"Dr. Lucy Vitava's residence and home phone number."

Will stared at the paper in his hands.

"Dr. Vitava usually works the graveyard shift: ten to six. Today, though, it was six to two." Teddy looked at his watch. "She's probably home by now." He pulled Will's cell phone from his shirt pocket and handed it to him.

Will felt queasy. "I don't know about this."

"Don't know what?"

"Just calling Lucy out of the blue."

"Why not?"

"For one thing, she's probably asleep."

"How could you possibly know that? And why do you care?"

"Let me think about this for a minute."

Teddy exhaled through his nose. "You aren't asking her out on a date. You just want to know if she is the mother of my long-lost cousin."

Will held up the scrap of paper. "How did you get this, anyway?"

"I checked a few databases." Teddy glanced at him over the tops of his sunglasses. "She's a doctor. Doctors tend not to have unlisted telephone numbers." Long pause. "She's in the Montgomery County phone book."

They rode along in silence.

"I can't just call her up," Will finally said.

"I can."

"No."

"All we need is the answer to *one* question."

Will gazed out at the road.

"I'm beginning to wonder if maybe you don't want to know the answer to that question, Uncle."

"You're wrong," he replied.

"Then what's stopping you?" Teddy paused. "Are you scared?"

Will considered the question. Scared of what? That Lucy might hang up on him, that she might refuse to talk to him or get angry or burst into tears? That she might tell him that all of this was a fantasy of his that indicated a deep-seated inability to form intimate human relationships? That she might cry out in delight at the sound of his voice? "Of course I'm scared," he said.

"We're talking about something that happened a long time ago. Before I was born," said Teddy. "The statute of limitations is up."

"I want to think about this."

For reasons Will couldn't explain, the ferreting out of this news had to be done slowly and methodically. There was a proper sequence of events. Obviously he would have to talk to Lucy before he could contact Charlotte. But before he could call Lucy, he needed to consider all the different ways she might react. And there were other questions to mull over, too. Such as, what was the chance that Lucy had told his mother that she was pregnant, and his mother had helped Lucy and never told Will? And how had Charlotte Cameron managed to find him, anyway? The answers to these questions would fit together like a puzzle; all Will needed was the right place to start.

He said, "How about we begin by paying a visit to your dear mother."

In his mind he had fast-forwarded to the climb up the switchbacked driveway to Marianne and Tom's Zen retreat. Teddy would back the truck up beside the fish pond, and he and Will would make their way down the heavily mulched path to Marianne's board-and-batten sculpting studio. She would be standing outside, goggled and masked, Stihl chainsaw in hand, engulfed in a cloud of sawdust as she worked to release the arboreal soul from a sectioned trunk of an old black-walnut tree. In Will's mind, he and Marianne and Teddy would sit on the back porch of her studio, gazing out at the Potomac. They'd be sipping one of Teddy's nut brown ales. In the middle of his story, Marianne's look of puzzlement would suddenly melt away. "Now that you mention it, I *do* remember a phone call," she would say.

"Mom won't have a clue about this," said Teddy.

"What makes you so sure of that?"

"My mother and secrets?" He shook his head. "She doesn't miss a thing. If she knew anything at all about this you'd have had a report from her years ago. Not to mention that if we head over there and tell her what you think might have happened, you might as well phone Grandmom and tell her yourself."

Teddy was right, as usual. Though Marianne had blasted off to college that day like a guided missile aimed at Philadelphia's Main Line, she would have had an ear cocked toward home. Had Will's mother or Lucy telephoned her at Swarthmore that fall, Will would have had a report from Marianne before the line was cold.

"Well," he said, grasping at straws, "maybe we don't tell her anything. Maybe we just talk to her."

"About what?"

"Stuff," answered Will.

Teddy's nostrils flared in disgust.

"What if I were to be honest?" said Will. "What if I were to tell her that I couldn't explain why I was asking what I wanted to ask until I got further along?"

Teddy cupped a hand to his ear. "Hey, Ma, any chance you know of something that might have happened in 1975 that has Uncle Will sweating bullets?"

"Or we could call the organizations for MIA families and see if Charlotte Cameron has been in touch with any of them. Begin by trying to find out what she knows," Will said.

Teddy shook his head sadly. "You're just dicking around with this. If I told you that I'd seen the name *Charlotte* spray-painted on Chain Bridge, you'd want to drive over right away to have a look at it."

AN HOUR LATER found Teddy and Will in the black Acura with the Thule bike rack, Will behind the wheel, parked on Thornapple Street behind a silver Honda station wagon with a Sidwell Friends sticker in the back window. Will wondered if this might be Lucy's car, then thought: *no.* People can change in dramatic ways over twenty years, but not in his wildest dream could he imagine Lucy Vitava as a private school chauffeur and soccer mom. It would have been as ludicrous as picturing her in white skirt and visor, part of a Thursday morning neighborhood foursome at the tennis club up the road.

Then again, according to Teddy's research, she *did* live in this neighborhood of old sycamores, slate roofs, solar add-ons, Volvos and Range Rovers.

"That's it."

Teddy was pointing at a buff-colored gabled house with two huge pots of red geraniums on either side of the front door. The flagstone walk was bordered with liriope. At a corner of the house stood a lilac bush in bloom. There were impatiens spilling from raised beds beneath the two dogwoods that screened the front porch. In all, the landscaping had the tidy, soulless look of a lawn service. No doubt Lucy was married to another doctor, both of them too harried and exhausted to take care of the yard themselves. Will couldn't imagine Lucy weeding or raking leaves, but then he couldn't picture her cooking dinner or changing bedsheets, either.

"Well," said Teddy breezily, "I guess now we've verified that Dr. Lucy Vitava lives in a house."

Right then Will was thinking about Lucy's mother's house, half the size of this. He recalled the matching picture windows in the living room—in the living room of every house on the street—which had lent the neighborhood a cartoonish feel. He thought about the stack of cardboard boxes in the foyer, and the bare walls in every room but Lucy's bedroom, which was covered with posters of Jimi Hendrix, Joni Mitchell, the Beatles.

"I'll take a quick snooze," said Teddy. "Feel free to wake me whenever you've finished your offices."

"Just now I was wondering what this house looks like inside," Will replied.

"We could knock on the door pretending to be Mormon missionaries and try to find out. Or sit tight until she leaves, and then sneak around back and peek in the windows."

"We don't even know that she's home," said Will.

"If we sit here long enough, the cop who pulls up behind us ought to be able to tell us," Teddy replied.

Will took his point. Two men hunkered down in a parked car on this neighborhood-watched street would be viewed with the same degree of suspicion as, say, a well-muscled young man in a ski mask pushing his way through the front doors of a convenience store.

"Question, Uncle."

Will looked at him.

"Why is this part so hard?"

"I walked away," said Will. "It just doesn't seem right to be barging back into her life."

"But this isn't about her life. It's about Charlotte Cameron's life. Barge in and then barge out. All we need is the answer to one question."

"It's never just one question."

"What are the other questions?"

"For starters: What did I know and when did I know it?"

"You think you knew all along?"

"Why run away, unless you have something to run from?"

"Could be that it just didn't feel right with Lucy. Taking off is cowardly, but it's also fast."

Will was shaking his head. "I was afraid. Scared out of my wits. So scared I didn't even admit it to myself."

"Did you love her?"

Will looked at the house. Then he said, "This is all wrong. Let's get out of here."

But in the next instant Teddy had the cell phone in hand, and had punched in a number, and then set the phone on Will's leg. Will's first impulse was to swat it away, like a wasp. But a sudden queasy spike of joy made him pick it up instead.

"Hello?" he heard a woman say. "Hello?"

"I'm trying to reach Lucy Vitava," he managed at last.

Silence. Then, hesitantly: "Yes?"

"This is Lucy?"

"Who's calling?"

At that instant Will recalled walking with her alongside a creek in the mountains around Lexington. But then he realized that she'd never visited him at Washington & Lee. Or had she? Could he have forgotten something like that? Maybe it was just that he'd often thought about her whenever he took that walk. "A voice from the past," he said.

"Will Gerard." Her tone was neutral, unreadable.

"How are you, Lucy?"

"Surprised," she said. "No, make that *shocked*."

"I guess I have to admit that I'm a little shocked, too."

She waited.

"I didn't think I'd have the nerve to call."

Teddy pretended to stifle a yawn. Lucy waited some more. Will could hear the sound of her breathing.

Finally he said, "I was in Boston last weekend. I ran into Alex Pine. We talked about Bangkok, the kids at school there. Your name came up. I thought I'd try to get in touch. It turned out to be pretty easy to find you." He was staring at Lucy's front door. "The Internet," he added lamely.

"How is Alex?"

"The same. I get the feeling we're all the same."

"I don't know about that," Lucy said warily.

"Look, if this a bad time . . ."

She let the comment hang in the air for a moment, before finally saying, "No, it's okay."

"Alex told me that she'd heard that you went to medical school."

"I did," she replied.

"Doctor Vitava," said Will. Teddy closed his eyes, shook his head. "And to think that all these years I've carried around this image of you as a pilot." Will looked at the blooming lilac bush. "Congratulations."

"Congratulations to you, too." Pause. "I saw the article in the *Post*."

"The truth is, I'd been thinking about you even before I ran into Alex. I'm calling because I was hoping to catch up." He paused. "It's been a long time." Silence. "Maybe we could we meet for a cup of coffee."

"I'm awfully busy," came the quick reply.

"I could come down to the hospital."

Teddy stirred in his seat, grabbed a clipboard from the backseat, and scrawled in giant, furious letters: "ASK HER!"

"Where are you?" asked Lucy.

Out front, thought Will. Gazing at your rose-colored door and beige drapes and purple lilacs like some kind of crazy fool. "I live out in Cabin John. Hard to believe we're almost neighbors." When she didn't respond, he said, "You free anytime tomorrow?"

"No."

"Wednesday?"

"Look," she said. "We knew each other a long, long time ago. As far as I'm concerned it was another lifetime. The truth, Will, is that you and I don't have anything to say to each other anymore."

"Just ten minutes."

The line went dead.

Aᴛ ᴍɪᴅɴɪɢʜᴛ, still wide awake, Will sat in the kitchen before a soggy bowl of Shredded Wheat and walked himself through a short course in personal ethics. How far could he push it with Lucy? He had called her up and she had told him to get lost. Did this mean he was obliged to get lost? Was this the moment to flush the scrap of paper with her address and phone number? Or was it possible that his reason for calling had the same moral standing as her desire to be left alone? By the time the dinosaur on the bottom of Teddy's favorite plastic bowl had come into view, Will believed that it did. The Catholic education he had endured at home and at school had not left him with a particularly acute sense of right and wrong—gospels, parables, commandments, daily mass and weekly confession notwithstanding. What he had come away with instead was a deep need, and a formidable ability, to justify whatever action he might choose to take.

In the middle of a bowl of Cheerios Will finally admitted to himself that the existence of Charlotte Cameron had never been a surprise. He had always known about her, not literally perhaps, not in any way that could damn him before a jury of his peers, but really, he had to ask himself now, what difference did that make? He had been young, to be sure, but again, *so what?* No younger than Lucy. Not too young to create a child. Not too young to have buried his own father.

If confirmation wasn't the issue, then what did he want from Lucy? Forgiveness, he supposed. Or if not that, then to have her sit through his apology. He wanted to tell her that he knew he should never have gone off to Europe without seeing her, and that this wasn't a recent revelation, but something he had carried deep in his soul all these years. He wanted to say that he knew he had compounded the sin by fleeing to school. Twice he had run away. Was it too much to insist that Lucy know all of this? That she hear it directly from him?

Of course it was.

The alarm was set for five o'clock, and Will awoke two minutes before. He ate a banana and drank a glass of orange juice, shaved and brushed his teeth while the kettle came to a boil. Coffee in hand, he stepped outside into a fog so thick it hid all trace of the trees in the front yard. Clouds of mist were billowing up the street from the river as if pumped by a machine. The drive down MacArthur Boulevard was excruciatingly slow, through patches of fog so dense Will had to brake to a crawl, his gaze fixed on the glowing tail lights of the early commuter ahead of him.

A trip that normally would have taken fifteen minutes took thirty that Tuesday morning. It was close to six o'clock when he reached Georgetown Hospital. He parked in the garage and hurried toward the entrance of the emergency room, feeling panicky, as if, indeed, he truly had some sort of medical emergency.

"Can I help you?"

The woman at the front desk looked weary. Her blank stare suggested that she had been up all night.

Will said, "Ah, I have a question for Dr. Vitava."

"Yes?"

"She, um, stitched up my son. His . . . chin." Will ran a finger across his own chin, as if he was speaking to someone with a poor command of English.

The woman imitated him. "His chin," she said.

"Dr. Vitava," said Will.

She pointed to a woman wearing hospital greenies who was standing thirty feet away.

Will looked. The first thing he noticed was a blond ponytail, cinched loosely, hanging to the middle of the woman's back. She held a clipboard in her left hand. Her fingers were slender. She was leaning forward to examine an older woman's face. In a moment the doctor turned slightly, and Will saw her face in profile. It was Lucy.

The woman at the desk called wearily, "Dr. Vitava!" But too late, as Lucy had already disappeared through a swinging door. To Will, the receptionist reported, "Dr. Vitava must be going to her office to finish her paperwork. I'll page her."

"No, no. Let her finish. I'm not in a hurry. I can wait."

He took a seat across the room, eyes glued to the swinging door. Five minutes passed. Will reminded himself of the new reality in medicine in these United States—the death of Marcus Welby, the HMOing of America, and all the paperwork spawned by this transformation— and realized that he might be sitting there for an hour. Twenty minutes passed. The weary receptionist remained at her post. Will considered taking her up on the offer to page Lucy, but he couldn't bring himself to ask. He looked at other doors, and through a plate glass window at the green-clad crowd moving on the sidewalk. Then it occurred to him that the location of Lucy's office down a certain hallway did not mean she would have to exit through this particular door. Thirty minutes had passed. Will went outside and sat with the smokers, perched like crows on a low brick wall. It was light now, blue sky and a promise of sunshine.

Lucy was gone; he would have bet a thousand bucks on it. Away from this second-hand smoke, he scolded himself. Away from the misery of the sick and the injured. Go home, old man.

And then, at last, he did rouse himself. He had started toward the parking garage, when he turned back to the hospital one last time, and spotted the doctor with the blond ponytail, still dressed in greenies, exit the front door of the emergency room. And suddenly he realized that he hadn't planned for this moment, hadn't a clue what he would say to Lucy, not even an opening line. She veered off to the left. Will thought about moving to intercept her, but stayed rooted to the pavement, even as a car rounded the circle and passed by close enough to touch.

Lucy was looking at the ground, then looking ahead. She was twenty feet away, almost past Will's line of sight, when she appeared to stumble. But it wasn't a stumble; it was a doubletake: suddenly Lucy was looking directly at him. And in that instant it was clear to Will that if he didn't say something, she might keep on walking.

"This won't take long," he said.

A shake of the head. "Sorry, I've got to get home."

Her face was the face Will remembered: the high forehead and wide cheekbones, blonder hair atop darker hair. Lucy had aged, yes, but not in the pinched way that most people age. Her features seemed sharper, her gray eyes more luminous. The way she looked at him then, he could see her at work, making a quick assessment of a medical emergency.

"Please," he said.

"I've been up all night. I'm exhausted. I need some sleep."

"You must be hungry, too."

"No," she replied.

"Something to drink—coffee or juice?"

"Damnit, Will, you're not listening to me."

"I am," he said.

"And if I say no, what will you do? Show up at my house?"

If I say no—

He waited.

Her shoulders dropped. "The cafeteria," she said. "I really don't have much time."

In the corridor of the hospital, she added, "Look, I'm not angry at you, despite how I sound. It's just that I don't need this. It has taken me a long time and a lot of work to get to where I am right now. I like it here. You called me up to talk about the past. That's just something I don't want to do."

Will said, "I didn't think I was interested in the past either. But sometimes it's hard to ignore. Sometimes you can't ignore it."

"Of course you can, Will. Whatever and whenever." She finally looked directly at him. "You of all people should know that."

She went to the soda fountain and poured herself a glass of water. Will stayed beside her, made Lucy stay with him while he poured coffee. He paid the cashier, and they took seats at a table in the middle of the empty room. He took a sip of coffee, his hand trembling so much he set down the Styrofoam cup.

"The reason I tracked you down," he finally said, "is because I want to apologize."

She closed her eyes momentarily. Will couldn't read the expression. There seemed some element of calculation in it, like a card player. Weariness, too. Perhaps Lucy had always been this complicated, and Will had never realized it, had never seen her for who she was. She looked at him, looked straight through him, but said nothing. To respond to his statement in any way opened the door to the question he had come to ask. "I'm fading," she finally said.

Will noted the ring on Lucy's left hand. "You're married, I take it."

She had finished her glass of water. She reached into a shoulder bag and pulled out a quart bottle of Evian, unscrewed the top, and took a sip. "I have a husband, a little boy, a basset hound, a parakeet, a house in the suburbs." She shrugged. "All in all, a regular life."

"Alex said that Susannah Hamilton ran into you years ago."

Lucy looked at Will, waiting for him to continue.

Will took a sip of coffee. "It was Susannah who told her that you were in medical school. That's how I found you. Through the article you wrote. On the Internet."

"I believe you mentioned that."

"I guess I did." He smiled sheepishly.

She stood.

There was no graceful way to ask the questions that had brought him here: *Did I get you pregnant? Did you have a baby girl on December 23, 1975? Did you give her up for adoption?*

"Lucy, there's one more thing."

"Sorry," she said. "I've got to go."

"Do you hate me?"

She considered the question. "No," she finally said. Another pause. "I adored you, Will. You have no idea." She picked up her bag. "But that was ages ago. Ages and ages ago. Back when we were kids."

"The reason I called," said Will, "the reason I ambushed you this morning is to say that I'm sorry." Lucy's back stiffened almost imperceptibly. "That summer," he went on. "When you called me at school. I ran away. I know that. I knew it then. I just never admitted to myself *why* I was running away."

The expression on her face suddenly went fluttery. She glanced toward the exit. "Look, it's just not important. Not to me. Not any-more."

"I think it is," said Will. "Last week I got a letter—"

But she was already gone.

He sat there for a moment contemplating the sludge at the bot-tom of his cup, feeling heartless and inept. This conversation had gone exactly as he imagined it would. No surprise there. At least, as Will thought about it, he couldn't imagine why he might have hoped that it would go differently. What else could he have expected from her? A smile and a hug? Arm in arm together through the streets of George-town, wistfully recalling the good old days?

Will would have preferred to skip the full report of this sorry encounter with Lucy to Teddy. But this was not to be. Young Ted was seated at the kitchen table when Will arrived home. He wore a wrin-kled white shirt with button-down collar, rolled at the sleeves, black Levis, no shoes. There was milk at the corners of his lips, and little pompadours of curly black hair on the knuckles of his big toes. And on his face, an expectant grin: "You saw her! You talked to her! So what did she say?"

Will shrugged. "We chatted for about fifteen minutes."

"And?"

"And then she ran out of the cafeteria."

"That's it?"

He nodded.

"You sat face-to-face with Lucy Vitava for fifteen minutes and never even *asked* the question?"

"Didn't have to." Will was addressing the floor now. "Anyway, it was probably closer to ten." He looked up. "I wanted to ask her, Ted. But I just couldn't."

Teddy stopped chewing. The scrap of pink marshmallow stuck to his lower lip dropped into his lap. "Why not?"

"Her expression. Something about the way she looked at me. I felt as if I was responsible for screwing up her life twenty years ago, and had lost the right to ask her anything about that now."

"Your child, Uncle."

"I walked away."

"Unfuckingbelievable," whispered Teddy, his mouth overflowing with Lucky Charms.

A shower helped. Will's skin tingled pleasantly from the loofah scrub. He arrived at his desk with high hopes of turning the corner on this mood, of getting some work done, but within seconds he knew that plan was doomed. He was a mess. His life was falling to ruin all around him, and his response to this was to behave as if nothing was wrong. To pretend to be interested in a proposal for an illustrated book on the history of baseball! Worst of all, for Will, was the inescapable feeling that stupidity was at the root of his troubles. Stupidity, obtuseness, insensitivity, and a callow disregard for his own emotions. It was true. He knew it was true. Not that this realization solved anything. But it got him moving. It got him out of his seat, and forced him to reflect on the mess that his life had become. Will stood at the window of his study, gazing out at the empty bird feeder, and concluded that there was no one to blame for any of this but himself. He had to do something. Something bold, even foolhardy, something from the heart.

He paid a visit to Teddy in the shed out back.

"Call Annie's office. I want you to set up an appointment for me."

"Huh?"

Will stood in the doorway.

Teddy's eyes remained fixed on the screen. "Sunday night," he went on. "Correct me if I'm wrong since I didn't catch every single word she said, but at the end there, didn't she break it off with you?"

"She did."

"You don't think she meant it?"

"Oh, she meant it."

"Well then, isn't it likely that she might not want to see you right now, Uncle Will?"

"Very likely. Which is why you are making the appointment."

Teddy turned. "I'm lost."

"Get me through the door. Whatever it takes. Use an alias."

The springs in Teddy's chair groaned as he leaned back. "His old, old girlfriend refuses to talk to him, so he ambushes her at her place of employment but neglects to ask the critical question; and his new, new girlfriend won't talk to him, so he decides to get around this by sneaking into her office under an assumed name." He spun the chair around to face Will. "Is it just me, or is there a pattern here?"

"It's you," said Will.

Teddy shook his head. "I have so much to learn."

"Go through the main switchboard number at Annie's firm. If Stephanie asks, tell her that the matter I wish to discuss with Ms. Leonard is confidential."

"Mr. Flood." Teddy spoke in an affectedly genteel tone of voice. "Mr. Wilbur Flood wishes Ms. Leonard's counsel on a highly confidential matter, a personal issue"—*iss-you* was how he pronounced the word. "Look, Uncle, maybe you ought to leave me your checkbook so that I can make bail in the event that she calls the cops."

"Another thing," said Will. "St. Jerome's. It's a home for unwed mothers in Silver Spring. Find out if it's still there, and get me a phone number."

Teddy's nose was already buried in the Yellow Pages. "The firm," he called out. "What's the name again?"

"Crosby, Stills, Nash & Young."

"Cosby, Steele, Holcomb & Brown?"

"Bravo, Theo. The game is afoot."

"Don't *ever* call me that," snapped Teddy. "I *hate* that name."

WILL HAD NEVER been to Annie's office. He had never set foot inside the grand atrium at its entrance. This was fortunate. For had he already trod those green marble floors, had he ascended the four open stories in that wood-and-glass elevator, or lounged even one time on this lawyerly leather couch upon which he now found himself, he would never have attempted this ruse. But here he was, not two hours later, feigning interest in that Tuesday's edition of the *Wall Street Journal*. It was absolutely quiet in the Cosby, Steele reception area: the sort of depthless silence that devours sound. The receptionist wore the briefest of telephone headsets, and the acoustical properties of the room were such that Will couldn't hear a single word she said. No doubt there was a white noise machine gobbling up her conversation. Gazing around this airy anteroom, with its gilded mirrors and sculp-

tural plants, the Frankenthaler painting, the coffee-table-sized book of
Ansel Adams photographs, Will came to the realization that Marianne
and Tom didn't have a thing to worry about with that boy of theirs.
Teddy would make a success of his life, with or without a Princeton
degree. The kid got things done. He had arranged this appointment
with Annie, and an "informational interview" at St. Jerome's Infant
and Maternity Home, all within the space of fifteen minutes! Teddy
was smart; he had the chutzpah of a native New Yorker.

"Mr. Flood?"

Will missed his cue the first time; he looked up finally when the
receptionist spoke this name again, louder, and he realized that he was
alone in the waiting room.

"Yy-ess?"

"Ms. Wells will show you to Ms. Leonard's office."

The receptionist raised a hand and a young woman materialized
in the entrance of a hallway. "Mr. Flood?"

Will mumbled a greeting as he launched himself to his feet, eyes
averted, unable to look directly at Ms. Wells, who was better known to
him as Stephanie, for fear that if Stephanie were to look into his eyes
she would somehow know that the two of them had spoken together
many dozens of times on the telephone.

"Right this way, sir," the sweetly familiar voice announced.

Will prayed that this wasn't going to turn out to be one of those
Washington offices designed around Pentagonesque corridors that
rambled for miles. The fact that Annie was a senior partner at Cosby,
Steele meant that Will and Stephanie wouldn't be strolling for too
many of those miles, but the fact that Annie was a woman meant they
probably wouldn't happen upon her office anytime soon.

"It was quite a lucky break that Ms. Leonard had a cancellation
this morning," said Stephanie.

"Ah," replied Will, in a gargle.

"Right here."

She ushered him from the windowless hallway into a large sunlit
room. It was so bright Will was blinded for an instant. He took
another moment to find Annie, who wasn't seated at her desk, but at a
small conference table across the room. Her head was down. She was
writing.

Stephanie knocked on the open door. "Ms. Leonard, Mr. Wilbur Flood."

What Will recalled of the next moment was this: his feet glued to the floor and Annie frozen in her seat, an affable smile fixed on her narrow face. Time passed. Hours, it seemed. Pretty soon Annie's smile became impossible for Will to look at. The door closed behind him, so quietly he never heard the click. Instead he experienced a hallucinatory flashback to that moment of terror inside a confessional when the priest's grate quietly scraped open. The memory was so vivid he could actually smell the Aqua Velva. He felt the urge to get down on his knees. *Bless me, Father, for I have sinned . . .*

At last he said, "There was something I had to tell you."

She considered this, nodded toward the telephone. "You might have started there."

"I did. Yesterday."

"You didn't leave a message."

"This is something I have to tell you in person."

"So you barge into my office?"

"I made an appointment."

"Mr. Wilbur Flood?"

"Would you have seen Will Gerard?"

She rested her chin on a hand. "Nope," she said finally. She thought some more. "Definitely not today."

"I had to talk to you today."

"You're going around in circles, Will."

"I didn't want it to end the way it did. On Sunday." To unlock his knees he took one step forward. "The thing I need to say is that I can't imagine my life without you."

She didn't respond, not in any way that Will could see.

He went on, "I also have to tell you that you were right. I didn't know what I wanted. I haven't made any room for you in my life. Not that I don't want there to be room, but somehow I just didn't know how. And I never slowed down for a second to try to figure that out. I've been sleepwalking, Annie." He paused. "Yesterday I woke up."

They stared at each other.

"Aw, shit," she said.

Will felt lightheaded. Perhaps it was a result of his shoes again feeling as though they were glued to the floor; that and, when Annie's jaw suddenly relaxed, the sense he had that a cloud had parted and a host of angels would soon alight upon his head. It was his turn to speak, but he didn't know what to say. Annie waited. Will felt his arms lengthen. He felt ape-like standing there. Inexplicably, he got down on his knees. Annie looked puzzled, then slightly alarmed.

Will said, "I know I'm doing this all wrong. But I had to see you. I had to show you that I'm serious."

"I see, I see. Now would you please stand up?"

"I want you to come with me," said Will.

Annie didn't respond. Instead she glanced away.

"Right now," he added.

She looked at him. "What does that mean? Are we talking broadly about *life,* or a cup of coffee at Starbucks?"

"Both," said Will. "There are things I need to tell you."

"Up," she commanded. "If Mr. Perkovich from the mail room were to knock on the door right now, the sight of you on your knees would be enough to turn my office into a pilgrimage destination." She touched the chair beside her.

Will felt like an old man climbing to his feet. "The thing I finally understood is that it wasn't about commitment. Or settling down. Or having a child. None of that. I thought it was. All along I pretended that it was. But it wasn't. I was fooling myself." He sat down. "On the way over, I turned the situation around in my head. I said to myself, what if it was me who wanted kids, and you couldn't have them? Or didn't want them. What would I do in that situation? Do I leave, or do I look at this as fate—the course that my life has taken? Do I simply accept that and get on with the business of living?"

Annie stared at him.

"I came to understand that what we've got—all we've got right now—is us. What we *had,* I mean. I don't mean that a decision to have a child is something to take lightly, or that making that decision is easy, but once love was part of the equation—once we *knew* that— then you and I had to come first. I missed that. I see it now. That's what I came here to say: I want us to come first."

Her eyes were opened as wide as he had ever seen them, glassy and unblinking.

"What I mean is, everything between us should depend on whether or not we love each other," said Will. "That makes it straight-forward. If I love you and you love me, we work it out. That's our starting point. It makes things simple, really. I don't know why it took me so long to get that. I don't know why I thought sitting around on my hands was going to help me sort anything out." He looked at her. "Especially when there was nothing to sort out."

Annie's chin quivered. When she finally spoke, her voice was sub-dued. "I'm going to Chicago, Will. I have to go to Chicago."

"Okay." Then: "I'd like to go with you."

She looked at him, just kept staring.

"I've never spent much time in Chicago. Who knows? Maybe I'll like it." He paused. "I wouldn't try to tell you what to do."

"You'd drop everything that's going on in your life right now and go to Chicago with me? Today?"

"In a heartbeat, Annie."

Her face relaxed. "No," she said quietly. "No."

Quietly, too, Will replied, "Look, just because I deserve to be dumped doesn't mean that you are required to dump me, or even that your dumping me is the best thing for you to do." He got down on his knees again. "Come live with me. Or let me come live with you. I want to grow old with you." He paused. "We'll get married as soon as your divorce comes through. Or not." Another pause. "But we can have kids. Start trying anyway."

She was shaking her head.

"Can't you think about it?"

"I've thought about it."

"You made a decision on Sunday. Maybe it was the right decision. All I'm asking you to do is reconsider it. In case it isn't still the right decision."

She looked away. "You know what I wonder? Honestly?" Will was pretty sure he didn't want to know what this was, but he nodded nev-ertheless. "I wonder what you're really feeling right now. Whether it's love—or loss."

"I want to *be* with you."

"It's too late, Will. Can't you understand that? It's just too late." She began to shake her head. "Go meet your daughter. Pull your life together, and make a huge success of it." She picked up a pencil. Will thought for an instant that Annie was intending to write something on the yellow pad before her, but instead she drew one square, then another, and another, and another, all of them interlocking. "Damn you," she said softly. "Damn you, damn you, damn you."

He sat there like a stone, feeling damned.

She looked up. "Why didn't you say any of this before? Why save this for now, when it's too late? Or was that the point? Maybe this isn't about loss. Maybe you're one of those guys who won't say what's in his heart—doesn't even know—until it's too late. Until it doesn't matter anymore."

"No."

"Maybe this is how you push me away and still feel good about yourself."

"I feel awful, Annie."

"Go," she commanded.

He stood.

She said, "Right *now* you feel terrible. We both do. But what about tomorrow? How will you feel then? Maybe this is your way of running away from the pain and still getting to let yourself off the hook. Which is something I get the feeling you're pretty good at."

He stood there and absorbed her anger. She had a right to it, as far as he was concerned. And yet, in his heart, he thought she was all wrong. At the door, he said, "I won't argue with you. But understand one thing: I'll never let myself off the hook. Not about us."

She put down the pencil. Then she picked it up, tapped it lightly on the pad. Then she looked up at Will, and flung the pencil at him from across the room.

WILL COULDN'T SAY what, exactly, he had expected of St. Jerome's Infant and Maternity Home. An ivy-covered brick mansion, perhaps, a New World version of Miss Clavell's Parisian boarding school for girls in the Madeline books? Certainly not the fortress-like monument to the fifties that stood framed in his rearview mirror, with its grid of tiny windows and the cube-shaped chapel elevated on pillars above the entryway. He sat parked in his car in St. Jerome's sunny lot, and consumed the last bites of a ham-and-cheese sub as he thought about the conversation ahead, all the while lamenting that he hadn't asked the Sandwich Man to hold the raw onions. In the glove box he found a packet of Tic Tacs with two remaining. Both were permanently glued to the bottom of the plastic container.

St. Jerome's would be immaculately clean, of course. It would smell like Will's Catholic grammar school, the linoleum hallways buffed to a glossy shine with some cleaning product that was used throughout the diocese. It struck Will as odd that there were so few cars in the spacious lot. In this age of rampant unwed motherhood, wouldn't a place like this be fully booked? But then he realized that St. Jerome's was a relic of another time, and that he was of that time, when the stigma of unwed pregnancy was so embarrassing to a

Catholic family that a pregnant daughter had to spend most of her term in hiding.

Will checked his watch: five to one. He took a sip of warm ginger ale, swished it around in his mouth, and swallowed quickly. Then he stepped out into the hot sun.

The director's office was near the front entrance. The door was standing open. In the outer room, a white-haired woman was crouched at an open file cabinet. She wasn't a nun. Will saw that right off. A lay worker, he figured: a woman whose houseful of kids was grown and gone, whose husband had passed away, and who now had dedicated her life to the Church. When he knocked at the open doorway, the woman spun around with alarm.

"I didn't mean to startle you," said Will. "I have a one o'clock appointment with Sister Catherine."

"It's one already?" The woman struggled to her feet. "Let me see if she's free."

No sooner had Will settled himself on a shiny vinyl couch than a door directly in front of him flew open, and a woman who had to be Sister Catherine marched toward him. She wore regular clothes—a simple gray dress—no jewelry, and a wide white headband that pinned back her hair, which was reddish brown with streaks of gray.

"Mr. Gerard?" He leapt to his feet. Sister Catherine's grip was like a vise as she pulled him toward her office. "Have a seat," she said, pointing to a wooden chair that faced her desk. Will sat. On the desk there were crosses, some standing upright and others laying flat, and a collection of miniature statues, a bust of Pope John XXIII, a large thorn suspended in Lucite, which magnified Sister Catherine's right hand to grotesque proportions when she took a seat behind it.

"Mr. Conroy is a dear friend of ours," she began. "I take it he must be a friend of yours as well?"

"An acquaintance," said Will. "A good friend of a friend."

Francis X. Conroy, Esquire, was a long-time member of the board of trustees of Catholic Charities. He also happened to be Marianne and Tom's next-door neighbor. Teddy mowed his lawn. For years he had acted as Fran Conroy's computer consultant and St. Patrick's Day bartender. And so, hours earlier, Teddy called him and asked him if he might be able to set up a meeting for Will at St. Jerome's. "A favor for friend in need," Teddy had explained.

Sister Catherine said, "This morning on the telephone I told Fran—and I should begin by telling you, Mr. Gerard—that there is very little I can do for you beyond explaining the search procedure. We have an information sheet. I could have faxed that to you and saved time for both of us."

"Do you get many requests?" he asked.

"Many, many, many." She smiled wearily. One front tooth was slightly discolored. "I view this as testimony to all the young women and children St. Jerome's has assisted over the years."

"How many years is that?"

She studied him. "Have you been here before, Mr. Gerard?"

"No."

"Perhaps you should begin by telling me how I can help you."

"I am looking for my birth daughter," he said.

"Are you familiar with the search process?"

Will shook his head. "I've literally just begun."

"Why did you wish to see me?"

He recalled Fran Conroy's words of advice, delivered to Teddy: "You can't fool this lady, but I'd advise your friend to tell her the truth as slowly as possible."

"I believe the girl's mother spent the last months of her pregnancy here."

Sister Catherine studied him. "You're not certain of that?"

"Close to certain," said Will.

"You will find this helpful."

She handed him the information sheet, prepared in a question-and-answer format. A glance at the questions, and Will saw that it contained all the information that a person in his situation would need to know. He looked up. "Sister Catherine, do you know my mother, Mary Gerard?"

She seemed puzzled.

"She lives in Charles County. St. Ignatius Parish. She supports a number of Catholic institutions," said Will. "I thought you might know her."

The nun smiled. "I should like to know her."

"But you don't?"

"Mr. Gerard, were you involved in the adoption decision?"

He took a moment, then shook his head.

"Is your name on the original birth certificate?"

"I'm not certain."

"Usually that means no."

He waited.

"If your name doesn't appear on the original birth certificate, then you would need the birth mother's cooperation for any sort of search."

"I understand," he said.

"Is she willing?"

"I'm not certain."

"Have you asked her?"

"Not directly," he said.

"Mr. Gerard—"

"I just got in touch with her, Sister. Yesterday. We hadn't spoken in twenty years. Her name is Lucy Vitava."

The nun's face gave away nothing. She said, "As the sheet I gave you explains, birth parents seeking to locate a child whom they have placed with an adoptive family have two search options."

Will stared blankly at the sheet for a moment, then looked up at Sister Catherine. "Do the children who were born here ever come back?"

She nodded slowly. "Of course," she said.

"Could you tell me if a young woman named Charlotte Cameron has come here seeking information about her birth parents?"

"No."

"No she *hasn't,* or no you *can't?*"

Sister Catherine pursed her lips. "Let me finish," she said. "Birth parents can seek non-identifying information about a birth child. The occupation of the adoptive parents, for example. Or else they may initiate a full search for the purpose of reunification; that is, a face-to-face meeting. For that, a birth parent would need to petition the court in the jurisdiction—"

"I won't need to do that."

The nun looked puzzled.

"I know where she is. My birth daughter, I mean. At least I think I do. The reason I came here is to see where she was born. To verify that this *is* where she was born, I mean. And learn something about her. Anything, really."

The nun sat there with a bland expression. "To initiate a full search a birth parent would need to petition the courts in the jurisdiction where the adoption was finalized to have the adoption files opened. That can take some time."

"I'm assuming that my birth daughter could do this, too?"

Sister Catherine nodded. "An adoptee must be eighteen if acting alone."

"How much information might the adoptive parents receive at the time of the adoption?"

"It can depend."

"Might they be told that the birth mother was an orphan?"

She nodded.

"Or that a grandfather had died in the Vietnam War?"

"Technically, no. But those of us involved in this ministry are human beings, Mr. Gerard. I won't say that it's impossible."

"Would they have access to any information about the birth father—about me—if my name isn't on the original birth certificate?"

"Unlikely," replied Sister Catherine, "but again, it all would depend upon the circumstances, I suppose. I can't say that it's impossible."

Will sat forward. He put his hands on the edge of the desk. "I was away at college, Sister. When Lucy was pregnant. I believe that she went to my mother. I believe that my mother brought Lucy here."

But even as he was speaking, Will realized this statement could not possibly be true: his mother had never set foot inside this building. He couldn't say why he knew this, nor what had prompted the revelation. Perhaps it was a sudden realization that Lucy would never have asked his mother for help, or that his mother wouldn't have accompanied her here. Or else a sudden awareness that if his mother had come with Lucy to St. Jerome's—had once sat in this same chair—she would have experienced the loss of this child so directly that she would never have been able to keep this secret all these years.

Sister Catherine stood. "Mr. Gerard, I'm afraid that is all I can tell you."

Will remained in his seat. He gazed at the wall behind Sister Catherine's desk, at the two bookshelves filled with binders, and between them, the dozen framed photographs. Most were groupings of people, priests and nuns, some in clerical dress and habit. There were names handwritten beneath in black ink. Will imagined religious retreats, workshops, farewell picnics. His brain was a muddle. He suddenly lost heart. Perhaps he was all wrong. For all he knew, his reason for coming here had nothing to do with the hunch that Charlotte was his child. Maybe it was penance: a sense of guilt and shame blown all out of proportion. It was possible that Lucy was never pregnant, or else she was coming to his mother's house that day in August to tell him that she had had an abortion. Or—

"Feel free to call me directly if you have any further questions, Mr. Gerard." Sister Catherine stood at the open door.

Will got to his feet. "Perhaps I'm wrong. You see, I was never actually told that Lucy Vitava was pregnant," he said.

"Ah," said the nun.

"These reunions," he went on, "the ones that turn out badly—"

"Could I give you some general advice, Mr. Gerard?"

He nodded.

"Keep in mind that all of this happened a long, long time ago. If there is a child, he or she would be an adult now, with parents, family, a whole life about which you know nothing. A birth parent's relationship to a birth child is real, but limited. These limits will always be there. You must approach this person with the utmost respect, more mindful of his or her needs than your own. Don't ever make the mistake of thinking that somehow you can recapture the past."

"If you were to have a file on a girl born December 23, 1975, to a woman named Lucy Vitava, would you add a note with my name and telephone number, and my wish to meet her?"

"I'm sorry, we have very strict rules."

"She would be my daughter."

"Mr. Gerard—"

"Couldn't you at least tell me whether a child was born on that day?"

"No, I can't. Good day, Mr. Gerard."

Will smiled weakly. It was crazy how he was going about this.

What had he thought he would accomplish coming here? That he would stumble upon some residue of Lucy's sadness, preserved in the hallway all these years beneath a coat of paint? There was only one reason to come to St. Jerome's, and that was to see where she had been, and Charlotte, too; if indeed Lucy had ever been here.

The car, baking in the sun, smelled so strongly of onions that Will had to hunt up a trash can for the bag with the remains of his sandwich, and then head across town with the windows rolled down. He was feeling depressed, in no mood for the long drive to Orange, or the wrestling match with Norton that was certain to ensue over delivery of his manuscript.

Stopped at a light at Dupont Circle, Will reached for the cell phone. Stephanie answered Annie's line.

"Will here. I need a quick word with the boss."

"I'm afraid you're too late. She just walked out the door."

"When do you expect her back?"

"Thursday morning. She's, um, on her way to the airport."

The light changed. Will's car didn't budge until a horn behind him sounded. "Oh, right," he said.

"She'll call in. I'd be happy to give her a message."

Will thought. "Tell her that I'm off to Virginia," he said.

"Sure thing."

"And tell her that I wish she was going with me. *Really* wish she was going with me." In the silence, Will could hear the galloping fingers on Stephanie's keyboard. "Or that I was going with her to Chicago." He paused. "Tell Annie that I know that I've been a fool. And that I would do anything right now to turn back the clock." He took a deep breath. "Tell her I was serious about what I said this morning."

"Got it," said Stephanie brightly.

"Something else."

"What's that?"

"Tell her that I love her. With all my heart."

There was a long moment of stunned silence.

"You bet, Mr. Flood!"

Crossing over the Potomac, Will had the sense that he had forgotten something: eyeglasses, say, or his jacket. Or the bulky leather book that was filled with the addresses and phone numbers of every person in the world of importance to him. But he drove with one hand on the wheel and was able to account for all of those things. What then? He saw himself entering St. Jerome's: empty-handed. He saw himself in the doorway of Sister Catherine's office gazing at the blue and red binders on the bookshelves, noting the religious geegaws on her desk, meeting Sister Catherine's serious gaze, talking to her, listening to her as he gazed at the wall of photographs behind her desk, then being hustled out into the sunshine.

Lucy had gone to his mother's house. She had waited. His mother had come home. Then what happened?

Miles of Route 66 passed beneath his car, as did miles of corrugated concrete walls on both sides of the highway; miles of doubts and regrets, too. Will listened to music on the radio, then to a talk show about the origins of rock 'n' roll, and then to nothing at all. And it was during this stretch of silence that it suddenly dawned on him that helping Lucy would not have required his mother to accompany her to St. Jerome's. Not if she had called on someone else for help.

Of course she had.

All at once it became obvious what had happened, so obvious to Will that he had to wonder why he had thought for an instant that his mother had taken on Lucy's terrible dilemma all by herself.

Teddy put him on hold. Will, at the wheel, stewed. He drove with the phone parked at his ear for one mile, then another.

Simple call waiting was too limiting for Teddy. Two lines and a hold button gave him real options: the conference call, or indulging in his favorite pastime of juggling phone calls, or putting two parties on hold while he wandered off to the kitchen to make himself a baloney sandwich. It went without saying that Teddy had insisted that Will purchase the sort of high-end equipment that would allow him to reenter the conversation without a click or a pop. That moment of return always felt to Will as though Teddy had crept up behind him in the dark, and quietly whispered in his ear.

"Uncle," he said.

Was there another boss in America who allowed himself to be treated like this?

"Exactly how much is this costing me?" asked Will.

"Too much to talk about right now," young Ted replied.

"That better have been New York."

"Well, no," he said. "Toward New York, but not quite so far north."

"Who?"

Teddy sighed. "I took it upon myself to leave a message with the roommate of one of your correspondents."

"Goddamn it, Teddy, you didn't call her!"

"Of course I called her. Someone had to call her. Charlotte Cameron lives in an apartment in College Park. This happens to be exam week at the University of Maryland. For all we know she could be gone tomorrow."

"What did you say?"

"I just left a perfunctory message about how I needed some more information for Mr. Gerard. Please call at your earliest convenience, blah, blah, blah."

Will said, "Put your hand on that stack of *Wired*s next to your desk and swear to me that if Charlotte calls you back, you won't breathe a word of this to her."

"I am the soul of discretion," Teddy replied.

"I have another job for you," said Will. "I need you to find my fourth-grade teacher."

"Who?"

Will said, "A nun. Her name is Sister Mary Bartholomew. That was back then, when she was a Sister of Charity. She left the order. I don't know what her name is now."

Dead silence, the silence of disbelief. "Let me get this straight: you want me to find a nun who isn't a nun whose name you don't know?"

"You got it."

"So what do I do? Take your class picture down to the Bethesda Metro at rush hour, and ask everyone getting off the escalator if they recognize the woman in the habit standing off to the side?" Before Will could reply, Teddy added, "Or maybe I just call the world head-quarters for the Sisters of Charity—"

"The motherhouse."

"Maybe nuns get vested in pension plans like everyone else. Or else Sister Mary Bartholomew—"

"She went by Bart."

"—Sister Mary *Bart* has a pen pal at the motherhouse. Or maybe there's an alumni newsletter. Wait a minute, I could just check their *database*."

"It'll be easier than that," said Will.

Teddy waited.

"She's an old, old friend of Grandmom's."

"You think Grandmom called on her for help?"

"I'm guessing she did."

"So what's our reason for needing to get in touch with your fourth-grade teacher?"

"Sister Mary Bart saw the piece in the *Post*. She's finishing a book on the history of capital punishment. Grandmom thinks she needs an agent."

"So this is a basic business call."

"You got it."

"Here's my question," said Teddy. "Is your love of clandestine activity a *result* of Granddad having spent his career at the CIA, or did Granddad go to work for the CIA *because* the Gerards are genetically predisposed to clandestine activity?"

"You got me."

"I hate lying to Grandmom, Uncle Will. Especially in my own voice." He thought for a moment. "Couldn't I just pretend to be an intern at the motherhouse calling at the behest of Sister Immaculata Hosanna who is putting together an alumni newsletter?"

"Something tells me they don't have male interns working at the motherhouse. Not yet, anyway."

"Then I could get Jill to call."

"Who is Jill?"

"Hold on."

Will was exiled to hold for a few seconds.

Teddy crept up behind him and whispered, "Jill is a person I just met."

"*Another* new friend?"

"Affirmative," replied Teddy. Then, again in a whisper, "We ran into each other this morning on the towpath. Her dog had a cut on its paw. I happened to have a bandanna in my pocket. I was the good Samaritan."

"Still are, from the hushed sound of things," said Will.

"Long John is resting."

"*Long John?*"

"The dog," snapped Teddy. "Long John is the name of the *dog*. Jill and I have just been *talking*."

"With Long John resting, and the Good Samaritan talking, who pray tell is at work?"

"Newt just brought a dead mouse to the front door," Teddy replied.

WILL HAD LEFT Washington under a blue sky. Now there were cottonball clouds in the west, and overhead, a pale blue sky that faded to white in the distance. At the Culpeper exit, Will became so engrossed with the white-capped sky that he missed the turnoff to Orange. The highway passed beneath an overpass and suddenly the Blue Ridge Mountains lay before him, breathtakingly close. The afternoon sun highlighted each peak, each fissured canyon. When the cell phone sounded, Will pulled to the side of the road, less for safety's sake than to savor this view of the mountains.

"Moira Higbee," Teddy announced triumphantly.

"What is this, *Jeopardy?*"

"What is the legal name of the former Sister Mary Bartholomew?" he asked.

"That was quick."

"Because I'm quick," he said. "Grab your pencil and I'll give you her number."

"A Post-It on the refrigerator will do just fine."

"You'll want it now, Uncle. It's an 804 area code."

"Where's that?" asked Will.

"Where are you?"

"Culpeper."

"That means you just left the 703 code, are passing through a short stretch of 540, and about to enter 804. The former Sister Mary Bart lives north of Charlottesville. She's a sociology professor at the University of Virginia. You want to take down the number, Boss, or should I patch you through?"

"Give me the number," said Will.

He punched it in a few seconds later, and took a deep breath. The line rang exactly once.

"Higbee," barked a voice.

"Gerard," Will barked back.

"Gerard who?"

"Gerard comma Will."

He could hear a baby crying in the background, and another woman's voice, cooing. The baby settled down.

"Will Gerard? *You've got to be kidding!*"

"Sister Mary Bart?"

"You rascal."

"How are you?"

"In bedlam. How the heck are you, Will?"

"Hard to complain on a beautiful day when you're sitting at the roadside staring at the Blue Ridge Mountains."

"Where are you?"

"Not far from Charlottesville."

There was a pause. "And why is that?" Another pause. "Don't tell me your dear mother put you up to this!"

"She did mention a book. And I would love to see it." He thought about Fran Conroy's advice to tell the truth, but slowly. "I was on my way to Orange to fetch a manuscript when I discovered that I was in your neighborhood."

"Now how did you happen to discover that?"

"Via my dear sweet mother," he said.

"You tracked me down."

"I cannot tell a lie, Sister. Not to you. Never could."

"What's up?" she asked.

"Could I stop by?"

She went silent.

"Truth is," said Will, "I'd like to talk to you about something that happened a long time ago."

The silence went on and on. In Will's stomach, it felt as though the car had lurched back onto the roadway, but there he sat, gazing out at cottonball clouds and corduroy hills.

"This is a pretty bad time to drop in," she finally said.

"Sis—"

"Mo—Bart to my old friends. Take your pick."

"Ten or fifteen minutes. I promise."

"I don't know, Will."

"Please."

Bart covered the phone and said something. A woman replied. It went back and forth. Finally she came back on the line.

"Straight down Twenty-nine," she said. "Left on Thirty-three, right on Twenty, third left on a gravel road. It's unmarked. Look for it after you pass a dilapidated house with a wrought-iron fence. We're about three-quarters of a mile beyond the top of the first hill, on the right. The name's on the mailbox."

Will never glanced at the directions. Some ancient part of his brain had leapt to attention the instant Bart began issuing instructions. He was transported back in time to every single afternoon of fourth grade: "Homework assignment," Sister Mary Bart would announce. All murmuring would cease. Spelling words, arithmetic problems, a science question: she would recite the assignment just once. Only Ralph DeCosta, who rocked in his seat and would no doubt be diagnosed today as ADHD, received a second, private recitation. After just a week at school, Will found that Sister Mary Bart's words would reverberate inside his head for hours. He never looked at what he had written down. He didn't have to. It was as if his brain had dedicated a special place to store the words uttered by this incomparable voice; and thirty years later he was astonished to discover that this region was still taking messages.

The mailbox resembled a dollhouse: weathered cedar, shingle roof with copper flashing, and an oversized front door to admit the mail. A sign affixed to it read "Higbee/Lang." There was a fresh coating of pea gravel on the long driveway, which looped uphill through hemlocks to a clearing. Every square inch of this clearing, it seemed, had been landscaped with ornamental trees and brilliantly colored flowers. The house set at the center of it had a steeply pitched tin roof, dormer windows, and a wide porch that circled the two sides Will could see. The instant he opened the car door he heard a chorus of dogs: first on the scene was an Australian shepherd, then a mutt with a black Lab or two in the family tree, then a basset hound. A Jack Russell terrier remained on the porch, barking itself in circles without uttering a sound.

Will stood at the car door for a moment to let the hounds run their olfactory inspections; then he started forward. But the basset, who was as big as a pig, pressed his muzzle to Will's kneecap, letting him know without even the hint of a growl that a superior sense of smell required a more thorough examination.

"Help," called Will.

"Ruby, knock it off," came a loud reply.

Will started forward again, and the sheepdog feinted to the right, ready to herd him.

"Help again," he called.

"Ruby, Sapphire, Opal! Back on the porch."

At once, the three dogs sat down. They formed a semicircle between Will and the house. He stopped. Across the lawn, he saw a vegetable garden enclosed by a beautiful fence made from deadfall. At the center was a scarecrow wearing a golden carnival mask.

"Bart," he called. "It's Will."

A screen door slammed, and suddenly she was standing beside the overwrought Jack Russell, which was bouncing like a ball. The former Sister Mary Bart still had those thick dark bangs, but her face was so much softer now, brighter, more open. What an effort it must have been all those years ago to wear the austere expression of a Sister of Charity! Or did she always have this look? Perhaps Will's mental image of her been colored by her voice, which hadn't changed a bit: one snarl from Bart and the dogs seated before him scattered.

She wore blue jeans and a gray flannel shirt, sleeves rolled, no shoes. Her toenails had red polish. Her hands were on her hips. She was grinning.

"Well, well, well," she said. "I guess we've both changed."

"You seem younger now," said Will.

"And you're shaving!"

She came down the steps, took both of Will's hands, studied his face before embracing him in an un-nunlike hug. She held him tightly for a long time.

"How long has it been?" she asked.

"Twenty-one years," he said.

"Your dad's funeral." She shook her head. "Twenty-one years! I felt old then. I feel older now. About a thousand years old." She turned toward the house. "A newborn will do that for you, I guess."

Starting up the steps Will heard the baby cry. It was a piercing wail of profound unhappiness.

"Yours?" he asked.

Bart nodded. She put an arm around his shoulders. "Eight weeks old today," she said.

For a man whose livelihood depended upon the creative juggling of numbers, it was embarrassing how mathematically inept Will could sometimes be when caught off guard without a calculator. While figuring a simple restaurant tip, his mind often slowed to a crawl. So too, now. Bart looked to be in her mid-forties, but she had to be older. Will figured he was ten in fourth grade, which meant that was thirty-one years ago. Sister Mary Bart had to have been at least twenty then. Which would put her in her early fifties now.

So how in heaven's name could she be the mother of an eight-week-old?

She regarded him with a warm smile, the ghost of Sister Mary Bart apparently still able to read his mind. "I'm a parent," she explained. "Not the biological mother. Gerry is Jasper's mother. My partner, Gerry."

"Oh," replied Will.

"I guess your mother never told you that after I left the convent, I came out of the closet."

"It's, um, not the sort of thing I'd forget."

"You're shocked," she said.

"I'm shocked to be calling you Bart."

For the third time in as many minutes he saw that broad Irish grin of hers. This was new. Will simply did not recall this smile from fourth grade.

"Gerry's inside," she said. "I want you to meet her."

The house seemed of a piece with the gardens in that both were meticulously designed, nothing out of place. From outside, this building had seemed like a renovated farmhouse, but inside Will saw that the structure was new. Every surface was smooth, pickle stained or painted with muted greens, grays, or yellows. The layout was modern, and the center stairway was too wide for the late-nineteenth or early-twentieth century. In a den they found Bart's partner seated cross-legged on a couch, nursing the baby.

"Gerry Lang. Will Gerard," Bart said. They nodded to one another. "Oh, and that little bundle of joy and urination is Jasper Lang." She turned to Will. "You've noted the gemstone motif? Had he arrived as a girl we figured we'd be stuck with Rose, for rose quartz, or Morgan, for morganite. I'm afraid we used up the good names with the dogs."

Gerry whispered, "Quiet, now." She rose fluidly, like a cat, carrying Jasper close to her belly as she started up the stairs. Will watched her stockinged feet disappear around the corner. A moment later she returned with a pair of hiking boots in one hand. She retrieved a baby monitor from the kitchen.

"Another time, I hope," she said to Will. "I love to hear about Bart's days of religious disguise."

"I was in the convent," Bart explained. "So well cloistered I didn't even realize that I was in the closet, too."

Gerry smiled the incredulous smile of a woman who has known all her life that she is gay. "That's what they all say," she told Will.

She put an arm around Bart and kissed the side of her head. Bart seemed at once embarrassed and grateful. Gerry handed the monitor to Will.

"In case you two go outside," she said. "Dear Moira forgets."

"A little unhappiness teaches a kid to be assertive," said Bart. "Isn't that right, Will?"

"In fourth grade we all became assertive," he replied.

"Assertiveness training is not something this little boy needs," Gerry said. Then to Bart, "I've got the phone if you need me."

They followed her outside and stood on the porch as she headed across the pea gravel toward a big magnolia. Two cars were parked beneath it, a VW Jetta and an Isuzu Trooper. The Trooper spun up gravel as Gerry sped off down the driveway.

Will said, "Life must be full with a baby on the scene."

"It feels as if Gerry and I haven't had fifteen minutes alone together since Jasper was born." Bart shrugged. "Something every couple goes through, I guess." She rested her hands on the rail. "The upside is that we've been together for seven years, and I've never felt closer to her." She smiled at Will. "Nothing like having a long-term project, I guess."

"Like building a house."

She glanced around. "That only took Gerry three years. Thank heavens she can't make this boy grow any faster than he does."

"So all in all you like being a parent," said Will.

She looked at him for a moment, then looked away. "I'm not one of those women who went to pieces at forty. At forty, I was feeling as though my life had just begun." She paused. "Having Jasper was Gerry's idea. Of course I agreed to go along with it. Not that I wasn't scared: I was. I'm not a natural. But Gerry is." She smiled. "I never did understand it when mothers would talk about how, with infants, you get more than you give. I mean, look at the work—the diapers, the feedings, the baths, all day dressing them and then undressing them, up four times in the middle of the night. It just didn't make sense. Still doesn't." She looked at Will, shrugged. "But it's true."

They walked together to the Jetta, where Bart retrieved a pack of Marlboros from the visor. "Three a day," she said. "This is number two. God and you are my witnesses."

They started across the lawn. Bart took the baby monitor from Will and turned it on: nothing but a low hiss. The sun was out now. They walked past the vegetable garden with its debauched Mardi Gras reveler of a scarecrow in sequined jacket. Ahead was a trellis, thickly draped by a leafy vine with tiny purple flowers, and beneath it, a wooden bench.

"Jasper might give us twenty minutes," said Bart. "If we're lucky." She took a seat and lit a cigarette with a pink Bic lighter.

"Gerry's what?" asked Will. "A designer of some kind?"

"Graphic artist." She blew a plume of smoke away from him. "This is all her doing." She waved her cigarette to indicate the house, the grounds. "I guess that must be obvious."

Will recalled Sister Mary Bart's classroom: uncluttered, orderly, shiny. His mind's eye saw the room in black-and-white, the domain of a young woman who rose from sleep before dawn, immediately made her bed and said her morning prayers.

"We always thought of you as being austere, and more than a little grouchy, but then you would come out to the playground with a basketball and throw us all for a loop."

"The clothes, the lifestyle, closer to Jesus, and all that," replied Bart, with a rueful smile. "I've changed a bit since then. Hope so, anyway."

"Why did you leave?"

"Why did I join?" She shook her head. "I was the oldest kid in the family. My mother and father raised me to become a nun. I couldn't disappoint them." That same rueful smile again. "Turned out that fulfilling one's parents' expectations doesn't qualify for what we nuns used to describe as 'having a vocation.'"

"Was it hard?"

"To leave?" She blew smoke into the leaves above. "It was awful. But I didn't have any choice. I woke up one day and realized that the life I had didn't suit me anymore. Not at all."

Will said, "In third grade, I wanted to be a priest. Fourth, too. But by fifth grade . . . ." He shrugged. "I was too young to understand the implications of a vow of celibacy, but somehow I just lost interest."

"At twenty," said Bart, "I was exactly where I wanted to be."

"I used to pray for you every night. Marianne did, too. We prayed together."

"Fell short on the Hail Marys, apparently," she replied, deadpan.

"What was it like?"

"St. Thérèse wrote, 'We always lived as if we were in a volcano.' That about captures it." Bart turned to Will. "So what's been up with you?"

"This job and that job in and around publishing. What you might call a checkered career. I'm finally doing something that feels as though it might stick."

She looked at Will, her eyes betraying a hint of disbelief. "No wife, no family?"

"No closer than a few years living in sin."

"Ah, well, let's both hope that the Creator is as forgiving as Jesus would have us believe."

"I suspect my mother might point out that you don't have an alternative, whereas I do."

"Funny thing," said Bart. "She has." A wide grin now.

There was a piercing cry on the monitor, then windy static. A fraction of a second later they heard the same cry from Jasper through an open window. Then he quieted.

"Sometimes it's only gas," Bart said wearily.

Jasper roared.

"And sometimes it's not."

They started toward the house, Jasper's cries in the monitor reaching them just ahead of his voice out the window, doubling and echoing his fury, which sounded wounded now, though apparently it must have been normal, as Bart didn't pick up the pace.

The nursery was pale blue with billowy, cream-colored curtains. Jasper's crib and changing table were bright white, the rug on the floor a mottled, cloudlike gray. Bart lifted the angry baby to her shoulder, and softly cooed at him, but he was not mollified, not for an instant: what he wanted she did not have. She rocked him and rocked him, and he screamed and screamed. Will followed her down the hallway and through a messy bedroom to a small balcony. Outside in the breeze, Jasper suddenly quit crying. You saw the grown man in the baby's face right then, in his downturned lips and petulant chin. In a moment an amazing set of light blue eyes fluttered open. They were magnified by his tears. Jasper was perched on Bart's shoulder, peering at Will like some strange creature from Dr. Seuss.

"He thinks I'm an alien," said Will.

"Well, around here," replied Bart, not finishing the thought. She turned. "Maybe we should get right to why you drove out here, Will."

He detected impatience in her voice. He recalled this impatience from the classroom. It was not to be trifled with. Telling the truth slowly was no longer an option. Bart knew why he had come to see her, and she wanted Will to get on with it.

"A hunch," he said. "I came because of a hunch." Bart's mouth tightened. "I think I'm a father," he went on. "I think I have a daughter who is a grown woman. Only I'm not one hundred percent sure of that. About ninety percent. Maybe ninety-five percent."

She waited.

"When I was in college, I slept with a woman whom I had known in Bangkok when we were kids. I think she got pregnant. I think she gave up the baby for adoption."

"Have you talked to her?"

"Yes."

"What did she say?"

"I didn't ask directly."

"Why not?"

Will looked out at the scarecrow. From above he could see that it had been propped up on a couple of bales of hay, one arm resting on a tomato stake. Then he looked at Bart. "I'm not sure. Still in shock, I guess. I only found out about this four days ago."

Bart looked right through Will.

"Her name is Lucy," he said. "Lucy Vitava. I think my mother helped her."

"Why do you think that?"

"Because Lucy came to the house soon after I'd left for school."

"Did you ask your mother?"

He shook his head.

"So what do you want to know from me?"

"Whether I'm right."

"Why should I know the answer to that, Will?"

"My mother talks to you."

"Well, she didn't."

"I was a coward," said Will. "I ran away."

Bart gazed out at the magnolia tree. And then softly: "I know," she said.

He looked at her, and suddenly couldn't think of another thing to say.

"Your mother didn't say anything to me. She didn't have to. You see, I was there. I was living in the barn that summer. That was the summer I left the convent."

"You saw Lucy?"

Bart shook her head. "I need to talk to her first."

Will said, "All I want is to know that it happened."

Suddenly there were tears in Bart's eyes. Will looked away, gazed down at an azalea that had begun to shed its dirty white blossoms.

"I've been to St. Jerome's," he said. "Talked to Sister Catherine. An informational interview. Sitting in her office, I somehow knew that my mother had never been in that room. And that if Lucy went there, she didn't go by herself."

Bart said, "The first thing you have to understand is that that was another lifetime. There's no other way to describe it. Right before I left the convent, when I called my parents to tell them what I was planning to do, they started crying. Both of them. They went into mourning. You would have thought I had died—I felt as if I *had* died. I couldn't go home. Your mother was there for me. She made me come live with her. She lent me money for college that fall. I would have done anything for her."

Will waited.

"When I was a kid, the nuns told us that life was a long, steep flight of stairs that you had to walk up. Toward heaven, of course. Toward God. The focus was on choice, on exercising one's volition. Moving forward. Doing the right thing. But you know something, Will? It's just not true. Life isn't a flight of stairs. It's an escalator. Sometimes you wish you could get off, and then you discover that you can't, or not when you want to. What you think you should do isn't always the same as what you do, and even looking back on the things you regret, sometimes you just can't figure how you would have done anything differently." She looked at him. "Lucy needed help. I couldn't refuse."

"My mother called you?"

She shook her head.

Will was baffled. "What happened?"

"I made a promise. I need to think about this."

Suddenly Jasper was in his arms and Bart was gone. Will stood there, dreaming again of that long ago day. *She came to the house, she waited, she saw my mother* . . . This scenario had played in his head so many times now it seemed as real as a piece of film. He saw Lucy's VW Bug parked in the shade, his mother arriving home, encountering Lucy on the patio; he imagined them talking at the kitchen table, then Mary going to her office, picking up the telephone, calling Bart—

What did it mean that Bart was involved, but his mother had not called on her for help?

Jasper regarded Will with a crooked smile—it was a facial expression that might be categorized as a smile, anyway. Then it quickly transformed into a deeply primal look. His face went pink, then beet red, then it felt to Will as if Jasper's rear end had suddenly erupted. Will called out to Bart at the very instant the screen door slammed. The house was quiet again. Jasper smiled. Definitely a smile this time. There is a God, thought Will. This was penance.

From the window of the little boy's bedroom Will could see Bart beneath the trellis, furiously lighting up cigarette number three.

At the changing table, he took a deep breath and gently set Jasper on his back. The whole room smelled of warm yogurt. Will took another deep breath, positioned a black-and-white patterned mobile over the boy's face in the hope that it might keep him occupied, then went to work. He felt like a surgeon. And scrub nurse.

Jasper's clothing amazed Will: when he located the row of snaps on the smart little outfit, it came apart like a sprinter's warm-up suit. He opened the box of towelettes and peeled off a dozen, stepped open the diaper pail and the hamper. A farmhand shearing a fidgety lamb would have had an easier time than Will had cleaning up this uncooperative boy. Jasper wriggled and kicked; he flailed his arms; he went rigid. Will had broken into a sweat long before he had even figured out how to reattach the Velcro tabs of a fresh diaper. How tight should it be cinched? And how to get this tiny T-shirt over such a large, wobbly head? How to make those small, pumping arms thread the narrow sleeves of a tiny orange UVA pullover?

At last he had the boy clothed, at last his own hands and fingernails were clean, at last the lids on the hamper and diaper pail were clamped shut, at last Will was breathing normally again. He marveled that Jasper hadn't cried out once during their struggle. He felt proud of himself for this, as if Jasper's silence reflected some measure of trust that the little boy had had in him. He marveled, too, at the focus he'd had for this job. No manuscript ever got that much of his attention. Thoughts of Bart beneath the trellis, fretting and smoking as she tried to decide what to tell him, had simply vanished from his mind. The Zen of babies, Will thought. You feed them and care for their every need, and in return they teach you to live in the moment.

He had Jasper nestled in the crook of his arm when the little boy's lip curled upward in another smiling grimace, and he farted, softly this time. Very softly, Will told himself, so softly as to hardly be considered a fart at all. He hurried down the steps and out the front door as fast as caution would let him go, to deliver this boy with the volatile bowels into the arms of one of his mommas.

Bart held Jasper face down, right hand supporting his chest, his head resting in the crook of her left arm. She spoke to Will at the window of his car.

"To be honest I've thought about trying to contact Lucy over the years. Dozens of times. To try to convince her to talk to you." Jasper fussed, and Bart shifted him to the other arm. "The fact is, with this sort of promise, there has to be a statute of limitations. Back then it was Lucy's decision. But now you have a right to know. This child has a right to know." She looked at Will. "Yes, she was pregnant. She went to your mother's house looking for you, and found me instead. She needed help. I gave her help. I called St. Jerome's. Lucy and I went there together. She was counseled. Adoption was her decision."

"And my mother?"

Bart shook her head. "Lucy didn't want her to know. She didn't want anyone to know. I stayed with her through the delivery. After that, she wouldn't talk to me. She left the hospital the next day. I never spoke with her again."

"The baby was a girl?"

She nodded.

Jasper opened his eyes, and just stared at Will.

"Born at Christmastime. Two days before. A beautiful kid. Seven pounds, ten ounces. Nineteen and a half inches. Thick dark hair. I will never forget that baby as long as I live." Bart's eyes filled with tears. "I don't know what else to tell you, Will, except that I'm sorry. But there was nothing else I could have done."

THE TWO-LANE ROAD to Orange was bordered on both sides by white fences, veering left and right, up and down, through darkened woods and open pasture, mile after mile. Soon the fences gave way to screens of scrub cedar that were interspersed with perfectly spaced bradford pear trees rising from islands of mulch. A mileage sign put Will about twenty minutes from Ruthie's motel. I have a daughter, he thought. A twenty-year-old daughter. The words played in his mind like the scrap of a song.

At Montpelier, he pulled off the road and stopped in front of an old gas station that had been converted into a gift shop, the ancient faded Esso sign still hanging. He took out the cell phone and called home.

"I am dripping wet," Teddy droned. "I have a towel around my waist. There is shampoo in my hair. The only reason I got out of the shower to answer the phone is because I figured it had to be you."

Will glanced at the clock. It was almost six-thirty. A shower before dark could only mean one thing: young Theo had another date. Two dates in three days! "You've got plans tonight, I take it?"

"No comment."

"Would these plans include the aforementioned Jill?"

"In a word, yup."

Two dates with two different women in three days!

Teddy sighed. But this sigh was expansive, so steeped in pride that Will felt obliged to beg his soapy nephew for a full report.

The thing was, Teddy explained, he and Jill weren't complete strangers. They had attended the same high school, a fact which Jill apparently didn't recall (and Teddy, being two years younger, thought best not to mention). He had recognized her at fifty yards on the towpath: the auburn hair and red lipstick, the histrionics over injured Long John. Jill looked like someone trying out for a play. But then she had always looked like someone trying out for a play. In high school she had been a theater person. High-strung, to put it mildly. Enormously appealing, too, at least in Teddy's eyes. And magnificently unapproachable. Her boyfriends tended to be the men of Teddy's school: the guys with cars, the guys who were shaving every day at sixteen, the baritones and jocks. All of this had flashed through Teddy's mind as he approached Jill on the towpath, Jill on one knee wailing about poor wounded Long John.

The cut on the pad of Long John's paw wasn't deep, nor did it bleed excessively. But this didn't stop Teddy from wrapping it in the bandanna that he happened to have in his pocket (Julianna's red bandanna, he informed Will), and carrying the little mutt a half mile back to the house, Jill beside him the whole way, so emotionally drained by the ordeal that she finally had to take Teddy's arm.

He could have walked like this for days.

Immediately Long John curled up on a pillow and drifted off into a deep sleep from which Jill was loathe to wake him, which meant she and Teddy spent most of the afternoon together. She walked around the house, gazing in wonder at all the books, and at the stacks of manuscripts, all of which she blithely assumed would one day be transformed into books. (Seeing her excitement at finding herself in a place where books were actually *born*, Teddy elected not to explain that most of these manuscripts were unsolicited, and so in all likelihood were destined for the landfill.)

Jill was a junior at Frostburg State, a communications major. So Teddy impressed her with his communications skills: telephone calls to and from his boss on the road, heated conversations with Very

Important Editors and Publishers in New York City. In between Jill talked about herself. She mentioned the existence of a young man named Kenny, a football player at Frostburg State. Sort of a boyfriend, she explained. The tight end and the leading lady, the First Couple of Frostburg: Teddy got the picture.

Ex-boyfriend, that is: Jill announced that she was furious at Kenny.

Teddy offered her a beer, which Jill wanted to split. He did not admit to brewing this beer himself, somehow realizing that Jill would be more impressed by an exotic import. The label he had designed for this batch (called Bad Aussee, after a town in Austria) looked like any other professional microbrew. Jill had admired it. All at once it struck Teddy as the creation of a nerdy kid who spent way too much time on his hobbies.

"This tastes wonderful," she said. "Where did you get it?"

A shrug. "It's not sold over here, sorry to say." A smile. "I happen to know the guy who brews it."

They split another Bad Aussee and sat together on the couch. Jill was telling Teddy about Kenny when the phone rang. That Teddy ignored the phone, ignored it absolutely, brought a smile to her face. She told him that her parents were away for two weeks; she was housesitting for them. Alone. Her leg touched his. Oh, and she was definitely finished with Kenny—Kenny whose major life goal was to be drafted by the Green Bay Packers, and who had been spotted in a bar in Cumberland the previous night with a cheerleader sitting on his lap. Jill had gotten this news from a friend that very morning. The telephone call had prompted the hike on the towpath, which meant the injury to Long John's paw could be blamed on Kenny, too. Her anger was of the soap-opera variety: all gritted teeth and venom. Small, pretty teeth, Teddy couldn't help but note. He didn't know what to say to her—certainly not what was on his mind—so he opted for *supportive*.

"Sounds to me like this guy ought to have his head examined."

Jill beamed. She thanked him with a hand on his arm. The hand moved.

Then suddenly she had to check on Long John. Still asleep, she reported a moment later. Sound asleep. There were three messages on the machine.

"Don't you need to get them, Ted?"

"In a minute. They won't go anywhere."

She was like a cat, coming toward him and then veering off to look at a bird on the window feeder, at the cover of the latest *New Yorker,* at a piece of wood that stood in the corner of the room that had been sculpted by Teddy's mother, which Teddy didn't mention, since he had also neglected to mention to Jill that the guy he worked for was his uncle. Teddy simply watched her, and somehow his watching her brought her back to the couch. She was leaning against him now, then threw her head back and sighed. "*Quel jour!*" she exclaimed. First the news about Kenny and then this! "Relax, relax," said Teddy, and damned if Jill didn't do just that. One moment her eyes were open and next she had drifted off to sleep! Teddy stared at his new friend a bit longer than would have been considered polite, wondering what he should do, wondering and wondering until finally coming around to the obvious conclusion that there was nothing to do but let the poor woman sleep. He covered her with a cotton blanket and turned down the ringer on the telephone.

When Jill finally awoke Teddy was at work, lost in thought at the computer while composing a professionally admiring letter to the next William T. Vollmann. Jill walked up behind him and rested her hands on his shoulders. He was in the middle of a brilliantly convoluted sentence that he would never find his way to the end of again, were he not to get the words down now, so that's what he did. He didn't turn around when Jill touched him, nor even when she caressed his neck, didn't even start, *as if he'd been expecting this all along!* Which turned out to be just the right response, he was astonished to discover, as Jill kissed his neck, then his ear. Teddy's fingers flew over the keyboard, flew and flew until Jill kissed him on the lips. What else could she do, a long, sweet kiss being the only way to get this distracted guy to close his file?

"Come, let's sit on the couch, Ted."

Thank God for that failing grade in linguistics, he thought. Thank God for academic probation! And for the good fortune of having a pushy mom! And for Uncle Will, too, for his caving in to his sister's demand that he hire me, and for choosing this day of all days to drive off into the Virginia countryside! Thank God, too, for that two-timing bastard Kenny, and for the accident-prone, comatose Long John!

Will interrupted the reverie: "So what, if anything, has been happening on the work front?"

"Forget about it," replied the soapy Teddy. "You just don't want to know."

But he did. Or felt obliged to pretend he did, anyway.

Rita Corelli was looking for him—no great surprise. Apparently she was not content to sit quietly at her desk to await news of Norton's manuscript.

"The woman must be lonely," Teddy complained. "She's called me eighteen times this afternoon."

"*Eighteen* times?"

"Four," said Teddy. The other line sounded. "Five," he added. "Guaranteed."

"Beam her up, Scottie."

"Will! Will! Is that you?" Rita sounded as though she was calling from a window ledge.

"Rita! How are you?"

"I'm awful. I'm terrible. I couldn't be worse."

"Why? What's up?"

"Have you talked to Norton?"

"Within moments. I'm about ten miles from Norton's trailer as we speak."

There was a long pause. "You never, ever told me that he lived in a trailer, Will. You hid that from me."

"I don't recall that you asked."

Another pause. "Is it *silver*?"

"Light yellow. With a small patio and a flower bed. It's nice. Think of it as a boat for someone who lives in the mountains. Would it bother you if I told you that Norton lived on a houseboat?"

"A houseboat sounds intentional, Will. A trailer—I don't know—a trailer just seems like where somebody ends up after a string of bad luck."

"He had the family mansion, but got tired of keeping it up, so he sold it to his nephew along with the family newspaper. The trailer is rent-free in exchange for Norton keeping an eye on things at the airport."

"He lives at an airport?"

"An airstrip."

"Jeez," she said. "I asked you if this guy could go on the road and you absolutely *swore* to me that he could."

"I did and he can," replied Will, thinking, I will go with him.

"He called," she said.

"Norton called you?"

"Twice."

"He called you himself?" Ruthie had always been Will's conduit to Norton; it simply never occurred to him that Norton might know how to make a long distance telephone call. "What did he say?"

"Well," she said. "I was getting a little antsy. We're about to have our positioning meetings for the new catalog. I had to know where things stood. Word came down from Kathie that we had to have the completed manuscript. *Really* had to have it."

Will had a sinking feeling.

"Did you get that, Will?"

"What you're saying is that *you* called him."

"*Really, really* have to have it," said Rita.

"You didn't threaten Norton by any chance, did you?"

She was quiet.

"You got him pissed off, didn't you?"

"He called me back. He kept saying he was only a half day away *if the rail lines hadn't been cut.*"

"He talked about rail lines?"

"Does that mean he's coming here?"

"Of course not." Will paused to consider the truthfulness of this statement. "Norton hates long-distance travel," he said. And then: "New York City is the last place in the world Norton Tazewell would go all by himself." He took a breath. "Did he say anything about the manuscript?"

"I didn't get most of what he was saying. That accent." A pause. "He did write those hundred pages I read, didn't he, Will? You're willing to take an oath that he wrote the entire thing?"

"Every single word. Writers are quirky. We know that. It's the professional cross we have to bear."

"I just keep wishing this guy was a little more mainstream."

"No, no, no," Will scolded. "Mainstream is exactly what we don't want. The fact that Norton is offbeat will be an *asset*. He'll make Shelby Foote look like David McCullough."

"That's exactly what I'm afraid of."

"Take the long view, Rita. This book is going to sell and sell. Trust me. You'll be sick of telling the story about how it happened that you published it."

"Either that or I'll be sick of job hunting." Then softly: "It's a whole new culture around here. We're not book publishers anymore. We're *content providers*."

"A flock of blackbirds. Keep your head down and they'll be gone before you know it."

She sighed.

"Here's the plan," said Will. "Tonight I meet with Norton and collect the manuscript. Tomorrow I walk through it from *A* to *Z*, and off it goes to you. Thursday morning it's on your desk."

"You make it sound so easy. What if he's already gone?"

"He can't be gone. He's hosting the weekly poker game tonight."

There was another long pause.

"Will, promise me that you never gave this guy my home address."

"Never did."

"And swear to me that you'll call if he has left town."

"Immediately."

Teddy stepped out from his hiding place the instant Rita signed off. "Smooth," he said. "Not that she bought any of it."

"Nobody likes an eavesdropper, young man."

"Amanuensis," Teddy replied. "I looked it up. It's from Latin: *servus a manu*—slave at hand. This slave at hand thinks you're being much too nice to that woman. She needs to be barked at."

"Barking's not my style."

"Balls," said Teddy. "Anyway, it's not like I wanted to listen; I had to listen so that I'd know when you were done. I figured you might want the news that Ruthie called to tell you that she's had a *bad time of it* with Norton's manuscript. That's a quote."

"Shit," said Will. "Do me a favor and call Dewey—"

"I can't. I'm running late." Pause. "If this blows up with Jill because you made me work, I will never, ever, ever forgive you."

"Can't happen," said Will.

"Dear Abby you're not, Uncle."

"No, but I have had some experience. The main thing to realize right now is that you aren't completely in charge. There's a whole lot of luck involved. Fate, too. So rinse the soap out of your hair and push the envelope."

"To tell you the truth, I'm tired of pushing envelopes."

Will laughed. "Just enjoy yourself, kid. And try not to get too upset if things don't work out as you'd hoped. Life has a way of torpedoing your fondest dreams."

"What does that mean?"

"In my case it means that Annie has flown off to Chicago. It seems the law firm is going to make her an offer."

"She's really moving to Chicago?"

"Her sister lives there. The sister with the four-month-old baby."

"What will you do?"

"Carry on," said Will. "What else can I do?"

"Beats me. I'm still stuck at the part about how you get a woman to like you."

"You don't. That's something that either happens or else it doesn't. It's not up to you. Timing counts for everything."

"I'll try to remember that."

"Hold down the fort," said Will. "And go easy on the aftershave. And don't forget that on first dates, nonchalance counts for a lot. You have fun tonight."

"Chin up, Uncle. Life is full of surprises. That's what you're always telling me, anyway."

"Here's one," said Will. "The surprise that's no surprise. The former Sister Mary Bart answered the question: Lucy *was* pregnant. And the baby was born two days before Christmas. A girl. She was adopted by a couple from southern Maryland. He was a history professor at a small college. Bart never got his last name."

"Cameron," said Teddy. "Dr. Roger Cameron. Professor emeritus from St. Mary's College." Will's heart was in his throat as he waited for Teddy to continue. "I just got off the phone with her." Pause. "Charlotte's her given name. But she goes by Jodie." Another pause. "Jodie Cameron sounds like a very nice person."

"What did you say to her?"

"I asked how the writing was going. She got a little embarrassed and admitted that most of what she had written was still in diary form. I asked her to tell me about the story, how much research she intended to do, her family background, all that stuff."

Will waited some more.

"Vietnam War doesn't mean *Vietnam*, Uncle. Turns out what Jodie's parents heard was that her birth mother's father was a pilot who went missing in Laos."

There were rocking chairs on the porch of the old gas station, quilts and stained glass hanging in the windows, petunias in wooden barrels where the gas pumps once stood. After Teddy signed off, Will stepped out of his car. He stood beside it as though waiting for an attendant. His mind wandered. First he thought about Charlotte Cameron—*my daughter Jodie.* He tried to imagine what he would say to her, whether there was anything he could say to bridge twenty years. Her lifetime. Then he thought about Bart, the former nun and fourth grade teacher, now a mother, lover, and scholar of capital punishment. Bart was living proof that people can change, that with enough luck and perseverance any lost soul might eventually stumble upon the right path. It gave Will comfort to imagine life not as something fashioned, but located. Perhaps somewhere in his brain, too, was a tiny lodestone that would guide him, if only he would allow it. Across the road, in a leafless black walnut, he spotted a red-tailed hawk sitting upright, perfectly still. He thought, maybe we humans are no different than the birds and the fishes, all of us headed off on one migration or another, blissfully unaware of being launched on a journey at all.

Will drove on, his mind's eye now fixed on young Teddy, who at this very moment would be back in the bathroom, his chin aimed at the mirror, shaving for the second time today. Shaving and practicing various expressions of nonchalance.

Luck, thought Will: not timing; just luck.

It wasn't as if Teddy's good fortune of the past few days had been earned, nor had he suddenly blossomed into a suave young man; rather, the wheel of life had simply clicked to a stop on his number. Twice in three days his number had come up. This was how Teddy viewed his good fortune, too, which meant that any consideration of it during that long, glorious afternoon with Jill was immediately displaced by the thought that his luck could go sour in a heartbeat. So too now, mugging it up at the bathroom mirror: Teddy was terrified that the suave alter ego who had courted Jill so ably while Long John slept might desert him the instant she returned. He took a deep breath and reminded himself that the earlier suaveness wasn't suaveness at all. That was fear, too. Fear that, miraculously, had presented itself as an appealing sort of insouciance.

With Jill there had been kissing on the couch, lots of kissing, kissing that was constantly interrupted by the ringing telephone. This was a huge annoyance to Teddy, until the third or fourth interruption, when he realized that each time they resumed kissing, Jill's ardor was stepped up a notch. After a brief shouting match with Rita Corelli, Jill met him in the doorway of Will's office and locked a leg around the back of his as she kissed him hungrily. She had made these wonderful cat noises in her throat, and then pulled away suddenly and announced that she had to leave. "To feed Long John," she explained. "He hasn't even had lunch."

On the porch, she turned suddenly. "So, um, do you have plans tonight?"

Teddy pretended to think. "Hadn't gotten that far," he managed.

"Well, maybe we could have dinner together."

"Sure," replied Teddy. His voice sounded nonchalant, even to himself. "If you're free."

Jill smiled triumphantly. "You goofball! Why would I be asking if I wasn't free?"

"Beats me," said Teddy, furious with himself for being unable to think of anything else to say.

The phone rang.

"Shouldn't you get that?"

"It'll wait."

"What if it's your boss?"

"Then he'll wait. I want to finish this conversation with you."

"Well, I am free," she said. "Only I don't feel like going out. And I don't like to cook." This was a huge dilemma, her pout suggested. "I guess you don't cook?"

"Sure I do."

Sure I do?

Where in heaven's name had these words come from? Sure I do? This from a fellow who, both times he had hefted it, had been stunned by the weight of his uncle's cast iron skillet. A young man who would all but panhandle to avoid having to prepare his own dinner! Teddy was like a dog at the kitchen door the evenings Will was home. He called his mother routinely at six-thirty p.m. to find out what was on the stove at her house. He ate there often enough that Marianne always set a place for him.

"I guess you don't cook?"

"Sure I do."

Teddy worked as a volunteer at the food co-op up the street, not for any left-leaning political reasons, and not to save 20 percent on purchases there (most of which were made by his uncle, anyway), but in order to be with people who had a deep interest in the subject of food, always with the fervent hope (again, like a dog at the kitchen door) that someone might take him home and throw an extra tofu kabob on the grill for a hungry boy.

As Julianna had done two days earlier.

Teddy sat for twenty minutes on the front steps with Long John in his lap while Jill went to retrieve Daddy's Volvo, all the while wondering if fate had delivered him to this glorious and terrifying moment. *Sure I do,* he had told her. So by golly, he would. He planned the dinner with the small hound in his lap: chicken, pasta, salad, wine, Ben & Jerry's ice cream. Chicken with *something*. Arugula in the salad. Artichoke hearts, too. Red, orange, green, and yellow fusilli, his mother's dinner party staple.

The meal wasn't fussed over or fine-tuned, not for an instant. Nor, with this menu, would Teddy be slaving over a hot oven. If he fired up the grill at all it would be to scorch a few mesquite chips to bring the faint smell of the Old West into the house, but that was it. Chicken would be the main course because Teddy knew that on the other side of the Aqueduct bridge there was a guy who grilled mesquite chicken by the side of the road to sell to homebound commuters. The fellow next to him sold steamers that Teddy would buy for hors d'oeuvres; lettuce and early tomatoes from the man in the red truck. Now that Teddy stopped to think about it, he could buy most of the dinner in that lot, which these days had begun to resemble a Latin American market minus the trays of *tamales* and *pupusas,* and the plastic bags filled with Coke.

Not the entire meal, however. The fancy pasta and pasta sauce, the arugula and artichoke hearts, he would purchase up the street.

Teddy didn't arrive at the food co-op intending to rub Julianna's nose in the fact that he had a date tonight. Nor, he had decided, would he avoid her. There was no reason *not* to show off this sparkling good mood. He circled the store about six times, eyes peeled for a red bandanna, all the while imagining the conversation that would ensue when Julianna spotted the Newman's Own organic sauce in his basket.

"You *could* buy fresh tomatoes, spices, a little garlic and olive oil and make that yourself."

"You're right," he would reply. Then, an apologetic smile. "But I'm pressed for time."

"How's your uncle?"

"Oh, fine." Momentary pause. "Out of town right now."

Subtle, thought Teddy. He hoped not too subtle.

Unfortunately, there was no sign of Julianna. He peeked through the swinging doors leading to the kitchen. *Nobody.* He checked the protest board to see if she might be off at a demonstration. Nothing.

At the register, Carly with the tiny gold question marks posted to each nostril said to Teddy, "So, were you looking for Jules?"

"Not really." Step up the nonchalance, he scolded himself. But somehow he just couldn't summon it. "Is she around?"

"Nope. She's out on the river. Kayaking." Carly laughed. The gold star inlaid in her front tooth was always a surprise to Teddy, though not today, not as much of a surprise as this news anyway. Did Carly's trill of a laugh mean that kayaking on the river was the last activity in the world that *Jules* would undertake were it not for the fact that she was out there with some *guy?*

"I take it you don't kayak," he said.

Carly grimaced. "Are you kidding? I get queasy in a bathtub."

They smiled at each other. Grinned so foolishly that Teddy had to wonder if this moment constituted flirting. Suddenly the tiny star inlaid in her tooth and the gold question marks on her nostrils seemed, well, fetching. Even her aroma of patchouli was alluring. On the walk home, he marveled at this sea change in his life: for some inexplicable reason, young women had suddenly begun to pay attention to him. Luck was part of it, but not the whole story. The transformation felt chemical, as if a fairy of some sort had dusted him with magic powder.

It was prudence, not swagger, that motivated Teddy to retrieve the packet of condoms from the basket on top of his uncle's bureau—a measure of hope and desire, too. Best to tackle the most important chores first, along with the ones that were unavoidable. Attending to the constantly ringing telephone, for example.

First came a call from his mother, inviting him to dinner: "Honey, I thought we might pick up some of your favorite mesquite chicken tonight."

Teddy begged off.

Then Barry Valentine: "That uncle of yours gave me a deadline. I need to talk to him."

Call the Wilderness Motel, Teddy advised.

Then Rita Corelli: "Even if I asked you to connect me to Will in Orange, how would I know he was there?"

You wouldn't, Teddy wanted to say.

Then came the return call from Charlotte Cameron, who identified herself as *Jodie*. Teddy took that call in the kitchen, his heart in his throat and the packet of condoms in his left hand, astonished to find himself talking to a woman who might be his cousin. *Was* his cousin, he soon realized, as she began to describe the details of her adoption.

In the middle of his shower Rita interrupted again, this time demanding to speak to Will, wherever he was in the heart of Dixie, which required a soapy, highly irritated Teddy to try Will's cell phone. There was no answer. Rita made Teddy promise to try again in fifteen minutes, which was precisely when Will happened to call.

At seven-thirty the phone sounded again: Rita again. She had Will's cell phone number but he wasn't answering. She had to talk to him immediately. Right now, she informed Teddy, or the deal was off. "You've got exactly five minutes to find that uncle of yours," she barked.

"But Rita—"

Click.

He tried the cell phone. It rang and rang. Then he stewed. A round of vacuuming dissipated some of this anger, but Rita's shrill voice still echoed in his head. *Hold down the fort,* Uncle Will had said. Almost his very last words.

Teddy headed out to the shed to straighten up. He changed the sheets on his bed, stacked up all the old newspapers on the floor beside his desk, swept up the Chee-tos, and then went to work on a huge mound of dirty laundry, which he was astonished to discover filled two jumbo black plastic garbage bags. And beneath the laundry, lo and behold, he came upon his very own checkbook, which had been missing for weeks now. It gave him an idea.

He thought: Uncle Will would understand. He would have to understand.

The telephone rang again as Teddy was ironing napkins in the dining room, and this time he let the machine pick up. He heard a woman say, "Will." The voice was unfamiliar. Teddy set down the iron and started toward the machine. "Will, it's Lucy." He stopped. "Look, this morning I was caught off guard. I shouldn't have been, but I was." Teddy knew that he should cut in, knew that Will needed him to talk to her, to set up a meeting, *something.* But he couldn't move. He was thinking: This is the mother of my cousin! Which made Lucy an aunt of sorts. She said, "I'm calling because I want to see you. We need to talk. I'll be home tomorrow morning." Pause. "Tonight, too. Please call me, Will."

THE TRAFFIC LIGHTS in Orange were blinking red and yellow in the rosy hours of twilight. People were out, more people than Will could recall ever having seen on the sidewalks of this town. From the corner of his eye he caught sight of a woman in a hoop skirt, and two men in ill-fitting gray jackets. It wasn't until his car reached the center of town, and Will glanced over at the commemorative statue of a Confederate soldier, that he realized that one of the fellows he'd passed on the street had been wearing the same forage cap. Then he caught sight of a banner: "Welcome, Reenactors and Visitors!" And beneath, in smaller type: "The Wilderness/May 1864."

The offices of the *Orange Gazette* were above a barber shop. The reception area was empty. The newsroom, fully lit, was empty, too. Will found Dewey Randolph squirreled away in his tiny glass cube of an office in the far corner. Dewey was pecking at his keyboard with two fingers.

"With all the bluecoats set to arrive, you might think about locking some doors."

"Hey, Will!" Dewey smiled broadly. "Not this time. These Yankee fellas have cash in their pockets. Not a looter or marauder in the group, I bet. Nothing like good old-fashioned commerce to smooth over a hundred and thirty years of hard feelings." He hit the Save key. "Not that some lootin' and maraudin' wouldn't be just what this paper of mine needs. An airplane flips over in a high wind is about as spicy as it gets around here."

Dewey was stout. He had a florid, 150-proof, red-apple glow in his cheeks. He wore bifocals, red suspenders, a starched white shirt with tie askew and sleeves rolled. He was a Rotarian and a Baptist. Will had always thought of him as pushing fifty, but looking at him now he saw that he and Dewey were about the same age. Dewey had a wife in the Junior League, a couple of teenagers, a well-trained golden retriever, the antebellum Tazewell family mansion with two-hundred-year-old boxwoods lining the front walk, a newspaper of his very own, two late-model Fords and a 1966 burgundy Mustang convertible that he only drove on sunny weekends. The regular expression on his face was one of deep contentment: the look of a man who was about to head home to his favorite plate of pork chops.

Dewey pulled a bottle of Jim Beam from the bookshelf and poured two neat shots.

"So what brings you all the way from the big city? More news from Hollywood? Do I stop the presses?"

"Grunt work," Will replied. "Today I'm the literary equivalent of a stable boy."

"Lord knows," said Dewey, "if anybody needs a full-time shoveler, it's that uncle of mine."

"You've seen him?"

"Not two hours ago. Stopped in just before he went to see a man about a horse."

Will laughed uneasily and sipped his bourbon.

Dewey returned the bottle to the shelf. "Seriously, Uncle Nort's set to ride in the reenactment of the skirmish at Widow Tapp's farm. He's been on some sort of high-calorie diet that he read about in a bike-racing magazine, of all places. He's aiming to bulk up to look like Robert E. Lee."

Dewey hit a button on his keyboard, and up popped an image of the front page of the *Gazette* with the headline LEE ESCAPES! "Awful nice to get your lead story three days ahead of time."

Will said, "I spoke to Ruthie yesterday. She had Norton's manuscript. I asked her to drop it off here."

"Ah, the manuscript." Dewey's arched eyebrows and tight smile indicated bad news.

"What's up?"

"Let me put it this way, Will. In the past week Uncle Nort's gone from can't stop talking about Moses Pugh to won't utter his name."

"You mean he hasn't been out traveling the route again?"

"Near as I can tell he hasn't stepped outside that trailer of his for the past ten days."

Will's heart thumped. He saw madness. He pictured a white-haired old man in a dirty undershirt wielding a broken bourbon bottle to keep the police at bay.

"Is he drinking?"

"No more than usual."

"Angry?"

Dewey shrugged. "The same."

"Tell me something, is the book done? Has he finished it?"

"I thought he had. Now I'm wondering if maybe he just got to the end of his rope."

"Ruthie said there's a card game tonight."

Dewey nodded. "Round about nine, same as always."

"At the airstrip?"

"Upstairs," Dewey replied.

"Do me a favor," said Will. "If you happen see that uncle of yours before I do, don't mention that I'm in town."

A few minutes later, after a brief stop at the Happy Garden restaurant, Will sat behind the wheel of his parked car, a paper box of crispy chicken and vegetables in his lap. He nibbled baby corn and snap peas, and sipped from a quart bottle of club soda, all the while contemplating the many ways in which the task before him might end up as a three-day siege. Perhaps this moment called for bold action. Perhaps he should break into Norton's trailer while the card game was in progress, steal the manuscript, and hope to reach Union lines before the crotchety old bastard realized that his book was gone.

A man passed Will's car, a man walking with a small girl: father and daughter. She took two steps for every one of his. They reached a corner and waited to cross the street. Will studied them. He saw the father halt the little girl with a hand on her shoulder. The hand slid to her neck, caressed it as they waited for a line of cars to pass; and when the way was clear, as they started forward together, Will watched this child take her father's hand. There was nothing said, no looks exchanged, just this remarkable assurance: the earth would keep spinning, the sun would rise tomorrow in the east, the hot weather would come, then the cold weather; and at every critical moment a small hand would reach up for a big one, and find it there.

Ruthie's motel was east of town, just past the airstrip, set behind a dense row of evergreens. Approaching, Will saw that it was lit up like a county fair. Ruthie and her late husband, Roy, had bought the rustic lodge nearly twenty years earlier, shortly after Roy retired from the construction trade. Back then it was called the Orange Motel and had been painted the color of highway stripes. Roy had scraped and repainted the clapboard structure himself: oyster gray walls with butternut window trim and dark blue cornices and doors. He had supervised construction of two new wings—designated *North* and *South*—each with a dozen rooms, extending in a V-shape off the back of the main building. In the garden between the wings, Roy had built a scale model of the Wilderness battlefield.

There were pickups and campers parked on both sides of the long driveway, tents and fires dotting the wide field to the left of the motel.

Will edged into Ruthie's narrow lot looking for any small space where he might leave his car for a few minutes, and when he found none, he backed out to the highway and parked at the end of a line of cars.

Ruthie stood at the front desk as if frozen in a trance, gazing down at her reservation book. Her headband had slipped forward. She looked disheveled, confused.

"Ruthie."

She looked up suddenly, her mouth pinched, eyes shiny, nostrils flared, then looked down at her book. "Will Gerard," she said. "Don't tell me it's Wednesday already."

"It's Tuesday, Ruthie."

"But you're wrote down here for Wednesday."

"Oh," said Will.

"You did say Wednesday, didn't you?"

"I believe I said *tomorrow,* and that was yesterday. Monday," he added, feeling suddenly confused himself. "But if you wrote down Wednesday, then Wednesday's what I must've said."

She reached for a tissue and blew hard. "Oh, gosh. It's never been like this." She blew again. "Folks just keep giving me money and checks and their credit cards and I give them keys and try to remember to write down who's where and all, but . . . but . . . I tried to get Verna's daughter to help me, but she's been cooking with her mother for days to feed the folks that are coming." She looked at Will. "That're *here,*" she said.

The phone began to ring. Ruthie didn't budge.

"I don't see that I have a room for you, Will."

"That's all right. I'm hoping I won't need one."

"Why ever did I think I could run this place all by myself?"

"Shush," Will whispered. "You do fine almost every day of the year. This is just something to get through. Like a hurricane. Besides, I don't see anybody complaining."

"Stick around," she said darkly.

"Ruthie Ann, these guests of yours are guys whose greatest wish in life is to have been a soldier in the Civil War. Right now they're as close to heaven as they could hope to get on this earth. You run out of room and we can line up the extras under a tarp outside, and tell 'em they're sleeping in the exact spot where Jubal Early's men bivouacked on the night of May 4, 1864. Could even charge them a little bit extra, considering that it's sacred ground."

Her face wore the hint of a smile. "But that's not true, is it?"

"Close to true. More important is that those fellows *want* it to be true. We could ask ol' Nort to stop by after the card game and set the scene for the next day. Leave them with something awful to go to sleep on."

Ruthie's face went ashen.

"It's all right," Will said softly. "I was just over at Dewey's office. I know you didn't have a chance to get the manuscript to him."

"It's a whole lot worse than that," she replied. "You're going to murder me."

Will's mouth went dry.

"I tried to call Dewey like you said. That is, I *meant* to try. But it was like McDonald's after a softball game in here, everybody asking for something, talking to me, hollerin' at their kids. I couldn't keep a thought of my own in my head."

"You forgot. It's no big—"

"By the time I'd remembered that I forgot, it was too late. Norton's book is gone."

"What do you mean *gone?*"

"It ain't here anymore."

"So maybe the fellow who was reading it when I called—"

"Finished it. This was later. I was down in room twenty-two trying to fix the darn TV. When I came back, it wasn't here anymore."

"Somebody stole it?"

"Somebody borrowed it is how I'd like see it."

"But you don't know who took it."

She bit her lip.

"What's the chance that Norton might have picked it up himself?"

She shook her head slowly. "Not in that loud truck of his."

Right then Will wanted to go out to the front porch and strip the fellow in the rocker of his Remington muzzleloader, march everybody on the grounds to the gazebo, line them up, let no man, woman, or child return to their quarters until every page of Norton's manuscript had been collected. But his native good sense prevailed: he decided to man the front desk, and have Ruthie canvas the troops to see what they might voluntarily surrender.

Will paced. He let the telephone ring. He told a couple who inquired if they might have a second room key that they were out of luck. He thought about Norton. Whatever writerly angst Norton was currently in the throes of would evaporate with the news that Moses had gone AWOL. Why was it, Will wondered, that Norton could walk in Moses's footsteps, fight his battles, live as tightly as was humanly possible in the shadow of a man who might have lived over a hundred years earlier; then struggle valiantly to tell his story, write and tear up the stirring tale a dozen times before it was finally finished; yet not have the wits to march that manuscript over to a copy shop and get it *duplicated*?

Self-reproach kicked in. The only way there would be a copy of this book, Will realized, was if he had paid someone to steal the manuscript from Norton at regular intervals and copy it for him. He had failed Norton, had failed Rita Corelli, the honchos at CastleBooks, their new owner, the new owner's shareholders, not to mention the millions of readers who devour books about the Civil War. He should have paid closer attention to this loose cannon of a client. He should have come sooner.

St. Anthony: Was he the patron saint of lost articles?

Will dimly recalled that he was. But he would have had to call his mother to verify this. And according to Teddy, right about now Grandmom was strapped into an airplane, gliding above the continent, on her way to Arizona to watch hummingbirds. This age was miraculous enough to allow telephone calls *from* airplanes, but not so miraculous as to allow calls *to* them. It hardly mattered. St. Anthony's intercession wouldn't count for much out here in Baptist country. Tonight Will's salvation would require a tent evangelist, a snake handler, a miracle worker of the holy roller sort. Someone who, if the manuscript had truly vanished, could pull a fresh copy off Norton's brain.

The phone rang again. It rang and rang.

Nothing is really lost anymore, Will reminded himself. The hard disk in your computer crashes and a utility program retrieves the data.

An airplane falls into the ocean and every last piece of it is vacuumed from the seabed. Surely there must be a faith healer in the vicinity who would know how to retrieve Moses Cadwallader Pugh's adventures from Norton's own blue-and-gray matter.

Will was standing outside on the front porch when Ruthie returned. She was out of breath and empty-handed. Tears had welled up in her large blue eyes.

"And to think that all I had to do was take that darn box to my room and put in on the shelf, and there it'd be right this very minute!"

Will said softly, "A four-hundred-page manuscript is as big as a phone book. It'll turn up."

"It'll turn up if it happened to grow legs and walk out of here, and then decides to walk on back."

"Here's what we do. You take a look at the registration book and try to remember who arrived at what time yesterday. Maybe come up with a list of the folks who might have been in here alone while you were fixing the TV. Meanwhile, I'll go over to the airport. Dewey said that Norton is set to play General Lee this weekend. He should be home now."

"Lord knows," sighed Ruthie. "Maybe it'll turn out that Norton fooled us all and had a copy made."

Will brightened. "You think it's possible?"

"How much would it cost?"

"Twenty-five or thirty dollars."

Ruthie's head shook slowly. "Not in my lifetime," she replied.

THE NIGHT HAD grown cool. The moon was up, moving in and out of the clouds. From Ruthie's porch, Will could see the flashing red beacon that marked one end of the airstrip. The light seemed as close as his car on the highway, just a five-minute jog. All that stood between this motel and Norton's trailer was a narrow stand of trees and a wide, sloping field.

The forest turned out to be a nightmare: pitch black, dense with saplings, the ground a minefield of fallen limbs and slick leaves. Will stumbled with every step. Out of the woods, as he passed behind the animal shelter, he noted an eerie silence. Then he tripped on a concrete culvert, and all at once a dozen hounds began to howl. This wasn't the full-throated, animated bark of watch dogs, but the mournful wail of the condemned.

Will started to run. The grass in the sloping field before him was up to his thighs. He kicked through it easily, his head up, eyes fixed on Norton's yellow trailer. But then the ground went mushy, and his feet were instantly soaked. The earth made disgusting sucking noises as Will madly continued forward toward higher ground. Soon the tall grass gave way to gravel, and the moonlight revealed that his brown loafers were covered with muck. His feet smelled so rank that after rapping on the door of Norton's darkened trailer, and circling around back to see if the old man might be hiding out in his tiny writing shed (and stepping into a soft pile of what he guessed to be the turds of a large grazing animal), Will gave up and went looking for a hose.

It was almost eight o'clock.

As coincidence would have it, at this same moment, one hundred miles to the northeast, young Teddy, too, had gone looking for a hose: he'd overdone it with the Old Spice. He smelled like an overripe, musky pear. In Will's bathroom, he dipped his face to the running faucet, then scrubbed and scrubbed. Ten minutes later he stood at the window of his uncle's darkened bedroom, peering out at every car that passed by on MacArthur Boulevard, hoping and praying that one of them would slow to make the left turn, one whose boxy silhouette would reveal itself to be Daddy's Volvo.

Uncle Will's fancy Guatemalan tablecloth adorned the dining room table; an oriental screen masked the shelf in the living room piled high with manuscripts; and three CDs had been cued up: Ella Fitzgerald, Lou Reed, 10,000 Maniacs, the best Teddy could manage with a music collection that seemed to him to have terminated abruptly in the mid-1980s.

And so he waited in the dark. Waited and waited. At eight twenty the telephone rang again. Bad, bad news, Teddy told himself, his heart sunk all the way to the hard toes of his newly polished boots. This was certain to be awful news.

"Oh, God. He *called*. I just got off the phone with him."

Not *Hi, Ted, this is Jill*. Not *Sorry I'm late, but I got hung up*. No clarification about who *he* was, not that Teddy needed clarification.

"You won't believe it. He tried to lay this guilt trip on *me*! The bastard. We talked for an hour. Right now I am sooooo pissed." That awful Maryland *so*, spoken through sphinctered lips, the mere contemplation of which left Teddy feeling even more deeply glum. "I can't even think straight," Jill hissed. Long pause. "Something tells me I'd make really lousy company tonight." A longer pause, then softly: "Ted, I hope you're not mad."

Me mad? he thought. Sure I am. But right then *mad* seemed to be the least of how he was feeling. He was also confused, frustrated, upset, wounded, buffaloed. *Roget's Thesaurus* would have a thousand words to describe his state of mind right then. So why, he wondered, at such a moment of high drama and anxiety, did he sense the approach of a yawn? He stifled the front end of it; but then it mastered him, and Teddy nearly honked.

He felt embarrassed; but grateful, too, for this moment to collect himself.

"Not to worry," he said. Almost brightly. "We'll do dinner another time." Say, when hell freezes over, is what he was thinking.

"I hope you didn't already buy a bunch of stuff."

Jill wanted him to have bought a bunch of stuff. Grocery cartfuls of stuff. She wanted Teddy to tell her that the house smelled like Thanksgiving. To admit that tears of anguish had begun to course down his razor-burned cheeks. "This and that," he lied. "Nothing that won't keep."

"Oh."

The weak petulance of Jill's *oh* made Teddy's spirits soar. Why hadn't anyone told him that conversations between boys and girls could go back and forth like this? That bad news could be brushed off so easily, that shame was something you could hide away in the back of a closet like an old brown suit.

He depressed the disconnect button.

"Oops," he said. "Another call. New York, no doubt. Gotta run. Listen, after you get things straight with Kenny"—*that tight end of yours*—"give me a call. That is, if you want to. Maybe we could take a walk on the towpath sometime."

"What if I want to take a walk tonight?" Jill's voice was small, small, small.

"Well, let's see," said Teddy, his voice gusty with good cheer, "I was free earlier. Back when you thought you might be free. But then when you didn't show, and didn't call—"

"Not even a little bit later?"

"I need to make a quick call," Teddy replied. "Let me get back to you."

But he didn't get back to Jill. Not that this move was calculated on his part. Teddy simply forgot to call her back. And the reason for this was that as soon as Teddy hung up the telephone, he was summoned to the front door by a tentative knock.

* * *

MEANWHILE, back in Orange, Will had taken a seat on a huge tire, stripped off his shoes and socks, rinsed everything with the hose, rinsing and wringing and then rinsing again. He beat his shoes against the tire to get rid of some of the water, all the while asking himself what in heaven's name he was doing out here in the Wilderness in the dark on this Tuesday night. *All this for a book?* No, of course not. That was just the surface of things. He saw himself clearly now: he was exactly like his father. Both of their lives were compartmentalized. Everything had its drawer, and somehow Will had never taken note of this, never even admitted it to himself. He had run away from Lucy and Jodie; now Annie, too—and from himself as well. He slipped wet shoes onto wet socks and trudged toward the hangar, his shoes squish, squish, squishing the entire way. The steady stream of cars sped past on the distant highway. And from the makeshift campground beside the Wilderness Motel came the sound of a bugle: a halting rendition of taps.

In his mind's eye Will saw Norton hiking through field and forest, marsh and meadow; he pictured the old man trudging alongside highways and logging roads, traversing parks and cemeteries; fording rivers in the heat of the day and the dark of night; all in an effort to follow the actual route of Grant's army. Will thought: *he is a madman.* Nothing short of madness could explain why Norton had undertaken this obsessive campaign. Nor why he had stayed with it all these years. So how, wondered Will, might this mad client of his react to news that his magnum opus had vanished? What if this weren't news? What if, in a funk of depression, Norton had retrieved the manuscript himself, marched it to the banks of the Rapidan, and pitched ten years of work into the muddy waters? No, he decided. There is a limit to craziness, even for Norton. The manuscript was here, *somewhere.* In the morning he would find it. He would search every car on Ruthie's property. Tents and campers, too. He would announce a bounty. And if that didn't produce results he would hire a hypnotist and march Norton back across the sacred ground. With *Ashokan Farewell* looped on a Walkman, with enough johnnycakes and Jim Beam to fortify him, Norton could probably channel the story: he would speak it aloud and

Will would tape-record the recollection. Perhaps he had read from the work-in-progress at the library in Fredericksburg, and someone in the audience had taped that!

Three cars were parked near the door to the hangar. Will laid a hand on the hood of one of them: still warm. So the card game had just begun. Nobody had lost big, not yet. Spirits would still be up; so too the bourbon, at the neck of the bottle, or close enough to hope that Norton might still be willing and able to hold up his end of a conversation.

Inside, Will climbed a steep flight of metal steps and rapped once on the door to the office.

"Airport's closed," came a gruff reply. Norton's voice.

Will pushed open the door. There were four men seated around a desk that had been pushed to the middle of the tiny room. Norton was shuffling cards, head down. Behind him, running the length of the wall, was a plate-glass window that looked out on the darkened runway.

"Hey, Will Gerard," said Lester Shifflet. Grover Payne, in his VFW cap, saluted with two fingers. Dewey Randolph, awaiting his cards, smiled uneasily.

Norton dealt the hand before looking up at Will. Recognition seemed to take a moment.

"Howdy, Will."

"Hey there, Norton."

Norton took a 150-proof sip from a Dixie cup. He gazed around the table. "Who's in?" he asked.

Everybody pitched in a quarter.

Norton ignored Will. He was punishing him. Will understood this. He had burst unannounced upon a regular card game in a sleepy hamlet in the dark of night. North or south of the Mason-Dixon line this sort of get-together must be considered the most intimate of male-bonding events. One simply doesn't crash parties like this one. Not ever.

At the very least Will knew that Norton was going to make him wait. Will moved to a low counter near the window and took a seat. He sat there quietly, hands folded in his lap, as if to underscore that he couldn't be shamed from the room.

Dewey said, "Uncle, maybe you and Will want to take care of business before we get too—"

"Your lead, Nephew," snapped Norton.

Dewey smiled apologetically. Will shrugged, then motioned to Dewey and the others to ask them to tank this hand. The only thing worse than trying to negotiate with a horse-weary Norton Tazewell teetering on the brink of fatigue and sobriety would be trying to negotiate with a horse-weary, teetering Norton Tazewell who was ten bucks in the hole.

A white lie seemed in order.

"Ruthie tells me that it reads like the wind," said Will.

"Exactly where it oughta be," Norton shot back. "Now who wants cards?"

Dewey wanted two, Grover three, Lester none: he folded. The others matched Norton's bet without much enthusiasm, and then allowed him to take the pot with two kings. He grinned.

"Norton, I'll be honest," Will said. "I'm in a little bit of a hurry."

Norton toasted Will with his Dixie cup. "Travel safely, young fella."

He won the next two hands. By now Grover had begun to snort his unhappiness. Dewey gave Will the sidelong glance of a hostage who has just come to realize that, the risk of death notwithstanding, this is the moment for action. Norton began to chuckle. He guffawed. "Let's see some cards now," he told Lester.

Will cleared his throat. "Fact is, friend, I can't leave until I make a pick-up."

"Can't you now?"

"The manuscript was due last week."

Norton harrumphed.

"How about you just tell me where you've got it squirreled away," said Will.

"Forget about it," Norton replied.

Will gazed up at the fluorescent lights until the white tubes appeared to slither across the ceiling. He closed his eyes and imagined Norton Tazewell dressed as Moses Pugh: Moses facing a firing squad. "Well," he said finally. "There're a few ways we can go here, but forgetting about that manuscript just isn't one of them."

Norton won another hand. "You gotta trust me on this, Will," he said.

There was an opening. In Norton's voice Will heard the plaintive cry of a wounded writer.

"Everybody loved the first hundred pages," he said.

"Sure they did. It was going like a brushfire there for a while. Like a hound with a scent." Norton finally lifted his head to look at Will. "Turned out like it does at the races."

"I don't follow."

"I was chasing a *bait sack*."

Will looked to Dewey. His tight expression counseled against asking for a translation.

"I'd like to take a look at it."

Norton put down his cards. "What I'm trying to tell you is that you *can't*. This story's past fixing. Like a car that's just fine going along down the road and then slams into a tree. Too many things got broke all at once." He shook his head. "I let a good man down, Will."

"Who's that?"

"Moses," he barked.

Will's skin tingled. Every follicle of hair on his body stood upright. Please stop talking about Moses as if he *exists*, he wanted to shout. Because he doesn't. You made him up. You made up his whole life. You can change any of it. It's just words on a page. A quick bit of cutting-and-pasting and Moses *doesn't* take a bullet in the heat of battle. He can make a mistake and *not* pay the ultimate price. Moses can do everything but tell Robert E. Lee how to win that damn war, and goodness knows, you could have him do *that*, too, so long as Bobby Lee ignores the advice.

Gently, gently, gently, Will said, "Let me take a look at it tonight, and then we can talk it over at breakfast in the morning."

"Uh-uh," said Norton.

"There's an awful lot on the line here. I don't have to tell you that. But if you're suggesting that I just walk away from this, I'm going to have to go outside and get the biggest stick I can find, and hit you over the head with it twenty-five times."

"You're not listening, Will. This book's history. It's already been walked away *from*."

"So walk back."

"Can't do that."

"You're a perfectionist. A perfectionist with the jitters. That's understandable for somebody who's been living with this story as long as you have. I expect that it'd be harder to send your own boy to Cold Harbor than to send Moses out into the world."

"He ain't going out into the world," Norton said flatly.

"He's got to go. You signed a contract that said that he would go. You've been paid a lot of money."

He shrugged. "Like you told me, we can always send it back."

At this, Norton's poker partners, upstanding citizens and men of commerce all, collectively blanched. Dewey's eyes rolled backward. Lester's downturned mouth seemed to be asking whether a self-respecting businessman like himself could participate in another hand of cards with a fellow who had just announced that he was going to walk away from $300,000. Grover the banker clutched at the plastic pocket protector shielding his heart. His deer-in-the-headlights gaze said *Words! Just a bunch of words!* When Norton's book deal was announced in Dewey's newspaper a few short months ago, Grover had hooted as if his old friend had just won the lottery. And now, it seemed, that same dear friend had just announced to the world that he would send back all the lottery money because he didn't like his *string of numbers!*

Will read the business pages. He knew all the stories about sports agents who put their clients' money in limited partnerships, real estate deals, any sort of speculative venture that kicked back a nice commission and *just might* earn a decent return, with the end result usually being that the athlete lost a big chunk of money. Will had even looked into a few of these schemes when Norton left it up to him to invest the first draw on his advance. And he'd rejected them all. Norton's $100,000 was locked up tight in two CDs that were insured by the federal government. Which meant that Norton actually *could* pay the money back and walk away from this deal.

Will thought: I have failed him. If only I had done the risky thing and thrown this money to the wolves, then we wouldn't be having this conversation at all. If I'd sunk the cash in a galloping thoroughbred or a farmhouse on a few dozen rolling acres, then Norton would have bills to pay. Right now he would be strapped to his desk, banging out volume two of the adventures of Moses Cadwallader Pugh, figuring out how to coax a third book from this story, begging me to turn in his manuscript so that he could collect the next draw of his advance.

"Norton," said Will, "I want you to tell me what's wrong with the story."

Norton sighed. "Don't know exactly. It's just that when Moses is walking those last miles toward the North Anna, it seemed like something was going wrong. A grim foreboding. I couldn't put my finger on it. Like the smell of fish that ain't gone bad but ain't quite right either."

"Just the sort of problem a good editor can help you solve."

He shook his head. "Too late for that."

They heard a door slam, then footsteps on the metal stairs.

"You start fussing about Moses's final march, and it gets you depressed, and as a result of *that* you're ready to ditch the whole book?"

"Not *ready to*," he replied. "Did."

There was a tentative knock on the door.

"Wait," called Will, then to Norton, "What did you say?"

"I got rid of it, Will."

Another knock, this time rat-tat-tat.

"Hold on," Will barked.

Norton said, "I don't even want to tell you what happens."

Moses turns out to be a pedophile, Will thought. Or a double agent. Or both. "What?"

"Moses died." Norton looked up at Will. His face reddened. "I didn't think that could happen. And when it did, it just tore me up."

Will's head was spinning. All he could think to say was, "Norton, I'm so sorry. What happened?"

Norton's white beard seemed to be floating upon his skin as he worked his jaw from side to side, struggling to keep his composure. "Moses was caught up in the fight at Todd's Tavern. You remember that?"

Will nodded as if he did.

"Well, Moses took a bullet in the calf that day. 'Course he didn't see to it properly, and the wound infected. Little Phil's adjutant tried to send Moses back, but he wouldn't go. I think he saw what was coming. Honestly I do. He fooled everybody for a good long while, including me. That was Moses's genius, of course. But after North Anna it got so bad Moses couldn't see straight. On the way to Cold Harbor, when they were crossing the Pamunkey, Moses slipped on the barge and went over the side. It's right there on the last page. One minute he's sayin' his prayers, and the next he's gone. Nothing I could do. Nothing anybody could do. All I could figure right then was that I must've done something grievously wrong with the whole story to have it end that way."

The only way Norton could see to hold on to Moses was to destroy him.

"Rita's one of the best in the world with this sort of problem," Will said gently.

Norton shook his head.

"Listen to me," Will went on. "This is a story—"

"It's Moses's *life* I'm talking about," Norton snapped.

"Fine, it's his life. Let's talk about that. Things happen in life. Good things and bad things. Some things you can control and some you can't. The same's true for Moses as it is for all of us. But he survives. And the reason he survives is because he's paying attention. He's got resiliency. He's gonna get hurt, knocked down, knocked into the water, what have you. But that won't be the end of him. He'll get back up. Get through the things that need to be got through. For a good long while, anyway. That's just his character. That's what we love about this man."

Norton smiled unhappily. "It's too late."

Will shook his head. "Look at what you've written. Look at the story. It's about perseverance and courage. It's about the lengths to which one man will go to fight for what he believes, even if that cause is doomed. Even if he's doomed, ultimately. Moses understands something about life. He knows he's got no choice but to stand up for who he is. To act on his beliefs. I'm not saying he won't die, Norton, because he will. Just like we all do eventually. But he won't die just yet. Not here, not now. Not at the end of the first book."

"Will, Moses *is* dead."

Lester said, "But he's just a fella in a story, Nort. He's never been alive so he can't be dead."

Will said, "All I've heard is that he went over the side of a barge. Disappeared. That everybody *thinks* he's dead. "

Norton looked at him.

Will continued: "There's screaming and hollering. And Moses is gone. Next morning, the soldiers search downstream. Nothing. They hold a service on the river bank. It ends with a prayer. *The end*. And below that, in ten-point type: *to be continued*."

Dewey smiled. "I get it: Pharaoh's *ghost*."

A twitch in Norton's cheek suggested that he, too, was warming to the idea.

Will said, "Next book could open with Moses washed up on the shore. It's morning. Flies all over his face. Dead as can be, you'd think. But then a young woman going for water happens—"

"Soldiers," corrected Norton, with some indignance. "A band of Confederates caught behind the Yankee lines. They take Moses prisoner. Finally he's able to convince them that he's one of them. At least he *thinks* he's convinced them."

"That man's got nothing but tricks up his sleeve," Grover said.

"Put together a fifteen-page outline and that opening scene and we'll bank some more of the advance," Will added.

Norton smiled sheepishly. "To be continued." He shook his head. "Live and learn, I guess."

There was a note of resignation in his voice that sent a chill down Will's spine. "Now then, about that manuscript," he said.

Norton seemed embarrassed. "You got to understand, I was awfully angry at myself, what you might call depressed even."

"Where is it, Norton?"

"Well, you see, it was already packed up to send to you. And then I just started thinking about it. And suddenly—"

"Where is it?"

"It ain't." Norton chewed his lip for a moment. Then he looked away. "Got pitched into a campfire yesterday afternoon."

Will's face burned. He wanted to cry. And to scream. He wanted to howl. He wanted to fling himself across the table and grab Norton by the throat. Strangle the crazy old bastard with his bare hands. Give Dewey the front page story of his dreams. Will wanted to murder Norton right now and then saunter off into the night, climb into his car, drive deep into the heart of Dixie. Maybe take a room in a boarding house in some small town in Tennessee, teach Latin at a prep school—

The reverie was interrupted by another knock, then Ruthie Ann called out, "Will Gerard, we don't got all night!"

The door swung open. A man entered. He was short and stocky, with small round glasses, and a Confederate forage cap gripped in front of him with both hands, like a codpiece. He wore an ill-fitting gray uniform that looked as though it had been made from Army surplus blankets. He looked terrified.

Ruthie stood behind him in the doorway. "This fella Wayland has got something to tell y'all," she said.

Wayland shuffled forward to face Norton, who had set down the deck of cards and sat there impassively, his mouth drooping just a bit, eyes as soft and inscrutable as Bobby Lee's.

Wayland fidgeted. "You see, sir, I'm new to this—this being the first time I actually dressed up and all. What I mean to say is that I didn't really understand all the rules about when it's make believe and when it's not? At least not like I do where I work—at the library, that is."

"What happened?" Will asked.

Wayland faced him. "We had our campsite set up and Darleen was resting in the tent—Darleen's my wife—and I was just then commencing to light a fire when I heard a commotion, and a soldier ran by saying that General Lee was heading our way. Well, of course, Darleen would want to see the general, too, so I went for her, and that's when I came out the tent, and nearly knocked right into a horse—Traveller," he added to Norton with a small grin, like a student hoping to pick up extra-credit points. "And General Lee—this gentleman—actually stopped. That's when I got a little worried, because I didn't know how privates are supposed to talk to General Lee, or even if they do. So I just saluted—"

"Tell Will about the package," said Ruthie.

"I made a turrible, turrible mistake," Wayland said.

"What package?" asked Will.

"Well, General Lee here pulled it out of his saddle bag and just gave it to me. He was in quite a state. He ordered me to dispose of it posthaste. Said to throw it in the fire. Suddenly it wasn't pretending anymore. It wasn't like listening to the fella in the next tent tell about how he lost his leg skirmishin' at Saunders Field. I mean there he is with half a leg actually, and you listen like you believe he did lose the rest of it on the fifth of May, but of course you figure that he must've lost it changing a tire on the interstate."

Will said, "What happened to the package?"

Wayland's back stiffened. "After the general took off, I marched it over to the fire with the order in mind. But something happened along the way. Maybe I heard a siren on the highway, or a plane was landing right then. I can't say exactly. It's just that by the time I actually got to that fire, I wasn't Private Macon Shuey of the Thirteenth Virginia Infantry anymore, but my old self, Wayland Sinclair. And being a librarian for years and years now—an archivist, actually—I couldn't bring myself to burn up any kind of papers to do with this war. I just couldn't do it."

Will's heart fluttered. "So what did you do?"

"Like the general said, it was all wrapped up, even to having an address on it."

"What address?" asked Will.

"I don't recall excepting that it was a little bit queer. A *shack* of some kind."

"Cabin John?"

"That's the fella."

Will grinned. "This was yesterday?"

Wayland nodded. " 'Bout four in the afternoon. Didn't know what else to do, so Darleen and I drove it over to the post office." He grimaced. "I mailed it."

Will had to resist the urge to shout for joy as Norton slowly roused himself.

"Private Shuey here disobeyed orders," he said.

Grover said, "Or else he was just improving on his orders. Wasn't it Longstreet who was famous for just that sort of thing?"

"Wayland," said Will, "I'll straighten this out with the general. Why don't you head back to your camp. And see that you leave your address with Ruthie so I can make sure you get a signed copy of the general's book."

As Wayland was tromping down the stairs, Will said to Norton, "It's out of your hands now. You don't worry about any of this. Just rally the boys on Saturday, and make sure the Federals don't grab ahold of you at Widow Tapp's farm. Forget about Moses for a while."

"Can't hardly forget a fella when the last thing you saw of him is a hand sticking out of the water," he replied glumly.

Nor will the reader, Will thought. Nor will the reader.

"As sick as Moses was, I just don't think he'd a survived that river. That was spring runoff. It was cold."

"Unless of course he wasn't sick."

"He was delirious, Will."

"Or else he just *appeared* delirious."

Norton perked up. "You gettin' at something?"

"Could be that Moses knew that he had to cross back through the Confederate lines."

"You suggestin' he *staged* the wound at Todd's Tavern?"

"Beats me. You're the writer," said Will, starting toward Ruthie at the door.

"Will."

He turned in time to see Norton roll his head from side to side, unleashing in his neck a volley of cracks and pops.

"All I'd be needin' with that manuscript is a day or two." His gaze lowered. "See, Moses knew that Grant was moving his base of supplies from the Rappahannock to the Pamunkey. Lee would need to know that. Which would explain why Moses went into the water right then."

"Rita will turn the manuscript around quicker than you can say Ambrose Burnside. How about if you fix it then?"

Norton smiled. It was his dangerous smile. "What I'm sayin' is that I want to fix it *before* she sees it."

"I don't have it, friend."

"You'll be getting it."

"And I'll be sure to send you a copy."

"What I'm sayin' is that I don't want the lady in New York to see it just yet."

"I promised it to her. Rita doesn't get that book this week, then she'll be down here to retrieve it herself. I'm telling you, Norton, she'd make Grant's campaign in these parts look like a stroll through the woods."

"That so?" Norton wore Robert E. Lee's expression of dignified surrender. He tugged at his beard. He frowned. "Well, then maybe we ought to send it along to her," he said. "Mark it as a draft."

"How about if I take care of that?"

"Suit yourself," replied Norton.

Outside, Ruthie said to Will, "This time I ought to send you a bill, Will Gerard."

"I expect you to. And I'll pay."

"No you won't. But next time you come visit, you bring me another one of those sailing books. Right now I'm about to find out how Captain Jack Aubrey is going to keep himself alive put out in that wine-dark sea. Poor man." She looked to Will. "You want me to call over to Jimmy Luck and see if he can track down Norton's package?"

Will shook his head. To roust the postmaster of Orange from his bed at ten o'clock on a school night would risk provoking the malevolent spirits of the U.S. Postal Service. The best course now was to take a deep breath, and let this package meander the post road without prejudice.

Ruthie said, "Oh, and you had a couple of messages I almost forgot about: a fella named Valentine called, and Norton's lady in New York, and that sweet nephew of yours."

"Teddy?"

She dug around in the pockets of her dress for various scraps of paper. "Could I give you a little bit of advice?"

Will nodded. "I'm sure I can use it."

"Those shoes you got on," she said. "I'd bury 'em. Socks, too."

THE DRIVE HOME was one long spasm of leg stretches, seat adjustments, and gas station coffee, Will driving with his head pressed to the ceiling of the car, or else stuck out the window, bellowing Jimi Hendrix's "All Along the Watchtower" at the top of his lungs—even the guitar solos—anything, in short, to keep this exhausted driver awake. Midnight found him rolling through the quiet streets of Cabin John, eyes glazed, his spine fused after a full day behind the wheel, a day that had begun right here in the fog, some nineteen hours earlier. Now the sky was clear, brilliantly clear, not that Will noticed the stars or the moon, or anything but the double line at the center of the roadway that ran off into the distance and looked as if it disappeared into the trees. The whole way home Will had been thinking about the news from Teddy: Lucy had called. He'd been wondering why she called, and what she'd said to Teddy; wondering when he could call her back and what she would say to him. And what he would say to her. As dazed as he was right then he gave some thought to turning the car around and driving straight to her emergency room. Bust through the front door and throw himself on a gurney—

Exhaustion.

It was exhaustion that was robbing him of reason. And perspective. For at this moment it seemed to Will that the relationship with Lucy Vitava had fallen apart days ago, not twenty years ago. But the sad, strange thing to contemplate—what suddenly became clear to Will despite his exhaustion—was that the relationship with Lucy had never ended. Their romance had been interrupted, twice. It had been swept away when they were kids, the day Lucy vanished from Bangkok, and again when Will fled to Europe, and to school. But there are some people you walk away from, walk and walk and walk and walk, and somehow never reach the horizon.

The existence of Jodie was partly to account for this sense of connection. Will wondered what sort of life the three of them, together, might have had. Not that he could imagine that life, as consumed as he was by . . . what? Guilt, of course. Guilt and some ineffable feeling for Lucy, a feeling that left him puzzled and wary—secretly thrilled, too. A feeling that had kept him awake these past two hours, and delivered him finally to his own driveway, home at last. Why hadn't he called Lucy that fall? Or ever considered calling her in all these years? Why hadn't he ever asked his mother if Lucy had called for him? Because he knew the truth and didn't have the guts to confront it? *No.* It was worse than that, much more damning as far as Will was concerned. He *didn't* know. He hadn't a clue. Not once had it crossed his mind that she might be pregnant.

And then: I went over the side of the goddamn barge and didn't even try to swim. Didn't *try.*

And the reason for this, Will suddenly realized, was because opening his heart to Lucy meant trading the life he had for a more complicated life that he didn't want, at least not then. With the death of his father, it had felt as if adulthood was suddenly upon him, and Will's response to this was to cling to the notion that somehow he could remain a child.

Darkness. Blackness above, the blackness of leaves through which was arrayed a leopard pattern of stars.

There was cold gravel, the rubbery vapors and tick-tick-tick of an automobile engine cooling in the night air, bare toes surprised by dew-covered grass, and the glorious feeling of stretching one's legs to their full reach, stretching like a cat. Will was so tired he could have curled up on the wet lawn right then and fallen fast asleep. Sleeping in his own bed was almost too glorious to contemplate. Life seemed marvelous for an instant, until the next step, when his foot came down on a slug, and he nearly slid to the ground. The move should have torn hamstrings or thrown out his back; it should have left him flat on the ground, howling in pain. But it didn't. Instead, Will instantly popped back to his feet as if this little moonwalk step had been intended all along.

Near the house, he saw a dim light through the front window, the bluish fluorescent light in the kitchen, the customary sign that Teddy was wolfing down a few bowls of Corn Pops after an evening in cyber-space. But then Will recalled that young Theo had a *date*! He tiptoed back across the driveway to Mr. Richmond's yard to peer at the shed: the lights were on, the shades drawn.

Suddenly Will could see Teddy's future perfectly: he would return to school, graduate from Princeton with honors, fall in love with someone as wonderfully peculiar as he was, marry the dear woman, go to work for a computer company, father children, make regular contributions to a 401(k), run baths, supervise homework; he would attach flea collars to the family dog at regular intervals, send his children off to camp and college, attend their weddings, baby-sit the grandkids, grow old with the sweet lady he had married. Teddy would have a fine life. Once, years earlier, Barry Valentine had admitted to Will that the thought of having sex with the same woman week in, week out, year in, year out, had terrified him at first. And he admitted that boredom had been partly to blame for the few rocky years that he and Diane had had. But then, inexplicably, something changed. Suddenly their sex was lovely. In the early years, lust had been a constant for Barry, never a surprise. Now it was. Now, too, Diane's libido had picked up—suddenly *she* was coming on to *him*! Barry had grinned at Will. Life has a funny way of blindsiding you when you least expect it, he said.

Quietly, like a kid arriving home hours past his curfew, Will climbed to the porch.

"So what's with the Huck Finn look?"

Annie.

He found her finally, in the shadows, sitting in a rocker. She was barefoot, wearing jeans, and one of his white shirts rolled at the sleeves. There was an empty wine glass at her side, and beside it, a brass candlestick, the candle burned to a tiny nub. No reading light, no book, no radio: just Annie and her burned-out candle and empty wine glass, waiting. Waiting for him.

"I thought you went to Chicago," he said.

"And I was beginning to think that you'd ended up in a highway ditch."

"Almost," he replied. "Somehow I made it."

She shrugged. "I guess that goes for me, too."

Will didn't know what to say, or what to think.

Annie stood. "I went out to the airport. I got all the way to my gate. I was intending to go. I thought I had to. I just couldn't justify to myself not going. You send out feelers and somebody picks up on them and wants to talk to you—well, you should go hear what they have to say, right? But there was this other voice in my head telling me to walk away. To take that chance." She smiled. "I tried your system: I flipped a coin. Heads I go, tails I stay. It came up heads. So I called Steph for my messages. She told me that you'd telephoned. What you said. How you sounded. We talked about how I was feeling. About what I should do. Steph suggested flipping the coin again. It seemed like a good idea."

"And that time it came up tails?"

"No. But by then my flight was gone." Annie shrugged. "I went home and took a shower, and then came out here."

"You saw Teddy?"

"Teddy and I had dinner together. He cooked it himself."

"Teddy cooked dinner?"

"Mesquite chicken, pasta, arugula salad. A regular gourmet feast. He was awfully proud of himself."

Will peeked through the front window. He could see the Guatemalan tablecloth, the other brass candlestick, a half-empty wine bottle. Teddy had cooked a gourmet feast? All by himself? Will flashed on old Rip Van Winkle just home from a twenty-year snooze, and had to wonder if the same cruel fate had befallen him as well. Perhaps the house was in Teddy's name now. Free and clear, too. No doubt the Gerard Literary Agency would have a thousand clients, and three floors of a skyscraper in downtown Bethesda.

Will stepped inside. "I'm lost," he said.

"Teddy had a date, then he didn't have a date, so he and I ate dinner together; then the date who stood him up called to say that she really, really wanted to see him, and fifteen minutes later she showed up at the front door."

Will stood at the kitchen door, looking out at the shed. "Teddy's out there with a woman?"

"I took a walk when he got off the phone so I can't swear to it." Annie glanced at the clock. "But the lights are still on, and it's going on two hours without a bathroom break."

She knew everything. Young Ted had given her a full rundown of the events of his momentous day: the wounding of Long John, the afternoon with Jill, her off-again, on-again, now off-again relationship with the tight end from Frostburg, the telephone calls from Jodie Cameron and Lucy Vitava.

The shower could not be made hot enough. It was scaldingly hot, yet Will needed it hotter still, hot enough to scrub away the day. He was fading. He didn't want to be fading, not with the deep joy he felt at having Annie at his side, their quiet domesticity unburdened by talk of the future: whether she would stay the night, or if they might do something together tomorrow, or next week. But there he was after a few bites of pasta and chicken, and a sip of wine (a tasty pinot noir that Teddy had purchased with his own money!), nestled beside Annie on the bed, as dreamy-eyed as a toddler at naptime. By this point in the conversation, Will's contribution had devolved to little more than a series of *uh-huhs*, artfully placed, he hoped, and thoughtfully delivered.

Annie was talking about baby lust, about how, when she had been out in Chicago the previous winter to attend the birth of her niece, something had clicked inside her. Before this, motherhood had been a concept, something to be deferred to the future; now suddenly it was something she had to face right now. It felt like hunger. Then followed four months of grappling with the idea of having a baby, when the real issue, Annie had lately come to realize, was motherhood. Attending to the next stage of her life.

"Uh-huh."

Yesterday, she'd had another long conversation with the friend of a friend who had adopted the Chinese baby.

"Uh-huh."

Annie had made some calls. She had set up an appointment with an adoption agency. "I think it makes sense, given our situation."

"Uh-huh."

"Which isn't to say that later we couldn't have a child of our own. If both of us wanted to, I mean."

"Uh-huh."

She would figure a way to cut back on her hours. She would find a Chinese woman to care for the baby and teach her Chinese. "Teach all of us Chinese," she said. "When the baby is older we could travel to China. As a family."

"Uh-huh."

"We can talk about it tomorrow."

"Uh-uh."

Pause. "Will, was that a *yes* or a *no*?"

His eyes were closed.

Softly, Annie said, "I want us to have a chance, that's all."

The next thing Will dimly recalled was Annie shifting his legs, sliding them beneath the cool sheet. Then his face was pressed to the back of Annie's neck. He draped an arm around her waist. In his dreams he saw trees, the tops of trees, a carpet of treetops, as he passed just overhead. Thinking back on this dream, he might have expected to look down and see North Vietnamese soldiers in the clearings, or grizzled men in blue and gray doing battle in fire and smoke. But there was nothing threatening or dangerous in the world below, just a thick carpet of trees stretching to the horizon in all directions, so wonderfully peaceful that Will finally relaxed. And in that moment of this dream it occurred to him that he was inside a helicopter. Then he looked over to see who was flying it.

The pilot was Lucy.

WILL FOUND HIMSELF awake at two in the morning. Exhausted to the very depths of his being, but somehow still wide awake. He went to the kitchen for a glass of water, and stood at the back door as he drank it, gazing out at the shed, whose interior light still blazed.

It had been a gift to have Teddy living here all these months. It was a joy to witness his fidgety transformation from kid-overwhelmed-by-college, kid-flummoxed-by-girls, to this new young man, whoever he was. This was the human version of the *zugunruhe*, the restlessness of birds just before their migration, and it recalled for Will another fussy moment of passage, back when Teddy was just a year old. Marianne and Tom had gone off together to New York. It was their first night apart from baby Teddy, and Uncle Will had been prevailed upon to baby-sit. Teddy had woken up howling at three in the morning. He howled louder at the sight of Will leaning into his crib, and louder still when Will attempted to change his dry diaper. Little Teddy was inconsolable. So Will quit rocking him. He carried him downstairs and set him on the kitchen floor with a tray of Cheerios before him. This move surprised Teddy, and soon he quieted. He sat there like a buddha, eyes glistening with tears; he glanced at Will, glanced at the Cheerios before him, then suddenly began eating them with both hands. And in this feeding frenzy a Cheerio had ricocheted off Teddy's nose and rolled out of reach. Teddy glared at it. He looked for a moment as if he might start bawling again. But then he leaned forward on his hands and pushed himself to his feet, and staggered over to pick it up. Those were his first steps.

Barry's gift packet of condoms had disappeared from the basket on the bureau, not exactly a huge surprise to Will.

In bed, he curled in beside Annie. She turned in her sleep to face him. Her hand found his beneath a pillow.

"You awake?" he whispered.

"Ummmm," she replied.

Will kissed her, first on the forehead, then the nose. "The light's still on in the shed," he whispered. "You think maybe it's time to call 911?"

She laughed softly, pressed her face to his neck.

Then she was asleep, or quiet enough that Will thought she might be asleep. Or else he was asleep, and dreaming all of this. One or two days ago he could not have imagined Annie the litigator going all the way to National Airport, and *not* getting on her plane. Nor could he have imagined that look on her face when she came toward him on the front porch, a look that said she had given in to the hope that they might have a future together. That she would take that chance. The Cheerio had ricocheted off Will's nose and, brave fools that they had somehow managed to become, they had struggled to their feet and staggered off together in slow pursuit.

The odds, whispered a voice in Will's head. The odds! Here he and Annie stood at the threshold of midlife, two people, two separate lives, two autonomous worlds fully furnished: roomfuls of beds and chairs, two sideboards, two drop-leaf tables, dozens of house plants and small appliances, bookcases overflowing with books which had been bought in a fever but never read, separate CDs and cassettes, LPs that they couldn't listen to anymore, the memory of animals that had spent full lives in their care. They had different taste in toothpaste, pasta noodles, salad dressing, breakfast cereal, apples, dish soap, cat food, toilet paper. The notion that two such lives could be merged beneath one roof seemed as improbable as the chance that two great ocean liners might come upon one another in the open sea, and sail off together side-by-side.

Yet now Will and Annie were kissing. Sleepy kissing. Kissing in that soulful way in which neither of them had kissed since the long-ago days when kissing was the whole point. But this wasn't the good old days, nor even a hazy reenactment of those days, and pretty quickly the kissing turned a corner and gave way to all the crazy impulses. The sex went on and on, so quietly and tenderly it felt sacred to Will, like a marriage act.

And then, as if to balance the sacred with the profane, he and Annie did the deed again, raucously and joyously this time.

It had all felt so much like a dream that when Will woke up in the gray hours his first thought was that it *had* been a dream. But then his knee found the wet spot on the sheet, and he sidled up to Annie. He turned onto his back, and lay quietly beside her, as the full catalog of worries about what the coming day might bring settled upon him like a small child kneeling on his chest.

Morning arrived slowly. Will's internal clock stood him upright before he was awake, or else his body had responded to the whir of the grinder from the kitchen, and the smell of coffee. There was no talk with Annie about decisions made, new paths taken; no sideways glances or conspiratorial smiles from either of them, nothing but orange juice and strong coffee sipped side-by-side on the front steps to whispered conversation about Teddy, conversation that drove Will, finally, to undertake the paranoid parental act of creeping across the wet lawn and pressing his cheek to the window of the shed. A light bulb burning at two in the morning was one thing, but a light bulb burning at dawn—

It was off.

The day was cool and damp, the morning far enough along now that sunlight slanted through the trees, briefly illuminating each commuter who drifted up the street.

Will told Annie of his campaign in the Wilderness. He described how Ruthie had saved the day: she had discovered hoofprints beside the front porch of her motel, and had tracked Norton's new horse to Wayland and Darleen's tent, where Wayland the archivist and Christian motorcyclist, who was engaged in private researches into the religious fervor and mass conversions that swept the Confederate army in the winter of 1864, had made a full confession.

Annie was not a religious person, nor was Will, not in the sense that he still held to the Catholic belief in the existence of a God so powerful as to actually be able to exert control over one particular parcel on its perilous journey through the labyrinthine corridors of the U.S. Postal Service. Still, they both observed a moment of silence for the safe delivery of Norton's manuscript.

Annie said, "Is he unusual or are all writers like this?"

"Norton is what the folks in Hollywood would describe as a high concept."

"What you mean is, a nut."

Will nodded.

It was eight-thirty, then almost nine, and still there was no sign of life out back.

Annie took his arm. "So who do you call first?"

"Good question." A moment later, Will said, "I was thinking we might drive out to St. Mary's City this morning, and see where Jodie grew up."

"Call the poor girl," Annie said softly. "Just punch in the number and get it over with. Don't even think about what you're going to say."

"I thought it might be easier if I had a sense of who she is."

"She knows you know. At least Teddy thinks so. She's probably sitting by the phone right now. Don't let her call you."

"Maybe I should call Lucy."

"Maybe you need to flip a coin."

"Heads I call Jodie right now," he said. "Tails we go to St. Mary's."

"Heads you call Jodie, tails you call Lucy."

Will took a penny from Annie's outstretched hand and flipped it. It came up tails.

Annie went for the cordless phone. She used it to call a cab, then handed it to Will.

He said, "I wish this was over. All of this."

"It will be soon enough."

"Thank you, Annie."

She kissed him hard, looking into his eyes the whole time.

He said, "So what are you doing tonight?"

"No plans."

"Let's make some."

"Call me. I'll be at the office."

"Will you sneak out early?"

"Depends."

"On what?"

"On who's asking," she replied.

He had always assumed that a good marriage required equilibrium, that it had to be rooted in some amorphous notion of equality and partnership: two people coming together to form a single unit of some kind. But this was just an idea, as fixed or fleeting as the two characters involved. In fact, thought Will, he and Annie had begun a journey. A partner in life should be someone you want to travel with, regardless of the destination or the weather. Why had it taken him forty-one years to figure out such a simple thing?

Will sat staring at the cordless phone long after Annie's Yellow Cab had come and gone before he finally summoned the nerve to punch in Jodie's number. A young woman answered. Will asked to speak with Jodie Cameron.

There was silence. Then: "This is Jodie."

He took a deep breath. "Jodie, this is Will Gerard." Silence. "The book agent."

"Yes, yes." And then, a moment later: "I spoke with your assistant. Yesterday."

The sunlight reflecting off the wet grass made Will squint. The sunlight and the pressure of tears.

"I know," he said. "He told me." And then, "Jodie, I don't really know how to say this, so maybe I'd better get right to the point. I'm not calling about the book you want to write. It's about you. About you and me." He looked up at the trees, looked all around and couldn't find one single bird. "The birth father you're looking for," he finally said. "I think that's me."

She didn't reply, didn't utter a sound. Will sensed she was crying, and suddenly he was crying, too.

"Jodie, do you know if I'm right?"

"I'm not positive," she whispered. "But I think so."

"I didn't know about you. That is, not directly. I wasn't told."

She cried softly.

"I should have known," he said. "And in a way, I guess, I did."

After a moment, Jodie said, "Sometime I would like to meet you. So we could have a chance to talk."

"I'd like that, too."

"I know where you live. In Cabin John." Another pause. "I have a car. I could come over."

"When?"

"Whenever it's convenient."

"Today sometime?"

"Around noon?"

"I'll be waiting," said Will.

It was almost ten, which meant Lucy would be at home—home alone probably. Will knew that he should call her. But he couldn't bring himself to do that, not right away, feeling as peculiar as he did: strung out and strung together, all at once, almost incapable of conversation. Incapable of conversation with Lucy, certainly. So he walked up the street to a coffee shop, where he sipped another cup, read the paper, and spent most of an hour pretending that this was just any other day, a Wednesday morning in May like all the rest.

At home he met Teddy on the front porch. Teddy appeared agitated. As Will approached, he sensed that his nephew was blocking the front door.

"Jill's in the kitchen," Teddy finally admitted. "Cleaning up. She was, um, pretty adamant about not needing any help."

"These would be breakfast dishes?"

Young Theo nodded. He smiled sheepishly. "I made waffles from scratch."

Will, in a whisper: "You little bastard. When did you learn to cook? Why haven't you ever cooked for me?"

Teddy's face erupted in a devilish grin. Suddenly he looked ten years old again, the lovable ne'er-do-well whose idea of good summer fun was to drop a wad of bubble gum on the hot sidewalk in front of the 7-Eleven in Glen Echo and watch people track it across the parking lot.

But within five seconds the grin vanished. Teddy looked concerned. "What happen to Annie?" he asked.

"She went home." Will put an arm around his nephew. "Not to worry about us. Sometimes life turns out all right, just when you least expect it."

"And sometimes it doesn't," Teddy replied grimly. "I take it you haven't spoken to Rita yet?"

"I thought I'd wait for the mail. In the hope that Wade is delivering a package from Norton."

"You mean Norton's *manuscript?*"

Will nodded.

"You don't *have* it?" Teddy's voice suddenly filled with anxiety. "Listen, Uncle Will, I think it would be a *really* good idea for you to telephone Rita right now."

"Why is that?"

"The thing is," he began, "she called again last night after you talked to her. She had tried your cell phone but you weren't answering. So she called me." Pause. "I didn't start it. She dissed me first."

"What did you say to Rita?"

"Norton's book is *rock solid,* right? Isn't that what you've always said? A sure-bet, can't-miss bestseller. Quote, unquote."

There were three crows in the tree above. One of them dipped its head and called out in a raucous laugh.

"What did you say to her, Ted?"

"Nothing."

"You *hung up* on her?"

"She hung up on me."

"Why did Rita Corelli hang up on you?"

Teddy lifted his chin. "First you need to understand something: what I did was calculated. Let's not forget that you left me in charge."

"I said *hold down the fort.* You and I both know that holding down the fort is an extremely passive activity."

"I didn't lose my temper, if that's what you're thinking. She was the one who lost it."

"What happened?"

He sighed. "She tried to hold my feet to the fire. She said that Norton's manuscript was way overdue, and that if she didn't hear from you in five minutes the deal was off. I tried your line. You weren't answering. I figured I had to do something. That it was up to me."

Will felt lightheaded. He took a seat on the porch steps. The single crow perched on the branch above regarded him with a quizzical tilt of the head.

"Uncle," said Teddy earnestly. "I didn't cuss at her. I didn't get pissed. This wasn't a knee-jerk response or anything."

"What did you do?"

"Well, after she hung up on me, and after I had tried you, and after the five minutes were up, I figured I had to do something, so I weighed all the options. It came down to this: either Rita was bluffing or she wasn't. If she wasn't bluffing, then the deal was cooked, so it didn't matter what I said or did. But if she *was* bluffing, and she got us down on our knees over this, I figured she'd never let us stand up again." He brightened. "It was an easy call: I figured we didn't have anything to lose."

Will thought: he flamed her. He had arranged to have gift-wrapped and delivered to her office an enormous chocolate penis.

"What did you do, Teddy?"

He shrugged. "All I did was fax a check."

"You faxed Rita a check?"

"To make a point," he said. "It's not like she's going to cash a *fax*."

"Whose check?"

Teddy couldn't hide his smirk. "My check."

"A check for how much?"

Now he was studying his shoes. "A hundred thousand dollars."

Will laughed. It was a laugh born of nervousness, incredulity, and yes, a bit of mirth, too. The crow flew away, screaming indignantly. The next instant the telephone sounded.

Teddy jumped. "Let me get that."

He returned with the cordless phone parked at his ear and took a seat beside Will. Teddy sat there listening for a full minute.

"Look," he said finally, "Gwen and I have already been through this." More listening, now with his eyes closed. Then: "So what are you getting at?" Teddy looked at Will, the corners of his lips twitching into a smile.

Will could hear Barry's voice. With Jodie due to arrive in less than an hour, he wanted to put off this conversation. "Later," he mouthed.

Teddy said, "How about if I have Will call you when he gets in?"

Pause. "Later in the afternoon sometime." Another pause. "You can't call him. He's on the road. He's been gone so long the batteries in his cell phone are dead." Pause. Then: "Sorry, Mr. Valentine, he didn't mention anything about a deadline with the messenger service."

Barry was screaming now, hooting and hollering.

Will pointed at Teddy. "Handle it," he mouthed.

Teddy looked stunned for an instant, then extraordinarily pleased. He motioned for Will's pen and newspaper while Barry continued to rant. "Ballpark?" he scribbled.

Will held up six fingers.

"Well," said Teddy finally, "if you're interested, and you want to make an offer, I could note the time and pass it along to Will." Pause. "No, this isn't an auction." Pause. "Not yet anyway." Pause. "No, he isn't here." Pause. "No, this isn't a ploy."

Will smiled. Teddy's gaze narrowed as Barry revealed his number. Teddy's lips curled downward. He sighed. He actually took a moment to hold the phone with his shoulder and empty his nose into a handkerchief. Then, sourly, he replied, "Sure thing, I'll tell him." Another pause. "Okay, okay, since you and my uncle are old friends I guess it's okay for me to tell you off the record that we're too far apart. I think Will has pegged a preemptive bid at the one-twenty-five range."

Will sat up straight.

"Well, that's a *little* better," said Teddy. "Hardback only, right?" Pause. "Well, if we're talking about a hard/soft deal, we're still too far apart to wrap this up right now." Pause. "How about if we freeze the conversation right here, and you and Will finish it?" Then: "Wait a doggone minute. We're in luck. He just pulled into the driveway. Hold the line, Mr. Valentine, and I'll see if I can put him on."

They sat together in silence for a moment. Teddy wrote down "$75,000," and underlined the number three times. Then he handed the phone to Will.

"Barry," said Will breathlessly. "You won't believe it. I talked to her."

"Iris?"

"Charlotte Cameron," Will said. "She goes by Jodie. My *daughter*."

"Great, great," came Barry's instant reply, so deeply mired was he in the wheeling-and-dealing mode. "Listen, buddy, I'd feel a whole lot better if we settled the number on this right now."

"She'll be here any moment. Think of it, I am about to meet my twenty-year-old daughter for the first time."

"You can absolutely forget one-twenty-five," said Barry.

"We'll talk about that later."

"We'll talk about it right now, chum. Your deadline, in case you've forgotten."

Teddy had started for the driveway. In a moment Will saw Jill there, too, as she emerged from the side of the house trailed by a limping Long John. She was heading toward a silver Volvo that was parked on the street. Jill had short reddish hair and porcelain skin. From Teddy's demeanor at the car door—the casual slouch, the way he braced his hand on the roof of her car—Will knew for certain that he had slept with her. And the slightly pinched expression on Jill's face as she lifted Long John into the backseat indicated that this romance was of the night-blooming cereus variety: daylight had spoiled everything. No doubt Jill had known this from the outset. No doubt she knew that her tight end had driven through the night to make amends, and that he was parked in her parents' driveway at this very moment. There would be shouts and recriminations on the front lawn when Jill arrived home with wet hair, then tearful confessions on both sides, and more wounded howling, and then hours and hours of sex.

Teddy's face was etched with a dignified sort of bereavement as he watched Jill's car disappear around the corner.

"Goddamnit," shouted Barry, "are you listening to me?"

"Barely," Will replied.

"With Teddy, I was willing to go to seventy-five. With you, I can do eighty. But that's for everything. Everything but film rights."

"I'll fax Iris."

"She lives in the middle of the jungle, for God's sakes. You decide."

"Honestly, it sounds low."

"Eighty thousand bucks is more than the cost of an average house in *our* republic. In the one Iris lives in it'll buy a whole bloody town."

"I'll think about it."

"Ninety. But that's it."

"I'm about to meet my long-lost daughter, Barry. I'm not even in the mood for this."

"Don't bullshit me, Will."

"Look, I'll have Teddy call off the messenger service. We can finish this later."

"One hundred even. But that's hard/soft, worldwide."

"Gotcha."

Silence. "Old friend," whispered Barry, "you can go straight to hell. Do not pass go. Do not collect two hundred dollars." Then: "I take it we have a deal."

"I need to think about it."

"One hour."

"Two," said Will.

Teddy stood quietly on the front walk, like a bad dog facing the rolled-up newspaper.

"Should I telephone Rita right now?" he asked.

Or maybe just fax her a smiley face, thought Will.

How many times in the past four months had he rued the decision to hire Teddy? How many times had he wanted to call off the experiment and send the kid home with a two-week severance check? At least a dozen, Will figured, probably two. And here was one more occasion. And yet he knew he wouldn't let Teddy go. Couldn't do that, now or ever. There was a surface tension about the lad, a vibrancy that energized the place. He was a loose cannon, yes, but often pointed in the right direction. This deal with Barry would account for half of Teddy's salary. For a first novel! A novel for which Will would have taken Barry's first offer, and felt satisfied if he had managed to squeeze out an additional 10 percent to cover his commission. In the long run Teddy would belong to the world, but in the short run Will figured he could use him right here.

"You pinched my rubbers," he said.

The tiniest smile appeared on Teddy's face. It grew. "The thing is, I figured that if you thought you'd need them at this point, that would mean you *wouldn't* need them. Only you might not realize that if they were lying around. In the heat of the moment, I mean. So then my taking them was really doing you a favor."

"Say that again?"

"Can I ask you a question, Uncle Will?"

"Shoot."

"Is it normal that afterward I felt sad?"

Sure it was. The cosmic wheel had just cranked forward another notch. Every moment of bliss is tempered by a heightened awareness of life's fleeting nature. "Could be that's when you realized that this might turn out to be a one-time thing," Will said quietly.

"A two-time thing," Teddy reported, with a measure of pride.

"So how do you feel right now?"

"Like I was trying too hard. Like I wanted to hold onto Jill, and knew that I couldn't, and in a way knew that even if I could, it wouldn't be the best thing anyway, but somehow couldn't stop myself from trying. I just couldn't get myself to do what I knew I *should* do. You know, playing it cool, as if none of this mattered at all."

"Either you can or you can't, Ted. Don't hold it against yourself. And don't run through all the things you said or did, and then kick yourself for not saying or doing something else. It'll just make you feel worse."

"Just now I was thinking about calling her. I guess I shouldn't do that."

"It's up to you."

"No," he said finally. "I'd probably end up taking Long John for a walk all by myself."

"Everybody ends up taking Long John for a walk all by himself."

It took Teddy a moment to get the joke. He grinned. Inside the house, a chime sounded. It was midday.

"Maybe we should talk to Rita's machine," said Will.

They performed the message in his office, Will chatting above Teddy's simulated wind, his rolling tires, his droning auto engine. Will played it upbeat and not completely truthful about the whereabouts of a much-sought-after manuscript. "Everything is under control," he said. There was no mention of the literary pyre, nor how all would depend now on the smooth operation of the U.S. Postal Service.

Afterward, Will and Teddy returned to the front steps.

"When Lucy called," said Will, "what did she say?"

"It was just a message on the machine."

"Neutral, annoyed, angry?"

"Not exactly neutral." Teddy thought. "It was more like she had something to tell you. Like she really wanted to see you all of a sudden." He looked at Will. "Is Lucy the reason it's taken you so long to settle down? Is it because you've never gotten over her?"

Will considered the question. A week ago he would have denied that. Denied it absolutely. But now he shrugged. "It must be part of it," he replied.

The world grew quiet then: no squawking birds, no traffic on MacArthur Boulevard, no jet planes overhead. Even Mr. Richmond next door took a break from his regular Wednesday noontime chore of tuning up his powder blue Bugatti.

"Maybe you should call her," Teddy said.

"Lucy?"

"Jodie."

"Already did," answered Will.

"You did?"

He nodded. "She'll be here any minute."

"Holy shit. Are you going to be all right?"

Will turned to him, shook his head. "Not a chance," he said.

Teddy looked toward MacArthur Boulevard as a blue Toyota began its turn. He put a hand on his uncle's shoulder as he leapt to his feet, then an instant later the screen door slammed.

Will watched the Corolla slow to get an address as it rolled past the house. It turned into Mr. Richmond's driveway, backed out, and came to a stop directly in front of him. He stood, began walking toward the car, then stopped when the driver's door came open. Suddenly he couldn't move. Suddenly he feared coming unglued at first sight of this young stranger.

Her hair was his color brown. She was tall and long-limbed like him, too. She wore stylish round sunglasses. My daughter, thought Will. Holy shit. She stood frozen at the door, her left hand resting on the roof of the car, gripping her keys. She had his lips, Lucy's milky coloring and long neck.

"Jodie?" he called.

Both of them were moving slowly, swimming through the air as they struggled to keep their composure.

Her hand shook, the keys rattling as they met on the walk. "I don't even know what I should call you," she began.

"Will," he said.

She looked at him, then looked away, her head shaking. "I'm sorry. This just doesn't seem real. I can't believe this is happening."

He was half-turned toward the house, thinking he should invite her inside. But he couldn't stand the thought of going indoors right then. At this moment they would need as much space as the whole world had to offer.

"Listen," said Will, "would it be all right with you if we took a walk down to the river?"

She nodded quickly.

So they walked together. They passed Mr. Richmond, his eyes closed, head swinging in time to a Sousa march on the boom box as he polished his beloved Bugatti; they passed the cluster of nouveau Victorians with the immaculate lawns and color-matched mailboxes at the end of the street. Traffic on the parkway was light, so they dashed across, Jodie three steps ahead of Will, her stride long and graceful. She wore tan jeans and brown clogs, a sleeveless denim shirt. On the shady lane that led down to the towpath, Will finally spoke. He said, "I have walked this street a thousand times and not once has it occurred to me that one day I would find myself walking here with my grown-up daughter."

Jodie looked up at the trees, then at him, then back at the trees. "I've been here, too," she said. "Just once. Last week." She looked at him again. "You were sitting on your front porch with a young guy when I drove past."

"Teddy," said Will.

"Your assistant? The one who called me?"

He nodded. "Teddy's your cousin, too."

She looked stunned. It was all she could do, Will sensed, to hold herself together.

The road ended, and they descended toward the river on a path as rocky as a streambed. At one point Jodie tripped, and then caught herself. She turned in time to see Will stumble, too.

"Bad genes," he said.

"Big feet," she replied.

"Big feet and my head in the clouds."

Just weeks earlier the canal had been ravaged by an early spring flood. Now it stood empty with whole sections of the towpath washed away. So Will and Jodie continued forward on a silty path that led through the scoured landscape toward the river. At the water's edge the flood-damaged trees sat two feet above their exposed roots. The Potomac was still carrying a heavy volume of water and debris. A branch the size of a canoe sailed past, glancing off a small rocky island. At the impact, a nesting goose complained loudly.

"Jodie," Will finally said, "I don't know where to begin."

"Do you mind if I ask some of the questions that have been on my mind?"

"Of course not."

"Why didn't you know about me?"

He listened to the geese. "I ran away." He looked at her. "From the news about you. And from myself, too. It's a terrible answer. I wish I had a better one. But I don't." He paused. "How did you find me?"

"I saw the story in the *Post*."

"You *guessed?*"

She shook her head. "Not right away. Only when it came in the mail." She looked out at the geese. "I'm not sure, but I think it was Lucy who sent it to me." She turned to Will. "Have you talked to her?"

He nodded. "Yesterday. For the first time in twenty years. We didn't talk about you," he added. "Yesterday I wasn't sure about you."

"And today you are?"

He nodded. "Yes."

Jodie stared at the water. Will heard a jet overhead; and when it passed, the staccato call of a pileated woodpecker.

She said, "This is hard. This is really, really hard. I didn't think it would be. I don't know why I didn't think it would be."

Will nodded.

She faced him. "The toughest part about being adopted is that even if your life is okay—like mine is—there's still this hole. This huge hole. It's just there. All the time. Every hour of every day."

Again he nodded. Again he was fighting tears.

"There was a nurse at the hospital. Holy Cross. An old friend of my parents. She checked the records for us. That's how I got Lucy's name."

"Have you talked to her?"

Jodie shook her head. "I went to see her. At the hospital where she works. She looked at me with this funny expression as I walked up to her, and I knew she knew who I was. And then, suddenly, she hurried away. This was just before Christmas." Jodie looked at Will. "On my birthday." She paused. "After that I wrote to her. I told her that I wouldn't keep bothering her. That I didn't want anything from her besides whatever family medical information she could give me. And the name of my birth father. I sent that letter to her in January and never heard back from her. Then a few weeks ago, out of the blue, the article about you arrived in the mail. No note, no return address."

Softly Will said, "Lucy and I were friends in Bangkok—boyfriend and girlfriend in eighth grade. Her father was a pilot. His helicopter disappeared in Laos. The day the news came, Lucy was taken out of school. The next morning she and her mother left Thailand. I lost touch with her. I found her again when my family came home to the States. My father died in 1974, and then a year later, at the end of March, Lucy's mother died. That's when you were conceived."

"Did you love each other?"

He thought for a moment. "I don't know. I didn't know much at all about love back then. It felt more like Lucy and I needed each other." He looked at Jodie. "That's what I told myself anyway."

Will felt crushed by regret. That night long ago he and Lucy had made a terrible mistake. And yet, before him stood this beautiful young woman who would not be alive in the world but for that mistake! How utterly different his life would have been had he not run away all those years ago. And so strange to realize that, right now, he would have traded this life for that one, sight unseen. He would have traded lives in a heartbeat. For all he knew the hand of fate might have him and Jodie out together on this very day—right here, too—only instead of introducing themselves, she would be telling her father about her semester at school, about her classes, about a problem with a roommate or a boyfriend. Will would have his arm around his daughter's shoulders. They would be laughing. They would talk about her summer plans.

"What was it like to grow up in St. Mary's City?" he asked.

She looked at him.

"Yesterday I went to see the woman who helped Lucy get to St. Jerome's. She was a nun back then—an ex-nun, now. She told me that your father was a history professor at a college in southern Maryland. Teddy told me the rest."

"St. Mary's was pretty quiet," Jodie said.

"Someday, if it's okay with you and your parents, I'd like to meet them. See where you grew up."

"My dad's retired. He's thinking of moving." She looked at Will. "You see, last year, my mom died. She had breast cancer."

"I'm sorry."

"I'm sure my dad would be glad to meet you. He's okay with this. In fact he encouraged me." A pause. "Not my mom. I think she felt pretty threatened by my wanting to find you and Lucy."

They were walking now, climbing toward the towpath. The sun was out. The tulip poplar blossoms scattered across the ground and covered with ants looked like enormous clumps of candy corn. Will described his family to Jodie—grandparents, parents, Jonathan and Marianne. He told her that his father had died at the age of forty-seven of a heart attack, and that his grandfather had died young of a heart attack, too; and as they climbed the rocky slope to the parkway in silence Will had to wonder if that would be his fate as well.

"You aren't married?" she asked.

He shook his head.

"And no other kids?"

He smiled. Fair question. "No."

"Do I have any other cousins?"

Another shake of the head. "Lucy was an only child. Jonathan's divorced, no kids. Teddy is Marianne's son. Another only child."

"Is he into computers?"

"He told you?"

"Not exactly," she said. "It's just the way he talks, the words he uses. And his sense of humor."

"And what are you into? History, like your father?"

She smiled. "My dad says that those who cannot remember the past are condemned to repeat it, and those who make a career of it are condemned to spend their life wishing they had done something else." She brushed a lock of hair from her face. "He nudged me toward science. I started out pre-med but then drifted toward biology. Right now it seems I'm going to end up in the field he wishes he had pursued."

"What's that?" asked Will.

"Ornithology." She gazed around. "I grew up looking at birds."

Will smiled. He didn't know what to say.

On the walk home, they talked birds: the nesting habits of ospreys, the lek of cranes, a pellet study of great horned owls that Jodie had just read about. She told Will that lately she had been involved in a research project to determine the percentage of bald eagle chicks in the Potomac River watershed surviving to adulthood.

"So your father's a serious birdwatcher?"

"It's a passion. He has thirty years of observations in his notebooks. That's one reason he wants to move to the shore: more birds."

Jodie told Will a story. A few months after her mother died, she and her father were sitting in the car one morning, coffee mugs in one hand, binoculars in the other. This was near their vacation cottage in Delaware, which happened to be only a few miles up the Broadkill River from Lewes. They were stopped at a roadside, spishing for redheaded woodpeckers. Jodie was telling her father about the diary she'd begun in high school to sort out her feelings about being adopted. Her father asked if she thought she'd ever want to try to find her birth parents. The look in his eyes assured her that he wouldn't be threatened by this. She nodded. A few months later, as she was packing up to head back to school, he came to her room and gave her a folder. In it was a sheet of paper with Lucy's name, her home address and phone number, her office address and phone number at Georgetown Hospital, copies of two articles on emergency medicine that she had published, and a photograph of her that Jodie's father had downloaded from Georgetown's on-line directory. "In case you feel like writing to her," he'd said. "Or want to go talk to her."

Will thought back on his own life at twenty, at thirty, at forty. Raising a child would have changed him in fundamental ways, he was certain. It would have tested him; no doubt broadened him, too. Still, he felt sure he could not have been as good a father as the father Jodie had. This thought was a comfort at first, but soon it left him feeling inexpressibly sad.

Jodie said, "I saw that article in the *Post* when it came out. I actually read it—I really *have* thought about publishing my journal. And then Lucy sent it to me, and I read it again, and all these things that I'd missed just jumped out at me: Bangkok, where I knew Lucy had lived. You were her age. And your family being Catholic, what with Lucy having stayed at St. Jerome's. Then I opened to the inside page, and saw that picture of you writing on a manuscript. Your profile, the way you held the pen in your left hand, with it almost pointing toward you." She looked at Will. "I showed it to my boyfriend, Alan. His eyes popped out. Right then, I just knew."

They walked.

Jodie said, "Did you ever think about Lucy? Afterward, I mean."

"Not in the sense that I ever thought about looking her up. Not until last week, when I got your letter. I was ashamed of what I did. Running away. I tried pretty hard to put it behind me. It seemed that I had. Things happen in life and you deal with them or you don't deal with them, and life goes on. That's how I was behaving. I wouldn't let myself get below the surface of this. Even now it's hard—with Lucy, I mean. I couldn't ask her directly about you when I saw her yesterday. It was as if I didn't have the right. You do. But I don't. Not now, after all these years, what her husband and son—"

"She's divorced."

Will was stunned. "She told me she was married," he said.

Jodie shook her head. She didn't ask the obvious follow-up question—*Do you still love her?*—but Will saw it in her eyes. He saw the answer there, too.

Of course he did.

Will thought about the ties that bind parent to parent, and parent to child; he thought about the biology of love, and the notion that science might someday find a gene that inclined a person to, say, watch birds. He thought about Jodie's boyfriend, who might become her husband one day, and the father of her children—his own grandchildren—kids who might be tall and thin, or left-handed, or dark-haired, or bookish, or solitary in the Gerard family way. It was a stunning thing to contemplate. The tree is the common metaphor for families, and Will had always loved the notion of the roots of a clan growing ever deeper as more of its tangled branches shot skyward. But really there was a better metaphor in the heavens: stars, constellations, whole galaxies wheeling across an empty universe, the precise relationship between any two bodies never fixed, but simply a function of time, and one's own position.

W ADE'S MAIL TRUCK was parked in Will's driveway, but Wade
was nowhere in sight. Nor was the mail. There was no sign of Teddy
either, but from the look of things, young Ted must have spent the
previous hour planting red and white impatiens in the flower beds on
either side of the front steps. Last night a gourmet chef, and today a
master gardener! Jodie followed Will up to the porch. She seemed
smaller there, frailer, as if suddenly overwhelmed, or disappointed. He
said, "Can I get something for you? Are you thirsty?"

She shook her head. "What I'd really like to do is just sit down for
a minute."

"Relax," he said.

Will found Teddy in the kitchen. Teddy was hovering near the
doorway, craning his neck to catch a glimpse of Jodie through the living room window. "Golly," he whispered. "She's gorgeous."

The intensity of Teddy's gaze spoke of the sort of interest one
should not feel for the daughter of a blood uncle. Either that, or else
this rapturous expression was the only one available to young Ted on
this particular morning.

Will frowned. "Your *first* cousin," he whispered.

"The czars of Russia always went for cousins."

"And look what it got them."

Teddy grinned. "It went okay, I guess."

Will glanced at the porch. "I don't have a clue. Right now I don't have much of a clue about anything."

"In that case, I'd better let Rita know that you were just called down to the White House to discuss a major pet memoir."

Will looked over at the kitchen phone. The hold light was blinking. "How long has she been there?"

"Fifteen or twenty minutes." Teddy shrugged. "I told her it might be a while. Waiting was her idea. And anyway, it's her assistant who's doing the waiting. I check in with Janice every few minutes. She and I are getting to be old friends."

"Maybe you should tell Janice that you see me coming up the street. Wade ought to be here any minute."

"Just keep reminding yourself that it was Rita who brought this on herself, Uncle."

"Sure she did. And since she's the buyer and I'm the seller I'm not supposed to rub her nose in that fact. Not if I hope to put this deal back together. This is one of those moments to tread lightly and make the best of whatever comes along."

"Must be our theme this morning," said Teddy. "You'll never guess what happened."

In Will's current frame of mind, his life teetering on the brink of happiness, he could only imagine terrible news: Marianne in an automobile accident, or some calamity with his mother's jet—

"Julianna stopped by. On her way to work. She dropped off those flowers that are out front. Sort of a present. For me." Now Teddy grinned. "She, um, asked me if I might want to go out with her this weekend. To pick wild mushrooms."

With everything in his life so tenuous and precarious, so fraught with danger, naturally the mention of wild mushroom picking brought to Will's mind the image of two black-clad figures sprawled lifeless on the forest floor, victims of amanita, the dreaded death angel.

"She knows what she's doing," Teddy added. "With mushrooms, I mean. Oh, and she lives in a group house in Brookmont. Mostly kayakers. A room has opened up there. I think I, um, might take a look at it."

"You would consider leaving me at the very moment when what I need most of all in the world is the love and support of my family?"

"Actually, the reason I bring it up is because I'm hoping to take the truck with me."

Will weighed the request for all of two seconds. "It's yours," he said.

"Julianna loves that truck. She wants to paint it canary yellow."

"You want some advice?"

Teddy's fretful expression indicated that he did not.

"Let her paint the truck," Will said. "Just draw the line at any bumper stickers promoting hemp."

Teddy brightened. "Can I give you some advice?"

Will nodded. "I'm sure I could use it."

"It's about Norton," he said. "You need to lower the boom on that man. He's got you convinced that this book means more to you than it does to him. If I were you I'd send that manuscript off to New York, and then cut him loose."

"Something tells me the folks at Mellon Mortgage might disapprove of that move."

"The guy's incapable of establishing a relationship with another agent. If he wants to write a second book, he'll be back. If not, nothing you do will change that. And cutting him loose for a while would do wonders for your reputation and self-esteem, not to mention the mileage on your car." Teddy put an arm around Will. "Now will you please introduce me to my cousin?"

When they reached the front porch, Wade had just arrived. He was already shooting the breeze with Jodie.

"Wade," said Will. "Have you two met? This is Jodie Cameron. My daughter. Jodie, Wade Peggett."

The ever discreet Wade, the postman who rings two, three, even four times, a man privy to all of the secrets and scandals of the neighborhood, didn't bat an eyelash. He looked at Jodie, then at Will, then smiled broadly. "Well, doggone it, I should've seen the family resemblance right off."

"Jodie, this is your cousin, Teddy," Will said.

Teddy beamed. He placed the cordless phone in Will's hand. "Remember, Uncle, Rita called *you*." Then he took Jodie's arm. "I believe we have some catching up to do."

They headed inside.

Will turned to Wade. "Please tell me that among those packages is one from Orange, Virginia."

"Tazewell, Norton," Wade replied. "That one sure looks like it's been though the war."

"Yes, it has," Will replied.

He borrowed Wade's pocket knife and cut open the box. Inside, wrapped tightly in brown paper, was Norton's manuscript: page 1 to page 489, upon which, in bold letters, Norton had scrawled in pencil THE END. Will riffled though the manuscript once to check to see that no big chunks of text were missing, then slowly, noting chapter breaks and pencil corrections.

At last he released the hold button on the telephone, only to get a dial tone. When he punched in Rita's number, she picked up the line herself.

"Are you sitting down, Rita?"

"I am lying on my couch with a bag of ice resting on my forehead."

"Rise and be healed," said Will. "Two minutes ago the mail arrived, and as we speak I have in my hands the completed manuscript of *Pharaoh's Ghost* by Norton C. Tazewell."

"Will Gerard, do you swear to me that you are telling the truth?"

He handed the telephone to Wade, and gave him instructions.

Wade said, "Ma'am? I can report that the package I just delivered to Will is from Orange, Virginia, and like he told you, it's got the name of Tazewell on it. It's a whole lotta pages, more than enough for a book."

Will took the phone.

Rita said, "Was that Teddy doing voices?"

"That was Wade, my postman. Teddy has been given an extended leave of absence to attend charm school." Long pause. "So what happens now?"

Her voice dropped. "Be straight with me."

"I am." He sighed. "Look, I'm sorry about the fax. Teddy's been under enormous pressure lately." He whispered: "*Serious* probation. His job's been on the line."

"I *knew* it had to be something like that," she whispered back. "He seemed so strung out."

"He was. A little less today, I'm happy to report."

"Poor kid."

"*Lucky* kid."

"He seems bright enough. And energetic. Why would he do something like that?"

"Sometimes you have to hit bottom before you can get a handle on your problems, Rita. Which he has. Enough, anyway, to understand that what he did last night was very, very wrong." Brief pause. "Now can we put that behind us, and get on with publishing a best-seller?"

"I was furious when I got that fax. But then I showed it to my assistant, and she started laughing. Janice laughed so hard she couldn't stop. I have to admit that put a smile on my face." Her voice dropped. "That, and the news that Kathie Link will be departing shortly."

"She got fired?"

In a stage whisper: "*Creative differences.*"

"So who's in charge now?"

"The VP for new acquisitions. Monroe Dabney."

Will said, "Is Monroe Dabney a Southerner by any chance?

"Galax, Virginia," Rita replied. "His family goes way back, I understand."

"This is a sign. This means you have to publish this book."

Rita said, "Monroe asked me if there was any mention of Moses owning slaves in Norton's book. I said there wasn't." She paused. "There isn't, is there?"

Will grinned. "Of course not. Moses's family is dirt poor. Some years they were lucky to have a roof over their own heads. Tell Monroe that in the sequel, Moses will make a discovery about his own heritage. There'll be a very affecting scene around a campfire with a black woman who turns out to be Moses's grandmother. She'll tell him that his nickname, *Weedy,* comes from *Ouida,* a city on the coast of Benin."

"Is that true?"

"Hard to say, but Monroe Dabney will be long gone before that book is published."

"So how did Norton end this one?"

"Moses slips off a barge into the Pamunkey River."

"The hero *dies*? Hasn't that been done?"

"Appears to die," said Will. "*To be continued.* Just like in Mailer's big novel about the CIA. We might want to think about putting the address of your Web site at the bottom of the page so we can create a mailing list for volume two. For now you just sit tight. Order a latté and bagel for tomorrow morning. FedEx"—he shrugged an apology to Wade—"will have this on your desk by ten."

Rita said, "By the way, Will, whatever happened to that other novel you were going to show me? The story about the woman who escapes to Central America with her daughter?"

"Ah," he replied. "Major second thoughts. It just doesn't seem like your kind of book."

"You *sold* it," she scolded.

"A little interest is all."

"Damnit, Will, I want to see it, too."

"The thing is, I have a feeling the chemistry would be all wrong. Did I mention that the author lives in the jungles of Guatemala? Iris is what you'd call a genuine eccen—"

"Maybe you're right."

"I could give you first crack at a novel I just got. This kid's the next William T. Vollmann."

"Whatever that means."

"Rita," said Will. "Rita, Rita, Rita."

"Who else has seen it?"

"Read *Pharaoh's Ghost* first. Then we'll talk. Better yet, I'll let Teddy pitch it."

"Have him pitch it to Janice," said Rita. Then softly, "By the way, how old is Teddy? Janice asked me to ask you."

"Early twenties," said Will with his fingers crossed.

"Perfect." Rita paused. "Any chance he might want to move to New York? Something tells me he could get work in this business."

"He has work in this business."

Rita snorted. "Are you really holding Norton's manuscript in your hands?"

" 'Moses felt exalted by the cold water,' " read Will. " 'Dizzy but exalted, as if the night sky itself had followed him into the churning brown waters of the Pamunkey.' "

"Praise the Lord," said Rita, signing off.

Wade said, "Will, I've got a favor to ask. Could I rope you into having a cup of coffee with me up the street one of these days? I'm looking for some advice. You see, lately I've been thinking about the Ia Drang and all that I saw there. I'm thinking it's time to put some of these stories down on paper. Leave something behind so that folks'll understand what really went on in that war."

"You want to write a book," said Will.

Wade blushed. "I guess I do." He nodded. "I really do."

"Let's talk," Will said. "Anytime."

The phone sounded. It was Barry Valentine again. "Yes or no?" he demanded.

"Where did we leave it?"

"Eighty for everything but film rights."

"We'd gotten up to a hundred, if I recall."

Barry howled. "Will, this is a *first* novel."

"The husband goes after her, Barry. We're talking mortal lock on movie-of-the-week."

"Spare me the Hollywood prognostications."

"Fine. Then we'll let the market decide. I'll peg the floor at a hundred, and give you topping rights."

"You've gone mad."

"One-ten and it's yours."

Another howl of indignation.

"Yes or no," said Will.

Pause. "No. And I don't want to be in your stupid auction, either."

"So long, Barry."

"Look, I might consider one-ten if Iris were willing to recast this as a memoir."

"Dear friend, if Iris were to recast this as a memoir, I'd be asking one-ten for *serial rights*. You want to talk memoirs, ask me about Wade's book."

"Wade who?"

"Wade Peggett. He spent two tours in the Ia Drang Valley. Special ops stuff. Traveling with mercenaries, calling in air strikes on Soviet helicopters. Bravery, madness. The war in the elephant grass."

Wade beamed.

"Nice title," said Barry. "Too bad nobody gives a shit about Vietnam anymore."

"That was last year. You need to get out with one of your sales reps and see what's shaking. Take the pulse of the business—you know, the semiotics of publishing and all."

"Go to hell." Quick pause. "So send me Wade's proposal."

"And what do I tell Iris?"

"That she's going to be published by a wimp. We can talk payout next week."

"What's to talk about? Half on signing, half on delivery."

"Sorry, amigo. We hold twenty till publication. New rules. Company policy."

"So make an exception."

"Word would get around," Barry said softly. "I have a reputation to uphold."

"No."

"Excuse me?"

Will said, "Why don't you take a minute or two to sit quietly and try to come to your senses?"

Thirty seconds later, the phone sounded. Barry hollered, "Goodness gracious, lad, what has gotten into you?"

"My life," replied Will.

"*Cojones,*" Barry muttered.

"Any chance I can interest you in a novel by the next William T. Vollmann?"

Click.

Will stood alone on the porch. He could hear Teddy and Jodie in the living room talking animatedly as Wade saluted from his truck and backed out into the street. Above the conversation Teddy called out in exasperation: "Damn, all the family pictures are in *shoe boxes.*"

Deep, deep feelings of shame had been lurking within Will's soul all these years, and only now did he even recognize them. To have run away from this young woman of intelligence and beauty who might spend her life making the migratory flyways safe for songbirds! He was still holding the cordless phone, regarding it now, thinking he had to use it, to call Lucy and take whatever sort of pummeling she would dish out, a pummeling he richly deserved, if indeed pummeling was what she had in store for him.

She was divorced.

Why hadn't she told him that? And why, after refusing to talk to Jodie, had she sent her the article from the *Post*?

Teddy and Jodie were trooping out the driveway toward her car, Teddy announcing to Will over his shoulder that he was taking his cousin to meet her aunt.

"Invite your folks to dinner tonight," Will called. And then to Jodie, "Could you have dinner with us? Alan, too, if he's free?"

"I'll call him," she said. And then: "Sure, I think that would be fine."

To Teddy, Will said, "So, Paul Prudomme, any suggestions for the menu?"

Teddy knit his brow. "*Gado gado,*" he said finally. "You cover the food and beverages, and Julianna and I will do the cooking."

Will took a seat in the rocker as they drove away. Teddy had an arm out the window, a hand tapping the roof. Will figured that it was long past time to face some music of his own. He picked up the telephone.

"Lucy, it's Will."

"Hello, Will."

Cool. Measured. Was that a note of warmth in her voice? Or was it triumph?

Teddy said you called—He just couldn't bring himself to begin this way.

"I met her," he said. "Jodie. We talked on the phone. She came over. We took a walk."

Lucy said nothing.

"Thank you," he added.

"For what?" She was miles away. Miles and miles.

"For telling her."

"Oh, go to hell," said Lucy. Same tone of voice, no venom that he could hear, which made it all the more painful.

"I went to St. Jerome's. I talked to Sister Mary Bart."

Silence.

"We don't have to do this, you know."

"Sure we do, Will. Every single bit of it."

"At first I thought you were calling to let me know that you had told Jodie about me. But something tells me that wasn't the reason."

"You don't get it, do you?"

"I guess that's been the story of my life."

"Well, wake up."

"Why didn't you tell me that you were divorced?"

"Let me ask you something: Do you think I'm mad at you?"

"Yes."

"Wrong again."

"You've seen her. She's an impressive kid."

Silence.

"She isn't furious. She isn't looking for parents. She just wants to get to know us a little."

"Stop it."

"What else could you have done, Lucy?"

"Think about it."

"I've thought about it."

"I could have been her mother."

The sudden catch in Lucy's voice took Will by surprise. He didn't know what to say.

"You know what pisses me off?" She paused. "What pisses me off is that I left you out of it. I went along with what you wanted. I thought that would be easier for me. And it was. At the time. And that makes everything okay for you now."

"No," he said.

"It makes things easier. You're more or less off the hook."

"*No.*"

"I disappeared on her, Will."

"I disappeared on both of you."

"And I guess it just isn't obvious to you who had it worse."

With that, the line went dead.

Annie was at work, in the lawyer mode, but surely not so deep in the lawyer mode, today, that she wouldn't put a client on hold to take Will's call. And he thought about calling her. But he didn't. Right then he felt a thousand miles away from Annie. This was what had to happen when you let yourself wander down those old hallways, he told himself. You get confused.

Will sat at his desk and read manuscripts for an hour, not because he was drawn to any of them, but as something to do. Then he shook out the Guatemalan tablecloth, set the table for eight, and walked up the street to buy wine and candles.

He waited for Jodie and Teddy on the front porch. He thought about Jodie, about this quest to find her birth parents, and whether she had had moments of doubt about the wisdom of seeking them out. It was possible, too, that the search hadn't been much of a burden at all; perhaps the note of trepidation he sensed in her was just confusion, or fear of rejection, or shyness. For as long as she had lived with the issue of adoption, there was every reason to guess she might have more perspective than he had, more than he would ever have. She wasn't looking for real parents, after all, just the man and woman who had conceived her.

The phone rang. The machine picked up. The caller hung up. Teddy had begged Will for caller ID, and he had refused, insisting that all calls needed to be answered; but right then he wished he had signed up for that service. And then he wondered what difference it would have made: even if he had known that it was Lucy on the line, he wasn't sure he would have taken the call. All he could say for certain right then was that if this reunion with Jodie had happened three months ago he would have called Lucy back in a heartbeat. So maybe timing did count for something in life. Timing and luck. He stared at her number, a number he had already memorized, picked up the slip of paper on which it was written, put it down. He thought about getting in his car and driving to Thornapple Street, knocking at her door.

She was divorced.

She had called to say leave me out of this, which was essentially what he had told her all those summers ago. So now they were even. Now they could have the conversation they had long needed to have. But not on the phone, not at her front door, not in the parking lot of a hospital. Where did she shop? he wondered. Perhaps he could arrange to run into her at a grocery store, or the farmers market. Or else none of that. Maybe this was the moment to behave like an adult, and bury all of these useless emotions. If Lucy eventually let down her guard with Jodie, and Jodie wanted to bring them together . . . well, it wouldn't happen often, Will figured, not often enough to force him to sort out why he felt tethered to Lucy by this rope that stretched across the years.

The phone rang, and Will picked it up.

"Hello again."

"Lucy."

"I want to see you," she said. "Right now."

She was on her way to the hospital, so they met at a playground in Georgetown. They sat at a picnic table, Will in a gray shirt, sleeves rolled, Lucy in a white T-shirt and khaki pants. She had this aura of impatience and instinct, and quick, expressive hands: Lucy the doctor. Will sensed she would be good in a medical emergency, and maybe not so good with a patient's family afterward.

She said, "You didn't ask me why I called."

"It seemed obvious."

A quick shake of her head. "It isn't."

He had brought an apple, which he began to cut into pieces. Lucy took one. "So why did you call me?" he said.

"To make sure you understood that this didn't involve *us*, not together anyway." She chewed the apple. "But then I realized I was wrong."

"Is that why you called back?"

"I didn't think about why I called back. That was impulsive."

"How much do you hate me?"

She smiled a weary smile, and took another section of apple. "I never hated you, Will. I hated what happened." She looked toward the tennis courts. "In the end I hated myself."

"What else could you have done?"

"I had three choices." She looked at him. "I just couldn't bring myself to consider the other two."

"You did the right thing for Jodie."

"What makes you so sure of that?"

"I've met her. I've talked to her." Then, quietly, "She's a beautiful, thoughtful kid. She came looking for us to find out who we are, not to say that she wishes things had been different."

"Oh, bullshit, Will."

He granted her that. He took a bite of apple.

"What about you?" she asked.

He looked out at the trees. "I can't even imagine," he replied.

She seemed curious now. "What if I'd come to you? What would you have wanted me to do?"

"I don't know." He thought. "Whatever you wanted, I suppose."

"I wouldn't have told you what I wanted." She kept looking at him. And then: "They told me a lot of things at St. Jerome's, but nobody bothered to tell me that I might never get over losing this child. All I know, all I've ever known, is that I should have kept her."

"All by yourself? Could you have managed that?"

Lucy smiled. "Don't be such a pessimist, Will Gerard. God knows, you might even have come through for me."

Now he let himself smile.

She reached across the table and took his hand. "I thought the world of you. You had no idea. Still don't, apparently." A pause. "It would make one hell of a love story, wouldn't it? Not a dry eye in the house." She let go of his hand. "Do you know why I never called you at school that fall?"

"Because I ran away."

She shook her head.

"Why?" he asked.

"You sure you want to know?"

He wasn't sure, but his head nodded anyway.

Lucy said, "I think you're Jodie's father. But I'm not certain of that."

Bullshit, thought Will. He couldn't stop his head from shaking. He was prepared for anything she might say to him right now, anything but this. "You've *seen* her," he said. Lucy wouldn't look at him now. "Why are you saying this?"

"You asked me why I never called. That's the reason."

He waited, studying her for the hint of a lie. But he couldn't find it.

"I had a boyfriend that spring. We'd broken up. The week before my mother died, he called. It was an awful time. I wanted company. I guess I was needy. We got together one last time."

Will looked at her. "I don't believe you."

"I'm not asking you to believe me."

"Why wasn't he at the funeral?"

She shook her head. "I never told him that my mother died."

"And he didn't see the obituary in the *Post*?"

"Maybe he did, maybe he didn't."

"What's his name?"

Lucy turned away.

Will said, "Why didn't you tell Jodie?"

She shook her head. "Like you said, look at her."

"Where is he now?"

"I don't know."

Was this true? Why would she make this up? "She's ours," he said.

"She was never ours," Lucy replied.

"Well, there's always a DNA test." Will paused. "If it mattered."

She didn't say anything at first. Then: "You tell me: does it matter?"

Will gazed at her, and in that instant felt something crack open between them. "No." A moment later, he said, "Why didn't you admit that you were divorced?"

"It was irrelevant."

"But you lied."

"I didn't like the way you sounded on the phone. As if you were calling to ask me out on a date or something." Lucy went on: "Things happen in life, Will. Some things you wish you could change. Wish with all your heart. But you can't. So you go on." She looked at him. "Not a birthday passed that I wasn't in mourning. Then, on the day she turned twenty, there she was, standing right in front of me and suddenly I felt as bad as I felt the day they took her away from me at the hospital."

"Talk to her," he said.

"She's not my daughter, Will. She's not yours either."

"Maybe not," he said, "but she's still family."

Lucy turned away. "I have a question for you. Do you know what happened to my father?"

He shook his head.

"You never asked your father?"

"No."

"How come you never asked me?"

"I always had the feeling that was something you didn't want to talk about."

"I *couldn't* talk about it. It's not that I didn't want to. And you're one of the few people in the world who might have understood. But you never asked."

"What happened to him?"

"For years and years I had this fantasy—"

"Please tell me what happened to him."

"He disappeared." She looked at him. "Don't you get it?"

"The story," said Will. "Tell me the story."

She straightened. She gazed past him for a moment, long enough that Will began to wonder if she might change the subject.

"There's a mountain in Laos near the North Vietnamese border. The U.S. Air Force built a radar station on top to direct the B-52s that were bombing Hanoi. As soon as the North Vietnamese figured this out, they started building a road through the jungle toward this mountain. Everyone knew about the road; the Air Force bombed it one day and the North Vietnamese rebuilt it the next. At some point the station should have been evacuated. But the military loved having a radar post five hundred miles from Hanoi, and the order never came. There were only a dozen guys up there. Everyone figured that if the mountain was attacked, there would be time to blow it up and evacuate. Not to mention that it was supposed to be impregnable. Turned out it wasn't. In March of 1968, North Vietnamese soldiers scaled the mountain at night and overran the place. A few Americans died on the spot. Others hid. My father flew in to bring them out. He rescued a few men, then went back for others. And that was it. His helicopter never came back. One Monday morning he walked out the front door of our apartment on Soi 16, and he never came home."

"Is that when your mother started drinking?"

Lucy shook her head. "She'd been drinking. That's when she *really* started drinking." She looked away. "My mother hated everything about our life in Bangkok, not the least of which was my father being gone all week doing what he loved while she was stuck inside an air-conditioned apartment wishing she had some other life. *Any other life* was how she put it once." She looked at him. "Then one day she got her wish. And that turned out to be worse."

Bangkok had felt like Disneyland to Will, full of energy, and pageantry, and somehow not quite real. Soldiers on R&R came and went from Thailand by the thousands. You sensed the war out there, somewhere close by, but not dangerously close, not close enough to change your life forever. Until it did. In Bangkok Will never talked about the war in Vietnam. Not with his father, not with kids at school, not with the American soldiers who coached his Little League team, not with anybody. Only now did he see the curtain that had encircled his childhood in Thailand. Mafia kids must have the same sort of life, he thought. You don't press your father about the details of his work life. You never ask questions whose answers you don't need to know. Will had never asked Lucy about what happened to her father for the simple reason that he knew he shouldn't. Ernie Vitava flew for Air America, and Air America was run by the CIA.

"For a long time," said Lucy, "I had this fantasy that my father didn't die on that rescue mission. I imagined that life had gotten to be too much for him—the war, the fights with my mom. I convinced myself that he had planned his escape from all of that. That his helicopter didn't disappear in Laos, but he flew it down to Pattaya instead, and ditched it at sea near one of those islands where we used to go snorkeling. I imagined that he spent the night on the beach, and hitched a ride the next day on that glass-bottomed tourist boat. Somehow he'd gotten himself to Australia, and started his life over there. Was there still, flying. I went to sleep thinking about that. For some reason it made me feel better. Then I got a little older and considered what that fantasy meant in terms of his leaving *me*." She looked at Will. "Then I got a little older still, and realized that it was entirely possible that he did escape to Australia. When push comes to shove, it isn't as hard as you think to walk away from anyone, even the people closest to you. I learned that firsthand. And so did you. And I kept asking myself how I would feel if I suddenly heard from him after all these years."

"There's a difference," said Will. "For one thing Jodie came looking for you."

"No." Lucy was shaking her head. "She came looking for someone else." Then she shrugged. "To be honest"—now she looked up at Will—"I guess I did, too."

She was still seated across the table, but Will could see that she was already somewhere else. Yes, they had loved each other, loved each other enough to still feel a tremor of that love echoing down the years. And yes, the two of them had created Jodie. Jodie was the central organizing principle of their past together. Of their whole lives, perhaps. Only they had responded to all of this in different ways. Will romanticized the past, and Lucy seemed determined not to let herself be touched by the romance at all.

"I held her, Will. I held her long enough to know that I was about to make the worst mistake that I was going make in my whole life. And that I would have to live with that. I went to medical school because I wanted a job that I could get lost in. Something a whole lot bigger than my own life. And you know something: most days it works. Working in an ER teaches you to pay attention to what's in front of you. That's where your focus has to stay if you want to be any good. After a while you even stop second-guessing yourself when something bad happens. Instead, you try to learn from it." She stood. "You learn to be grateful for every small accomplishment. Like not passing up this chance to say good-bye."

Aₙₙᵢₑ ₘₒᵥₑd ᵢₙ with Will two days later, and two days after that, Teddy moved out. He had taken a room down the road with Julianna and the kayakers. In June Will signed a lease for office space up the street, a suite in the old firehouse adjacent to the food co-op. The Gerard Literary Agency prospered. Will sold two books before the official start of summer: the novel by the next William T. Vollmann (bought not by Rita Corelli, but by a young editor at Gothica who had spotted the chapter that Teddy had posted on Will's Web site); and *American Patriots*, a journalist's account of a near disastrous attempt to infiltrate a right-wing militia group. The Gothica sale was noted in *Publishers Weekly*, and two editors called Will out of the blue to ask him to lunch.

At the end of May, Annie thought she was pregnant (was almost certain of it, and positively glowing at the prospect), only to wake up two days later in the swell of nervous irritation that always heralded the arrival of her period. Will said, "Not to worry. We'll just have to try harder." Annie didn't smile. She couldn't smile. There was no possibility of humor in this for her. A little bad news on the reproduction front could only be a sign of more bad news to come. That night Will cooked pasta marinara for Annie. There was candlelight and a good merlot, and long stretches of unhappy silence, too.

In June Annie and Will struck out a second time. They resolved to stay upbeat, to eat healthier meals and get more sleep. Annie kept running. She signed up for a yoga class, and looked into acupuncture and hypnosis. Friends and family came forward with their own infertility treatments. Marianne dropped off vitamin C for Will and B-6 for Annie. Julianna brought various herbs and tinctures. Teddy downloaded an article from the Web which indicated that scientific studies had found a link between a woman's lack of body fat and the absence of a luteinizing hormone essential to conception. (Annie quit jogging, and Will laid in a supply of Ben & Jerry's Rain Forest Crunch.) Michael and Alejandro petitioned the saints on Will and Annie's behalf with an offering of walnuts, Hershey's kisses, anise seed, and two Kennedy half-dollars placed before a small statue of St. Michael that had been in Alejandro's family since the days of the Spanish Conquest. When this didn't produce the desired result, the statue was turned to the wall and threatened: Miguelito would not face the world again until Annie Leonard was carrying a child.

Once more came the agitation that preceded her period. Timing and luck, Will reminded himself. Trust the stars. But as the hot weather arrived, and the possibility of pregnancy seemed more remote, Will began to wonder if he and Annie had waited too long.

Infertility treatment began with a sperm test. As if having to masturbate into a cup wasn't enough of an embarrassment, Will had the misfortune to be referred to a urologist at Georgetown Hospital. He all but donned a disguise to deliver his sample to the lab.

"Post-vasectomy?" inquired the attractive young woman at the desk.

Will smiled tightly, "Actually, no."

Early in July, Will and Annie drove out to Lewes. This time there would be no break-ins, no assaults with flashlights, no interpersonal missteps of any kind. But lovemaking with the aim of procreation, a depressing activity anywhere, seemed all the more dispiriting to Will in this particular beach house: the air of solemnity where once they had played, the absence of spontaneity and lust in the very place that had been consecrated by spontaneity and lust. The thermometer resting on the bedside table atop the dreaded basal temperature chart made the whole endeavor feel like a science experiment. In Lewes the second morning, Annie's temperature spiked, and a groggy Will roused himself from a deep sleep to perform like a trained seal. Afterward Annie lay still for twenty minutes; then they trundled out to the car and drove three hours to a fertility clinic in Washington.

There were two other couples in the waiting room. The mood there was furtive and rivalrous, as if Dr. Feltzer had a limited number of babies in his supply, and every couple in the room was vying for the same child. The results of Annie's postcoital exam were so promising that the nurse in charge summoned Will to have a peek through the microscope at his energetic sperm. Well-formed, she assured him with a smile. Abundant. And highly motile. How could he not be encouraged?

But Dr. Feltzer himself proved a disappointment: cool and relaxed, capped teeth sparkling white, well-tanned, with the crinkly crow's feet of a weekend sailor. All through the conversation he remained aloof, detached, as if daydreaming about a new sloop that he was planning to buy. The pocket protector in his lab coat featured a cartoon sperm. Just like mine, thought Will: abundant perhaps, and well formed, and highly motile, but somehow still too frivolous for the job. The news that Will Gerard was Will Gerard of the Gerard Literary Agency brought the good doctor out of his seat. He suddenly became animated. He had a book idea to pitch: *Having Your Baby*.

Toward the end of July, Will and Annie decided to spend their next dancing days in Pennsylvania. They would camp in Amish country. Teddy hunted up a campground in cyberspace and made a reservation for them. ("It's between Intercourse and Paradise," he informed his uncle. "That's got to be a decent omen.") But a crushing heat wave settled over the mid-Atlantic that week, and Will and Annie opted for an air-conditioned road trip instead. That Tuesday morning they drove to Orange, ostensibly to deliver Norton's edited manuscript, though the real purpose for the trip was to present seventeen volumes of Patrick O'Brian's Aubrey-Maturin sea novels to Ruthie as a long overdue thank-you present. Norton was out of town. (July 30, Will recalled: Petersburg, the Crater.) But Ruthie reported that he had spent the previous two months shut up in his writing shed, and had already finished four chapters of the new book. Moreover, the Wilderness Motel now owned a copier, and Ruthie proudly presented to Will an up-to-date version of Norton's manuscript. The book had a title: *Pharaoh's Heart*.

Pharaoh's Ghost and *Pharaoh's Heart*, thought Will. Next would come *Pharaoh's Land*, or *Pharaoh's Revenge*, then *Pharaoh's Lament*, *Pharaoh's Sins*, *Pharaoh's Betrayal*, even *Pharaoh's Pharaohs*. Norton could write eighteen volumes on the Civil War—eighteen volumes on the year 1864 alone. At the end of each book Moses Pugh would seem to die, only to be resurrected again, and again, and again. Ol' Moses might live forever. Will and Annie would retire to a gated kingdom in Florida on the hyperkinetic wanderings of this immortal spy. They would name a cat after him, and perhaps a sloop of their own.

That night Annie and Will had sex in the Wilderness beneath the implacable gaze of Robert E. Lee; the next morning, too. It was playful for once, which left Will feeling lighthearted and hopeful. He had come awake that morning to the sight of Annie asleep beside him, a hand clutching the corner of her pillow, the mischievous sleep smile on her face; and lying there he realized that he would rather try and try and try and fail miserably at making babies with this woman than make them successfully with anybody else. "Just because we can't control the outcome doesn't mean we shouldn't work on our technique," he whispered to Annie when she stirred. "All we can do is make our nest of spices, set it on fire, and hope a phoenix rises out of the ashes."

"*Phoenix*," mumbled Annie. "I like that. It's different."

They raced across the Virginia countryside through the sultry heat later that day, past dead possums and battlefield markers, nail salons and Confederate memorabilia shops. In the commercial nightmare west of Fredericksburg, the traffic lights were strung together like Christmas decorations. Will and Annie had lunch at a restaurant called the Bikini Weenie, and then went looking for a bookstore so that Annie could check one of her many reference works for information about the timing of implantation.

"I feel something," she said. "I'm sure it's too soon, but . . ."

Six days, the book reported. But six days was the *average,* which meant that Anna Sophia Leonard, valedictorian of her high school, *summa cum laude* in college, law review editor, first female partner at Cosby, Steele, Holcomb & Brown, could no doubt accomplish the task in two.

It was possible.

The ocean lay miles and miles to the east. Just outside Fredericksburg Will sensed its presence in the gray sandy fields, and in the birds: the gulls and killdeer, the lone osprey wheeling above the Rappahannock. Soon they reached a bridge stretching across the Potomac toward the red cliffs of Maryland. Beyond it was a rest stop and tourist information center. While Annie surveyed the countless vacation opportunities in the Free State, Will borrowed a telephone directory for St. Mary's City from the white-haired woman at the desk. Roger Cameron was the only Cameron listed. Will copied down the address and phone number.

A few miles past the tourist stop they left the highway and rode through the landscape of Will's youth: the tidal marshes and deep green tobacco fields dotted with silver gray wooden barns as shiny as metal in the noontime sun, some patched with new cedar boards that from a distance looked like the stripes on a wild animal.

St. Mary's City was no city at all, just a small college set on the bank of a river inlet, the seventeenth-century stockaded town that gave the place its name now an archaeological site. Will parked in a visitor lot, and he and Annie walked through the campus to a grove of bald cypresses at the bank of the river. There were more ospreys here, and sailboats riding the gentle chop of the incoming tide. Across the inlet they saw houses ringing the shallow harbor. A map at the post office revealed that the road behind those houses was Jodie's road.

It was newly black-topped, apparently widened and spruced up to service all the new houses, whose perfect lawns looked as if they had been rolled out the previous day. There were older houses on this street, too, and Jodie's parents' house turned out to be one of these. It was brick, two-story, with a steeply pitched roof, set behind an untended thicket of trees. The driveway that circled behind the trees was covered with rusty pine needles. There was a freshly painted shed screened by rhododendrons, and a hedge of azaleas along the front of the house. Beside the mail box was a "For Sale" sign, with a realtor's name and number. There was no car in the driveway, and no curtains in the windows.

Will and Annie sat there for a moment, studying the empty place like any house-hunting couple who was trying to decide if this one was worth a walk-through.

Will said, "I don't suppose anyone would mind if we walked around a bit."

Annie had another idea. She picked up the cell phone and punched in the number listed on the sign. In a moment someone answered. Annie glanced at the sign: "Irene Walters, please." And then: "Irene, my name is Annie Leonard. You don't know me. My fiancé and I drove down to St. Mary's from Washington for the day. To sightsee. We noticed the houses on the river. The ones you can see from the college. And we found this one for sale with your name—"

She listened.

"Are you sure that wouldn't be an imposition on such short notice?" Annie paused. "Why, thank you. That would be wonderful."

They were standing in the driveway, gazing at the house when a horn sounded, and an old Cadillac with a dented front bumper rolled to a stop behind Will's car. Irene Walters had frosted blond hair and high heels that did not fare well in the carpet of pine needles, but she hurried nevertheless.

"What luck," she called. "You caught me just as I was headed out the door!"

Annie stepped forward to take the sell sheet. Will wandered away. He paused at a gnarled old dogwood, gripped its rough bark, and wondered if Jodie had climbed this tree. Then he stood at the threshold, and in the entryway, content for a few moments just to take in the scent and mood of this old house.

"Late nineteenth-century," Irene explained, "but in *excellent* shape. New wiring, plumbing, air conditioning. The roof is only ten years old."

"Are most of these houses weekend places?" Annie asked.

"More and more. This one is owned by a professor from the college. Retired professor. He has already moved to *his* weekend place. *Delaware,*" she added grimly. "Hours and hours away. You really have to adore the sand and saltwater to go back and forth with all that beach traffic."

She guided them to the kitchen, which opened into a sunroom with a spectacular view of the water. Irene touched Will's arm, and gestured. "Honestly," she went on, "I think Dr. Cameron needed a change of scenery. With his retirement. His daughter is grown and his wife passed on last year, I'm sorry to say." She quickly added, "They loved this house—the elegance, the views of the water." She gestured again. "I guess a person just comes to a point in his life sometimes when it's time to move on to something new."

She muscled open the back door and the room was instantly filled with the rivery smell of the inlet. "If you have any questions . . ."

Of course Will had questions, dozens of them, all of them inappropriate: *Tell me all about the Camerons, Irene: What did they do on the weekends? Did they laugh a lot? What sorts of books did they read? And Roger Cameron, what sort of father—*

Annie said, "How long did the Camerons live here?"

Irene pursed her lips. "Well, they moved in shortly before they adopted Jodie, and she's the same age as my Mitch, who is going on twenty-one." A shake of the head. "Time does fly."

Will drifted away.

He stood in the front hall again. He climbed to the second floor on the same worn steps that Jodie had climbed as a toddler, hand over hand on the balusters. Upstairs, he wandered through the rooms where she had slept: the small one as an infant, the spring of his junior year at Washington & Lee; the larger one a few years later, while he was working at Tenleytown Books. He ran a hand along the wall of the narrow hallway, the corridor that Jodie had learned to navigate in the dark of night. He stood in the doorway of the large room where her parents had slept, the marks of their double bed pressed into the wide pine floorboards. This was where Jodie had first colored, where she had dressed up in her mother's clothes, and had spent her days of flu and chicken pox; where she and her mother had talked about puberty, about boys and sex and all the mysterious emotions of adolescence; and still later, just a year ago, where they had held hands as Jodie sat with her mother through the end of her terrible illness.

"Will." He turned to find Annie in the doorway. "Irene has to run to pick up her daughter. She was offering to come back to lock up after we left."

"Be glad to," Irene called up the stairs. "It's on the way. No trouble a-tall! And do call if you have any questions. And you be sure to let me know the next time you're in town, so I can give you a proper tour!"

They had had three of the four seasons descend upon them that day. The morning had opened in high summer at Ruthie's motel, nothing moving in the warm damp July air but gnats and mosquitos. There were pewter clouds at Fredericksburg, and a sudden rain squall. Maryland had delivered a burst of spring, gusty wind and air suddenly so clear the leaves on the tobacco plants seemed to vibrate in the sun. The heat wave had broken. Now clouds were blowing in from the northwest, and there was a blustery hint of autumn in the air as Annie and Will strolled across the overgrown lawn toward a small dock.

They held hands.

Will had never been much of a hand-holder, had never gotten to that place in a relationship when hand-holding happened effortlessly. But holding Annie's hand now felt natural. And notwithstanding the chord of sadness about this tour, his life felt rich, and full of promise. Enough promise to imagine that Annie might actually be pregnant, that together, somehow, they might have created a cell that was right now dividing into two, four, eight, sixteen, thirty-two, sixty-four cells; soon hundreds of cells, then thousands and millions, each one taking its place according to the cosmic plan, the tiny head, hands, and heart all in their proper place. Life is a journey from the unrecalled to the unknown; it begins and ends abruptly. All the more reason, Will figured, to be sure not to let any small miracles pass by unnoticed.

After a long silence, Annie said, "Well, shit. Let's just buy the place."

He smiled. At that very moment, it seemed a blessing that he didn't have the ready cash for a down payment, or else he might have done just that.

The swath of lawn ended at a sea wall, which Annie and Will followed to a path, overgrown now, a backyard nature trail. Along it were planted live oaks, cedars, cypresses, sassafras. There were swamp mallows and dozens of other plants that Will couldn't identify. Fifty yards ahead the trail ended at the river. There, atop a creosoted pole anchored in the shallows, was an osprey nest. Two fledglings gripped the edge of the cup, testing their wings in the steady breeze. The mother bird sat upright in a nearby snag.

That bird knows Jodie, thought Will.

High above, the male circled, sounding its call: *kyew, kyew, kyew.* Will wondered what it saw from that great height. Was the world viewed simply as *fish* and *not fish*? Or did these animals see things that Will could not even imagine? Upon returning to this nest four months ago, had these ospreys been confused by all the changes in their native landscape: the new houses, the new black ribbon of road, all the trees felled by chainsaws or knocked down by winter ice? Had they noted the absence of the older woman of the house? And that the older man had suddenly stopped coming out in the morning to greet them? Did they miss the girl who once dug in the garden and swam in the river? Or were all of these changes noted, and understood in some birdly way as being the order of things? Perhaps these well-traveled creatures had seen enough of the world to know that it was always in the process of becoming something else.

Jodie was in Colorado now. She and Alan were spending the summer in the Rockies, counting golden eagles. Will had received a few postcards from her. For the most part they were breezy reports of their summer adventures, written in Jodie's wonderfully precise hand. "Saw my first western tanager yesterday. A crossbill last week." Will had saved the cards, and had reread each one dozens of times. Too many times, he knew. But he couldn't make himself put them away. He couldn't see them as the small things they were: four cards with images of birds. Hummingbirds, hawks, condors and golden eagles. The past and present and future suddenly felt seamlessly connected to him. He knew this wasn't true, and that it could never be true. Jodie had sailed into his life like a young osprey just home from the winter migration—to alight only briefly at its natal ground before continuing on to find a nest site of its own.

Already she was moving away from him, moving on into the life she had created for herself, the life she had found. And Will was moving on, too. But not so quickly that he didn't pause at times to sense the shadow life he might have had with Jodie. And to realize that what little they had together right now was all they could hope for: it was a beginning. And so as Jodie was counting eagles, Will was counting the days. Twenty-two until she would return east. Tomorrow, twenty-one.

ABOUT THE AUTHOR

KARL ACKERMAN is a novelist and screenwriter. He is the son of a career U.S. diplomat and has lived in Norway, Taiwan, and Thailand during the height of the Vietnam War. He has worked in a variety of jobs in publishing, including bookseller, sales rep, editor, and book reviewer. His first novel, *The Patron Saint of Unmarried Women,* was selected as a notable book of the year by *The New York Times.* He and his wife, writer Jennifer Ackerman, live with their two daughters in Charlottesville, Virginia.